I0582289

Also in the Orlell Chronicles

Book 1 - Guardians of Gayrile

Book 2 - The Jewel of Power

Book 3 - The Quest for Drisilas

Book 4 - The Shard and the Shadow

Book 5 - *coming soon!*

Book 4

The
Shard

and the

Shadow

Alice G. Bjornstedt

*For my mom,
who taught me
to hope.*

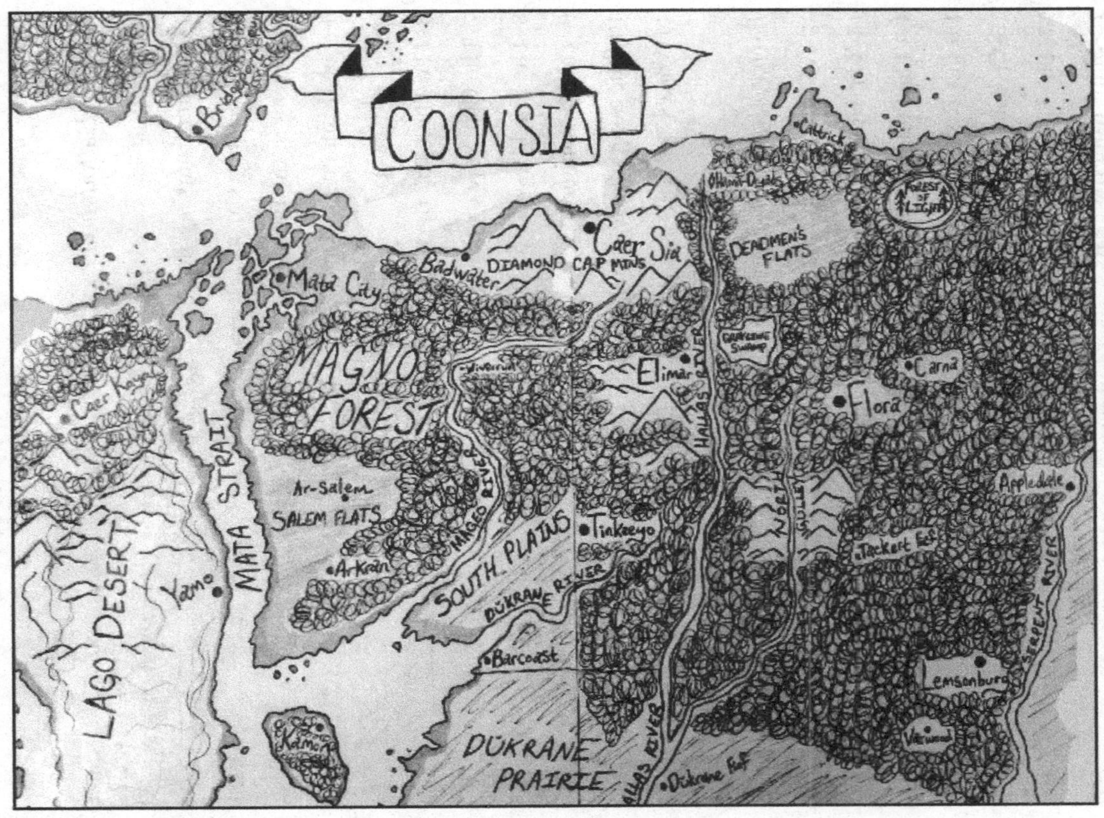

COONSIA
Bria
Catbrick
FOREST OF ELZINA
Caer Sia
DIAMOND CAP MTNS
DEADMEN'S FLATS
Badwater
Mata City
Caer Hogan
MAGNO FOREST
Elimar
Carna
Flora
Ar-Salem
SALEM FLATS
Appledale
Arkran
SOUTH PLAINS
Tinkaeyo
DUKRANE RIVER
Tackart Er
LAGO DESERT
Yamo
MATA STRAIT
Barcoast
Lemsonburg
Kamon
DUKRANE PRAIRIE
Dukrane Faf
SERPENT RIVER
5

Table of Contents

PART 1

Daffodalion

Prologue

Fog hung low in the silent wood.

It dampened the budding limbs of the dogwood trees, floated suspended over the dewy grass, and glowed gold with morning sunlight. A few beams of light filtered through the haze, touching down like delicate fingers on the solitary figure that rode through the wood. His steed, a glossy black mare, dipped her head to crop at the fresh grass that grew alongside the trail.

"Not here, girl," Dandio murmured to the horse with a gentle tug on the reins. "I hear it's forbidden to harm any living thing in the Forest of Light. We're almost there."

He glanced around at the misty forest. It had been a long journey. He had left Caer Sia five days ago, traveling east to meet with two Dwarve tribal leaders. Trouble had plagued the Black Dwarve tribes for years, but now, with the trouble surrounding Terrax all of nine months behind them, the situation was finally looking up. Dandio had left weeks ago to negotiate an alliance between the Liznees of Caer Sia and the Dwarve tribes. The negotiations had gone smoothly, and the Dwarves had been satisfied with the proposition Dandio had brought. Jan would be glad to hear it, he thought, smiling slightly to himself.

His horse whinnied softly as they moved through the trees, bringing his thoughts back to the present. Caer Sia, the capital of Coonsia, was about sixty miles from the Forest of Light. Dandio could probably cover half that distance today on horseback. They would reach Elimar tonight, then go on to Caer Sia and hopefully arrive home before dusk tomorrow.

It was necessary to stop for water, though, and he guided his horse toward the spring in the center of the glade. Fresh water bubbled out of the earth and filled the stream that ran through the forest. The mare bent her head to drink eagerly. Dandio swung out of the saddle and stretched stiffly. It had been a long journey, and he found himself looking forward to returning home.

The horse raised her head suddenly, her ears flicked back as she listened to the sounds Dandio could not hear. She gave a low, uneasy nicker. Dandio patted her neck lightly, calming her, then knelt to fill the water flasks.

He had just finished when the birds went silent abruptly, and the forest plunged into ominous quiet.

The mare snorted again and pawed the ground anxiously. Dandio stood and listened. He could hear nothing. But the silence was so sudden and unexpected that it set his ears ringing. As the moments stretched on, a feeling of dread began to grow in the pit of his stomach.

Something was terribly, inexplicably wrong.

He swung his gaze around the wood, his hand resting on his sword hilt as his keen green eyes sought for the source of unease.

Nothing. The sunlight shone down upon the glade, casting uncertain shadows among the trees as the branches and the fog shifted in the slight breeze. The movement played with his tense mind, but he saw no danger.

Then one of the shadows detached itself from the woods and swept forward.

The mare reared with a shrill whinny of fear, wrenching her bridle from Dandio's hand, and shied backward. Her cry pierced the silence, startling a group of robins from their hiding place in one of the trees. In a flurry of feathers and anxious chirps, the birds fled the forest.

Dandio drew his sword in a flash. In the same instant, a chill unlike any he had ever experienced clutched the air around him. The low-scudding clouds were swept across the sun by a sudden breeze, and the foggy clearing filled with gray light. The horse reeled away as sheer panic overcame her loyalty to her master. Dandio reached after her, but his attention was drawn back by movement ahead.

A shadowed figure moved forward through the fog. Tattered black robes, tossed by the wind, swept around a withered frame. A being utterly sinister, watching and waiting. An unknown shadow darker than the night itself. A biting cold radiated from its form.

Dandio took an involuntary step back, gripping his sword hilt. "Stop where you are," he ordered, setting his stance. "I am on official business for the High King, and I order you to stop and identify yourself." The words made a cloud before his lips, standing out in the frigid air.

The figure paid the words no heed and continued to move toward him, slowly yet surely. Dandio couldn't make out any features beneath the hood. Whoever or whatever it was, it seemed to move with a slight sway, almost like the very breeze would sweep it away.

"Last warning," Dandio said, raising his sword. "Stop and identify yourself. If you are an enemy, this place is forbidden to you."

The hooded figure stopped three paces away from him, and Dandio peered through the haze, trying to see it more clearly. Black robes, shimmering slightly as though coated in frost, wreathed its hunched figure. A deep cowl covered its head, the face beneath completely obscured by shadows. Claw-like hands with skin the color of charcoal reached up and removed the hood.

Dandio's sword slid from his grasp as the light reached the face beyond, and he staggered back.

A face out of time, decayed and rotted by the darkness it had embraced. An ancient power that overwhelmed every good thing in this world. He hid his face from the horror as the fog at its skirts swept onward, wreathing him in a biting cold. Through blurred vision, he saw the face contort into a smile.

Forbidden? A low voice echoed in his head, banishing all other thoughts, searing within his skull. *How very… interesting.*

With a strangled cry, Dandio fell to his knees. The voice spoke once more in his mind, the words nearly indecipherable past the pounding of his own heart. But he heard them still.

Tell me, mortal… what do you know of the Prophecy of Three?

The figure's hands rested on Dandio's head, and white-hot pain flared behind his eyes. He could not speak, could not resist, yet he knew, beyond a doubt, who he now faced.

And then the fog was gone as his consciousness faded away.

Minutes later, the intruder's accomplices stepped hesitantly toward their hooded leader. At his bidding, the armored figures lifted the Liznee's limp body and carried him away. The shadowed figure stood for a moment longer, his hidden eyes studying the brightness of the wood with contempt. Then, after a pause, he turned and vanished through the fog and the freezing air.

Only Dandio's sword and pack were left, all alone in the grass, as the Forest of Light was slowly swallowed by ice and white fog.

1

A Letter from Gayrile

"I think you had another bad dream."

Mel looked up at his younger sister's voice. He sat on the stone steps of their front porch. The midday sun and early summer breeze rumpled his messy red hair, and he pushed it back from his face to see Misty. She stood there, arms folded, concern on her eight-year-old face.

"I did?" he asked in reply to her statement.

Misty shrugged slightly. "You were yelling in your sleep last night. I couldn't really hear what you said, though." Her brow wrinkled with worry.

Mel forced a smile to reassure her. "Well, I don't remember what it was about at all. Do you want to play chess before dinner or not?"

Misty seemed satisfied and nodded. "Yep. I'll go get the board." She skipped back up the steps and inside their little home.

Mel rested his chin in his hands and took a breath. He hated keeping secrets from her. But the truth would only make her worry more.

It had been nine months since the two of them had embarked on the quest to return the High King's sword Drisilas. Nine months since they had watched as the beautiful city of Caer Sia fought her enemies. Nine months since the terrible wraith known as the Darkness had met its end.

Misty, thankfully, had been in the palace, away from the fighting during the battle. Mel, on the other hand, had been in the courtyard, where he and Rygal had watched the bloody struggle unfold.

It wasn't even this battle that occupied his nightmares now, though. Of course, the pain and fury and bloodshed still filled his mind occasionally, accompanied by a nauseating sensation of helplessness. But at night… at night, only one thing repeated itself in his mind, over and over again, forbidding him to forget it.

We shall see each other soon, I think.

The voice in the void. A being from a place beyond any Mel could imagine. He had thought about it, long and hard, and about the conversation with King Jan just after the battle. Yet even the Liznee king, normally so calm and collected, who always knew exactly what to do, had been uncertain about what this might mean. The only thing they were able to conclude was that the battle was far from over.

It was a hard truth to face. The general populace believed all was well—by every outward appearance, the Darkness had been destroyed by Jan's sword Drisilas, as everyone had hoped. The battle had been won. Only Mel knew the truth—that the wraith had been ordered to stand down, to surrender, by the strange voice beyond the void.

Now is the hour of us. Now is the hour of your master.

Since the events following the quest, there had been no word of danger. The northwestern kingdoms of Orlell, for the first time in decades, felt the satisfaction of peace. Now that the Darkness was destroyed, and the rebel warlord Terrax defeated, it seemed there was nothing left to fear.

But Mel couldn't believe this. Not after seeing the face in the void, and hearing those ominous words. As much as he had hoped he would forget about it all once he was back home, he knew everything had changed the moment he had first laid hands on Drisilas all those months ago.

"I found the chess board," Misty announced importantly, drawing Mel out of his thoughts. He smiled as she plopped down on the step next to him and placed the chess board between them.

It was a beautiful day, the sun shining in a clear blue sky. The fruit trees along Appledale's roads blossomed pink and white. School had ended five days before, and now summer had really begun. Well, for Mel at least. Misty had decided she wanted to do summer school, to jump further ahead in her studies. She would be attending a boarding school in Lemsonburg—a large city several miles south of Appledale—over the next three months.

"When do you leave for school?" Mel asked her as they set up the chess pieces.

Misty beamed up at him. "After dinner. Mama says we're going to take the late carriage tonight and sleep at an inn near Tackert Fief.

Remember Tackert Fief? We went there with Dandio. Mama said that the carriage will follow the river south and if it's warm enough, we can stop and swim along the way."

Mel smiled at her eager chattering. "The water will probably be cold."

Misty shrugged. "Yeah, maybe. But I want to do something fun before I get there. Mama says they're having a placement test on the first day, to figure out where everyone should go." Her face fell, nervousness in her hazel eyes.

"You're going to do great," Mel said encouragingly. "You're a whole year ahead of most of the kids your age. You'll totally conquer that test."

"Okay," Misty said, smiling again. Nervous or not, Mel could tell she was excited. Misty had always been bookish, with a knack for learning quickly. Mel was sure she would thrive in the Lemsonburg school, which offered a wider range of subjects than the little Appledale study house could.

They played in silence for a little while. Mel's earlier thoughts distracted him; Misty had him in checkmate after only a few moves. "Best of three?" Mel asked, setting up his pieces again.

Misty nodded eagerly. "What are you going to do while I'm gone?" she asked, returning to their original conversation. "Do you know what trade you'll pick?"

"I knew you were going to ask that," Mel said with a short laugh. He hesitated. As was custom in the area, unless a student had a specific goal of academic study in mind—like Misty did—they would select a trade study at age twelve. The only problem was, Mel had no idea what he wanted to do. He wasn't good at studies like Misty was, and beyond that, he felt… well, stuck. After the excitement of the quest, going back to mundane activities like school and plans for the future seemed quite dull.

"You could do book-binding, like what Dad does," Misty suggested helpfully. Their father owned a small bookshop in town.

"Maybe," Mel said slowly. He guessed that was what his father hoped he'd choose. But while Mel hated to let his father down, he also didn't want to spend his next few years of study doing something he didn't like.

"Seamstress, then, like Mama," Misty said with a giggle.

"Misty, I'm horrible at sewing." He shook his head, smiling. "I thought blacksmithing might be neat to learn. If I'm too young to be trained with a sword, I could at least learn to make them."

"But Appledale doesn't have a blacksmith," Misty pointed out. That was the drawback of trade school—the trademaster offered free training, but only to local students. Since Appledale was a small town, and his family didn't have the money to send him to a larger city for training, Mel's choices were severely limited.

"I'll probably decide later," he said out loud with a slight shrug. His twelfth birthday wasn't for a few months yet, so he still had time to choose. Besides, trade studies typically lasted four years at most, and they didn't necessarily dictate what occupation you ended up with. But it didn't help that the one thing Mel did want was out of the question.

Mel wanted to return to questing. He'd felt that tug right after he left Caer Sia last autumn, and now it was stronger than ever. Despite the peril that had filled the adventure, the experience had awakened a new strength and determination inside him. Along with it was the call to action to help people, the way Dandio did. He had looked up to the Liznee warrior for as long as he could remember, and after joining him to fight against the Darkness, Mel longed more than ever to be like him.

Misty beat him in the next game, which Mel excused as having too much on his mind. She looked quite satisfied with herself as she packed up the game and stood up. "Mama asked me to get the mail, so I'm going to the post office. Want to come?"

"No, that's okay. I'll put the game away." Mel took the chess board from her and carried it inside the house. The window directly above the kitchen wash basin was open to allow a breath of cool air inside. Even in the early weeks of summer, their house could get quite hot.

His mother, Elonie Smallbutton, stood at the wash basin, up to her elbows in suds. "Did Misty go to the post office?" she asked as he came inside.

"Yep, she just left. What's for dinner?" Mel asked eagerly.

"Vegetable soup and bread, and it'll be ready soon," Elonie said. She brushed a stray strand of blonde hair out of her eyes and turned back to scrubbing dishes.

Mel walked down the hall to put the chess board in Misty's room, then returned to the kitchen. By the time he did, his father had arrived home from work.

"Lovely day today," Joseph Smallbutton commented cheerfully. "It smells delicious in here, my dear. Where's Misty off to?"

"The post office—wash up and we'll eat once she gets back," Elonie told him, making room at the wash basin so that her burly husband could stand beside her. Mel smiled at the two of them. Even if his everyday life was slow at times, his home and his family were two things he would always cherish.

Misty came skipping in through the door, carrying a few letters. "Hi, Dad! You have a letter from Aunt Patricia." She pushed the envelope into her father's hands, which were still sudsy. This resulted in soap water splashing onto the floor, and made Elonie shake her head wearily.

"Aunt Patricia will wait—I'm hungry," Joseph declared and sat down at the table.

Misty set the other envelopes aside and sat down at the table. Mel ate hungrily, enjoying the savory stew. He noticed his sister had barely touched her food.

"Try to eat something, Misty. It'll make the nerves go away," Joseph said encouragingly.

"I don't feel hungry," Misty said glumly.

Mel snatched a piece of bread from his sister's plate. "Better hurry, or I'll eat it all," he warned, grinning.

Misty whisked her plate out of his reach and took a tiny bite of stew. "Do you think the test will be hard?" she asked anxiously.

"It's just a placement test, dear," their mother said with a gentle smile. "It will show what sort of things you're strong at, and what subjects you'll need to work on."

"And there probably won't be many of those," Mel added with a grin. A smile finally appeared on Misty's face, which raised Mel's spirits too. He hated to see his sister upset. Nervous or not, though, he had no doubts that Misty would do quite well.

They finished dinner, and Mel helped tidy up so that his mother could finish packing. Misty stood by the door, her book bag in one hand and her oversized backpack weighing down her slender shoulders. At least she was smiling now and looked excited to go.

"I'll be back tomorrow evening," Elonie said, as Joseph escorted her to the door. "Make sure you bring in the laundry—oh, and Mel, could you water my flowers?"

"Yep. Bye, Misty," Mel said, giving his sister a quick hug.

"And the mail—I should be expecting a letter from your grandmother soon—watch for it, will you?" Elonie added as she very slowly made her way out the door.

"We'll be fine," Joseph said, giving her a kiss. "Have fun, you two. Good luck, Misty."

With a few final hugs, the two left the house, leaving Mel and his father alone in the kitchen.

"Peace and quiet," Joseph murmured, winking at his son. "I'll be in the parlor. Might want to water your mother's flowers before it gets much darker."

Mel nodded, filled the watering tin, and headed outside. The sun had set, and the early summer sky was streaked a brilliant pink. The quiet of the house and yard felt strange. Without his mother's soothing presence or Misty's chattering, a little of the liveliness seemed to have faded away.

He shook the gloomy thoughts out of his head and poured water over the peonies and rose beds next to the house.

"Happy evening, Mel," a man's voice called.

Mel looked up. Patrick, Appledale's postman, strolled down the road to their house. "Hi," Mel said, setting down the watering tin and walking over to meet him.

The postman grinned. He was short and stocky, and wore his official uniform. He held out an envelope to Mel. "This arrived for you, lad—came in just after your sister left. I imagine she's gone now?"

"Yep, all the way to Lemsonburg," Mel told him.

"That you, Patrick?" Joseph appeared through the front door. He walked down the steps and clasped the other man's hand in greeting. "Come in if you've got the time. It's dreadfully quiet without the ladies here, and I've a mind for a game of cribbage and a beer."

The two men strolled inside the house. Mel looked down at the letter absently, then did a double take. His heart skipped a beat as he recognized the handwriting.

"Mel, do you mind watering my vegetable garden while you're at it?" Joseph called from inside.

"Um—sure Dad," Mel said quickly, stuffing the letter inside his pocket. His hands trembled with excitement as he finished watering the plants outside the house.

He knew the slightly scrawled handwriting, written in dark blue ink, was Rygal's, one of his companions on the quest. Unknown to either of his parents, Mel had kept up a correspondence with the young warrior. But the letters had only consisted of one topic—information about possible threats to the Liznee kingdom. In Appledale, any news took weeks to circulate through rumors, and it was usually outdated and inaccurate. It had been months since Rygal's last letter, which had detailed a very brief uprising in southern Coonsia and was nothing to worry about. But whether or not the news was interesting, Mel looked forward to each letter with great anticipation.

He felt guilty for lying to his parents about it, but he figured it was the best thing to do. If his parents knew about these letters—letters that could potentially call him back into some form of danger—they would only worry. Mel couldn't blame them, either. There were so many terrible things he and Misty had witnessed, so many times they could have died. His parents were only trying to protect him.

But protection or no, waiting in silence for outdated rumors about his friends was far worse than keeping secrets. Mel sat down on the front steps and opened the folded page.

The first sentence hit him in the chest.

Then he was reading as quickly as his eyes could take it in.

To Mel Smallbutton of Appledale, Daffodalion.

Dear Mel,

I'm skipping formalities for the urgency of this message, but you need to know—Dandio is missing.

We don't know much more. Jan has some guesses, but we'll discuss those later. By the time this letter has reached you, it will be nearly two weeks since he's disappeared. But the most important thing you should know is that our world is once again in danger, and we are threatened by an entirely new foe.

There will be a council in Flora, Daffodalion, on the 15th of the sixth month, an hour before noon. I hope by then we'll have more news on Dandio too, but that's not the only reason for the council. Something else has happened that requires our immediate attention. After this meeting, we will select members that will embark on a quest—that's all I've been told about it.

I hope you'll be able to attend. The council is private, and you'll need a password to enter. You will also need to present this letter to the guard when you get there—so DON'T LOSE THIS LETTER. The password is Lumolyn.

I also need to warn you that there will be spies. Be watchful of them. This new threat we face is unlike anything we've seen before, so keep the council a secret to anyone that asks.

And most of all, be careful. It's not safe anywhere, not now.

Good luck, and I hope to see you soon.

—Rygal of Gayrile

P.S. You might meet a friend of mine on the road. He is known as the Hummingbird. You can trust him.

Mel read the letter through, then read it over again to make sure he had missed nothing. He didn't feel excitement, or hope, or even frustration over how he could convince his parents to let him go.

All he felt was dread over those three words.

Dandio is missing.

Missing…where? Dead? Captured? Lost?

Lost didn't seem like a Dandio tendency. Dandio was smart, strong, and an incredible warrior. So…dead?

No. No. Mel couldn't bring himself to believe that.

That left captured. By whom? The new foe Rygal mentioned? And…this new foe was worse than anything they had faced before? Rygal had faced a lot—warlords, dragons, Sirens—so if Rygal, who was probably the bravest person Mel had met (with the exception of Jan or Dandio, of course), was worried, they were facing something really terrible. Worse than the maddened kragon Adderstrike? Than the maniacal traitor Drona? Than the Darkness itself?

Mel didn't know. All he knew was that Dandio, the one person they would need most in this situation, was missing.

He forced himself to calm down and think, to face the bigger, scarier possibility the letter introduced.

Dandio's disappearance was not the only problem, not if a new threat had indeed arisen. Rygal had stated that there would be a council in Flora in two days. During that council, many topics would be discussed. In the end, a group would leave on a mission of some kind—likely, in defense or challenge of their mysterious new opponent.

And Mel might have to join them.

2

A Carriage to Carna

Mel folded up the paper and slid it back into the envelope, then took a deep breath. Never mind the possibility of a quest, he thought. His priority now would be to get to the council and learn what he could about this new threat Rygal spoke of with such dread. For the sake of Dandio, he needed to be there. He knew that without a trace of doubt.

The real problem now, he knew, would be convincing his father to let him go. While Joseph wasn't a natural worrier like Elonie, that wouldn't make the task any easier. In fact, it might be harder. Mel had disclosed more details about the horrific battle to his father, and with that in mind, Joseph would be even more hesitant to let his son go.

He walked inside slowly, not sure what to do. Patrick, the postman, sat at the kitchen table across from Mel's father. Both men were happily engaged in their cribbage game. He would have to wait until they had finished and Patrick left, which could be a while.

Mel walked down the hall to his room and sat on his bed. Now that the shock of the news had passed, his mind reeled with questions. Dandio missing, a secret council, some new threat, the looming possibility of another mission… for what? What would their task be?

The minutes ticked by as he sat, restless with thoughts, worried and confused over what it could all mean. Flora was roughly a day and a half journey by carriage from Appledale. That meant he would have to leave tomorrow morning to get there in time. He would leave before his mother got home, though maybe that was a good thing. He could imagine exactly how his mother would react to the news: *Mel, you're too young to face this kind of thing! It's a war council—let the warriors deal with it.*

"I don't even know *what* we're facing, Mom," Mel argued back mentally. Neither did Rygal, apparently. He figured Jan would have some ideas, and wished more than ever that he could speak with the Liznee king the way he had after the quest. Their conversation then had answered some of his questions, eased some of his fears after he'd heard the voice…

Are you sure you want to play this game?

Mel jolted upright, realizing that he must have drifted off. The light had faded outside. The faint glow of candlelight came from the parlor, and he got up.

Joseph sat in his favorite chair by the fireplace, reading. He looked up in surprise as Mel entered the room. "Everything all right, Mel? You were asleep when I walked in." He frowned slightly as he noticed the letter in Mel's hands. "What's that?"

Mel's words tumbled out over each other, each more urgent than the last. "I got a letter from Rygal, Dad—I'm sorry I haven't told you—I just didn't want to worry you and Mom, or make you think I was going to disappear again, because I'm not—but now I don't know—"

"Whoa, whoa, slow down." His father moved to him, concerned. "What are you talking about?"

Mel pressed the letter into his father's hands. "It's—this is from Rygal, and he has bad news, Dad—Dandio's gone missing and he might be captured or hurt or dead—we don't know, but Rygal says there's some new evil and it's worse than anything before, and we're having a council to decide who's going to stop it—and I have to go! Tomorrow, so that I can get there in time!"

Joseph took the letter and scanned Rygal's hurried handwriting in silence. As Mel had expected, he looked stunned. "Rygal of Gayrile sent you this?" he said finally. "How long…"

"The last few months," Mel said. "I—I'm sorry I didn't tell you, but Rygal promised to send me any updates on what's going on in Coonsia. I wanted better information than the rumors we get here," he added, a little ruefully.

Joseph looked up, worry written in every line of his face. "This is serious, Mel. I know you helped find the sword, but this is different. I can't let you go throwing yourself into another Coonsian scrape."

Mel kept his voice calm, but it was hard to hold back his growing desperation. "It isn't just Coonsia's problem—if it was, Rygal wouldn't have written me at all. And what about Dandio? I have to help."

His father looked torn. "Son, you came back last time covered in bruises and telling stories that would scare grown men silly. I'm sorry about Dandio, but I can't let you go through this again." He hesitated. "We're very proud of you for everything you did on the quest. But this is another thing altogether. Especially if they intend to send you back out there."

Mel took a deep breath. "This isn't about the quest. This is about Dandio. I owe him, Dad—he saved both me and Misty about a hundred times on the quest. He almost died doing it. I need to help him now. Please."

Tears prickled at the corners of his eyes, and he looked down. It had been months, but he still didn't like to think about the day they had crossed Deadmen's Flats. Dandio had been seriously injured protecting Mel from a bloodthirsty serpentine. Mel still felt the guilt of it sometimes. Now was a chance to repay that debt.

There was a brief pause. When Joseph spoke again, his voice was tight. "All right. Whether I like it or not, I can see you're right." He squeezed Mel's shoulder tightly. "And I'll trust you to be very careful, understood?"

Hope lit in Mel's chest. "I will—I promise. It's just a council. I'll be back before you know it."

"Well, I won't count on that, from what you've told me of Rygal," Joseph replied dryly. But he seemed convinced, and that lifted Mel's spirits. "Now, can I see that letter again?"

Mel handed it over. His father read it, then looked up. "Hmm,

Flora. That's about a two-day travel by carriage, so you're right, you'll need to leave tomorrow morning if you want to get there on time."

Mel nodded. "I can pay for my carriage there."

"And I can send you with extra money for an inn tomorrow night," Joseph said. He looked back at the letter and tapped a portion of it. "Have you heard of this Hummingbird fellow?"

Mel shook his head. "No. I wonder who he is."

"Well, I'd assume he's a ranger. I've heard the rangers use birds as codenames—keeps their true identity safe."

Mel raised his eyebrows. That was interesting. He didn't know much about the rangers, but he thought he had heard Dandio talk about them once or twice. Supposedly, the rangers were only ever called in to help in truly perilous situations.

Joseph handed him the letter and stood. "Let's work out the rest of the details in the morning—it's getting late."

Mel's heart felt lighter as he walked back down the hall. He would go to Flora, find out what he could, and perhaps, just perhaps, help find Dandio.

"One more thing," Joseph called. "What do you expect me to tell your mother?"

Mel thought, then shrugged. "Tell her… tell her Rygal came and stole me away in the night, or something like that."

Joseph raised an eyebrow. "Hmph. And I just watched?"

"No, you were playing cribbage," Mel said, grinning.

"I don't think she'll like that," Joseph murmured, but he returned the smile. "Try and get some sleep, son."

Mel returned to his room and flopped back on his bed, a storm of emotions swirling inside him. Excitement at the coming journey and seeing his friends again. Uncertainty following Rygal's news about the new threat. A deep sense of concern for Dandio, wherever he was.

Finally, he slept. In his dreams, a face with reddish eyes peered through the darkness at him, the face distorting in a triumphant and wicked smile, and he heard the voice echoing in his mind.

Now is the hour of us. Are you sure you want to play this game?

......

Mel woke up early the following morning. His sleep had been brief and not especially restful, but excitement for the journey ahead gave him energy. He got up, dressed, and packed quickly. *"Trail packing—pack light."* Rygal's words floated through his mind, and he managed to gather everything he needed into his leather back-pack. He wasn't sure how to wear the dagger Rygal had given him, but slung it to his belt as best he could.

When he finished, he scribbled a quick note for his mother. She would still worry, he knew. But at least he could assure her that he would be home soon.

Unless you get sent on a quest, a little voice nagged at him. But he shook it aside. It was highly unlikely that would happen. From what Rygal described, there would be quite a few people at the council, all with a lot more experience than him. Whatever the mission was, he guessed there were others who had been chosen for it.

Joseph was already up and had made an egg and potato hash for breakfast. "You've got that fastened on the wrong side," he commented, nodding at Mel's dagger.

Mel looked down and adjusted the weapon clumsily. Joseph walked over and undid the clasp, then positioned the dagger correctly. "You're right handed, so keep it on your left hip. That way, you can draw it quickly if you need it."

"Thanks, Dad," Mel said with a smile. There was a brief silence as he got his plate of breakfast. He could tell his father was still processing the reality of what was happening. "I'll be okay," he said awkwardly, to fill the silence.

Joseph managed to smile. "Be sure that you do. Make good choices and don't go throwing yourself into a fight, all right?" Mel nodded and sat down to eat.

"I stopped by the station," Joseph said after a moment. "The next carriage north leaves in an hour. You'll go to Carna today, spend the night there, and go on to Flora tomorrow."

"Sounds good. Thanks," Mel said in between bites. Now that the morning had come, his uncertainty had faded, and he only felt eager for the adventure and the answers that would accompany it.

They finished breakfast, and Mel followed his father out the door as they left for the station. "Dad... if I do end up being gone longer..." Mel began, then hesitated, not sure what to say. He had kept quiet about that up till now, but small chance or not, there was still a possibility he would be gone for longer than any of them thought.

Joseph smiled down at him. "I know we fret—both your mother and I. But it's because we love you, son. And you need to know that if you are selected to go, we trust you." He squeezed Mel's shoulder. "But that doesn't mean we won't worry for you while you're gone."

They reached the station, a simple wooden building with a stable to one side and a porch where travelers waited for their next ride. Only a few people were there now, and the two of them sat down on a vacant bench.

They waited in silence until the carriage pulled up, with the driver announcing rides west to Carna. Joseph pulled him into a bear hug and spoke seriously. "Listen, Mel. If Rygal's right, and this new enemy is half as bad as you think, then you'll need your wits as well as your blade. Use your head and think every action through. That's just as important as fighting physically."

"I will. Thanks, Dad," Mel said.

"And good luck finding Dandio," Joseph added. Mel gave him one more hug, then shouldered his pack and jogged over to the carriage.

The seat cushions were a little lumpy, the floor slightly stained, but it was clean enough and the wheels carried it quickly. As they rolled away, Mel pressed his face against the window and watched as the station disappeared around the corner.

Here we go again, he thought wryly. And here he was, leaving home to go and face the potential of yet another deadly foe that he knew next to nothing about.

"Am I seriously doing this?" he muttered to himself.

"Eh?" grunted the driver.

"Nothing," Mel replied, and pulled his knees up as the journey began.

3

∽ ∽ ∽ ∽ ∽ ∽ ∽ ∽ ∽

Rumors in the Pastel Inn

Rain spattered the cobblestones as the carriage bumped into the town of Carna. Mel straightened stiffly from his position leaning against the window.

The carriage had stopped briefly once or twice in the smaller fiefs to the northwest of Appledale, picking up passengers who were headed to a neighboring town. After they had been dropped off at their destination, the carriage had picked up speed and headed steadily toward Carna. The winding roads and soft jingle of the harness must have lulled Mel to sleep.

Now they reached their destination. Carna was a medium sized town—larger than Appledale, but considerably smaller than Flora. The strong smell of wood smoke and damp stone reached Mel's nose as they passed by shops and houses that lined the road. Through the haze of rain, the lamps had been lit, casting the town in a yellow glow. Next to the road was the market, and Mel could see the vendors packing up their remaining goods in preparation for the night.

The driver reined in the horses, slowing the carriage, then turned in his seat. "Where you headed, laddie?" he asked.

"The Pastel Inn, please," Mel replied. The driver nodded, then clicked to the horses and brought the carriage forward again.

In a few moments, they stopped and the driver swung down from his seat to open the door. Mel stepped down stiffly, legs sore after the long ride. The inn stood above him, a simple two-story building painted a light gray. Warm light flowed from the lower windows. A signboard bore its name just outside.

Mel shouldered his backpack and walked inside. The smell of baked bread and meat reached his nose, and his stomach rumbled. Aside from a few snacks he'd packed for the journey, he hadn't eaten since breakfast that morning. The lower half of the inn served as a cozy tavern and eating place, and there were already a few groups of people sitting at tables, talking while they ate.

Mel made his way to the counter. A serving girl paused as she saw him. "Good evening. How can I help you?"

"Hi," Mel replied. He squared his shoulders and tried to stand a little taller. "Do you have a room available?"

The woman frowned slightly, unaccustomed to youngsters coming in and asking for a room. But she seemed to push it aside. "Yes, we do," she replied. "How many nights?"

"Just one," Mel said. He paid with the money his father had given him.

The woman seemed satisfied. "If you're hungry, we've got beef stew and freshly baked bread ready soon," she offered.

Mel's stomach rumbled again. "That sounds great. Thank you," he said, taking the room key she handed him. Then he headed towards the dining room.

There were about a dozen men seated at three separate tables, all talking and drinking ale. Farmers, he guessed, judging by their muddy clothes and worn boots. Mel sat down at a table in the corner, feeling awkward. This was a small town, and newcomers would be subject to conversation. Mel would be asked where he was from, where he was going, and—most likely—how old he was. All were things he didn't want to answer. He huddled down at the table, trying to look as inconspicuous as possible.

Thankfully the farmers were all engaged in their separate conversations. A young man came over and gave Mel a glass of water, telling him the dinner was nearly finished. It was as Mel was raising the glass that a word hooked him into the farmers' conversation.

Dandio Ki. Mel almost choked on the water. He hadn't heard the context of the name, but now he was listening as intently and as discreetly as possible.

"I don't know what happened. All I heard was that Dandio Ki went on a trip and hasn't come back." That was a muscular farmer with a shaggy mustache.

"Well, that could be nothing. I ain't been on a quest before, so I don't know how long it would take." A tall man with a pipe in his mouth leaned back nonchalantly.

"But surely he'd have arrived back by now? I heard it was a short errand, not a quest." The words came from a wiry fellow with a straw hat.

"That's what my missus said she heard. Me missus never told a lie," said the first speaker.

The waitress brought Mel his soup; he ate slowly, listening hard.

"Whatever has happened, it'll be no good, I warrant," murmured an old man in the corner.

Everyone except the mustached farmer and the man with the straw hat sighed heavily and rolled their eyes in the old man's direction. "There's Old Isaac for you. If a leaf falls, something terrible's bound to happen," said another farmer, whose large nose was badly sunburned. The others nodded in agreement.

Old Isaac shook his head urgently. "No! There's been a rumor in the streets, I tell you." He leaned closer and lowered his voice to a hissing whisper, but Mel still heard. "They say a great evil has infiltrated the Forest of Light."

Now everyone rolled their eyes in exasperation. "Not possible," scoffed the straw hat man. "Nothing evil can even enter the wood. At least that's how the legends go."

"Aye," agreed the mustached farmer. "Me missus had a cousin who knew a man that once tried to enter the wood with naught but a pocketknife, an' he was thrown out, I tell you." There was silence as everyone tried to decide if they could trust the word of the farmer's wife's cousin's friend. "He did like a good drink though," the farmer admitted after a suspenseful pause. The others laughed.

Mel finished his meal, then headed upstairs to his room. Once inside, he thought for a long time. As of now, Dandio's disappearance was a rumor, but should it spread, the country would go into pandemonium. As if there wasn't enough to worry about already! Now, on top of everything else, the council would also need to concentrate on keeping the public calm and the news secret. If not, well…

He lay awake long into the night, thinking of everything that had happened, watching the rain fall through the dim light of the lanterns.

······

Morning dawned bright and sunny, with no traces of last night's dark rumors. Mel gathered his belongings together and headed downstairs. The council was today, and he knew he had to get an early start. The thought sent a hopeful thrill through him.

He stopped by the market on his way to the station to get something for breakfast. In the warm days of early summer, the farming community of Carna thrived. Mel purchased a small block of cheese and a box of plump strawberries. Then he sat on the small bench just beside the station porch and read Rygal's letter once more as secretively as he could.

The council, he guessed, would mostly deal with the new threat Rygal mentioned, and with Dandio's disappearance. Maybe there would be more news about the rumors he'd heard last night about the Forest of Light. Or maybe all of those things were connected, caused by the same dangerous foe. That would make sense, depending on what the unknown enemy was.

Something was watching him.

He felt it, more than saw it, from his place by the station. Somewhere in the market, unfriendly eyes had fixed on him.

Mel's head snapped up, and he looked around swiftly. He saw nothing out of the ordinary. But something had been there, he was sure of it. Something sinister. He had felt that before… that chill, that hate.

He stood and walked back toward the market, his eyes scanning the crowds. Still he saw nothing. A boisterous group of children ran past him to reach a vendor selling sweets. Two men argued over the price of whiskey. A few women exchanged the local gossip while sipping tea.

Nothing out of the ordinary. Perhaps he had just imagined it.

Then he saw it.

A thin, spidery shadow, slithering along the side of a brick building across the street. Practically shapeless, it looked like liquid darkness as it crept along soundlessly. Mel stared at it in both confusion and fear, unsure what he was looking at. His curiosity got the better of him, and he took a hesitant step forward.

The shadow stopped, then straightened up like a wolf catching a scent. It vaguely resembled a hooded figure, whose unseen eyes fixed directly on Mel, as if staring into his mind—

That's the one. The one we saw before. How strange.

Mel reeled back as the low voice echoed in his thoughts. Panicked, he ran back to the cover of the station, then whipped around to face the unknown speaker again.

Gone. The rising sun had reached the shadowy areas under the eave of the brick building. The creature had vanished.

The voice…

Mel's heart pounded, and he sat down on the bench to steady himself. The voice—it was the very same one he had heard inside the Darkness all those months ago. Low, clearer than before, maybe. But it was the same, he was sure.

The clatter of horse hooves and creaking gear reached Mel's ears, and he looked up to see the carriage approaching. Good. The sooner he was at the council and could talk to someone—Jan hopefully— the better. All he wanted now was a quiet, safe ride to Flora, away from this town that had suddenly become sinister.

Mel stuffed the letter back into his bag and took a deep breath to calm himself, then opened the carriage door. And froze in his tracks.

A cloaked and hooded figure was already seated there. Waiting.

4

The Hummingbird

The hooded figure made no sound from inside the carriage. The head turned slightly toward Mel, then looked away again. For an instant Mel stood still, totally at a loss.

"Coming, boy?" the driver asked, sounding annoyed.

"Yes—sorry," Mel stammered, quickly passing him the coins for fare. He shook his head to clear it. No matter what, he had to act like nothing out of the ordinary had just happened. He sat across from the stranger and set his bag down on the floor. *Calm down.* It was the second time that morning that he'd needed to remind himself.

The stranger remained silent, head bent slightly. Mel realized this wasn't the wraith-like shadow he had seen creeping along the building in the market. No, the stranger was human, and that made him relax. But only a little.

The driver clipped the reins to the horses' backs, and the carriage bumped forward again, heading west. Mel looked at his hands, casting an occasional quick glance at the man across from him. He wore a mottled green and gray cloak that wrapped around his frame, and his boots were travel worn and slightly battered. The face was hooded, so Mel couldn't make out any features.

The long silence grated on his nerves. He couldn't stand the uncertainty of not knowing if this man was an enemy or not. If the stranger was dangerous, then Mel would rather know now.

"Where are you headed?" he asked finally, for the sake of conversation.

The man raised his head slightly. His voice was quiet, with a very slight Coonsian accent. "Flora. And you?"

"Me too," Mel said, leaning back in his seat and stuffing his hands in his trouser pockets. "I'm, um, visiting friends."

"I see." The stranger studied him from under the hood, meeting Mel's eyes. "Friends at the council, I imagine?"

"Yeah," Mel said without thinking, then realized with a shock what the stranger had said. "Wait—no, I'm—what do you mean?"

"I assumed such from your letter," the man told him quietly.

Mel looked down and almost fainted with guilt. Sticking out of his leather bag, in plain sight, was Rygal's letter. True, he couldn't actually read too many details…but the signature, *"Rygal of Gayrile,"* was practically announcing Mel's destination to everyone in Orlell. He shoved the letter into the bottom of his bag, under his clothes and money, and had the fleeting, horrible thought that this man would take his letter.

"Relax. I'm going to the council too." There was the slightest hint of amusement in the man's voice as he showed Mel an identical letter from the pocket of his cloak. He pushed off his hood. "Who are you?"

"I'm Mel—I didn't realize—" Mel stammered, still flustered. He looked up into the stranger's face as he realized, gradually, that if this man was a spy, he wouldn't have received a letter himself. That made him relax, though it made him no less embarrassed.

The stranger's mouth twitched with a subtle smile. "I won't tell Rygal," he said.

Mel set his bag aside, then straightened. "I'm Mel Smallbutton, from Appledale," he said, trying to salvage a little of his dignity.

The man extended a hand. "My name is Aryion Paya, ranger of Elimar."

Mel shook his hand, noticing a thin scar on the palm. "You're the Hummingbird," he guessed, remembering Rygal's note.

The ranger raised an eyebrow slightly. "Yes. How did you...?"

"I've heard of you—well, sort of. Rygal mentioned you," Mel explained.

"Oh, did he," Aryion said. "I hope it was all good."

Mel laughed and nodded quickly to reassure him. Aryion, he judged, was likely in his early thirties, though the worn lines on his face made him look older. He had a small, scruffy beard that shaded the lower half of his face, keen features, and deep brown eyes. His dark hair, the same color as his beard, was messily cut, and brushed his shoulders. Now that his cloak had been pulled back slightly, Mel could see the hilt of a sword at his belt.

"Rygal mentioned you as well," Aryion said after a brief pause. "You went on the quest to find Drisilas with him?"

"Yep," Mel said proudly. "That's the first quest I'd ever been on," he admitted. "I'm not really sure why I was invited to the council at all."

"Well, that makes two of us," Aryion replied.

Mel looked up at him curiously. "Didn't Elimar send you with the ruling lord?" Typically, he knew, a ranger worked as a special officer to the kingdom, working under individual barons or lords depending on the area. But Aryion shook his head.

"No. In fact, only those personally invited by King Jan were sent from the Elimar Council."

Mel frowned at that fact. "Rygal said there might be spies," he said slowly. "That's probably why Jan wants to keep it secret."

"I guessed the same. The last thing we need is confusion and lies spreading among the public and causing panic," Aryion pointed out.

Mel nodded, remembering the conversation he'd overheard last night. "I think some people have already heard about Dandio going missing," he said slowly. "But I guess it'd be hard to keep something like that quiet."

Aryion looked surprised. "Really? In Appledale?"

"No—I heard some men talking about it last night in Carna," Mel told him. "Just local gossip, but if people hear that it's true…" he trailed off, not entirely sure what would happen.

There was a moment of silence before the ranger spoke again, voice low. "Have you heard anything more about his disappearance?" he asked.

Mel shook his head, feeling a sharp pang of worry in his chest.

"No. Only what Rygal said in his letter, and that wasn't much." He looked up. "What do you think happened to him?"

Aryion leaned back, his face thoughtful. "Well… I have my theories. But I think it may have something to do with what happened to the Forest of Light."

Mel frowned slightly. "What do you mean? What happened?"

The ranger looked up at him, and there was a look in his eyes that made Mel wonder if he wanted to know. Then Aryion took a deep breath, and when he spoke, his voice was barely above a whisper. "The Forest of Light has been destroyed. Completely engulfed in white ice. I traveled past it on my way here."

"Ice?" Mel repeated, baffled.

Aryion nodded. "You could feel the cold even from the path, over a hundred feet away. I don't know what could have done it—I don't even know what sort of creature has the power to do that, not since the Darkness. This… this was something else entirely."

Mel's mind whirled in confusion as he tried to make sense of this information. It wasn't the Forest's destruction that worried him, though it was concerning. It was more the principle of it. Something had come and obliterated the last remnant of the High Light's glory set on Orlell. "The farmers last night said something about an evil entering the Forest. I've only heard a little about it—it's said that nothing evil can get in. Usually."

"Usually," Aryion pointed out. "It is an old legend, as old as the Forest itself. But it states that any who enter the Forest with cruel intentions will forever bear a terrible curse." The ranger paused, thinking. "But if the creature who destroyed it is anything like the Darkness, they will care little for the legend."

Mel thought of the Darkness, of the sweeping fog and pale ice, and shivered at the thought of such a creature returning. "I wonder what could do that," he said aloud. "But… if Dandio was there, maybe he was captured."

"And I believe he was there," Aryion said. Mel looked at him, and he continued slowly. "As I said, I only have a theory. But I found tracks in the Forest, preserved in the ruin. A horseman rode in and stopped at the spring. He appeared to step away from the water, at which point his tracks vanished. The horse, from its tracks, was startled and fled. It turned up in Caer Sia later."

A prickle of fear ran down Mel's spine as he remembered the creeping black shadow he had seen in the market, and the way it had vanished. If it had been the same…

"Did you… did you see anyone else there?" he asked slowly, trying to keep the worry out of his voice.

The ranger frowned slightly and shook his head. "No. Most of the animals have likely fled the area, just like the horse did." His dark eyes studied Mel carefully. "Why do you ask?"

Mel shrugged as casually as he could. "Oh, nothing. Just wondering."

Aryion didn't seem convinced, only looked at him thoughtfully. He dismissed the matter. "Well, whatever the truth of it is, the High

King believes Dandio was captured—possibly by the same power that destroyed the Forest. The gear and the sword were confirmed to be his by Ĵan himself."

Something about the way he said this made Mel look up. "*You* brought the news to Sia," he guessed slowly. "You found Dandio's gear, and you reported his disappearance."

The ranger said nothing, only nodded very slightly. His face was grim. Mel instantly had a hundred new questions, but he couldn't quite put them into words. Nor was he sure that he wanted them answered.

"So… why'd you come east again?" he asked instead. If Aryion had originally traveled west, through the Forest of Light into Caer Sia, it was odd that he would have come back this way. Flora was closer to Caer Sia than Carna was, yet the ranger had come miles northeast to be in Carna.

Aryion looked at him—Mel saw a quick, fleeting look cross his face that he didn't understand. It was quickly masked. "The King requested that I return to the Forest before the council, to see if anything had changed or if there were any new signs. I bring that report to the council today."

Mel nodded, satisfied for the moment. He thought back to what Aryion had said about the destruction of the Forest. "You said it was frozen… destroyed," he began, and the ranger nodded in confirmation. "The only creature I would have guessed to have the power to do that would be the Darkness—but it's gone now."

Aryion nodded. "Yes, I've thought about that as well. I'll admit I know very little about these powers—likely less than you do," he added with a wry smile.

Mel fidgeted with the strap of his pack, thinking. He knew about such powers, though he wished he didn't. Images floated through his mind. The white ice of the Darkness spreading over the grass around Castle Sia; the charred skeletons of Terrax's warriors falling to the ground in its wake; the burning coldness of its touch as it had seized him and pulled him into its mass –

Now is the hour of us.

He closed his eyes briefly, and the face within the void smiled back at him as the echoes of its voice died in his mind.

Mel looked up at the ranger again. Aryion's dark eyes were fixed on him intently, his face as unreadable as ever, but Mel thought he saw both sorrow and compassion in his gaze.

"Jan will probably have a plan," Mel told him, forcing a smile. "He knows a lot about these sorts of things."

Aryion nodded in agreement but said nothing further. Mel looked out the window, watching as the terrain sped by, riding in silence for a little while.

He finally turned back to his companion, needing a change in conversation. "What does a ranger do, Aryion?" he asked curiously. "I've only heard a little about them."

Aryion leaned back against his seat. "Many different things, depending on the ranger. We roam through the kingdom, sending reports to the ruling lord of a city or fief if there is a threat. We are trained in strategy as well as battle, and sometimes a ruling lord will employ a ranger in times of war for that purpose."

"To help fight?" Mel asked, fascinated.

"Occasionally," Aryion said, one hand tracing the hilt of his sword. "More often to plan the battle itself. As I said, we are trained in strategy."

"Trained by who?" Mel asked.

"A mentor—another ranger, with experience. My father trained me himself, for a time." A quick flash of sorrow crossed Aryion's face, pain and grief from some old memory. It was gone just as fast, and he continued. "It takes years of training and work, but as far as trades go, it can be quite rewarding at times."

The carriage lurched slightly, slowing, and the driver called back to them that they had arrived in Flora. Mel swung his pack over his shoulders and looked out the window, excitement filling him, both that his journey was over, and that the time had come.

Today he would get answers, he told himself. Answers that only this mysterious council and those attending could give him.

5

Flora

A blaze of color met Mel's eyes as he stepped out of the carriage onto the patio of the station. The city itself, upon first glance, resembled the brightly colored Elven flower it was named for. The station, which was near the center of town, allowed for a wide view of the numerous markets that filled the village.

Flora, Mel realized gradually, was a trading center for the many merchants that traveled the northern roads of Orlell. Positioned between the prairie lands to the east and the wealthy northern cities, the vendors and shops sold every type of mercantile one could think of. The air filled with the shouts of the merchants and peddlers advertising their goods: "Exotic silk fabrics!" "Fresh fish straight from Mata City!" "Cinnamon! Ginger! Cayenne! Rare spices from the east!"

Aryion seemed to know his way around, so Mel followed the ranger's long stride as they walked through the crowded marketplace. Everywhere Mel looked, there was something new. A group of olive-skinned men with curled mustaches spoke in a lilting, musical language. Two desert-dwellers in brightly dyed robes heckled over prices with an Elven peddler. A family of Liznees stopped to talk to a man with blue skin and rust-red hair. A group of guards, wearing the uniforms of the Daffodalion army, patrolled the marketplace.

Mel realized he had wandered slightly while staring, and jogged to catch up to Aryion. "Where's the council going to be?" he asked.

"The baron of Flora has offered his meeting hall for the High King's use," Aryion told him. "Down this road… ah, here we are."

They faced a solid, two story building made of gray stone, surrounded by a well-kept lawn. For a baron's living quarters, it was quite plain. But as they approached, Mel noticed three guards stationed outside wore the armor of the Red Dawn. Likely, they had accompanied Jan east for the council. Along with the group of soldiers, a tall figure draped in a gray cloak stood just inside the doorway.

Aryion and Mel handed their letters to the guards, who admitted them in. As they entered, the man in the gray cloak stepped in front of them and asked, in a low but familiar voice, "Password?"

"Lumolyn," Mel and Aryion said in unison, and Mel added eagerly, "It's good to see you, Rygal! How was your trip south?"

Rygal laughed and pulled off the cowl. "Is my disguise that bad? Jan said I'm supposed to stay inconspicuous."

Aryion arched an eyebrow. "Inconspicuous, Rygal, is the last word I would use to describe you."

Rygal's smile widened. The last time Mel had seen Rygal, the young warrior had been fighting for each breath, his ribs badly crushed by Adderstrike. He was taller and broader than Aryion, though younger, and had dark hair and a small beard. His sword was slung at his side, and his easy, friendly manner lifted Mel's heart.

"So, who else is here?" Mel asked as they started down the hall.

"A few lords and dukes from Coonsia. Jan wanted them here to overview the defensive strategy, but they've already been a bit difficult," Rygal said with the slightest hint of disdain. Mel knew lords and dukes tended to be a tad…overbearing in situations like this. "Jan came, of course. So did several other of my comrades from earlier quests. And you two."

"Any news of what we're up against?" Aryion asked as they headed down the hall. Rygal's smile vanished.

"No—at least, not that I know. Jan has his guesses, none of them pleasant, though that's probably to be expected. Oh, and someone else came, a person of great importance."

"Who?" Mel asked.

"The Queen of the Stars, one of the Seven Servants. She arrived this morning."

Mel didn't need to ask who that was. Aryion drew his breath sharply. "Cahadras herself?" he asked in a low voice. Rygal nodded.

"I think Iriam requested for her to come, but it is difficult to make contact with any Stars. They're more reserved than your average Fyrocrian, which is saying something." Rygal shrugged slightly. "I don't really know particulars. But we can thank the Light she's here. Perhaps she can help solve our riddles."

Mel's mind spun with the impact of this. He knew so little of the Star people, the last race of Fyrocrians that still dwelt in their ancient kingdom in the sky. But he knew they had fought hard and strong in the Dividing War centuries before, and it was thanks to them that the people of Orlell had survived. He looked up at Rygal as they walked down the long hallway. "The Stars—do you think they'll help in this battle, then?" he asked in wonder.

"I don't know if they'll help us fight," Rygal said hesitantly. "To be honest, I'd be afraid to ask that. They're… strange people, very old and very proud. But good too. It's hard to explain." He paused, then started again. "I do know that if anyone has any idea of what we face, it'll be Cahadras."

"What do we know so far?" Mel asked him.

Rygal frowned. "Well, we'll discuss it soon. The council will start in a few minutes, and our questions will be answered." He glanced at Aryion. "I can tell you, at least, that we know the orc tribes are amassing at the southern border again."

Aryion's head snapped up at that. "All of the tribes?"

"I'd imagine so. From the report, it sounded like they have gathered in great numbers. Jan thinks they've joined with whoever is behind all this." Rygal paused. "They were led by Hagshrub."

Mel didn't understand the sudden interest in Aryion's eyes. The news just confused him. "The orcs haven't come this far west in years," he said slowly. "Don't they normally live in the Anozira mountains? Why would they fight us now?"

"The orcs will fight anyone if they're paid enough for it," Rygal told him bitterly. "But they're not the only ones. We've received word that several ships of Jenna warriors have left Sikhazi and sailed southwest, toward Esile Bay."

"Jenna?" Aryion repeated with a slight frown. "That *is* strange. The orcs are mercenaries, but they are a minor threat compared to the Jenna tribes. The Jenna will want war, after being forced back during the War of the Strait."

"Right, and there's thousands of them that have come this way so far," Rygal said. "We received news of it from Reedmount, but that was almost a month ago. Whoever this new warlord is, he's likely amassed quite an army by now."

A prickle of dread ran down Mel's spine at his words, and he found himself more eager than ever to learn what he could in the council.

They reached the meeting hall, and Mel, once again, hardly knew where to look. Within the room was such a swirl of color and noise that Mel found his head swimming slightly. And the color was not only in the clothing—the diversity of races and species was breathtaking. Mel spotted Elves, Liznees, Direns, and humans, along with other species. Several Coonsian dukes conversed with a group of tall, dark-skinned men. The Siren lord, recognized by the simple crown he wore, sat perched near the end of the table, three of his warriors sitting close by. They resembled the salamanders Mel had seen in his backyard, but much bigger, with an intelligent and proud air in their stance. He also noticed two Coopers, both about the size of a sheep dog, otter-like, with thick brown fur. One wore the chain of office as Lord, and the other, younger, sat nearby.

Aryion surveyed the crowded room and gave a low, impressed whistle. "You definitely did well in bringing them all here, Rygal. Was there any difficulty in getting them to come?"

Rygal sighed wearily. "Oh, there were plenty of arguments, I can tell you. Jan had to convince a lot of them to even consider it, let alone send representatives. But everyone's here." He was called aside by a tall Diren warrior and excused himself.

"Best get a seat while you can," Aryion advised Mel, then left to greet an Elf whom he seemed to know. Mel moved forward awkwardly, feeling very out of his league. The Sirens, silent in their study of the room, watched him with yellow eyes that seemed neither unfriendly nor welcoming. The desert-dwellers spoke quietly in their own dialect.

He finally took a seat next to the second Cooper he had noticed— the younger, judging by his lithe movements and glossy brown fur. His otter-like face was friendly, and he smiled as Mel sat down.

"Hello. Quite a few people here, don't you think?"

"Between Rygal and Jan, I almost expected more," Mel said with a grin.

The Cooper laughed and nodded. "Yes, that's true." He studied Mel carefully. "Rygal mentioned you, I think—he told us about your adventures the last time he visited. You're the one who went to return Drisilas with him, right?"

Mel nodded and held out a hand. "Yes—I'm Mel Smallbutton of Appledale."

The Cooper extended a paw and shook Mel's hand in greeting. "Jarus Puddlepaw of Mata City—good to meet you."

This name was familiar, and it took Mel a moment to place it. "Oh, I've heard of you too," he said as it finally occurred to him. "You helped Rygal stop Safacon—on the quest to find the Jewel of Power?" During the quest for Drisilas, Rygal had regaled both Mel and Misty with the thrilling story of the defeat of Safacon, the cruel sorcerer who had enslaved Gayrile for decades. Jarus, as Mel remembered, had been one of eight companions who had gone to find the Jewel itself.

Jarus nodded and smiled. "Yes. I guess we're all part of history now in one way or another, strangely enough."

"What about your other companions?" Mel asked eagerly. "Are they all here?"

"Not all of us, but a few. Rygal's here, of course, and Norrin came with him—he's the one that led our quest. Lammar was invited, but he's been called away on important business in the east and won't be here today." Jarus shrugged slightly, a little rueful. "As for the Brownaes, it's hard enough to get word to them in regular circumstances. But I've heard from King Casper of the Direns that Neely is quite well."

"And what about your wife Maya?" Mel asked.

Jarus smiled and shook his head. "She would have come in a

heartbeat, naturally. But she stayed in Mata City. Her designs for ships are being adopted by the Mata City fleet, so she's quite busy. And we have a child to care for now," he added proudly. "Little Ella will be one year old this next spring."

"Congratulations," Mel told him, smiling at the cheerful Cooper.

A sudden silence fell on the room, and everyone stood. Mel and Jarus quickly followed suit, turning expectant eyes to the door.

Jan Ki entered first, clad in a simple black jerkin over a dull red shirt. Drisilas hung at his side, Mel noticed with a flash of pride. He caught Jan's gaze; the Liznee king gave him a quick smile of greeting but said nothing. His silver face was worn, with dark circles under his eyes. The gravity of the times weighed heavily on him, along with worry for his brother. But his green eyes were alert and still held a spark of hope.

Jan surveyed those assembled and nodded respectfully. "I welcome and thank you all for coming. May I introduce our honored guest. Cahadras Maramoon, the Queen of the Stars."

Murmurs rose from the watchers. A woman, tall and graceful, entered the room. Her silver breastplate was engraved with the red and gold emblem of the Stars, and below it her long skirts brushed the floor. Her hair, white-blonde, was swept up into an intricate bun. Her face was proud, lined with the care of a thousand years. Yet it was her eyes that Mel was struck by. They were gray-blue, clear and calculating, and they flashed with a fire that spoke well of her power.

Even Ĵan bowed to her before taking a seat at the head of the table. Cahadras remained standing, studying the group assembled. She spoke finally, her voice low and tone brisk. "I have not come here for formalities, and any advice I have I will give frankly. Think you that you can combat this threat with mortal strength? I tell you to banish such thoughts from your mind. Your enemy will only turn it against you, and he would find such futile resistance amusing."

Several people looked around uncertainly. Mel felt a surge of nervousness. It seemed with every moment there was something new to learn about their unknown opponent.

Cahadras took her seat and nodded slightly to Ĵan, who cleared his throat and began. "This council will now commence. There are many grave matters to be discussed. First, it may be worth telling what we are up against."

Ĵan paused. "Not quite a year ago, as some of you have cause to remember, the wraith known as the Darkness met its downfall. But while this was a great victory, it has brought new questions to light. We have heard hints of another force before—something or someone that has been orchestrating everything that's happened in this last decade. Kado and the Hazes, Safacon and the Objects, the Darkness—they were clues, but many of our guesses toward their meaning were sadly incorrect. The Jewel of Power, for one, was not a mere weapon, as we had first believed. It was a gateway to another world, a realm whose powers Safacon hoped to gain for himself."

"But the Jewel was destroyed," Rygal said slowly, as though unable to keep silent any longer. "Why should it still be considered a threat?"

Cahadras arched an eyebrow at him. "The Jewel matters greatly in light of this, son of Maran. Safacon himself hardly knew its true strength. However, he did understand that the power it held, if attainable, would change the world of Orlell in ways you can hardly imagine."

"Safacon fell," Jan said, "and the Jewel was destroyed, as was the Darkness. But now… now we face something greater." Again, he hesitated. "You all want to know what we are up against now—indeed, what we have been up against all along. It's high time you all knew. I admit I did not expect this, and it is difficult to believe even now."

A few people muttered uneasily. The Siren lord snorted. "We have come for the truth, no matter how grim," he said. "It is better to be out with it."

Cahadras looked at him, and her steady words completely silenced the watchers. "He has come back. The one from a world beyond light. The ruler of the dead. Kahlifis, as he was once called, though now he uses another name." Her eyes flashed. "The Ace-Lord. The Aces have returned."

6

∽ ∽ ∽ ∽ ∽ ∽ ∽ ∽ ∽ ∽

The Choice of the Council

For an instant there was dead silence. *Aces?* The word was vaguely familiar to Mel, carrying a fear and darkness he couldn't explain, but he didn't know much more than the name itself. Creatures out of the darkest sort of mythology, mentioned fleetingly in history. But the shock and horror on the faces of the people around him told him that this evil was no myth.

One of the Diren warriors shook his head. "We are not here for you to sport with us," he said flatly. "Tell us the truth of it. The Aces cannot be back. It is impossible."

A skeptical smile crossed Cahadras' face. "*Impossible,*' I think you will find, means nothing in the weeks to come."

"I thought the same," Ĵan said, looking at the Diren who had spoken. "The Aces returned? It has been decades since they were last seen in the mortal world, and centuries before that when Kahlifis was thought to be killed. Deny it if you will, but this is the truth."

"Kahlifis is dead, Ĵan," the Siren lord snapped, disbelief evident in his tone. "The Dividing War was three hundred years ago, when he led the rebel charge. You ask us to believe that he still lives?"

"What... what are the Aces?" Mel asked in the short silence

following the Siren's words. All eyes turned to him, and he blushed nervously.

Jan took a deep breath and glanced at the skeptical lords. "I know this is difficult to believe. I hope we can better explain everything today. To answer Mel's question, I ask Iriam the Neutral to speak about the Aces."

A tall figure wreathed in black stood to Cahadras' right. Like the Liznees, his skin was silver, but a darker shade than Jan's. His eyes were purple-red, similar in appearance to the chilling face Mel remembered in the void. Mel felt a shiver of fear as he remembered it. But even as the thought crossed his mind, he noticed that Iriam's face held a different light. There was kindness and justice in his eyes. His deep voice was grim as he spoke.

"As the High King has said, many years have passed since the Aces last entered our world. They are not like the other Netrocrians—their power is a darker sort. Even before their rebellion, we trusted them very little. There are eleven known of such creatures, led by a twelfth, whose powers are greater than any we have faced before. He is known as the Ace-Lord, and I believe we will speak of him later.

"The Aces are ruthless, pitiless creatures, and as mortal fear of them grows, so does their strength. The more we fear them, the stronger they become. They exist to serve their master, and to kill and destroy whatever they can."

"Like the Darkness," Mel said slowly, thinking out loud.

"In some ways, yes. In others, not at all," Iriam said, his gaze resting on Mel's face. "Both Darkness and Ace had the power to alter the Essence—the very life-source of a person. The Darkness killed by rotting the Essence from within—thus it destroyed Terrax's army. Yet the Aces can do more, with powers unique to them. Their ice allows them to reach the Essence, to change it or rip it from their victim in an instant. It is a vile way to kill, but quite effective, I can assure you."

Mel's stomach lurched at the thought. Unbidden, a memory of Llyrion came to his mind, and he remembered anew the last agonized seconds of the Elven warrior's life before he died. Killed by the Darkness. Fury and fear filled him in equal parts, and Mel closed his eyes in an effort to push it away.

"The Aces first appeared in the Dividing War, nearly three hundred years ago," Jan said. "Many of them were killed in that battle. Their leader was believed to be killed as well—it was two hundred and fifty years before he appeared again, in central Coonsia."

"That can't have been the same leader," an Elven dignitary insisted. "Sire—think. Even if Kahlifis managed to escape in the aftermath of the war, how would he be alive today?"

"There are other ways to live," Cahadras said quietly. "Particularly if one has a power source to do so."

A bearded man Mel didn't recognize looked up thoughtfully. "You believe he had the Jewel, my lady?" he asked Cahadras. "Safacon thought to use it to reach a realm of eternal life. But… that was centuries before Safacon."

"Indeed it was, Norrin," Cahadras told him. "But the Jewel existed long before Safacon."

That got everyone's attention. Next to Mel, Jarus straightened, his furry face wrinkled in absolute confusion. Even Norrin looked shocked. "*Before* Safacon?" the wizard repeated finally, staring at the Star Queen. "How is that possible? Safacon created the Jewel—created it from the heart of a dying Star, as the legends go. Its power came from the Land Immortal, did it not?"

"So it did," Cahadras said. "But Safacon did not create it, contrary to your stories." She paused. "What none of you, nor any mortal, knew was that the Jewel was already here, before Safacon or even the Dividing War. I understand your confusion. The truth was kept from history."

A turmoil of emotions showed on Norrin's weathered face—the shock of this revelation had hit hard.

"Safacon spoke of another power before his defeat," he said at last, half to himself. "I wish I had given it further thought." He turned to the Star Queen again. "If Safacon did not create it, where did the Jewel come from?"

Cahadras studied all those assembled. "The Jewel was one of three Star-Stones, made, with its sisters, to be a beacon of hope and unity for the rulers of the ancient world. Isilas, the fire-stone, was given to the Fyrocrians, to Lord Sindian of the Liznees. The Blue Stone was created for the Cantrians, and was given to King Grisham of the humans."

She faltered a moment before continuing, and Mel thought he could see the pain of the memories in her eyes. "The Jewel… was the third, and it was given to Kahlifis, lord of the Netrocrians. Unknown to any of us, Kahlifis knew of another world, another source of power. The Dark Realm, as it is simply called, for there is no name better fitting. Kahlifis twisted the magic that filled the Jewel so that it no longer drew its power from the Land Immortal. Instead, it served as a gateway between the mortal world and the Dark Realm. It is these powers that Safacon tried so hard to reach."

Rygal looked at Norrin, searching the old wizard's face for confirmation. Mel could see how hard it was for them to accept this stunning fact. For his part, Norrin still looked surprised, but understanding had begun to dawn in his eyes. He spoke again, slowly. "And what about the Dividing War? How did Safacon find the Jewel after that?"

"Kahlifis sought to take over the mortal world of Orlell with his newfound dark magic," Cahadras told him. "This sparked the Dividing War. Along with his followers, Kahlifis rebelled and fought against the loyal servants of the High Light. However, he was defeated, and the Jewel was believed lost."

She paused, then continued. "The secret of the Dark Realm was kept hidden. When Safacon first rose in skill, centuries later, he meddled too much, with too many things he did not understand. By the time he realized his folly, it was too late. He was made a pawn, his life sold to the ruler beyond—the Ace-Lord, ruler of the Dark Realm, master of the Jewel."

Jarus looked up sharply. "Norrin, the voice—just before the Jewel was destroyed, we heard a voice—even you weren't quite sure who it was."

"No, though I am beginning to guess now," Norrin told him.

Mel barely heard the wizard's voice. His mind had hinged on one word. "A voice?" he repeated, looking at Jarus in disbelief. "What do you mean? What did it sound like? Did you see anything?"

Jarus looked at him, startled by his intensity. "No, I didn't see anything. Right before we destroyed the Jewel, I heard a voice speaking, warning us not to interfere, that kind of thing."

"But you didn't see anything? A face?" Mel pressed, needing to be sure.

"No…" Jarus said, totally confused now.

"Why do you ask this, lad?" Norrin asked gently, his brow furrowed with concern.

Mel turned to face him, unable to form a coherent sentence. "I—the Darkness—the void—I heard—I thought— Jan," he broke off, looking at the Liznee king for help. "I heard the voice, remember, right when the Darkness was destroyed—"

"What does he speak of?" one of the barons asked, irritated. "Voices and faces—there is no sense."

"It's all right, Mel," Jan said quietly, meeting Mel's eyes. "Tell them what you saw." His low voice reassured Mel's racing heart.

Mel took a breath and spoke as calmly as he could, sensing everyone's eyes on him. "When we fought the Darkness, it grabbed me," he said hesitantly. "It pulled me inside itself, into the fog. I thought it was going to kill me, but it didn't. Everything went dark, and then I heard a voice."

"What did it say?" Jarus asked expectantly as Mel paused.

"Well, first I heard it talk to the Darkness. The voice ordered it to surrender, to stand down and let itself be defeated. By Drisilas," Mel said, looking at Jan again. "I saw a face, too—red eyes and gray skin. And then the voice spoke to me…it told me that it would be here soon." Images surged through his mind as he said it, and he stopped, wincing at the terror of the memory.

An uncertain silence had settled over the council. "What does this mean, Jan?" Norrin asked. "I have no doubt that it was the Ace-Lord's voice they heard, both Jarus and Mel. But why would the Aces want the Darkness to surrender?"

It was Cahadras who answered. "Because the Ace-Lord had no further use for the Darkness by then. At that point in time, the wraith had served its purpose." She paused. "The Ace-Lord has no favorites among his servants—he deals only in usefulness. Once that usefulness runs out, he removes them from his plot."

"The voice said that the Darkness' death would pave the way," Mel said slowly.

Cahadras nodded thoughtfully. "And so it has, quite well. As did the Jewel's destruction, which did little except return the Jewel's power to its original master." She looked at Jan. "You used the word 'orchestrating' earlier. It is a fitting description. All these years you have fought against the dangers presented and unintentionally fit yourselves perfectly into the Ace-Lord's scheme."

The words hit Mel in the stomach, and for a moment he struggled to believe them. But he could see the truth. He thought about the quest and everything that had happened: allowing the Darkness to pursue them into the caves, later unknowingly leading the wraith into Caer Sia. Even the battle at the end of the struggle had been part of the plan. The Ace-Lord needed the Darkness out of the way. There could be no threats to his coming empire. And what better way to do that than to use the companions as pawns, to make them think they were fighting for good?

Everything they had fought for, all this time, had been in vain. And now the Aces had come.

"We had no other choice, Cahadras," Iriam said, his deep voice quiet. "Many would have died had we chosen to do nothing. Nor could any of us have known the truth. The best we can do now is fight against the real danger."

"Indeed," Jan said, clearing his throat. "The Aces are here, and they have worked quickly. Already we have heard many reports of our enemies rushing to join them."

"Yes," the baron of Flora agreed grimly. "We have seen clans of orcs passing through our lands of late."

"Acting as if they owned all of Orlell," snarled the Siren lord.

"And the Jenna!" chimed in one of the dark-skinned nobles Mel had seen earlier. "A great host of Jenna warriors traveled through the outskirts of our kingdom in the Lago desert only a week before last. Our sources state they are joining with the orcs."

"So they have, most likely," the baron of Flora said. "But none of them could have destroyed the Forest of Light, could they?"

His words raised a chorus of questioning and concerned voices from the listeners. "Silence!" Ĵan ordered, standing. "I must confirm that these rumors are true. The Forest is destroyed."

"How?" Rygal asked, dumbfounded. "We know the legends—no evil can enter the Forest."

"The legend is true, but I doubt it would mean anything to the Aces," Ĵan said grimly. "Still, your questions would be better answered by another." He looked at Aryion, who had remained quiet up till now. "You first brought the news of its destruction, Hummingbird. Tell us what you saw."

Aryion stood slowly and hesitated, as though deciding how best to answer. "I know little of these matters, sire. What I can tell is what I saw. The Forest was frozen, killed as if by a sudden intense frost. And the cold… it seemed to claw at my very core." He paused again, gathering his thoughts, then continued. "There were a few tracks, though I could not make out their meaning. The only other sign was Liznee gear—a pack and a sword, which I brought to Caer Sia. There, they were identified as belonging to Dandio Ki."

Startled exclamations broke out immediately. "He was in the Forest itself?" a Liznee courtier stammered, shocked. "During its very destruction?"

"There were no signs of struggle?" Norrin asked, looking at the ranger. Aryion shook his head.

"Captured," Rygal guessed determinedly, but he looked doubtful.

"He might not have fought. Maybe he surrendered if he knew he couldn't defeat an Ace," Jarus suggested slowly.

"Dandio would never have surrendered without a fight," Jan said, his voice tight. The pain on his face wrenched Mel's heart.

"Maybe he was captured before he could fight," Mel said, desperate for a logical answer. "Or—or maybe the Aces changed the tracks to make us think he's dead. Maybe they want us to give up."

He thought the idea was a weak one, so he was startled to see a wry smile cross Cahadras' face. "That is a very wise thought, child. The Ace-Lord thrives on fear and uncertainty, and deception is his strongest trait." She looked at the others. "The fate of Dandio Ki is unknown as of now. Of him, I can tell you nothing further than what the ranger has reported already."

"But of the Forest," said a sandy-haired baron who seemed to be speaking for a group of people, "of the Forest, it seems we are overlooking a possibility. Clearly, only a Netrocrian with great power could do such a thing. Yet the Aces are not the only Netrocrians we know of. The Darkness, I know, is dead, but..." he hesitated, and the others urged him on, "but what about that Neutral, who's dwelt rather conveniently close to the Forest all these years?"

There was a very tense pause as the baron threw a challenging look at Iriam.

"You are *severely* misled if you think—" Ĵan started, but Iriam motioned for him to stay silent.

The Neutral looked at the baron, studying him carefully. His voice was crisp and reasoning. "To understand you correctly, sir—you propose that *I* froze the Forest of Light?" The baron, who looked like he would like to be anywhere else, nodded hesitantly. Iriam frowned slightly. "Well, it is an option, although it would take great strength. But what motives would I have to do that? Taking over Coonsia, perhaps? Please believe me that I have no desires what-soever in that direction. In fact, I have advised Ĵan long enough to have heard every complaint to ruin any such appeal."

A few people chuckled. The baron's face was bright red. Iriam met his eyes, his tone calm as he concluded. "I give you credit for voicing that possibility, but I have long protected the Forest of Light. Now, it is my sole duty to bring its destroyers to justice. Rest as-sured, sir, that I am on your side."

The baron sat down again with a mumbled apology. He and his friends looked embarrassed, and Mel hid his grin.

"Thank you, Iriam," Ĵan said as the Neutral sat down again. A slight smile played at the corners of his mouth. "To be honest, I of-ten pity those who battle for a throne; I know what challenges they will end up with."

A ripple of laughter ran through the listeners, and the tension in the room eased as quickly as it had come. "Now," Ĵan said, "we will determine what should be done to counter the Aces' invasion." He looked at Cahadras. "My lady, you understand the Ace-Lord's character better than any of us. What do you think his goal is?"

The Star Queen stood again. "When he was mortal, Kahlifis sought the other two Star-Stones with a great passion. I have no doubt that he will try to gain them now. His servants draw their strength from the fear of mortals—their power grows daily. If there is any hope of stopping them, we must act quickly."

She paused, thinking. "The Jewel is gone; thus I assume the Ace-Lord will now seek the other two Stones with urgency. The Stone given to the Fyrocrians remains in the hilt of Drisilas." She nodded slightly at Jan. "The remaining Stone, the Blue Stone, was given to the humans. King Grisham of Arkran, upon receiving it, requested that it be rendered into two equal halves—two Shards—so that everyone in his kingdom could share its powers."

Jan nodded. "The Shards are likely what the Aces seek. One half was kept in Arkran, until the Darkness attacked the city. However, after Drisilas was forged and the Darkness driven back, we managed to recover that half of the Stone. It's kept in Caer Sia now."

"And the second Shard?" Norrin asked.

"In the island city of Kamon," Iriam told him. "It is a small village, but its people guard the Shard loyally."

Jarus raised his paw hesitantly. "What do the Shards do?" he asked slowly. "If Drisilas' Stone is fire and strength, and the Jewel is a gateway, then what powers does the Blue Stone have?"

Cahadras nodded to him. "A very important question. The Shards have remained separate for centuries, but they both possess powers from the Land Immortal. A gift to mortal man, they can heal any wound, treat any sickness, and, when joined together, draw a large amount of power from the Land Immortal itself. The Ace-Lord will seek to join them and use them to take power from the Dark Realm, as he did with the Jewel. But, if joined before that, the Shards alone may offer some chance of halting the Aces' progress."

She looked at the others. "Two parties shall be sent from here. The first will number fifty warriors, led by Norrin of Arkran. They will journey to Kamon, where they will recover the Shard. The second group shall be smaller, and they will go to Caer Sia, where they shall guard the second Shard. This group, as we have decided, will be led by Iriam and the High King."

Iriam nodded. "If you agree, madam, I suggest that our group will number seven in total. It is enough to discourage any attackers, as well as travel light and reach Caer Sia swiftly."

"It is a good number," Cahadras told him thoughtfully.

"The road to Caer Sia will likely have dangers enough," Jan added. "Once the Aces realize we mean to join the Shards, they'll send warriors after us."

"We'll give them a fight before we give up," Rygal said, echoed by fierce growls of agreement from the assembled warriors.

"That may be more difficult than we think." Everyone looked over, surprised to hear Aryion's voice. The ranger stood, his face troubled. "Your highness," he said quickly, bowing his head in Cahadras and

Jan's direction, "have you yet heard of the enchantment placed on the Ace-Lord's servants?"

Cahadras' face was unreadable, but Jan frowned and shook his head no. Aryion continued slowly. "It is but a rumor I overheard in Cattrick Fief, but I know it may be vital to our mission. I have heard that the orcs and men who serve the Aces now have pledged more than just their loyalty. They are altered, changed somehow. Enchanted was the word used by one source. It may be that—"

He was drowned out as shocked and fearful voices rang out through the room. Iriam stood. "Silence!" he commanded, and everyone fell quiet again. The Neutral turned his crimson eyes on the ranger. "Speak, Hummingbird. This news troubles me and will determine much."

Aryion nodded gratefully and went on. "It is, as I say, a rumor, but I will mention it here. I have heard that the Aces' servants—orcs, men, and many others, most likely—have been enchanted by the Ace-Lord. Their memories are completely removed, so that they remain loyal to death. And even death remains out of their freedoms. It is said that the Ace-Lord has made them immortal, unable to die."

"It is not a rumor confined only to the North," said one of the desert-dwelling lords. "One of my men returned earlier this month with a strange report of deathless orcs traveling through the sands. We dismissed him as fevered by the heat, but now I am not so sure."

"The Ace-Lord is powerful," Iriam said, "but the Shards equally so.

Until they are joined, we will be wary of their warriors, and try to avoid them."

Jan nodded. "We must reach Caer Sia swiftly if we are to protect the Shards. I have asked Aryion the Hummingbird to accompany us. He knows the terrain well, and his knowledge in strategy will be greatly useful while we prepare.

"I also ask Quinn Fireleaf to accompany us, if he is willing," Jan continued, nodding to the Elven ranger Mel had noticed earlier. "Together with the Hummingbird, I am hopeful that we may best plan our defense against the Aces."

Mel glanced over at Aryion. The ranger barely moved, only nodded slightly to the watchers. Mel was a little surprised—Aryion had said nothing about a mission on the carriage ride. But maybe Jan had asked him before the council.

He felt a familiar stir of both curiosity and unease in his chest. Whatever Iriam and Jan had said, he felt sure that the journey to Caer Sia would be more dangerous than they were letting on. Why else recruit not one, but two rangers for the task?

Iriam scanned the crowd. "These are treacherous times, unlike any we have known before. Thus, I ask you to search your hearts and decide if you believe yourself willing to join us."

There was a moment of silence. Then Rygal spoke, the ghost of a grin flickering across his face. "I have not forgotten the day that you guided me as a boy through Grayline Swamp," he said to Iriam, standing. "I pledge my sword, as a Guardian of Gayrile, to defend Caer Sia now."

The delegates from Gayrile looked pleased, and Mel noticed Norrin smiling in pride. He was startled to see Cahadras frown slightly as she studied Rygal. Almost as if she were trying to see his thoughts. "Be wary of your choices, son of Maran," she said quietly, as Rygal sat down again. "You are skilled, passionate. Beware that the Ace-Lord does not turn it against you."

A cold shiver ran down Mel's spine at her words. Rygal bowed his head in acknowledgment. "Yes, my lady. By my word, I shall do whatever I can to defend Caer Sia."

Jarus stood next, a little hesitantly. "Well, if you'd allow me, sir, then I want to go too," he said hopefully. "Since the quest for the Jewel, I've only heard about the battles happening in Caer Sia. I would be honored to help defend the city now." He paused, then added, "Besides, somebody has to keep an eye on Rygal."

Several people chuckled as Rygal pretended to look offended. Iriam smiled and nodded. "You may come," he said. "Your courage and cheerfulness will undoubtedly pass the Aces' tests. And now our number is nearly complete."

A long, expectant silence fell on the room. Mel waited, watching the many waiting faces while his thoughts wandered. Six people, waiting for the last person to volunteer. Six companions, some that he knew well, and others not at all. But they all had the same determination in their eyes that he felt. Willing to stand before the Ace-Lord and protect the Shard. Willing to die for the cause.

He remembered seeing the same light in Dandio's eyes, even as he faced off with the serpentine, or on Llyrion's face as he fought. He realized, in the same moment, that if anyone had reason to go to Caer Sia, it was him. Try as he might, he couldn't dismiss the simple truth. That feeling he'd felt, leaving Caer Sia after the last quest, re-entered his thoughts now. A call to return, to fight, to leave everything behind in order to defeat the dark forces at play.

Mouth dry, he stood. "I—I wish to go too, if I am allowed." His voice sounded very small in the wake of Jan's.

Everyone turned to look at him, and a ripple of questioning whispers ran through the room. Mel understood their hesitation. Here he stood, an eleven-year-old boy, having seen less of the world than most everyone here. Inexperienced. But willing. And that felt more important than the former. He kept his eyes on Jan's face.

The Liznee king looked thoughtful. "Why do you wish to come?" he asked finally.

Mel hadn't expected the question, and he scrambled for an answer for a moment. "On the quest for Drisilas," he began slowly, "Dandio saved my life, both mine and my sister's. I owe him that. Besides that," he hesitated, trying to put into words what he felt in his heart, "the Aces threaten all of Orlell, not just Coonsia or Caer Sia. If the Shards will protect Appledale too, then I'm ready to do what I can to protect them." He lowered his head, a little surprised at his own speech.

Iriam's deep voice was thoughtful. "Your youth does not diminish your courage, child. Indeed, I believe you are meant to come on this venture. To what ends, I cannot say, but I permit you to come."

"Now the number is indeed filled," Ĵan said. "Let us turn to new matters."

Excitement filled Mel's chest, and he couldn't prevent a grin from breaking out on his face as he sat down again. Dandio would be proud, he thought.

Then through a swirl of hopeful thoughts came the Ace-Lord's face, the smile lit by a distant blue light.

Are you sure you want to play this game?

Mel's smile faded, and he swallowed hard. But his unease was joined by a fierce determination. He would no longer shrink from the fight. No, he was committed now. Mentally, he looked the mocking face in the eye and answered firmly: *Yes, I am. I'm not afraid of you.*

Yet the voice in his mind laughed softly.

Ah, we shall see. We shall see.

7

A Company of Seven

Ĵan dismissed everyone except for the barons and lords. The rest of the meeting, Mel guessed, would be discussing the political and economic details that made up the complicated business of war. Not only that, the safety of the many fiefs and towns involved needed to be prioritized. No one was exactly sure where the Aces were presently. Most people guessed that the Ace-army was gathering in central Coonsia some twenty miles south of Mata City, Jarus' hometown.

"We haven't really seen anything suspicious," Jarus said when Mel asked him. "No Aces, at least."

"Did the Coopers fight the Aces when they appeared last time?" Mel asked. Ĵan had explained that the Aces had last been seen thirty years ago, when they had fought the Liznees before disappearing again. Mel had hardly heard anything about this battle—but then, he hadn't heard about the Darkness before, either.

"I think the Coopers might have helped," Jarus said slowly. "I don't know too much about it, though. I joined Lord Roan's court as a scribe after the quest for the Jewel, but I wasn't told anything about the Aces."

"I don't think anyone was told much" Mel said. He could tell from the startled reactions of the barons and lords when word of the Aces had been announced that they hadn't known. No one had suspected the truth, except Ĵan, Iriam, and Cahadras. Even Ĵan had seemed shaken. The only thing that Mel had seen concern Ĵan before had been the Darkness, which had caused trouble enough. But the Aces were a different matter entirely.

It still felt surreal. He'd heard of the Aces briefly—Dandio had mentioned them once or twice before. But it was always in passing, in the midst of a legend that never spoke of reality. Now he knew better. The Aces were no mere mythology. They were back, very real, and they were back with vengeance.

Aryion and Rygal approached them. Rygal was shaking his head, still stunned by the revelation of the council. "I can't believe this," he murmured to himself. "The Aces, back—no wonder Ĵan kept it so secret. If the public hears about this…"

"There will be chaos," Aryion told him grimly.

Rygal turned to Mel. "So, seems like you knew a bit more about all this than we thought. You heard the Ace-Lord's voice? Inside the Darkness?" He shook his head again, wide-eyed. "We thought you destroyed the Darkness on your own—with Drisilas, of course."

"I don't think the Darkness could have been destroyed like that," Mel said slowly. "The Ace-Lord just needed it to do his dirty work— weaken Caer Sia, and find out more about the sword, probably. Then he took away its power when it ran out of usefulness."

Rygal raised his eyebrows. "Well, you surprised everyone today with that news."

Aryion looked at Mel. His dark eyes were immensely thoughtful. "Did the Ace-Lord tell you anything else?" he asked. "And have you heard his voice since?"

"He said that the Aces were coming soon," Mel said. "Now I guess they're here. I… I haven't heard anything since." The strange occurrence in the market that morning, he thought, was too hard to explain. Besides, it scared him to think about it further. He hated to think that the Ace-Lord could access his thoughts that easily. What if he could hear them even now? What if Mel's presence at the council had betrayed everyone?

His stomach turned at the thought. "I have a question for Jan. Do you know when the meeting will be finished?"

"I'm not sure," Rygal said. "It might be a while. They're choosing warriors to accompany Norrin's party south to Kamon now." He whistled. "I envy him there. Kamon will be beautiful this time of year."

"I've never been that far south," Jarus said. "But it sounds amazing—sandy beaches and palm trees. I hear the fruit grows so large and plentiful they have to harvest it three times a day."

"Lucky Norrin," Rygal said, shaking his head.

"So, what will we do in Caer Sia?" Mel asked.

"The Shard must be guarded," Aryion said. "And the Red Dawn army of Caer Sia must be made aware of the threat. The Liznees will be prepared for war."

"Well, Caer Sia sounds nice too," Jarus decided. "Though I'll always be partial to the northern coasts."

"Ah, but you have never been south," came Quinn Fireleaf's voice. The Elven ranger had approached and overheard Jarus' words. He smiled. "After this adventure, I will have to show you Kamo Bay—it is only just west of my home town of Tinkeeyo. The water is always warm, even through the winter."

"Enough talk about water and beaches," Rygal said with a laugh. "What do you know of the Aces, Quinn?"

"Little, I am afraid," Quinn answered. "But my great-grandfather faced them in the Dividing War. His son, my grandfather, told us his stories. They were... strange, to say the least."

"I think there'll be a lot of strange before this is over," Mel said, and the others nodded thoughtfully.

Quinn looked at him, studying his face. "You are Mel, correct? You knew Llyrion Tarash?"

Mel nodded, surprised. "Yeah, he went with us to return Drisilas, before... before his death. How did you know him?"

"We knew each other when we were young," Quinn said. "He chose to train in the Red Dawn, and I apprenticed as a ranger, so our paths drew apart. I was grieved to hear of his death."

Mel was startled to hear this. "I didn't know you knew him. The Darkness killed him—he saved my life." A familiar pang of grief touched his heart, and he lowered his eyes.

The door opened, and a group of solemn barons left the room. Jan and Iriam came after them, talking quietly. "Norrin is determined to take the road through the Brown Woods, and then head south past the mountains," Iriam was saying, sounding slightly uncertain. "It will be a quick route, but it may be dangerous."

"I agree," Ĵan said. "Still, I trust Norrin's judgment. He is determined, and knowing Norrin, we probably won't persuade him otherwise." He smiled at the five others waiting for them. "Well, here we are. I want to thank you all for choosing to accompany us. In Caer Sia, we can best counter the Aces' advances."

"Do we have a plan of defense?" Rygal asked.

"Our plan as of now is to travel to Caer Sia and wait," Ĵan said. "There, the Shard can be protected, and we can fortify the city to stand as our base. As for the Aces, they are cunning creatures, but their true power is drawn from fear. Standing before them, with Caer Sia as our vantage point, they will hesitate to attack."

"Nevertheless, I doubt the Ace-Lord will hesitate long," Iriam said gravely. "He needs both Shards, and he will take them by any means necessary. Thus, we must be prepared for any attack he means to organize."

"I thought the Aces' soldiers are deathless," Mel said worriedly. "How are we supposed to fight them?"

"Immortals can still be pushed back," Ĵan told him. "From what we've gathered, this isn't like the Hazes, with powers as well as immortality. No, while these warriors might not be killed, they can still be defeated, in other ways."

"How?" Rygal asked uncertainly. "How do you stop an Ace?"

Iriam smiled slightly at him. "I have told you that the Aces thrive on fear. Take away your fear of them, and they can be battled as a common soldier."

"So we'll beat them by… not being scared," Mel said slowly. That made absolutely no sense. "What about the Ace-Lord?"

Iriam's smile faded. "The Ace-Lord is another being entirely. But he cannot hope to succeed in his conquest without the Stones. Once the Shards are rejoined, he will have to retreat and form a new plan."

"Is that how the Liznees beat them last time?" Mel asked, looking at Jan.

Jan hesitated. "No… no, we didn't beat them. They left." They all looked at him in surprise, and he continued slowly. "Dandio and I were young and did not fight in the battle. Our father the king led the charge himself. From what he told us, the Ace-army had suffered casualties. But the eleven Aces all still lived. Neither side showed any real advantage over the other. In the last light of the fifth day, the Aces simply vanished, leaving the Red Dawn to defeat the outlaws and vagabonds that had followed them. They were gone, and remained gone for thirty years."

Gone like the Darkness, Mel thought, and felt a chill go down his spine. Was that what had happened? Had the Ace-Lord simply decided to abandon the conquest? But why?

"If we can beat the Aces, we can beat the Ace-Lord," Jarus said, though he sounded worried.

"What are their tactics?" Rygal asked, looking at Ĵan. "How do the Aces fight? How can we best counter them?"

"Most of that will be decided in Caer Sia," Ĵan said. "And I have to admit, this isn't my area of expertise. If Dandio were here…" he stopped abruptly. A brief silence passed before he began again. "The last time the Aces were seen, they battled the Red Dawn in open combat for nearly a week. I am not sure if they will try this strategy again or not."

"Likely not," Iriam said. He studied Rygal. "You ask how they fight, son of Maran. I will tell you, for I alone have fought them before. The Aces rely on speed and silence, two of their greatest strengths. While we strive to keep their presence secret, they will encourage the spread of rumors as much as they can. In this way, fear and despair will do their work for them, allowing them to grow stronger. If they face any resistance, they will destroy it entirely."

It wouldn't be hard for them to do, Mel thought. If what Iriam had said earlier was true, then the Aces could strip the Essence right out of a person. Destroy them from the inside without ever needing to come near. A sensation of hopelessness filled Mel's chest, and he fought to push it away.

Ĵan turned to Rygal. "When the Liznees faced the Aces before, we did it as an organized battle, charge after charge, over and over until we weakened their line."

"And you beat them then," Rygal said, clearly trying to find some fragment of optimism.

"No. Even now the Red Dawn refuses to call it a victory," Jan said heavily. "It was a confusing end to a brief and costly battle, which is why it is barely spoken of now."

An uncomfortable silence followed. It was broken unexpectedly by Aryion's voice. "If we know their strengths, we might turn them against the Aces."

They all looked at him. "How so?" Jan asked.

"A head-on charge, like what the Liznees did before, will only lead to a stalemate, or worse," Aryion said. "For whatever reason the Aces retreated last time, I doubt they'll give up again. They'll slaughter any army fool enough to face them in line-to-line combat."

"What are you suggesting?" Iriam asked, frowning slightly in thought.

"Take away the shadows. Take the element of stealth away from the Aces entirely." Aryion paused. "If anything, it might be better to have the public made aware of the threat now."

"That's not what you said earlier," Rygal said doubtfully.

Aryion nodded, conceding the fact. "I know. And when the word gets out, there will still be fear, I can tell you that. But the alternative is allowing the uncertainty and rumors to heighten it. That will only give the Aces more power. If we tell the people what we know now, before anything horrible has happened, we might prevent some of the panic." He paused, seeming to gather his thoughts. "Fight the Aces with their own techniques. Take away their stealth and secrecy and teach everyone to beware of them."

"That could put everyone in danger," Rygal said, frowning. "You think we should just tell everyone what's going on?"

"There would be no more secrets," Aryion told him. "And the public is in danger regardless. That's the point of this mission."

"You make a wise point," Iriam said thoughtfully. "Fear often loses some of its power when it has a name."

But Jan shook his head. "I agree with you, but I think it might be wiser to wait to reveal the truth for now. Wait until we get to Caer Sia, until the Red Dawn has been assembled and prepared." He looked at the others. "We hope to leave tomorrow morning. We will not take pack animals, so everything we bring must be carried on our backs."

Tomorrow. Mel realized he should send a note to his parents and let them know what was happening.

"In the meantime," Iriam added, "we would do well to gather supplies."

Aryion offered to buy their needed supplies, and Mel went with him. Outside, the summer sun glared off of the cobblestones, and he squinted in the light. They moved through the busy market. Mel kept his eyes on the ranger's tall form—the last thing he wanted was to get lost in an unfamiliar city.

"Can we stop by the post office here, too?" he asked. "I need to send a message to my parents. They didn't know I'd end up going to Caer Sia." *Neither did I,* he added inwardly.

Aryion nodded. "Of course." He glanced down at Mel. "You have a sister, you mentioned?"

"Yeah—she's going to school in Lemsonburg," Mel said.

Aryion smiled. "I have a sister as well. Twin, actually."

"Is she a ranger, too?" Mel asked, interested.

He noticed that the slight smile vanished as quickly as it had come. In an instant, Aryion's face was as grave as ever. "No… not that I know of."

This answer raised more questions, but Mel somehow sensed that Aryion didn't want to talk about it anymore. "I'm glad you're coming," he said instead, grinning. "Between you and Quinn I bet we'll come up with a strategy to stop the Ace-Lord soon. Did you know you'd be asked to go?" he asked.

"Jan mentioned protecting something in Sia," Aryion said. "I promised to help in any way I could. Besides that, I have a long-standing score to settle with the orc chieftain Hagshrub. If the orcs intend to join with the Aces in the Ace-Lord's growing conquest, I am prepared to stop them."

The ranger's expression was dark and grim. They walked in silence until another question entered Mel's mind. "Do you know anything about the Star Stones, Aryion?" he asked. "Up till now, I thought the Stone in Drisilas' hilt was the only one."

"I've heard of them, but not much," Aryion answered, as they moved through the noisy marketplace. "The story that Cahadras told is an old one, and my father spoke of it once before. About how the Star King gave them as gifts to the rulers of the world, and how the Stone given to the Netrocrians was believed lost." He shook his head. "I didn't know that it and the Jewel were one and the same."

Mel nodded. Dandio had explained a little of the Star-Stone lore during his last adventure, along with the history of Drisilas. But Mel hadn't really thought much about it until now. Now the remaining Stones needed to be guarded, kept away from the Ace-Lord.

Almost as though he had guessed Mel's trail of thought, Aryion spoke slowly. "I assume the Ace-Lord has a plan to gain the Stones for himself. Why would he risk a second invasion, if he were not confident in his plan?"

"I think so too," Mel said. They purchased cornmeal and oats from the miller, and the conversation continued in lowered tones as they moved to another shop. "I don't know how we'll figure out the Ace-Lord's plans," Mel began again once they were past the crowds. "But when I faced the Darkness, when I saw the void… if that's the place the Ace-Lord gets his strength from, then I can definitely say we don't want to let him anywhere near the Stones. Not if he can channel that power through them and into our world."

They continued to walk through the town. Aryion pointed out the post office for him, and Mel walked to it while the ranger continued shopping. He borrowed a pen and piece of paper from a kind old lady inside and settled down to write.

The money he had brought, which had originally been for the return carriage home, would be enough to send his letter to Appledale with the next courier headed east. As for the letter itself… it took him a while to figure out what to say, knowing there were no words that would ease his parents' fears. In the end, he decided to keep it simple:

Dear Mom and Dad –

I'm going to Caer Sia with King Jan and Rygal. The plan is to fortify the city in preparation for the new enemy. I'll write you when we get there. I promise I'll be careful. Please try not to worry for me.

I love you.

-Mel

Mel signed the letter and sent it off with the first courier he saw. Aryion met him outside the post office, laden with the items he had bought, and they returned to the baron's living quarters. The council hall had cleared out, and the baron offered a space for the seven companions to stay before setting out in the morning.

Jan and Iriam were deep in conversation over the best route to take and asked for Aryion's advice, as the ranger knew the northern roads better than anyone. Mel helped Rygal pack the bags in the guest chamber. With the urgency surrounding the council, he hadn't had time to reconnect with his friend, and the two of them talked while they worked. The conversation soon shifted from catching up to discussing their coming adventure.

"Do you think we'll see any Aces on the way to Sia?" Mel asked.

Rygal frowned slightly. "I'm not sure. From what we've heard, it sounds like they're in the west, in the flatlands. Hopefully we don't cross them." He crammed a blanket on top of the rest of the supplies and forced the bag shut, then looked at Mel again. "So, what do you think of Aryion? You two seem to be getting along well."

Mel thought for a moment. He had known the ranger for all of twelve hours, and, in that time, had gathered a few thoughts. Aryion was quiet, grim-faced, matter-of-fact. His subdued manner worked well with Mel's own personality, which tended to be too outgoing for his own good. And yet Aryion had listened to Mel's chattering questions, given advice, and talked with him—not treating him like a little kid, but as an equal individual caught up in the same dangerous adventure. Just like Jan or Rygal or Dandio would. Mel knew there was only one answer to give. "I like him," he answered.

"Yes, I like him too," Rygal agreed thoughtfully. "I suppose the real question is, do you trust him?"

This time Mel thought for a little longer. Following the unexpected treachery of Jan's advisor Pellion Drona last year, it was hard to trust anyone. It surprised Mel to realize that despite their short acquaintance, he trusted Aryion just as much as he trusted Rygal.

"I do," he replied. "You've known him longer than I have, though." He paused before asking his next question. Aryion's reaction earlier, when Rygal had talked about the orc tribes, had caught his attention. While he guessed it was a personal matter, his curiosity got the better of him. "Rygal, what were you telling Aryion about the orcs?"

Rygal tightened the ties of the second pack, and hesitated. "Mel, remember how you asked me for information after the fight with the Darkness—to send you a letter if there was trouble?" Mel nodded, and he continued. "Well, Aryion and I have a similar pact. I give him news about the orcs, and he fulfills his end of the deal."

"What deal?" Mel asked, frowning slightly.

Rygal started to speak, stopped, then began again. "Something Jan asked him to do. You can ask him later."

This didn't really answer the question, Mel thought, but he didn't press. Instead, he asked, "So, why does Aryion want to know about the orc movements? And what about the chieftain you mentioned—Hags-head, or whatever his name is?"

"Hagshrub," Rygal corrected, and hesitated again. "And I can't tell you much. That's Aryion's business. If he's willing to tell you, that's between you and him."

Mel thought about this as they finished packing. He trusted the ranger, yes, but did he want to ask about the "business," as Rygal called it, with Hagshrub? He remembered the conversations he and Aryion had in the carriage and in the market. Both times, he had seen a flash of emotion cross the ranger's face when Mel had mentioned anything relating to families. And then there had been that barely subdued anger in Aryion's dark eyes at the name of the orc chieftain. What had he said earlier? *I have a long-standing score to settle with Hagshrub.*

Whatever the truth of the matter was, Mel knew it wasn't his place to ask. He would settle, for now, with wondering.

......

A light storm rolled in overnight, and the morning dawned gray and wet. A haze of rain drizzled down in a steady, soaking mist. Mel wrapped himself in his cloak to shield himself from the cold.

Norrin's group had left for Kamon last night, heading south. The seven companions had spent the night in the baron's guest rooms. The space was small, but the beds were soft and Mel had slept well. Now, the companions met outside. Mel offered to carry one of the packs, which, though heavy, provided some warmth.

Water dripped from the tips of Jarus' ears, and the rain ran off his thick fur. He looked content despite the damp. "In Mata City," he remarked to Mel, "it rains all the time. This is just like home."

"Don't you get tired of it?" Mel asked, rubbing his cold nose.

"Nope." Jarus laughed. "Don't worry. Summer is on its way, and I bet the weather in Caer Sia will be delightful."

Iriam approached them, and smiled at Jarus' words. "The trees will shelter us somewhat from the rain, as soon as we start on the road," he said, then turned to face everyone else. They all stood expectantly, waiting. "We will move quickly," the Neutral told them. "We must veer south slightly, in order to bypass the land of the Sirens, as we have received word of orcs congregating there. Then we will go north, through the mountains and down into the valley of Caer Sia. With any luck, Norrin and his group will rejoin us there in a few weeks hence, with the second Shard."

"In my experience, it's dangerous to count on luck," Jan added with a wry smile. "So we must be cautious."

With the remaining lords and barons waving their quiet farewells, the companions started down the road, following Iriam west, until they vanished from sight into the heavy fog.

8

∽ ∽ ∽ ∽ ∽ ∽ ∽ ∽ ∽

The Road Less Traveled

The same morning, in Carna…

The wagon driver strolled casually toward the station, squinting through a heavy fog that filled the township of Carna in the early morning. He carried a half-filled mug of coffee. His purse jingled at his side, filled with yesterday's pay.

Only a few passengers had gone west the day before. A noisy mother and her three children, who had insisted upon petting the exasperated horses before leaving. Later, he had dropped a few farmers off at their homes toward the end of the night. And there had been the two passengers early in the day: the tall ranger and the young boy who had boarded just after him.

The driver stepped up on the patio of the station and took another drink of coffee. The sun was just beginning to rise, and he felt the satisfaction of a new day approaching.

Movement caught his eye, and he turned to see a figure, hunched and hooded, make its way toward the station. Shrouded in rags, it shambled closer, head down. The wagon driver blinked. His tired eyes must be playing tricks; in the early light, the figure appeared to blur and shift, like a draft of smoke.

"Good morning to you," he called as the figure continued to approach. There was no answer. A beggar, probably, or a drunkard coming from the alley. Either way, someone of no interest to him.

"Off with you," he said briskly as his friendly greeting remained ignored. "I've no time for beggars. You'll have better chance when the market opens."

Still no answer. Uninterested, the wagon driver turned his back on the approaching vagabond. He raised his mug to his mouth absently—then flinched back. The coffee that met his lips was ice-cold, and a fine layer of frost coated the ceramic mug.

He turned sharply—a hand gripped his forehead like a vice as he faced the newcomer. White-hot pain filled his vision, and he let out a choked shout. Reddish eyes glinted beneath the hood, and the weak morning light glittered over the skull-like face as the stranger smiled.

Quiet, please. You don't want to wake your neighbors, do you?

The pain faded as his confused mind relaxed under the frigid grasp. Ice glimmered on the stranger's fingers and entered the man's mind. Sounds and glimpses floated through his consciousness, fragmented memories of the day before. He saw himself face the young boy yesterday morning, saw himself accepting the payment the lad offered— *"Coming, boy?"* His own voice echoed his mind again. He felt the familiar yet urgent need to be off, to deliver these passengers to their destination in –

Thank you, that's quite enough.

Ice glittered briefly over the images in his mind, then shattered them into a thousand glittering particles, gone forever. His last coherent thought was that he needed to drink his coffee faster next time, before it grew so cold.

The cloaked figure vanished, satisfied with the information it had procured. By the time morning light rose upon Carna, the only person on the station stoop was the wagon driver; he sat rocking gently back and forth, humming a tuneless song as the last remnants of his sanity slipped peacefully away.

••••••

The rain stopped around midmorning, and its sweet smell lingered in the forest. Clouds shrouded the sun, casting a white glow on the surroundings.

The seven companions had traveled west from Flora, following the battered path made by wagon parties and rangers long ago. Iriam led them. Behind him trotted Jarus, who occasionally paused to sniff a leaf or listen to a rustle in the foliage. Quinn strode next to Jarus, his eyes taking in every detail of the wood. After him walked Rygal, then Mel and Aryion. Jan had taken the rear guard position several paces behind them, his hand resting on Drisilas' hilt.

When they had started, Mel had tried to stay alert and attentive. He watched Aryion and Quinn, noting how their eyes scanned the path ahead as they walked. He had focused on copying the two rangers, mimicking their silent movements and keeping his eyes up for any danger. After awhile though, the excitement of the journey faded slightly, and his boredom grew. They traveled through the Brown Woods, a vast expanse of wilderness before the border to Coonsia. This forest, Mel decided, was well-named. The towering fir trees, sparse underbrush, and general muddiness of everything around them blended into a monotony of brown.

Iriam called a halt after a few hours. "We will rest for a few minutes," he told them. "Eat and drink if you will, but prepare to be moving again soon."

Mel sat down on a fallen log and stretched his legs. "How far is it to Caer Sia, Aryion?" he asked as the ranger sat beside him.

"Many miles," Aryion told him. "But if we keep up this pace, we should reach it in five or six days."

Mel nodded, digesting this information. He had a vague image in his mind of the geography of Daffodalion and could remember that once they crossed the border between the two countries, it was around a two-day trip north to Caer Sia. Longer, if the snowy passes through the mountains were blocked. But he guessed that the snow would be thawed now.

They started walking again. Quinn fell back in pace to talk to Aryion. The two rangers exchanged information they had noticed so far on the journey: tracks, wildlife, signs of trouble. Mel was startled to hear it all. "Where was that?" he broke in when Quinn reported seeing a fox in the brush.

"Right after we passed that tall oak with the three forked branches," the Elf replied. Mel's blank look made Quinn laugh, and even Aryion smiled. It was the first real smile Mel had seen on his face, and it softened his usually grim features.

"We are trained to notice everything," Quinn explained. "It's surprising how often the smallest detail can be the difference between danger and safety."

"So you saw all of that this morning?" Mel asked incredulously, still surprised.

They nodded. "There were other things, but nothing dangerous," Aryion told him. "If there was trouble, we would alert Iriam and prepare to fight."

Mel realized, with a twinge of guilt, that he had completely forgotten the very real danger that surrounded this mission. While they weren't going to face the Aces the way Norrin's group was, they still needed to be vigilant. He made a mental note to start paying better attention to their surroundings.

His thoughts were interrupted by Jarus' uncertain tone. "Iriam… come look at this."

The Cooper had walked a few feet off the main road, and now stood next to the trunk of a giant tree. The others grouped around him to see. Black streaks scored the bark, the scars from some forest fire in the tree's youth. But Mel could see what had caused Jarus' concern. Standing out brightly from the black, glittering slightly, was a fine coating of ice.

"It's been months since the last frost," Rygal stated uneasily.

Iriam ran a hand over the bark of the tree; his hand came away coated in white frost. It covered his palm for a moment before vanishing. "Aces," Iriam said quietly, nodding to himself. "They have been here very recently."

"Why?" Jarus asked, his brow furrowed. "Do you think they're tracking us?"

"There's nothing we have that they would track," Quinn said, equally confused.

Mel noticed that Aryion and Ĵan exchanged a quick glance; they both looked worried.

Iriam turned to face the group. "The Aces may be following Norrin's group. It is likely that they traveled this road yesterday. Still, it pays to be wary." He looked at the two rangers. "Aryion, Quinn, continue down this road and look for any other signs. Be cautious."

They both nodded and started down the path, keeping to the edges, and seemed to vanish completely into the trees. It seemed like a very long time before they returned.

"There's a crossroads ahead," Aryion reported. "I only walked part of the west road, which is the one we need to take. More ice on the trees, and one of the signposts was destroyed." He held up a chunk of broken wood, which bore a few scattered letters.

"It's a trap," Rygal guessed immediately. "They're waiting for us down the west road."

"Show me the signpost," Iriam asked. The companions followed as Aryion led them to the crossroads. A broken post and more scattered fragments, glossy with white ice, littered the ground.

"If they were attempting to lure us to them, this seems like a very obvious attempt," Jan said doubtfully.

Quinn had walked down the other road, which wound north, and now returned. "More ice that way. I don't understand. If they are trying to trap us, why place traces on both roads?"

Iriam straightened. "In all probability, the Aces do not want to lure us to them. This is a warning. The Aces want us to retreat." He nodded back in the direction they had come. "I would not doubt, however, that either they or their servants wait for us on both roads."

There was a heavy silence. "Is there any other way around?" Jarus asked. "Any other roads we could take?"

"If there were, we would have seen them on the maps," Jan said. He sighed. "The best we can do, I think, would be to go back towards Flora, and then veer north toward Cattrick."

"In that case, our options to cross the border would be either Grayline Swamp, or Deadmen's Flats," Aryion said wryly.

Mel shuddered. He'd traveled through Deadmen's Flats, a wide expanse of salt flats, on his previous trip. He had no desire to visit the strange area again.

"The road to Cattrick will lose us days of travel," Iriam said. "Perhaps weeks. Not only that, our sources tell us that the orcs patrol the northern roads heavily."

"Wonderful," Rygal muttered. He turned and paced back in the direction they had come, thinking. Mel saw him pause as he seemed to notice something. Rygal looked around at the terrain, then at what he had found, then back again. He seemed to be doing several calculations on his fingers.

Jan had moved to look at the destroyed way post with Iriam when Rygal's voice made them turn. "Wait a moment! I think I found our solution."

The companions jogged to his side to look. Rygal gestured triumphantly at a thin road leading off of the main road. "If my guesses are right—which they usually are—then we can follow this path. Not only will it take us around the Aces, it will also save us a good twenty miles of traveling south on the road we're on currently. The best shortcut we could ask for."

Mel studied Rygal's shortcut. It would be an exaggeration to call it a trail. In fact, it was more of a thin, uncertain track of dirt that eventually dwindled into patchy clumps of grass.

"You say this will save us time?" Iriam asked slowly, clearly uncertain.

Rygal nodded rapidly. "Yes. See, this road we're on right now is leading southwest, and will take us the long way around the mountains, along the edges of the Dûkrane Prairie. Then it'll cross the border just south of Elimar and curve north. That's a good five-day journey in itself, and it'll take another three to reach Caer Sia." He nodded at the path. "This trail will take us due west—skips the detour around the prairie, and rejoins the main road just inside the border."

"I see," Iriam said, still doubtful. He and Ĵan exchanged a look. Mel could tell they were uneasy about the path. At the same time, no one had planned to find signs of the Aces this early in the trip.

Ĵan finally turned to look at the others. "You are all on this venture with us. What do you think of this?"

There was a brief silence, then Quinn said hesitantly, "I do not like leaving the main road. But this seems like the best way around."

"I agree," Aryion said, but he did not look happy about it.

Jarus flicked his ears in annoyance. "I *would*," he said in frustration, "had not nine out of ten of Rygal's *'shortcuts'* done more harm than good." Rygal's smile faded somewhat, and he looked embarrassed. Jarus sighed. "But I agree that this may be our only option," he concluded.

Mel felt everyone look at him, and his face warmed. "I… I don't like leaving this road, but it might be better to risk the shortcut than risk the Aces," he said slowly.

Ĵan and Iriam exchanged another look, and Mel realized that the whole trip hung on their decision. He wondered briefly what would happen if the two leaders disagreed.

"We will take this trail," Iriam said finally. "Rygal, lead on."

9

The Messenger

Mel had grown so tired of listening to Rygal's hesitant, "Yes, I believe it's this way," or "No, we need to go back there" that he was wondering if his ears would burst. The sun had sunk below the horizon about an hour before, and the uncertain lighting did nothing to ease Mel's worry.

At first, the short cut had held much potential. The little grassy strip had widened into a gravel trail about eighteen inches across, leading due north. But then, a few hours before sundown, the trail had split. The companions paused, and after a long, indecisive moment, Rygal had taken the left road, which seemed to curve back towards the main road and the direction they needed to go. Which it had—for a few miles. Then, abruptly, the trail turned southeast. Now they were trekking through the forest in what seemed to be the wrong direction. Thick clouds covered the sky, so it was impossible to navigate.

Rygal refused to admit defeat, but Mel could tell his confidence had faded. They reached yet another fork in the road and Iriam called a halt. Rygal paced before the crossroads, muttering uncertainly to himself. "If we go left… no, that'll go back toward Carna… but the right will go too far south…"

"Rygal," Iriam said, in a low and dangerous tone, "where are we?"

Rygal looked up, his eyes scanning the surrounding area, and seemed to deflate. "Well, we haven't crossed the river, so I'd place us still in Daffodalion."

"That's not helpful," Jarus said. The Cooper had been wary about the shortcut from the start. He had been gracious enough not to say "I told you so," but now that night had fallen, Mel could see his patience was fading.

Iriam studied Rygal severely, then turned to the rangers. "Aryion, Quinn, have either of you traveled these woods before?"

Both rangers shook their heads unhappily. "If you want a guess, I place us around twenty miles from the border," Quinn said. "But in which area, I have no idea. After the sun set and the clouds covered the stars, it has been difficult to tell which direction we're going in."

Jan took a breath and nodded. "Fair point. In that case, I suggest setting up camp here. We can't see anything in this light anyway."

This was the best they could do, Mel realized, and he joined the others in setting up his bedroll. Aryion lit a fire, and Mel moved to warm his hands by the blaze.

Jarus sat next to him. "There's one good thing about Rygal's short-cuts," he said cheerfully. "They never go in the right direction, but sometimes they lead to something better. In this case," he nodded at the camp, "a fine place to rest on a summer night."

Mel grinned despite his weariness. "Well, you should tell Iriam that," he said. "I don't think he's too pleased with Rygal right now."

"Maybe not," Jarus admitted, "but he's tired too. We'll all feel better after a good night's rest."

Mel nodded, but he couldn't help feeling a stir of unease. This road was uncharted on all their maps, and if they went too far south, they would miss the road through the mountain pass entirely. All of this would only add time to their journey when speed was their best ally.

Jan walked down the trail to scout as far as he could into the shadowed woods. Rygal stood on the road, studying the ground and looking agitated. It was impossible to do more in the darkness, which clearly made him more frustrated.

"Come sit," Aryion called to him. "Jan and Iriam will sort this out. You are only tiring yourself further."

Rygal threw him an exasperated look. "I'm not tired. I'm looking. Something walked down this trail recently—the dirt's been torn up. But I can't tell what it is."

Aryion frowned and moved to him; Mel, curious, followed. Rygal nodded at the ground. Deep furrows scored the packed earth, scraping the covering of pine needles aside and creating thin lines on the path.

Mel had the strange sensation that he had seen those tracks before, but he couldn't remember when.

Aryion knelt to study them. "These are fresh—an hour old, I would guess."

Rygal nodded. He looked uneasy. "Aryion, this trail… I traveled it years ago, during the rise of Kado, when my group was heading to Elimar. I think it was abandoned in favor of the main road, which is why it's not on the maps."

Aryion looked up at him. "If it was indeed abandoned, that would have been almost ten years ago. In that case, it's rather well-tended for an unused road, isn't it?"

Mel frowned as he realized the ranger was right. While the path was overgrown and hard to see, it was still here. He remembered the broken signpost and the ice on the bark of the trees.

"What do you think?" Rygal asked.

"I think," Aryion said quietly, "that if the Aces meant for us to fall into a trap, they would have done a better job of covering their tracks at the crossroads."

Chills ran down Mel's spine. "Wait… you think they *wanted* us to go this way? But then…" He trailed off and looked at the strange tracks again. At the same time, he remembered with a jolt where he had seen those marks before. Etched into the kitchen floor at home, partly covered with a rug now but still visible; those tracks were accompanied by terrifying memories of running and hiding and hearing a hissing voice—

"Form up!" Jan's voice cut into the night air. They looked up to see the Liznee king jog back into the camp. Drisilas blazed in his hand, lighting his tense features.

"What is it?" Iriam asked immediately.

"In the trees—not Aces, there's a group of—"

A huge shape dropped from the trees in front of them, bat-like wings spread to catch itself, as it sprang at Jan. Quinn loosed an arrow; it sank into the creature's face at point-blank range and the beast fell with a familiar screeching hiss. The firelight reflected on mud-red, plate-like scales and a slithering body.

"Serpentines," Jan finished, unnecessarily.

Mel stood between Rygal and Jarus, his back to the fire, watching the writhing shapes just beyond the ring of firelight. It had been months since he had last seen a serpentine, but that made them no less terrible. Bulbous white eyes stared out of the darkness, and the light of the fire glinted on their curved fangs.

"I spoke too soon," Jarus whispered to Mel. "Rygal's shortcuts are terrible."

The serpentines circled the camp. There were five, Mel saw, and they hesitated to attack. Quinn's rapid and lethal shot had made them wary.

But they didn't hesitate long. Two spread their wings and sprang at the companions from opposite sides of the camp, and the other three lunged forward at the same time. Quinn loosed another arrow, missed, and was knocked down, pinned under the serpentine's claws. A blast of red fire from Jan struck the snake in the face before it bared its fangs at the Elven warrior.

"Don't let them bite!" Jan called, as Quinn kicked the body off and stood again.

Mel ducked as a serpentine swept overhead. He remembered the potent effects of the serpentine's venom all too well. A bite would be deadly this far from Flora.

A second serpentine fell, Iriam's deep blue ice glittering over its scales. Mel turned just in time to see another snake pounce on Jarus, pinning the Cooper to the ground. With a shout, he ran forward and slashed across the serpentine's snout. In the split-second distraction, Jarus wriggled free and plunged his short knife in between the scales of the serpentine's chest. The snake let out one last angry hiss before slumping to the ground.

"That was close," Mel panted.

"Watch your back, Mel!" Jarus yelled at the same time. Mel turned just in time to see another serpentine lunge out of the darkness, its claws gripping his shoulders and heaving him to the ground.

Mel fell sprawling, his dagger knocked from his grasp. He struggled frantically as the snake crouched on top of him, hissing in his face as venom dripped from the tips of its fangs.

A sword flashed at the same instant that the serpentine lowered its teeth. In a single, clean cut, the serpentine's head flew back into the woods. The body remained erect for a moment, then slumped down on top of Mel. Someone kicked it off and hauled Mel to his feet; he stumbled, gasping from the closeness of the encounter.

"Are you all right?"

Mel looked up, dazed. It was Aryion. Blood streaked his sword as he looked at Mel in concern.

"You…" Mel looked at the serpentine's headless form, then back at the ranger. "That was…"

"You're safe," Aryion reassured him as Mel trailed off. Mel nodded and took a breath to calm his racing heart. He looked around. The fifth serpentine crouched, hissing, facing off with Iriam and Jan alone.

"Speak your words, messenger," Iriam commanded.

The serpentine stiffened, then spoke in a hollow, echoing voice. *"Your journey is futile and will only cost you pain. What you protect, I shall take by force. You know what I ask."*

"And you know our answer, Ace," Iriam replied. The serpentine lunged at him; there was a flash of blue ice and yellow fire, and the snake slumped, impaled by both Drisilas and Iriam's ice.

There was a long, stunned silence. Iriam turned, surveying the camp. "Is everyone accounted for? Who is injured?"

It took a moment to regroup and assess injuries. Miraculously, no one had been bitten. Jarus had a deep claw mark that ran down his foreleg, and it was bleeding badly. Aryion rapidly set to work cleaning the wound.

"Are you all right, Mel?" Jarus asked, panting.

"I'm fine," Mel reassured him, "but that looks like it hurts."

"It's just a cut," Jarus said, but he winced as Aryion applied a cleansing balm.

The ranger arched an eyebrow. "You are very lucky it is 'just a cut,' as you said. Had it bit you, I am not sure you would still be here."

"I'll be fine," Jarus said. "It will heal."

Rygal and Mel had both suffered several small gashes from the serpentines' claws. Aryion finished helping Jarus, then tended to both of them in turn. "Thanks," Mel said as the ranger wrapped his injuries. "And thanks for saving me. I didn't even see you coming—I thought I was dead," he added with a rueful smile.

Aryion met his eyes and returned the smile. "Well, it would do no good for Jan to have brought you along if you plan on getting yourself killed. Never turn your back on an opponent. I am glad to help."

Mel thanked him again, then moved across the clearing to Jan. "The serpentines are trackers," he said slowly. "I bet the Aces sent them after us, but why?"

"I am not sure," Jan replied thoughtfully.

"Why go to all the trouble of stopping us from getting to Caer Sia?" Jarus asked with a frown. "If they want the Shard, why not pursue Norrin's group to Kamon?"

"Maybe they're trying to get the Shard that's in Caer Sia," Mel suggested, but he doubted that. If the Aces wanted the Shard in Caer Sia, they would attack the city, not send serpentines after the companions. He thought about what the fifth serpentine had said, the message it had brought.

"What's the Ace-Lord after?" he asked finally. "What do we have here that he could possibly want?"

"I am not sure," Jan said again. "But it would be worth trying to find out."

Yet Mel noticed he nodded shortly to Aryion before moving to talk with Iriam. Jan knew more than he said—Aryion did too.

Somehow, Mel was starting to guess that the Aces were after more than just the Shards.

. . . . . .

Jarus shook Mel awake the following morning. "Wake up, Mel! Good news," the Cooper said, grinning. "We aren't half as lost as we thought we were, or at least, we're definitely going west. See for yourself!"

Mel sat up and rubbed his eyes. Jarus pointed west, where the growing sunlight lit the tops of the trees. Beyond that, the purple-gray slopes of the Diamond Cap mountains rose in the distance.

"Just got a bit disoriented last night," Rygal said. His confidence had been restored with the light of morning. "We're closer to the border than we thought. Better get up, Mel, or Jarus will eat your share of breakfast."

"Only after I've eaten yours," Jarus threw back, and padded over to the fire, limping slightly on his injured leg.

Mel repacked his bag and joined the Cooper for breakfast. Quinn had cooked the bacon over the fire and warmed several cornbread muffins.

Iriam called them together once they had finished. "Jan and I speculated whether or not we are to continue on this path, or turn back," he said. "We have decided that time is far more important. This trail appears to be leading west after all. It is unmarked on most maps, so its exact destination is unknown. But as long as it takes us west, we will follow it."

"If the trail fails us, then we will seek to find and follow the Hallas River north," Jan added. "That will at least place us at the border."

Aryion frowned uncertainly. "It will be no easy matter crossing the river, especially at this time of year," he said. "The snow from the mountains will have melted and filled it to a rushing torrent."

"*If* this path is right," Rygal ventured awkwardly, "then there should be a bridge. After all, whoever made the path would have needed to cross the river all year long."

Iriam nodded. "Yes, there should be a bridge," he said. "If not, we will have to ford."

Mel's heart sank at that idea. Spending part of the day with wet clothes was not at all appealing. He found himself hoping that there would be a bridge.

They began to walk again in the same formation as yesterday. Rygal offered to carry Jarus, who was now limping painfully. At first the Cooper refused, but after stumbling over a root for the tenth time, he submitted.

Mel fell behind to walk alongside Rygal. Jarus wanted to hear the entire story of the quest for Drisilas. Mel and Rygal managed a fair recounting between them, reminiscing over the pleasant memories and trying to move past the bad.

They had only been walking for about an hour when Iriam stopped and motioned for silence. Mel's heart skipped a beat, and his hand gripped the hilt of his dagger. The only sound he heard, however, was a faint but welcome roar ahead.

Jarus' ears pricked up. "The river," he murmured.

Iriam nodded. "Yes, that would be the Hallas," he said.

They continued onward, the path leading them steadily towards the sound. At length, they rounded a bend and faced the Hallas River. Gray-green water lapped its rocky edges as its current carried stones along its bottom. Mel saw with relief that an old, oak-wood bridge spanned its banks. Iriam tested it carefully before deciding it was safe to cross.

After the bridge, the trail changed from mud to gravel. Here they rested briefly. Aryion checked Jarus' wound, then deemed that Jarus could walk on it, but carefully.

"We are growing close to the border," Jan stated as they started off again. "Still a few miles, but close." There was the eager light in his eyes of a king returning to his country.

"The real question is, where will we cross it?" Mel said. He knew they had come farther south than they had intended thanks to the unexpected detour. Since Caer Sia was in the northeast corner of the country, this could mean they would enter Coonsia even farther away than they had feared.

"Indeed," Jan mused. "We have yet to pass a landmark I have recognized, unfortunately."

"Look!" Quinn's excited shout came from ahead. For an instant, everyone snapped into attention, all poised for battle, then realized what was before them.

The trail became wide and pronounced, then, beautifully, intersected with a familiar, well-traveled road.

"The main path," Iriam said slowly, as though he could not believe it. "The trail joined back with the main path."

Rygal, far too late, forced a nonchalant expression. "Yes. Of course. I knew it would," he said. But a huge smile of relief spread across his face.

They had just set foot on the larger path again when a sound came from down the main road. In an instant, the relief was gone. The rhythm of pounding horse hooves and jangling gear grew louder, the sounds of a large host moving towards them.

"Get to the shadows," Iriam warned. "Wait until we know who or what we face." The companions quickly obeyed, slipping under the shelter of the trees.

"I can't tell who they are yet," Jarus said quietly, scenting the air. "Could it be Aces?"

Jan crouched beside Iriam, peering in the direction of the sound. One hand rested on Drisilas' hilt. "I can't be sure yet," he replied in a low voice. "It is likely. I doubt there is any other host of that size, in this area."

"The Aces have no horses," Quinn said at the same time, sounding more and more confused. "None would carry them."

Mel drew his dagger and hunched behind the trunk of a large hemlock tree. Aryion stood on the other side of the tree, his long sword held loosely, his keen dark eyes fixed on the source of the sound. With his cloak swept around his shoulders, he seemed to blend into the foliage.

The first three horses came into view. They cantered ahead of a larger group—scouts, Mel guessed. Behind them jogged the main force, some on horseback, others on foot. There were close to a hundred of them. It was impossible to make out any features yet.

The riders had nearly drawn even with them when Rygal stood bolt upright. "It's—it's Norrin's group!" he cried in astonishment.

"What?" Mel said, startled. The riders halted, their horses snorting and huffing. Then a familiar figure dismounted and hurried over to meet Iriam on the road. Mel recognized the rugged features of Norrin. The old man's eyes were filled with surprise.

"Well met, friends," he said, clasping Iriam's hand. "I take it your journey is going well." He glanced past the Neutral's shoulder and nodded to the other companions in bewilderment.

"Well enough," Iriam replied, as the others sheathed their swords.

Norrin shook his head in confusion. "They say your powers are great, Iriam. I wish you had come on the quest for the Jewel simply to save time. You might explain your secrets—how have you caught up to us? We left half a day before you."

"Rygal had a shortcut that actually worked," Jarus said incredulously.

"Well, that's a first," Norrin said dryly, arching an eyebrow at Rygal. But he smiled. "I'm interested to hear how you came here."

"Allow us to escort your riders for the time, then," Iriam said, gesturing to the path ahead. "At least until we reach the road to Caer Sia."

"We would be grateful for it," Norrin said. His face became serious. "And I would be grateful for your advice, Iriam. We have heard yet another rumor about the Aces, and I am afraid it raises even more questions."

10

The Song of the Stars

Norrin's group of riders eagerly welcomed the companions. The two parties rested for a few minutes while Norrin had the gear reloaded in a way that left enough open saddles. The pack horses, though smaller and shaggier than the elegant beasts of Caer Sia, could maintain a faster speed for a longer period of time. Mel sat in the saddle in front of Jarus.

"We've only run into one troop of orcs so far," Norrin said as they started again. "They were prepared to fight. As far as I can tell, they weren't with the Aces—they were mortal, at least. We drove them south. Three of my men were injured; we sent them back to Flora for healing. Hence, the riderless battle horses." He nodded at the tall horses Jan and Iriam rode.

"No Aces yet?" Iriam asked him.

"None so far," Norrin replied. "But I would not be surprised if they come after us soon."

"And it pays to be cautious," Jan said grimly. "In the meantime, where exactly are we? After we left the main road, we've lost sense of our direction."

"Well, you're not quite in Coonsia yet," Norrin said. "You've crossed the Hallas River just north of the prairies. We are around ten miles from the southern border. These woods are between the Magno Forest in Coonsia and the prairie lands towards the Southern Fiefs."

Mel clipped his heels to his pony's sides so that he could hear the conversation better. Iriam told Norrin about the shortcut, and the fight with the serpentines last night. Norrin looked startled.

"Five of them?" he repeated, and Iriam nodded. "Well, I am glad you are all still here. But why would the serpentines pursue you?"

"That's what we've been wondering," Rygal said.

"The serpentines brought a message," Mel reminded him. "But we don't really know what it means." He watched Jan's face carefully as he said this, but the king's expression remained passive.

"A message?" Norrin asked, turning in the saddle to look at him. "What sort of message?"

"It wants something from us," Mel said slowly. "It told us to retreat before it… causes pain." The message still didn't make sense to him, even now. Norrin frowned thoughtfully.

"Probably about the Shards," Jarus guessed. He was perched in the saddle behind Mel. "Maybe the serpentines meant to find Norrin's group. Maybe the message wasn't meant for us at all."

"I have never before heard of a serpentine tracking the wrong target," Jan said slowly. "But we will have to see."

Iriam looked at Norrin again. "Tell me this rumor you mentioned. Perhaps I can answer your question."

"If you can, I'd be grateful," Norrin said. "We came across a gypsy caravan yesterday morning, traveling east. We bought some supplies from them and exchanged news. Now, trust what you will of local rumors, but in my experience they're something to heed…" he trailed off.

"What was the rumor?" Jan asked.

"Aces, sire. One Ace near Tinkeeyo. Word is that it entered the local scribe house and shredded its way through every book and scroll there. It only took one scroll."

"A scroll?" Rygal repeated. "What was in it?"

"Well, that's the question," Norrin said wryly. "The scribe master was found babbling nonsense in the woods outside the city. Completely mad—though I imagine facing an Ace would have been far from pleasant." He rubbed his scruffy beard thoughtfully. "The scribe apprentices replaced the scrolls on the shelves the next morning and can report that one is gone. But they don't recall which one it was."

The story added yet another layer to the uncertainty in Mel's mind. Jarus frowned. "Why would the Ace-Lord want a scroll?" he asked slowly.

"That depends a great deal on what the scroll contained," Iriam said. He paused before continuing. "In the days before the Dividing War, there were Fyrocrians who still maintained contact with the High Light, like they did before the times of mortals. The Stars walked the land of Orlell, interacting with the lives of men. And occasionally, they brought messages from the High Light."

"What kind of messages?" Mel asked.

"It varied. Some were words of encouragement; others were dire warnings. And still others spoke of times to come—prophecies, spoken by the High Light through the Stars, His servants."

"You mean… messages for the future," Mel said slowly, both confused and interested.

"Yes." Iriam looked at Norrin. "I will speak with you further tonight. Together, perhaps we can make more sense of this news."

"If it's true at all," Jarus reminded them. "Gypsies are notorious gossips."

"Yeah, but that's what we thought during the quest for Drisilas, Jarus," Mel said. "Sometimes those local rumors hold more truth than we imagine."

"Well said," Norrin said. "It has piqued my interest, at any rate. So, yesterday, after hearing the news, I sent three men to Elimar to try and pick up any more news about the incident in Tinkeeyo. I also want to know how far this story has spread. We don't want the people to panic."

They traveled for the rest of the day, alternating between jogging or walking the horses. The purple gray of the mountains was visible periodically through the trees. Gray clouds wreathed their peaks. A storm had settled at their summits. Mel guessed by the time they reached Caer Sia, the rain would be long gone, and the city would be blessed with summer warmth.

Norrin called a halt at sundown. The western light lit the distant clouds with pink and orange. A few stars shone in the sky high above, peeking through the boughs of the fir trees.

They set up camp in a wide clearing. The riders tended to their horses and built a few fires. Mel rubbed down the pony he rode, then joined Jarus and Aryion next to a small fire on the edge of camp. A hearty dinner of venison stew had been prepared, and Mel ate hungrily. The warm broth was soothing in the chill of the evening.

Norrin came and sat across from them. Iriam and Jan had stepped aside to review the maps. Once they reached the crossroads south of Elimar, Mel knew he and his companions would go north. For now, though, they had the peace of numbers with Norrin's riders.

"Can you tell us more about the Stars, Norrin?" Jarus asked after they had finished eating. "I remember you mentioning them during our quest for the Jewel."

"Yes," Mel agreed eagerly, looking at the old wizard. "I didn't even know the Stars were real until we met Cahadras."

Norrin smiled. "Well, that is quite a long history. What do you want to know?"

"The years before the Dividing War," Jarus said. "What did the Stars do? You said they came to Orlell… they helped the mortals?"

"Indeed," Norrin said, nodding. "The Star-King gifted the Star-Stones to the three mortal rulers of Orlell, as Cahadras told us during the council. After that, a period of about fifty years passed. Several Star warriors and noblemen came to Orlell. Some of them helped the small settlements in Coonsia. Others, like Cahadras, acted as a neutral voice for discussions between kingdoms."

"Cahadras?" Mel repeated, in awe. "I knew she was old—I didn't know *that* old." He stopped abruptly as he realized how rude that sounded. Jarus laughed. "You know what I mean," Mel said, shaking his head at the Cooper.

Norrin chuckled. "Yes, Cahadras was here for the births of many of Coonsia's cities. She and another Star, Luet, helped ally both Caer Sia and Tinkeeyo with their neighbors in Daffodalion. They also brought messages from the High Light for those cities, and their messages were recorded, until the Dividing War." His face fell.

"What happened then?" Mel asked.

"After the Dividing War, many of the old scrolls were lost," Norrin said. "Destruction followed the wake of Kahlifis' revolt and sparked many wars between mortals that have lasted up to this day. Some of the messages were found, though, and kept safe in libraries and scribe houses. Some are sung to this day by the bards and minstrels of Coonsia."

"Like the Song of the Stars," Jarus said, nodding.

Mel looked at him, a little lost. "The song of..."

"The Song of the Stars," Jarus repeated. When Mel still looked blank, realization dawned on the Cooper's face. "Oh, that's a Coonsian song! You haven't heard it before." Jarus thought for a moment, recalling the words, then began:

'Ere the Ace-Lord in his line,
'Ere the Forest fill with light,
'Ere the world be told of time,
Then the Stars walked land and sky,
They in the Land Immortal dwell
.

'Ere the world was wrought from dust,
'Ere the dark woods cover us
'Ere the kings sit on their thrones,
'Ere foot trod on Elven roads,
They in the Land Immortal dwell.

'Ere the Dark ones leave His trust,
'Ere their hatred forged for us,
When War toiled, our minds forgot,
Kingdoms split as mortals fought
All they the Land Immortal dwell.

"There's four or five verses, depending on the version," Jarus added. "I don't remember it all." He trailed off, the air filled by the crackling of the fire.

Then Aryion's low voice filled the silence. "You left out the very last verse," he said, and recited softly,

When I fall where this road ends,

126

And lie in crypt beneath my lands
Don't weep for me, I'm not gone
I've flown away, but I live on
There in the Land Immortal dwell.

The quiet, haunting lilt to the melody sent chills down Mel's spine, yet the notes were somehow comforting too. He could not explain why.

"That was some fine singing," Norrin said to them with a smile. He looked at Aryion. "I haven't heard that last verse in years. They tend to leave it out—people don't like singing about crypts."

"Yes," Aryion said with a faint smile. "It was my mother's favorite, though. It ends the song with hope more than just history." He fell silent again, staring into the fire. The light played over his features and reflected in his thoughtful eyes.

Norrin stood. "Well, I must speak with Iriam before the night gets much older. Get some rest, you three. We'll be off again early tomorrow morning."

Mel set up his bedroll a short distance from the fire and lay on his back, watching as the clouds slowly covered the twinkling stars. The song played over in his mind, its haunting melody echoing in his thoughts as he slowly drifted off to sleep.

11

∽ ∽ ∽ ∽ ∽ ∽ ∽ ∽ ∽ ∽

Voices and Ice

Morning dawned gray and chill, leaving Mel's blanket heavy with dew. The fire had recently been stoked, and warmed him in the cold. For a moment, he lay in uncertainty as his mind tried to reconcile the sounds of the horses and the sights of the tents. Then yesterday's events came back to him.

Norrin stood on watch a few feet from the fire, leaning on his staff. "Good morning," he called as Mel sat up. "Sleep well, I hope?"

"Yep," Mel said. He shivered as he climbed out of his bedroll and quickly shuffled closer to the fire. "Cold today," he commented.

Jarus appeared from the forest, followed by Rygal, who carried a stack of wood. "I don't know, Rygal. You saw how the last one turned out," the Cooper was saying.

"Yes—it worked great," Rygal said.

"Ask Norrin's opinion, then. He'll agree with me," Jarus said confidently.

Norrin arched an eyebrow at Rygal, who had knelt by the fire to set down his load. At the wizard's inquiring glance, Rygal began. "Right, well—Norrin, this road leads west for a few miles before the crossroads. But there's another trail that cuts north before that. I

128

figured it might be better for us to take that one to Caer Sia instead."

Norrin smiled slightly. "Well, that would be a better question for Iriam, as you are currently following his orders, not mine. But I still suggest staying on the main road. It is not far to the crossroads, and you will have to go north then anyway."

"Told you," Jarus said with a grin.

Rygal shrugged, unabashed. "Jan always says time is our best ally, and in this case we can probably save more time. I'll ask Iriam."

Mel pulled on his boots and jacket as Rygal walked away. "How's your leg?" he asked as Jarus sat next to him.

"Not too bad," Jarus replied cheerfully. "It's still stiff, but Aryion said it should heal as long as I'm careful on it."

Norrin smiled. "I am glad to hear that, Jarus. Few have taken on serpentines and come out with only a claw mark."

"They were cowards," Jarus said loftily. "Mel and I sent them packing."

"Iriam helped too, of course," Mel added with grin.

Norrin's smile widened. "Well, whether or not Iriam had anything to do with it, I have heard that you fought well. Both of you," he added, turning to Mel.

Mel felt a flash of pride at the wizard's praise. He had spent most of the quest for Drisilas either running or hiding whenever there was a battle. It felt good to be useful on this adventure.

They gathered for breakfast, and Iriam called everyone to attention. "We will travel together to the crossroads, three miles or so from our current location. Once we reach it, we will part ways. My companions and I will continue our journey north to Caer Sia, while Norrin will lead the rest of the party to the island of Kamon."

Norrin stepped forward. "The roads west lead through miles of dense wilderness. There is no way of knowing how near the Aces are to us. Thus, we must be on the alert, for both Aces and their servants."

They packed up camp and mounted the horses. Mel clipped his heels to the little pony's sides to catch up with Norrin, who was speaking to Jan.

"If anything, the thing I want to know the most is what prophecy the Aces took," Jan said quietly. "That will determine much. If the Three are indeed in play..."

"There's no way of knowing that yet," Norrin replied in the same low tone. "But hopefully we will learn this from the scouts. They plan to rejoin us at the crossroads today around noon, with news from Elimar."

Mel remained quiet, though he was bursting with questions. He wasn't sure why the Ace-Lord wanted to steal a scroll from a library in the first place. Perhaps it held some key to his conquest? But what sort of prophecy could do that? And if it that was the case, why would Tinkeeyo keep a prophecy that held some sort of secret weapon for the Aces?

He glanced back at Jarus, who sat behind him. The Cooper's face was thoughtful, but he didn't say anything. Mel wondered how much he knew. The story Norrin had told them last night about the Stars and the prophecies was fascinating, but he couldn't connect it to their current situation. The Aces had risen in power and began a successful conquest some thirty years before. Why hadn't they taken control of Orlell then? What, if anything, could have stopped them?

Jarus spoke hesitantly, as though trying to tell how to phrase the question. "Jan… I've been thinking about the serpentines. The message they brought makes me think that they were after us all along. But why?"

Jan was silent, his eyes scanning the road ahead. "I am not sure yet, Jarus," was all he said.

In the same second he spoke, an arrow shot from the bracken and plunged into the shoulder of the pony Mel and Jarus rode.

The horse reared with a cry of fear, throwing both riders from his back. Mel landed hard on the ground; winded, he pushed himself up on his elbows and watched with shock and horror as a volley of arrows launched from both sides of the road. Riders cried out, horses screamed in pain, yet rising above it all was a reverberating, high-pitched howl that echoed over the trees.

"Form up!" Iriam shouted from ahead. "That is the cry of the Aces. Form up quickly!"

The cry sounded again, otherworldly, filled with hate. Mel clapped his hands over his ears, his heart pounding as sheer terror overwhelmed him for an instant. Then someone gripped his shoulder and pulled him up—Aryion. The ranger stood, sword drawn, beside

Rygal. "Up, Mel—stay close to me," he ordered. Shaking, Mel got to his feet and drew his knife.

Through the trees came the attackers, brandishing weapons and shouting cries of challenge. Muscular, gray-skinned warriors dressed in tattered leather armor and animal hides leapt through the underbrush. A strange triangular emblem was carved into their armor. Their brute-like faces were twisted with snarls as they attacked the circle.

"Orcs," Rygal panted; he stood next to Aryion, gripping his sword.

Across from him, Quinn released two arrows in rapid succession. Both found their target, burying themselves in the flesh of the attackers. But to Mel's horror, the two orcs wrenched the arrows free, and charged with a bellow of rage.

"Immortal orcs," Jarus corrected, his voice trembling slightly from fear.

Iriam and Norrin were both shouting, trying to organize the warriors into counter attack. The unexpected ambush had done its work well; the bodies of men and horses lay strewn across the path. Rygal parried the blow of the first orc that reached them, then thrust his sword into the warrior's torso. The orc stumbled back, unharmed, and sprang forward again.

"Stay close!" Aryion ordered again. This was easy to obey, as Mel was hemmed in on both sides by his companions and Norrin's warriors. He blocked the blow of another orc that charged at him. The sheer strength behind the orc's strike vibrated up his arm into his shoulder, and he winced. This orc was older and stronger than he was. There was a strange light in the orc's eyes—hollow and pale blue. Like the eyes of the serpentines when they had been possessed by the Darkness during his last adventure.

Aryion stepped between him and the orc and kicked the warrior back, sending him crashing into the fray of surging bodies. Still they kept coming—more and more attackers, seeping through the trees.

Then Iriam stepped forward. His black robes billowed around his tall frame, and a terrible light filled his eyes. He raised his hands. Ice crept along the ground, rushing to meet the oncoming warriors. It locked around their feet like chains, and the front line of orcs fell, struggling to escape the frigid grasp. Iriam lowered his hands until they were level with the warriors, and the ice locked over the fallen bodies. The orcs shouted and struggled, but they were caught. Trapped in a coffin of deep blue ice.

Jan moved next to Iriam. Red fire shot from his fingertips, and his other hand gripped Drisilas. For the first time the orcs hesitated. But it was only for an instant—then they charged forward, slashing through the onslaught of ice and fire as they battled to break past Jan and Iriam.

"Mel!"

Mel turned—someone had called his name, a voice he recognized but couldn't believe. He must have imagined it. It couldn't be—

"Mel!" The voice cried out again, tight with pain and fear but familiar—

"Dandio?" Mel called back, hardly daring to believe it. His heart was suddenly racing.

"Mel, please!" Dandio's voice was fading away, growing weaker–

"Dandio!" Mel shouted, and sprang away from Aryion's side. He heard the ranger call out, but ignored him as he sprinted into the trees and down a shallow draw. The dense woods made it impossible to see, and he ran on, calling Dandio's name.

"Mel!" The voice called him again, to the right, and he spun to follow it. It was getting farther and farther away, even as Mel ran. He continued on, shouting, but his cries faded into silence.

"Mel, wait!" Jarus' voice came from behind. The Cooper came running up after him, limping heavily on his injured leg. "What are you doing?"

"I heard…" Mel started, but he was cut off by a high-pitched scream that made his blood run cold. A shrill cry tense with terror, and yet another familiar voice.

"Misty!" he shouted, and took off again. Jarus yelled for him to stop, but he didn't listen, couldn't wait, because her scream sounded again and again in the distance as she sobbed with fright. She was getting farther away, he would lose her.

He tripped over a tree root and crashed into the ferns. For an instant he lay there, dazed. Voices shouted in the distance, first Dandio's, then Misty's again, panicking, crying out as if in agony.

"Mel, stop!" Jarus reached him and put a paw on his shoulder as he started to rise. "What's happening?"

"They're here!" Mel choked. "The Aces took them—they're here!"

Jarus looked at him blankly, shaking his head slowly. "There's no one there, Mel. No one at all."

Mel paused, tears streaming down his face, and listened. The distant shouts and clangs from the battle and the soft chirping of birds were all he heard.

Then Misty's scream filled the air again. He clapped his hands to his ears and hunched over, willing it to end. But now Jarus looked up, a wild panic in his eyes. "Maya?"

"What?" Mel said through gritted teeth.

"Maya!" Jarus sprang away down the hill, following a voice only he could hear. Mel got shakily to his feet and followed him, even as Misty's cries faded away. Almost sobbing from the horror of it, he stumbled on until he caught up to the Cooper.

"It's not real, Jarus," he stammered. "It's a trick—just wait." He squeezed his eyes shut as the voices began again in his head. This time it was his mother, then his father, then Misty again. He gripped Jarus' paw as they both huddled down, the agonized cries assaulting their ears and minds.

And then, mercifully, it all ended. Replaced by a new voice.

"Very impressive, child."

They both looked up as they heard it. As Mel's eyes found the speaker, the terror doubled in his chest.

Tall, wreathed in black robes. The cloak was tattered with decay, as though it had cheated death many times over. The armor beneath was tarnished, ancient as the world. The face was charcoal gray, withered until it remained only a grinning skull. The red eyes flashed in sunken sockets.

An Ace.

Mel remained still, frozen in place. The Ace stepped forward, glancing around, greedily taking in the sights of the mortal world. "I have long craved to meet you, child," he said, looking at Mel again. His voice was hollow and echoing, like a breath of ice. "He speaks so highly of you, the Master does. Of course, you have met him before."

"Stay back," Jarus gasped, getting to his feet and holding his knife out at the Ace. Mel could not move. The bone-chilling fear seemed to have locked him in place.

The Ace studied Jarus with mild interest. "Your voice is familiar, at least. We heard you when you broke the Jewel." He closed his sunken eyes and inhaled deep, a grotesque smile spreading over the withered face. "Your fear tasted sweet then—it is even richer now."

"Run, Mel!" Jarus yelled, lunging forward. Mel's heart leapt into his throat as Jarus—brave, cheerful Jarus—flung himself at the Ace. The Ace raised his hands. White ice sparkled on his fingertips as he faced the Cooper. Jarus stopped on the other side of the clearing, his eyes wide as the Ace prepared the finishing blast.

"No!" Mel cried, stumbling to his feet.

But before the ice left the Ace's hand, a crackling blast of sparks came from behind Mel, striking the Ace in the chest and sending it reeling back. Bright specks of yellow stood out on the black robes before they winked out.

Norrin stood tall behind Mel, his staff raised, eyes fixed on the Ace before him. "Get back, Jarus," he warned. Jarus retreated—the Ace, recovering from Norrin's sudden attack, let the ice fly after him, and it crashed into a tree just above the Cooper's head. The force of the blast flung Jarus back into the bracken, and he fell unconscious into the ferns.

"Jarus," Mel panted. He tried to stand, but his knees seemed to have turned to rubber. Instead he knelt, watching as the battle unfolded before him.

The Ace had turned to face Norrin, his face livid. Yellow flames played up and down the length of Norrin's staff, reflecting in the wizard's eyes as he stepped forward, standing between the Ace and Mel.

"Norrin of Arkran," the Ace said at last, savoring the words like a foul taste. "You are foolish to challenge us."

Norrin remained silent. The two opponents circled. The Ace studied his face, as though reading his thoughts. "So... they sent you to recover the second Shard, did they? But then... what is the purpose of the second party, so much smaller than your own? Why leave such a valuable asset so unguarded?"

The red eyes trained on Mel. Mel stared back, trembling, while his mind reeled with confusion and fear.

Then the Ace laughed. "Ah, *that's* why. Does the High King truly believe it wise to bring him back to Caer Sia? I thought the serpentines had delivered their message successfully, but clearly they have not."

Norrin spoke finally, his voice low and calm. "Your master has no power here, not without the Shards. The Stone will be your downfall." He lunged forward, spinning the staff in a pinwheel of sparks. The pale ice met the yellow fire with a hissing crackle, like a torch plunged into water. For an instant the two struggled against the other, then they broke away.

The Ace looked at Norrin questioningly, and then laughed again, long and low. "Not without the Shards?" he repeated. "You haven't heard, then, have you? Heard of the fall of the mighty gates, the toppling of the lovely towers, the cries of the lost echoing in the streets?"

Chills ran down Mel's spine. Norrin fired another blast of yellow flame, and the Ace stumbled back. "No more riddles. What do you speak of?" Norrin demanded. There was a growing note of uneasiness in his voice.

The Ace lunged forward, white ice in both his fists as he struck at the wizard. "Caer Sia, mortal fool," he hissed. "Caer Sia is ours. The Shard is ours."

"You lie," Norrin murmured, breaking away. The flame faltered for an instant.

"I only bring the words I was told to bring. I have only one purpose here. My final purpose. To deliver the words of the Ace-Lord to you who hear them." The Ace straightened, raising his chin. "This is the sign I bring." From the depths of the robes, he held up the tattered banner of Caer Sia.

Norrin clashed with him. Ice and fire struggled against the other, and this time ice was stronger—Norrin fell back for a moment, then charged again. "Hurry, Mel!" he ordered.

Mel stood and stumbled toward the place Jarus had fallen in the ferns. The Ace flung a blast at him, and Mel dropped flat just in time as ice whistled over his head. In the same moment, Norrin swung the long beam of wood like a bow staff and slammed it against the Ace's head. The black-robed figure stumbled back before launching a rapid volley of icy blue darts. Norrin deflected the blows rapidly, but Mel saw him wince as one of the darts struck him in the side.

Then another figure emerged to Mel's right. Rygal. The young warrior seemed unharmed, but he was out of breath as he gripped his sword. Mel saw him pale slightly and hesitate as he saw the opponent before him.

And the Ace's power seemed to double. Blast after blast of ice fired from his hands. Norrin fell back, giving ground as he deflected the blows. For an instant Mel didn't understand. Then he realized what was happening. The Ace grew stronger with their fear; now Rygal's worry for his mentor was being used against him.

Norrin saw Rygal too; for an instant he faltered, and the Ace knocked him back. Rygal lunged forward to Norrin's defense, and the icy bolt hit him across the knees, sending him sprawling. Panting, he straightened as the Ace raised his hands again.

A vivid flare of yellow fire hit the Ace in the back before he could strike Rygal a second time. Norrin stepped forward, forcing the

Ace's attention away from Rygal. Blood streaked his face, and his teeth were gritted. "Not him, you devil."

The Ace snarled and struck at him, and they clashed, ice against fire.

"Norrin!" Rygal yelled, getting painfully to his feet.

"Go!" Norrin ordered. "Get them out of here, Rygal!" He deflected another blast, and the force of it nearly knocked him down.

"I'm not leaving you, Norrin!" Rygal argued back.

Norrin fired another blast of sparks that sent the Ace recoiling, then turned to meet Rygal's eyes. There was sorrow there, but also love as he looked at the man he had raised as a son. "Go," he said, his voice firm.

Rygal shook his head stubbornly and charged at the Ace again. Norrin sent a wave of sparks that pushed Rygal back, out of the reach of the Ace's ice. Furious, the Ace rounded on the wizard again.

The two of them clashed. Norrin set his feet and pressed forward. Yellow fire licked along the Ace's robes, searing the flesh. A mad smile had formed on the skull-like face. Instead of countering the blow with ice, the Ace reached up and seized the center of Norrin's staff with both hands. The flames spluttered as ice spread down the length of the wood. Norrin let go and stepped back as his staff split in two, the halves of frozen wood clattering at the Ace's feet.

"Valiant," the Ace hissed, "but foolish. Much like this quest of yours." Norrin slashed at him with his wide-bladed knife; the Ace deflected the blow and shot a blast of ice that grazed the wizard's side. "You have lost," the Ace continued, as Norrin doubled over, stumbling. "You have lost the Shard, and your allies will lose this war."

Norrin raised his weary eyes and met the Ace's triumphant gaze. "Your master has destroyed the Forest of Light, and he will forever bear that curse," he rasped. "The Prophecy has already spelled out your doom."

"As it has yours," the Ace replied calmly. He raised his hands—a ray of white ice spanned the distance between his fingers and Norrin's chest, locking them together for a half second. Mel thought he saw something gold and glittering through the white ice, torn from the wizard's body, shining bright for an instant—then the white ice flashed and the light died.

Norrin fell, still and silent, ice glittering over his chest.

Rygal screamed, breaking the frigid silence. His wordless cry of pain and anguish echoed in Mel's mind, filled his dreams for weeks to come. Rygal lunged forward, sword raised as he charged wildly, blinded by grief and rage. The Ace turned to face him calmly and sent him reeling back with a blast of ice. Rygal got to his feet and the Ace knocked him down a second time, then raised his hands.

Before the Ace could strike him again, a tall figure sprang in front of Rygal and deflected the Ace's blast with a shield of crackling red fire. Jan stood, bracing himself as the ice collided with his shield. Then he let the bolt fly in a fiery arc at the Ace.

Rygal pushed past Jan and charged again. Jan fired at the Ace, then lunged forward and wrapped both arms around Rygal from behind, dragging him back. Rygal fought the restraint blindly, his sword nicking Ĵan's cheek, but the Liznee did not let go.

The Ace looked at the struggling pair, grimacing with hate. "He is already ours, Liznee," he hissed at Ĵan. Ĵan let go of Rygal to block the blast of ice that the Ace flung at them. This time the force of the blow sent both of them sprawling. The Ace raised his hands and struck at the unprotected Liznee king.

The ice was deflected mid-air by a deep blue blast that shattered it. Fragments of ice flew in all directions, and the magnified sound of breaking glass made Mel's teeth rattle. He turned—moving toward them, black cloak billowing behind him, Iriam entered the fight. The look on his face made Mel shiver.

"Leave now, Mel," Iriam ordered, his eyes fixed on the Ace. Mel forced himself to his feet and stumbled toward Ĵan. The Liznee king had reached Jarus' unconscious form and moved him to safety. Rygal had fallen a few feet away, and now watched in silence, blood streaming from a cut on his brow.

For the first time, a trace of fear appeared on the Ace's face. He let a blast of ice fly at the Neutral, who raised his hands and snatched it out of the air almost casually. Then he fired it back at the Ace, striking him in the chest. The Ace reeled back, then struck again. Iriam deflected the wild blows as he advanced. Finally he gripped the Ace by the throat, holding him upright.

The Ace choked, then let out a rasping laugh. "Look at you, Neutral. Fighting for a lost cause. How much are you willing to lose in defense of a cursed child?"

Iriam's grip tightened abruptly—there was a low crack, and the Ace's body tensed. It hung still for a moment before the last glittering ice in its body transformed to flame as it died. Fire enveloped the body. Iriam let it fall as it withered away into ashes.

A long, exhausted silence fell over the clearing. Mel sagged against a tree. He heard Jan's voice vaguely, as though coming from far away. He barely heard the words.

Rygal struggled to his feet, fell, and crawled the remaining distance. "Norrin," he gasped hoarsely. His face was drawn and pale as he lowered his face to the wizard's chest.

Figures appeared through the forest, beholding the aftermath of the battle. Aryion's face swam into Mel's vision—the ranger's voice was tense with worry, demanding if he was all right. A question Mel could not answer. He felt sick and weary, his strength drained by the entire horrific encounter with the Ace.

He closed his eyes, huddled back against the tree, and listened to the fragments of sound that filled the glade. He heard Iriam's voice telling Jan that the orcs had been driven back, heard the many questions from the surviving riders, heard the distant sound of the orcs' horns in mournful retreat.

His pounding, tormented heart was the last sound he was conscious of.

PART 2

§ § § § § § § § §

Kamon

12

A Company Divided

The survivors made camp at the crossroads. Mel slept haltingly, his sleep interrupted by nightmares of the recent images of the day and the battle in the woods. Again and again he heard Rygal's cry, saw Norrin fall, saw the blood on Jan's face left by Rygal's frantic struggles.

It was all so wrong.

Mel opened his eyes as the sun rose over the trees. His whole body felt heavy with weariness. Everyone here felt the same, he knew. All were weary from both the battle and from the toil of tending to the fallen. Nearly half of Norrin's riders had been killed. Their bodies had been gathered and set for a great funeral pyre, while their companions circled it in silent honor of their heroic actions. A stone was set beside the heap of ashes, a memorial to all the fallen.

A separate grave had been dug a little ways away from the pyre. Here they laid Norrin of Arkran, with the halves of his staff at his side, his name etched into a smooth stone that marked his resting place.

Jarus had sat there for several hours, grieving in quiet solitude, before finally going to sleep. He had suffered a gash just under his right ear, where a stray chunk of ice had rendered him unconscious. Inwardly, Mel was glad for the wound, glad that Jarus hadn't had to watch the battle.

Rygal had stood apart from everyone last night, a distant, glazed expression in his eyes. He hadn't reacted, hadn't even wept at Norrin's death yet. And as far as Mel knew, he hadn't slept at all, simply stood in silent vigil beside the grave, a hand on his sword hilt, staring at nothing.

Mel sat up stiffly. His body still ached, but any wounds he had received were minor in comparison to the rest of the casualties. Quinn was injured the worst out of the seven companions. An orc sword had slashed his shoulder, badly damaging the muscles and prohibiting his ability to shoot his bow. Iriam had assumed command of the weary group.

Even greater than the injuries and deaths was the much larger, heavier truth of what they had learned. The Ace's mocking words told that Caer Sia had been taken. The tattered banner the Ace had brought, crusted in ice, seemed only further proof of it.

Mel had refused to believe this at first, unable to accept the fact that they had failed. But the message had been confirmed late last night. Norrin's three scouts, who had gone to gather news in Elimar, returned in the wake of the battle with more bad news. The three exhausted riders recounted their report to Iriam, who had assumed command of both groups. The report confirmed the worst. It was true. The Aces had attacked Caer Sia two days before. The capital had been captured, the Red Dawn defeated, and—worst of all—the Shard placed in the Ace-Lord's hands.

There was no way to know the fate of the survivors, if there were any at all. The news was devastating to Jan.

The mounting horror and despair seemed to seep into Mel's very core. He felt utterly overwhelmed by it all, by the pain and defeat and the pure power displayed by the Aces. For the first time, the possibility entered his mind that Dandio might be gone forever.

"Oh, Dandio," he whispered, wondering if his words, by some magic, could reach the Liznee if he was still alive. "Where are you?"

Mel packed up his bedroll and shouldered his pack. Iriam stood on watch near the fire. "How do you feel?" he asked as Mel approached. His deep voice was gentle and calm.

Mel let out a long breath. "I'm all right. Just sore." He looked up at the Neutral. "Iriam… what are we going to do? We can't go to Caer Sia now, not if the Ace-Lord's there."

Iriam nodded, his face thoughtful. "Indeed. I have been thinking this over. I will tell you once everyone else is awake."

Mel nodded, too worn out to argue otherwise. He helped water and feed the horses—there were many empty saddles following yesterday's battle. His eyes strayed to the roads before him. One turned due north, toward Caer Sia, and the other wound west. He wondered what Iriam planned to do now.

Once the others were awake, they ate a brief and quiet breakfast. When the meal was finished, Iriam spoke. "I have pondered what is to be done next," the Neutral said. "If Caer Sia is indeed lost, then we can assume that the Shard there has been taken as well. The Ace-Lord has dealt us a heavy blow. But," he continued, and a light flashed in his crimson eyes, "we must not abandon hope. Such despair will only help the Aces further."

He studied the weary, battered faces before him. "We cannot stay here long. The Ace that led the charge yesterday is dead, and the orcs were driven back, but there is still danger for the residents of the area. We are very close to Elimar, and there is a chance that the orcs will raid there. This we cannot risk. Therefore, I ask the remaining warriors of Norrin's party to travel there and defend the town in case of attack. Get word to the authorities there as soon as you can, and have them on alert." Iriam's eyes landed on one face. "You, sir. What is your name?"

The rider he had spoken to hesitated. "Gareth, sir. Gareth of Caer Sia." He had a shaggy brown beard and a wide honest face. Mel had noticed him yesterday, helping organize the start of the counter attack.

"Norrin spoke highly of you," Iriam said. "And I also know you to be the captain of guard in Caer Sia. If you are willing, I ask you to assume command of the riders."

Gareth looked surprised, and shook his head hesitantly. "I—no, sir, I couldn't. I'm only a local soldier, not a war leader."

"Your men need you," Jan said from across the fire. His voice was hoarse. "So does your city. You are a leader, and we need you to take command now. Please," he added.

The heaviness in his king's voice made Gareth agree without further argument. Iriam nodded gratefully. "My companions and I will take seven of the horses. In the meantime, take whatever gear you need and ride with all haste for Elimar."

Mel glanced up. The companions weren't going back to Elimar with Gareth's group, it seemed. Nor could they continue their journey to Caer Sia. He wondered what Iriam planned to do.

The riders in Gareth's party stood and began to pack up the camp while the seven companions lingered by the fire.

Iriam studied them all. "What I ask of you is a dangerous and unknown venture, even to me. Our plans have changed greatly, and should you choose to go with Gareth and his men, I would not begrudge it."

"What are we going to do?" Jarus asked softly.

"What *can* we do?" Quinn said wearily. His arm was wrapped in a stained bandage, and his face was bruised.

Iriam looked at him. "Jan and I spoke last night, trying to best decide our next action. And here is what we plan to do." He looked into the eyes of each of them in turn as he continued. "We are going to the island city of Kamon to recover the second Shard."

There was a stunned silence. Of all the things Mel had guessed, this was the last possibility. He had expected that they would go back to Flora, gather allies somewhere, try to take back Caer Sia maybe.

"Why?" Rygal asked bluntly. It was the first time he had spoken all morning. His voice was low and strained, a harsh rasp. "What does it matter to us what happens in Kamon? We can't do anything without the other Shard."

"Neither can the Ace-Lord," Iriam told him. "If he plans to channel the Dark Realm's powers through the Stone, like he did with the Jewel, he must have both Shards. If you choose to continue, you will be challenging him to a race, and a dangerous one at that. We must reach Kamon before the Aces."

He paused again. "As I mentioned, this is a risky errand, and certainly not what any of you signed up for. Thus, the choice to continue must be yours alone."

There was a long silence. Mel's thoughts felt like a whirlwind. On one hand was the possibility of returning home to his family—a failed adventurer, but alive, which might be better in the long run. On the other was a long, hard road through miles and miles of wilderness until they reached Kamon. After that, they would face an even more difficult struggle when they inevitably clashed with the Aces. Mel couldn't help thinking it would be a fight with little hope of success, though. After seeing the Ace's powers yesterday, he hated to know what their leader could do.

Despite the thought, he knew there was only one choice. If the Ace-Lord recovered both Shards, the entire world would be his for the taking. Whether he was on this quest or not, his life and the lives of those he loved were in danger.

He looked at the others. They seemed to have come to the same conclusion.

Iriam saw the resolution on their faces and nodded in approval. "Good. Well, gather the gear we still need, and let us be off. It is a long road to Kamon, and we must make haste."

Mel had already packed his bag, so he helped Jarus gather up the food and water. The Cooper was uncharacteristically silent, but Mel couldn't blame him. The horror of yesterday was still fresh in both their minds, and neither of them seemed ready to talk about it.

He noticed Rygal standing alone on the edge of camp, and his heart ached for his friend. He finished helping Jarus, then walked towards Rygal hesitantly, not sure what he would say.

But a hand on his shoulder turned him aside gently. "Let him grieve," Jan said quietly. "There is little we can say to help. Only time will do that."

Mel met the Liznee's eyes and nodded slowly. His eyes were drawn instantly to the cut on Jan's cheek. The reality that it was Rygal's sword that had done it was more disturbing than the actual injury.

But what would Rygal do now? Of course, he would continue on the quest…but then what? There had been something in Rygal's eyes last night, after Norrin had been buried, that scared Mel. A sort of dazed numbness, barely masked by the pain still burning deep inside. Mel remembered a similar feeling after Llyrion had been suddenly ambushed and killed. That had all happened so fast, there was no time to even properly mourn. They had shed only a few tears, then continued on. That was the only thing they could do, after all.

Yet this loss had impacted Rygal even more than Llyrion's death had. Mel knew that without a trace of doubt. He had lost his mentor and the only father he had ever known.

They mounted the horses and started off, taking the road that curved towards the south. Coonsia's terrain seemed, at first, hardly different from Daffodalion's, but as they continued on, the land changed. Oaks and birches were replaced with towering evergreens, and the Diamond Cap mountains loomed to the north.

They stopped a few hours before dark. The camp was set up in silence, everyone either too tired or too discouraged to talk much. Mel laid out his mat, then rooted through the pack until he found a water flask.

Jarus set up his bed roll next to Mel. Mel waited awkwardly, not sure what to say. "How are you doing, Jarus?" he finally asked tentatively.

The Cooper shrugged slightly. "Not bad. My head hurts, but I'll live." He looked up, sensing Mel's real meaning. "And…yes, I'm doing all right."

Mel took a deep breath. "Okay…it's just…well…I'm here, in case you need me," he said finally.

Jarus gave him a slight smile. It was nothing compared to his usual cheerful grin, but it was something. "Thank you."

They both looked up as Aryion entered the camp. The ranger

had gone down the road to scout ahead, and his face was troubled. "Iriam, we might have a problem. There's a group of Black Dwarves ahead, moving this way. I don't know if they are on our side or not."

Mel's heart sank. The companions were exhausted from yesterday's battle. A fight with Dwarve warriors in the waning light was the last thing they needed.

"I'll go," Jan said after a pause. "We are in Coonsia now. They are under Caer Sia's leadership, and mine."

"Not alone," Iriam told him immediately. "Let us both go." He looked at the others. "The five of you, wait. Rest if you will, but stay on the alert."

The two of them headed down the path and disappeared into the rapidly darkening woods.

Aryion was the only one in any condition to do much. He re-did the bandage on Quinn's shoulder, then gave Jarus a draft of sweet-smelling medicine to help him sleep through the throbbing headache. "Go easy," he added as the Cooper settled down. "Your head will heal, but you'll have to go slow for a little while. Try to sleep."

"All right. But wake me up if there's trouble," Jarus said. He curled up by the fire.

"Can I help?" Mel asked the ranger. "I'm not hurt."

Aryion smiled faintly. "I am nearly finished, but perhaps you could water the horses. They will need their strength for this journey."

Mel nodded promptly and moved to do so. He saw that Aryion had not put away the medicine gear, but had instead gone to Rygal. The young warrior sat silent on a fallen log at the edge of the clearing; he looked up dully as the ranger approached.

"You will do no good if you wear yourself out," Aryion told him bluntly. He pulled out a balm and cleaned the gash on Rygal's forehead. "If you will not eat, at least take some of the draft I gave Jarus so you can sleep."

"Do we know anything more about the Aces?" Rygal asked him in a low rasp.

Aryion paused. "No. You should ask Iriam, if you're concerned. They've gone to check on a Dwarve patrol ahead."

"I know. I heard." Rygal's tone was irritable.

Aryion finished cleaning the cut and held out the same draft he had given Jarus. "Take this, and try to rest."

"I don't need rest," Rygal said abruptly, standing and pushing him away. "I want answers. I want to know where the Aces are, how they got into Caer Sia, if they're coming after us again. I want to know where the Ace-Lord thinks he can hide. I want to know how to kill them."

The last words dropped into silence. Mel looked at him uneasily. Rygal's face was flushed, his red-rimmed eyes full of fire.

Quinn spoke hesitantly. "Once we get the Shards and join them, the Aces will be defeated, Rygal. That should be our priority now."

"That's not good enough," Rygal snapped. His voice was raised, haunted and angry. "I'm going to kill him. The Ace-Lord. I'll kill him myself. I'll swear the Blood Oath."

He stomped towards the fire, a hand clutching his sword hilt. Aryion's low voice made him stop. "No, you won't. You aren't thinking clearly right now. Rest, and don't do anything until you are calmer." His voice faltered for a moment. "You know the Blood Oath is… not the answer. Revenge is not the answer."

Rygal rounded on him sharply. "Says *you*? You're the biggest hypocrite here, Hummingbird. Where were you yesterday? Where were you while Norrin protected *your* charge? You have one purpose on this quest, and this is what you do with it?"

"You saw what the Aces did to lure him away. Any of us would have fallen for it," Aryion said. His voice was still quiet.

Mel's mind had hinged on one thing Rygal had said. "Your… charge?" he asked slowly.

Aryion looked at him, at Rygal, and then at him again, and for the first time Mel saw true regret in his eyes. Regret for hiding the truth. In the same instant, the pieces fell into place. Aryion's strange journey back to Carna from Caer Sia, to escort Mel to the council; Aryion always watching out for him, no matter what else was going on; Rygal's explanation of the ranger's appearance after the council—"*Jan asked him to do something, it's Aryion's business, you can talk to him later.*"

And then, like a flash of lightning, the Ace's words yesterday echoed again in Mel's mind. *He is already ours. What are you willing to lose in protection of a cursed child?*

The Aces had lured *Mel* away from the others, him and him alone. They had pursued, tracked, haunted his mind ever since the encounter with the Darkness. The Ace-Lord's greatest asset to his kingdom wasn't some secret weapon. It was a fear-filled eleven-year-old, in over his head.

There is something in you I can use, child.

Rygal shook his head in reply to Aryion's words. "No, *they* fell for it, and you let Mel go. Norrin didn't fall for it, and now Norrin is dead." His voice rose as he stepped closer to the ranger. "You lost him. You broke your end of the deal because you stayed to fight the orcs—because you're still looking for Hagshrub. Isn't that right? He's your target. You swore the Blood Oath, and you're bound to that, bound far tighter than you could have been to that boy." Rygal pointed at Mel.

Mel's thoughts whirled in confusion, in fear, and, most of all, in a sickening feeling of betrayal. "What is he talking about?" he demanded, looking at Aryion.

Aryion was silent. His face was drawn and pale with anger, but he made no motion to speak.

Rygal looked at him in disgust. "The only reason you came at all was to protect Mel, which is inconvenient, isn't it, considering the circumstances. You have the gall to tell *me* I'm being irrational? *You're* the one with a Blood Oath to fulfill!"

"Rygal," Quinn said cautiously.

Aryion finally spoke, his voice quiet. "I can see the flaw in my actions. There is nothing more I can do. Though I doubt you will believe me, I can assure you Hagshrub was the last thing on my mind yesterday."

"You expect me to believe you? To trust you?" Rygal's voice was loud. "You failed him. Probably the same way you failed your father all those years ago, wasn't it?"

Aryion's face darkened. For the first time, his hand went to his sword hilt. Seeing the motion, Rygal drew his sword with a hissing flash. "Attack me, then, Hummingbird," he challenged—his eyes were wild.

"Don't!" Quinn shouted, limping to his feet.

"Stop!" Iriam's deep voice ordered at the same time. Mel, standing with his fists clenched, his whole body trembling, turned to see both Iriam and Ĵan walking into the camp. Iriam looked furious, Ĵan had his hands spread in a placating gesture.

"Rygal, put your sword away this moment," the High King ordered. "We cannot afford to be at one another's throats. We need to trust each other if we are to defeat the Aces."

Aryion looked at Ĵan and gave a short bark of laughter. "Trust? *Now* you bring up trust? This entire quest has been hung on secrets. There isn't an ounce of trust in this entire company, and you've noticed it just as well as I."

"Watch your tone, Hummingbird," Ĵan said in a low voice.

Mel barely heard him. The blood was roaring in his ears. Something inside him had snapped. "All this time, all this time, and you didn't think it relevant to mention—just once—that the Aces are after me?" he demanded, striding to stand in front of Jan. "You've known for—what, maybe nine months now, since we beat the Darkness—and you didn't even tell me?"

"Mel—" Jan began, glancing at Aryion.

"I'm sick of secrets!" Mel shouted. "I'm sick of it when they're secrets that put *my* life in danger. Everything's been full of secrets since the quest for Drisilas, and now you're wondering why we don't trust each other?"

"We only hid what we had to, Mel," Jan said gently. "We could not risk putting you in danger."

"No, you didn't," Mel scoffed. His anger made him completely forget his place, and he didn't care. "I'm obviously already in danger, but I guess I should have realized that sooner. You didn't want me at the council because you needed my help, and you didn't let me come on this quest for my help either. You just wanted me here to keep an eye on me—watch over me like I'm some sort of—some sort of weapon?"

Jan was shaking his head. "No…"

"He's been in my head!" Mel screamed at him. "The Ace-Lord's voice has been in my head for months and months now and I don't even get to know why! All I'm getting is half-truths at best—most of them are flat out lies."

He rounded on Aryion. "For all you talk about getting rid of the secrets and telling the public about the Aces, you kept everything from me. You didn't even have a *right* to keep some of those secrets! So maybe Rygal's right about you—I don't even know anymore!"

Out of breath, he spun away and went to sit by the fire. His whole body was shaking, his heart beating raw and painful. Anger and hurt and betrayal flowed through his mind like an angry storm. His eyes burned with furious tears that would not fall.

Jarus had woken up sometime during Rygal and Aryion's argument but said nothing to Mel as they sat there. Mel didn't care. He didn't want to speak with any of them. They had all lied to him. Yet the truth was so terrifying he almost wished he had never learned of it.

For whatever reason, the Aces were after him. *He* was the asset they were seeking so diligently. Without even realizing it, his choice to join the quest had bound him to the fight. From now on, nowhere on Orlell would be safe for him until this deadly struggle with the Aces was over.

13

The New Blood

Iriam and Jan's return ended the argument but did little to ease the tension. A heavy silence settled over the camp as evening fell. The forest grew cold, and a few stars twinkled through the haze of twilight. Jan offered to take the first watch.

Iriam reported that the Dwarves had only been passing through, and were not interested in disrupting their travels. It was one worry off the substantial list in Mel's mind.

Mel felt too angry and upset to eat anything, and instead wrapped himself up in his blankets as night fell. But he could not fall asleep. The initial anger was passing. Now there was only fear and regret, and a dizzying sense of confusion.

He realized he had gathered some ideas about the Ace-Lord's true motives over the past few days. The serpentine attack—and Jan's refusal to talk of it any further—had been an indicator that there was something else they weren't telling him. The serpentines had tracked Mel during the quest for Drisilas. It was logical that the Ace-Lord would send them to track Mel yet again on this adventure. But why? Evidentally, the Ace-Lord wanted Mel for something— some sort of plan.

He is already ours. How much are you willing to lose to protect a cursed child?

Mel had no idea what this meant. But he understood now that he had been chosen. Cursed. Hand-picked by the Ace-Lord during their interaction within the Darkness. Whatever task or purpose the Ace-Lord had in mind, Mel wasn't sure, but he was bound to it nonetheless. And there was nothing Mel could do to change that.

He closed his eyes and pressed his hands to his head. Why had he gone to the council? Why had he not seen the truth faster? He realized angrily that the choice to join the quest had never been his own. Even if Mel hadn't volunteered, he knew Ĵan would have asked him—and Ĵan knew that Mel would never think to refuse. No, it was Ĵan who had wiled him into this whole fiasco, brought him along to keep an eye on.

"Are you still awake?" came Ĵan's quiet voice. Mel rolled over. The Liznee king was kneeling above him, the moon lighting his solemn features.

"I'm sorry about what I said, sire," Mel mumbled sullenly. "I didn't think."

Ĵan didn't seem to hear him. "Let us talk, then, if you aren't too tired. I have a lot to tell you." He stood and moved to sit on a stump within the tree line.

Despite himself, Mel was intrigued. He stood and walked over, shivering slightly in the chill.

Ĵan studied him. "I was wrong, Mel. I can see that now. You must know, however, that my reasons for keeping the truth from you were not to slight you. So much of the Aces was yet to be learned after the quest for Drisilas. I only had a theory, and a weak one at that. It made no sense to tell you something that might have been false—especially something so serious."

Mel stirred the dirt with the toe of his shoe. "You could have at least told me your theory."

"Yes, I could have. But I did not, and I apologize for it now." He took a breath. "You ask to know the truth. So I will tell you as much as we now know. As you probably have guessed, the Aces are after you. They seek you with equal vigor as they seek the Shards. It seems you hold the key to next part of the Ace-Lord's plan."

"I do?" Mel asked, confused. "How? I mean—what do I possibly have that the Ace-Lord wants?"

Jan smiled faintly. "You're smart, brave, and determined. However, you are also… impressionable. The Ace-Lord wants your mind and your heart in equal parts. He believes you will join his side, when given the opportunity."

"I'd never do that, Jan," Mel said defensively. "You know I'd never do that."

"Yes, I know. Not willingly, at least."

"So the Ace-Lord thinks he can force me to join his side?"

"Force or trick. I am not sure which. I doubt the latter. The fight with the Darkness showed the Aces that you are clever as well as brave, and I doubt he thinks he can trick you," Jan said. "The Ace-

Lord learned a lot in that fight, actually. Particularly about you. When you were in the void within the Darkness, you heard his voice and saw his face, right?"

Mel nodded slowly. Jan continued. "During that exchange, some way or other, the Ace-Lord chose you. He selected you to be the asset he needs—the New Blood to join his forces."

"The New Blood?"

Jan paused. "There is a prophecy, Mel. One that speaks of the rise and eventual downfall of the Aces. It has been forgotten for decades. I have only learned parts of it. The last time it was revisited was around thirty years ago, the same time that the Aces appeared and fought the Liznees. I was young, but I can remember my father scouring the old scrolls then, sharing the hope of the Prophecy. The Aces fear and loath the Prophecy—we can assume now that this is what drove them to retreat last time."

He looked at Mel. "Since then, hardly anyone remembers the old prophecies, which is exactly what the Ace-Lord wants. If no one knows the truth, there is no hope for him to break through. Hope is powerful, Mel. The Aces cannot understand nor overcome hope—and this Prophecy will give hope."

"Then what's the Prophecy?" Mel asked.

"It is called the Prophecy of Three, but we know very little about it. First must come the New Blood." Jan thought a moment. "Decades ago, there was a village called Tiravale. There were eleven residents—simple farmers, it seemed. The Ace-Lord went to them, seduced them, and gave them great powers. And they sold their souls to him—they became the Eleven Aces, joining with Kahlifis, the Twelfth. In this number the Aces have their greatest strength, but there can be no more than that."

Mel was starting to feel a little lost. "What does this have to do with me?"

"The Prophecy of Three speaks of many things, Mel—many different people who must step into their roles in order for the Aces to be defeated. While the Ace-Lord despises its words, he is no fool, and thus far he has found ways to avoid the outcome of the Prophecy. For the one called the New Blood, it is described as a mortal, young and passionate, whose powers will overcome the Aces. So, to keep this from happening, the Ace-Lord wants to find this person and turn them into one of his own—the Twelfth Ace."

Mel remembered the Ace's words to Norrin yesterday—*I have come for one purpose, my last purpose.* That Ace was supposed to die, because the prophecy required that the Twelfth Ace be New-Blooded—young, inexperienced, and an excellent choice for the Ace-Lord's expanding kingdom.

How much are you willing to lose to protect a cursed child?

He felt sick. "How... how would the Ace-Lord do that?"

Jan let out a long breath. "It's unpleasant, Mel, and highly dangerous. The Ace-Lord's powers are greater than many of the other Netrocrians, darker and stranger. While the Aces all possess the power to destroy a person's Essence, the Ace-Lord can alter it—alter the very life and being of a person. To transform the residents of Tiravale into the Aces that they are today, he removed their Cantrian Essence, which was created by the High Light, and he filled them with his own dark powers. They are completely his now, pawns in his hand."

Mel closed his eyes, overwhelmed for a moment. He realized that if the Ace-Lord wanted him, there was very little he could do to stop that. Even Norrin had been powerless. Mel knew, too, that the longer he resisted, the more people around him would die. "Is there… anything I can do to stop him? I don't have any powers—not like what you said is in the Prophecy."

"Yes, you do." Jan gripped his hand and looked intensely into his eyes. "You have a choice. Every day from here until we face the Ace-Lord, you can choose. You choose whether you give up, or have hope and continue, no matter how dark it gets. It's difficult—trust me, it is difficult, but it might be the one thing that will slow the Ace-Lord down, and protect your own heart."

Mel studied him. Jan's tired face, lined with so many worries, held a question there. A question for Mel, if he would continue, even with so much against him.

"All right," Mel said softly. He took a shaky breath. "Is there anything important that I'm supposed to do in the Prophecy of Three?"

"I am not sure. I've only heard pieces of this prophecy, Mel," Jan admitted. "I do know that there was a copy of it in Caer Sia's library. Perhaps, if it survived the attack on the city, you may read it when we return north."

Mel nodded slowly. "I guess I'll just have to wait until then," he said. He doubted he would ever get the chance. If they ever made it to Caer Sia, it was unlikely they would live long enough for him to find and read the Prophecy.

Yet even with that thought, a little of his fear had faded now that the truth was out. His mind felt clearer. Determined.

You want me, Ace-Lord? You'll have to kill me first.

14

The Ranger's Story

The following morning brought no change to the despondency and heaviness that hung over the companions. Rygal's fire seemed to have gone; now he was silent, his eyes dull, face haggard. At a soft word from Jarus, he agreed to eat and drink a little before they started out again. Mel wished he had the words to say to him, but the argument yesterday made him feel awkward to talk with anyone much.

There was an underlying note of tension in the entire group. Mel wondered uneasily what would happen if conflict broke out among the companions again, and they had to pick sides. But he somehow doubted this would happen. No one seemed to want to argue or even talk as they saddled the faithful horses and began the ride west.

Mel felt tired too. He wanted to talk to Jan—he still had many questions for the Liznee king about the Prophecy. Still, the conversation last night had brought a new determination and life to Mel. The earlier despair and resentment had been completely replaced by raw will to continue the fight. He would not give up. That would bring swift defeat. He also knew that the companions would need to trust one another if they had any hope of beating the Ace-Lord. Mel decided that morning, as he watched the weary group pack up camp, that if there was anything he could do to help heal the broken trust, he would do it.

He glanced over his shoulder. Jarus was hunched in the saddle behind him, his bright eyes watching the passing terrain. His face was tired and sad.

At last, Mel could stand the heavy silence no longer. "How are you feeling, Jarus?" he asked softly.

"All right," Jarus replied in the same lowered tone, then paused. "Did you talk with Ĵan last night? I didn't mean to eavesdrop—I just heard your voices."

Mel hesitated for a moment. Then he realized that the secret would have to be out sooner or later. He summarized last night's conversation as best he could.

Jarus gave a low whistle as Mel finished. "That's intense, Mel. I guess that explains why the serpentines came after you, and why the Ace was there the other day." He paused, thinking. "It's a little odd, though…"

"What is?" Mel asked as he trailed off.

"Well… not that I envy your position at all—but I wonder why I'm not being tracked too. I heard the Ace-Lord's voice before, when we broke the Jewel. Technically, I could be the New Blood they're hunting."

"Maybe," Mel murmured. He hadn't thought of that. Why would

the Ace-Lord choose Mel, particularly? "I guess the Ace-Lord wasn't ready for the conquest when you broke the Jewel," Mel suggested finally. But he doubted that.

"True," Jarus said. The Cooper sounded thoughtful. "I wonder… it's a random thought, but… well, Mel, Jan said that you're still… 'impressionable' was the word he used?"

"Yeah," Mel said slowly. He didn't like that word. It implied he was too young and inexperienced to think for himself.

But Jarus didn't bring that up. "Jan said the Ace-Lord tricked the other eleven Aces too. Maybe he's planning to do something similar to you. I wonder…" he trailed off again.

"What are you thinking?" Mel asked.

"You said before you don't really know what you want to do—that once you turn twelve, you have to choose a trade study. I was older when I heard the Ace-Lord's voice, Mel. Not a lot older, but… I knew what I wanted by that part of the journey. The Ace-Lord might try to use some of that uncertainty in you." He shrugged unhappily. "I'm not sure. I just thought of it."

"Maybe," was all Mel said. He wanted to protest, but he didn't have much to argue. Jarus was right. Like it or not, Mel had come to a crossroads in his life—a time to choose. It was much bigger than a simple trade school choice. *I'm not going to choose the Aces, though,* he told himself furiously. *I have my family, and this quest. I'm not going to join the Ace-Lord.*

Yet he felt a flicker of doubt. Even if they joined the Shards and, by some miracle, recovered Caer Sia, what would happen then? He knew the Ace-Lord wouldn't just give up. The Aces would keep coming until they had what they wanted—first Mel, then all of Orlell.

They talked of other things for a while, alternating between jogging and walking the horses. Mel was exhausted by the time they set up camp. He started a small fire and helped Jarus start the evening meal. The conversation with the Cooper had refreshed him, no matter how dark the topic was. Perhaps it was the fact that the secret had been concealed for so long—now it was a relief to have it out in the open.

Mel ate his meal and watched the others quietly. Jarus sat across from him by the fire, talking to Quinn. Iriam and Jan were bent over the maps, engaged in a discussion over the best route to take to the coast. Rygal was asleep. The strain of the ride and the last few days seemed to have drained him entirely of his former strength. In the shadows of the trees, wrapped in his mottled cloak, sat Aryion. Mel could see the glint of his dark eyes as he scanned the camp in silence.

Now that Mel's main question about the Aces was answered, his mind promptly turned to the next mystery. His feelings about Aryion were conflicted. For one, he felt that the ranger had lied to him one too many times—lied about protecting Mel, lied about why he had come, lied about the orcs. And what about the oath that Rygal mentioned—the Blood Oath? Mel didn't know what that was, but he noticed that the mention of it had startled the others—even Quinn, who had known Aryion longer than any of them. Whatever it was, Mel assumed it was a serious matter.

Secondly, Mel felt disappointed by the whole situation. He had trusted and admired the ranger, and he hated to think ill of him. Not only that, he felt that Aryion had disliked keeping the truth from Mel, just as much as Mel had disliked not knowing.

Mel could no longer stand it. Uncomfortable matter or not, he had to talk to Aryion.

The ranger looked up as Mel walked over. "Did you speak with Jan?" was the first thing Aryion asked. Mel nodded. Aryion glanced away. "I assume he told you the truth of our arrangement, then."

"No, actually," Mel said. "He told me about the Ace-Lord hunting me, and why they want me. He didn't say anything about you." He took a breath before continuing. "That's why I wanted to ask you directly."

Aryion was silent for a moment. A slight smile played over his face as he looked up. "Ask me what, exactly?"

Mel hesitated only a moment longer. "I wanted to ask about the Blood Oath… and about your business with Hagshrub."

The momentary smile was gone in an instant, and the pain in the ranger's eyes made Mel feel a little bad for bringing it up. But he was committed now.

"The Blood Oath," Aryion said finally, and cleared his throat. "Yes." He hesitated a moment longer, then shook his head briskly. "Hang it all. I am tired of the secrets. So, I will tell you, if you promise to answer my questions about you."

Mel nodded quickly. Aryion paused again, gathering his thoughts before he spoke. "The Blood Oath is a promise. A serious one, made only for the most dire of circumstances. When a warrior takes the Oath, he is bound by it—either until he fulfills his promise, or until he dies attempting it. It's a cruel bond. There is no going back on a Blood Oath—failure is believed to lead to an eternal curse. That's why someone must think very carefully before taking it. I took it," he held out his right hand, nodding at the thin scar on his palm, "years ago, when I was not much older than you."

"And… your promise?" Mel prompted. If the Oath could only be taken for serious matters, he guessed that it was nothing good.

The ranger took a deep breath. "It's a bit of a story, Mel. But I will tell you." He thought for a moment before beginning. "I was born and raised in a small town outside of Elimar. My parents were poor. My mother was often ill, but she cared for me and my twin sister. My father was a ranger, but worked at the mill to provide for us. When I was twelve, he began to train me as a ranger too. Once I was old enough, he was determined to join the Ranger Order of Coonsia, with me as his apprentice. But times were difficult, so we lived there until the winter of my fifteenth birthday."

He paused, as though each word was painful. "There was a raid on our town that winter. It was a hard season, but we had plenty of food. The orcs did not. They came in the night and attacked.

Hagshrub, their chieftain, led them. My father joined the men of the village in counter-attack, but there were too many orcs. Hagshrub led a second group behind the defenders, and reached our home. My mother and sister had hidden there, with some of the other children and the women of the village. Hagshrub ordered his warriors inside… no one within had weapons."

Mel's heart lurched. Aryion's face was drawn, the memories of the day running fresh through his mind. "My mother was frail and sick. Hagshrub murdered her in cold blood, along with the other innocents that hid there. Then they set fire to the houses. By the time we realized they had attacked from behind, there was hardly anything to save."

Mel swallowed hard. "Did your sister…"

"She survived, thank the Light. She had pulled our mother from the fire, though by then it was too late to save her." The ranger's voice faltered for a moment before he continued. "Once the warriors of the town clashed with the orcs, Hagshrub ordered the retreat. My father, blinded by rage and grief, pursued them, and I followed him. He dueled Hagshrub in the woods as I watched." Aryion shook his head slowly, his eyes distant. "He might have won, if only had he had his full strength. He was old and weakened by the long night of battle already, and Hagshrub killed him."

He closed his eyes for a moment. "I…well, I tried to fight Hagshrub then, with my father's sword." He tapped the hilt of the blade at his belt. "Hagshrub left me alive—apparently he thought he had dealt enough death for the day. He retreated, but I believe he heard me. I swore the Blood Oath, over my father's body, with my father's sword—I promised never to rest, not until my dying day, until Hagshrub was dead and my parents were avenged."

Mel stared at him, startled. The truth of it all, the horror of it, was shocking. Yet now he understood the sorrow in the ranger's eyes, the grim expression, the unsmiling face. "So… you've been tracking him all this time?" he asked.

Aryion nodded. "It has been sixteen years now. Since the orc tribes are always on the move, they are difficult to track under regular circumstances—hunting down one chieftain is even more so. We have met only once since the death of my father. Hagshrub managed to evade me—that was around two years ago. After that, I knew I would need help to pick up his trail again."

"So… you asked Rygal," Mel guessed slowly. He remembered Rygal and Aryion's conversation before the council—Rygal had told Aryion about the orc tribes. The intense interest Mel had seen in the ranger's eyes made sense now.

But Aryion shook his head. "Well, not yet. I wasn't sure what to do. Until a few months ago. I traveled through the Forest of Light and found it in ruins—that part of my earlier story is true, at least. I brought the Liznee gear back to Caer Sia—I didn't know whose it was. When I delivered it, I was interrogated by Jan. He explained a little of his theory about the Aces." He shook his head. "I admit I didn't believe him then, about the Aces being back. Not until I heard your side of the story at the council, about the Darkness and the face in the void, did I think it could have been the Ace-Lord."

"So Ĵan hired you… to protect me?" Mel asked.

"It was the agreement we settled on. Rygal was there too, actually, when I brought Dandio's gear back. He wanted to be the one to escort and protect you, but Ĵan said it would be too obvious. If the Aces saw Rygal traveling east to Carna, they would track him and intercept him on the way. Instead, I was sent back to ensure your safe arrival to the council. In exchange, Rygal and Ĵan told me what they knew of the orc movements, and promised to help me find and kill Hagshrub. Iriam promised too, later."

Mel thought about the conversation in the carriage on the way to the council. Everything in Aryion's story now lined up with Mel's unasked questions then. Mel's anger had faded, though he still felt a little hurt. "Why didn't you tell me this earlier?"

"Ĵan asked that we remain silent until our suspicions were confirmed. Another part of the deal that I regret now."

"What happened to your sister?" Mel asked after a pause.

Aryion let out a breath. "We parted ways after burying our parents. I left immediately to pursue Hagshrub, to fulfill my vow. She resented my choice to swear the Blood Oath. We have not seen each other for nearly sixteen years now—last I heard, she went south."

There was a heavy silence. Mel spoke hesitantly. "So, you're still going to kill Hagshrub?"

"I must attempt it, upon any opportunity. Kill him or die trying."

Aryion's voice was distant. Then he looked up, meeting Mel's eyes intensely. "But from now on, my first priority is you. If in any way I can save you, know that I will. Please know, too, that Hagshrub was not on my mind during the ambush from the Ace. I lost you, and I am as much to blame for Norrin's death. In that, Rygal isn't wrong."

Mel shook his head, but didn't say anything. It was his own fault, if it was anyone's. He had been led astray by the Aces and brought Jarus into it too. Norrin had fought fearlessly to protect them. Mel guessed that the outcome would have been the same, even if Aryion had been there. The ranger would have been killed too.

Aryion straightened. "Well, there is my history with Hagshrub. Now I have a question for you. Yesterday, you said that the Ace-Lord has been… in your head. That you have heard his voice?"

Mel exhaled and hesitated before nodding. "Yeah… I should have said something about that earlier, I guess." He thought for a moment. "I was worried for a while that he could track us through my thoughts, but I'm not sure if that's how it works. I haven't heard the voice since Carna, though."

"Carna? Before or after we met?"

"Right before," Mel said, a little guilty. "I… I think I saw an Ace in the shadows. It looked right at me, and the Ace-Lord spoke through it. He sounded surprised to see me there."

Aryion raised his eyebrows. "You are very lucky it did not choose to attack then. I doubt I could have deterred it, if it had come for you. Most likely it was there to scout."

Mel nodded. He had guessed as much by now. "Is there anything else you want to know?"

"Not unless you have anything else to share." Aryion smiled slightly. "No more secrets?"

"No more secrets," Mel agreed, and shook his proffered hand. The small smile widened, lighting the ranger's tired face. The trust between them, broken briefly by yesterday's confusion, was restored.

Jan assigned the watch schedule as they all settled down for the night. Mel and Aryion took the first watch as the moon began to rise. Mel still had one more question. "Can you tell me more about the rangers—and your training?"

Aryion nodded, and their quiet conversation lasted long into the night.

15

∽ ∽ ∽ ∽ ∽ ∽ ∽ ∽ ∽

The River Dûkrane

The weather grew increasingly warmer as they traveled farther southwest. The persistent overcast of clouds lingered over the forest, until the humidity and heat were almost unbearable. Mel's cloak was damp with dew each morning, and by evening he was drenched in sweat.

It had been five days since the confrontation with the Aces. Thanks to his conversations with both Ĵan and Aryion, most of Mel's questions had been answered. But while this eased his curiosity, it had done nothing to take away his fear. If anything, he felt more anxious, knowing that the Aces were after him, knowing that they could strike at any moment.

He wished he could read the prophecy Ĵan had told him about—the Prophecy of Three. But it sounded like there were only two existing copies of it. One had been kept in Tinkeeyo, but that copy had most likely been either stolen or destroyed by the Aces when they had raided the scribe house. The other was in Caer Sia, as Ĵan had said. Mel realized there was about as good of a chance of reading that copy as there was to recover the Shard. The Ace-Lord wouldn't destroy the Shard—he needed it to channel the Dark Realm's pow-

180

ers. But there was no guarantee that the prophecy had survived.

Jan only had parts of the prophecy known by memory, but the lines were scattered and made no sense without the context. Now, as Mel rode down the muddy road lost in thought, he decided to talk to Iriam that evening. The Neutral knew more about the Land Immortal and the Stars than anyone else here. It was quite likely that he would know more about this Prophecy, too.

Mel walked up to him when the group stopped for an afternoon break. "Iriam, I've been wondering. Do you know anything about the Prophecy of Three—anything that you can tell me?"

To his surprise and disappointment, Iriam shook his head. "Not yet, Mel. I cannot tell you anything about the Prophecy until we recover the Shards."

"What?" Mel said in disbelief, louder than he had intended. He took a quick breath to calm himself, then continued. "But, Iriam, if I'm the New Blood that the Prophecy talks about, how will I know what to do without it? The Prophecy will tell me what I have to do, right?"

"In a way. But if you knew it now, you would no longer be the New Blood," Iriam said.

Mel frowned, confused, and Iriam continued. "Mel, the Prophecy states that the actions of the New Blood must be unaltered by the opinions of others. You cannot be turned one way or the other—the choice to stand against the Aces must be yours alone."

"But... how am I supposed to do something if I don't even know what it is?" Mel asked.

"The Prophecy calls for a 'nameless New Blood,'" Iriam said. "It also says that this person will know their call. Thus, I know that when the time comes, you will know what to do."

And Mel knew that was all he would get out of him for now. Iriam believed in him, and that was encouraging. Still, he couldn't help wondering. What exactly did the Prophecy of Three require of him? Something bad? Something painful? He felt a shiver of fear.

The rain, which had let up for the past few days, started again in another few hours, and before long it developed into a torrent that battered down on them. Mel was soaked through by the time Aryion discovered a small cave in the side of the hill. They couldn't afford to ruin the precious maps, nor risk injuring the horses on the slick road, so Iriam had them stop inside the shelter. Quinn lit a fire, and Mel scooted close to the blaze to try and dry his clothes.

"Now what?" Mel asked Jan as they watched the rain pouring down.

"Now we wait," Jan said. But he didn't sound happy about it. Mel knew that waiting anywhere too long was dangerous, especially since they still had no idea where the Aces were. Time wasted on the road would only aid the Ace-Lord's progress.

After a few minute's rest, with no sign of the rain letting up, Jarus stood and stretched. "Well, if we will be here for a while, then I'm going out. I haven't swum since the council, and this rain is close enough to it." With that, he trotted out into the rain and spent awhile romping around in the wet, splashing in puddles and occasionally stabbing mock blows with his knife at invisible enemies.

Mel took a drink of water and glanced around at his other companions, their faces lit by the yellow glow of the fire. Rygal sat in the shadows, wrapped in his cloak. Since his argument with Aryion, he had remained silent, barely eating anything. Completely engulfed by loss. His eyes were dull and lifeless, the usual spark that was Rygal extinguished.

It cut to Mel's heart to see his friend like this. Cahadras' words at the council were all too true. The Ace-Lord knew exactly how to break down their spirits, and he would do so until the resistance despaired and surrendered to his reign. That thought was even more disturbing than to think of the rest of the Aces' powers.

Mel's mind was full of uncomfortable ideas as he wrapped himself in his cloak. The rhythm of the pouring rain filled his ears as he fell asleep.

. . . . . .

Iriam was on watch when Mel woke up early the next morning. The rain had stopped, and the sky was mostly clear. The wet forest glistened in the bright sunlight.

There was a faint roaring sound that Mel couldn't place. For a moment, he lay in confusion, not sure what it was. Then it came to him, and he sat up, straining his ears. "Is that the river?" he asked.

Iriam nodded, his eyes scanning the forest around them. "We are a half mile or so from it still. But it is undoubtedly the Dûkrane River."

Mel stood stiffly, moving to the mouth of the cave to stand next to the Neutral. The faint roar came from far ahead, through the trees. From their position up on the hillside, Mel could almost see the slight dip in the land where the hills sloped down into a draw. The Dûkrane River flowed west through that draw, carrying the snow melt to the sea.

The other companions awoke shortly after. Now that the rain had stopped, everyone could hear the distant thunder of the river. Jarus' keen ears were perked up as he listened to the sounds the others could not hear. His face was uneasy. "It's very full," he said. "I can hear it lapping at its banks."

"Yes," Iriam said. He looked like he was thinking hard. "By the sound, it is flowing faster than I expected."

"But there's a bridge, right?" Mel said, not sure what the concern was. "We can still cross it?"

"Most likely," Iriam said.

"We will have to cross it either way, Iriam, unless we want to detour thirty miles northeast and cut through the mountains," Jan said heavily.

Aryion looked at Mel, answering his earlier question. "There is a bridge, Mel. At least there should be. But the Dûkrane is a difficult river to predict. It flows through a steep valley, which makes the water drain down the hillside and weaken the soil. Sometimes this makes the whole hillside slide down, washing the bridge and most of the road downstream."

Mel gulped. "That's not going to happen now, though, is it?" The thought of a whole hillside crumbling down on top of them was a disturbing one.

Quinn, who was packing up the cooking utensils, shook his head. "It is nearly summer now. The trees and spring growths will have strengthened the hillside with their roots."

"Yes, if there was going to be a landslide, it would have already happened," Aryion said. "The only question will be the condition of the bridge itself."

Iriam turned to face them, seeming to make a decision. "Our only option is to go on, bridge or no bridge. At this point, turning back would be foolish, and dangerous. We have no idea how close the Aces are, and the detour Jan mentioned would take us too close to Caer Sia. Let us continue."

Mel shouldered his pack and mounted the pony in front of Jarus. The Cooper's ears were perked up, and his nose scented the breeze as they rode down the road. The morning chill was gone, and the sticky, muggy heat had set in again. After several minutes of riding, Mel was dripping sweat, and the distant babble of the river was starting to sound more and more appealing.

"Maybe we can just swim across, if the bridge is washed out," he suggested to Jarus.

But Jarus shook his head. "I wouldn't trust this river at all. Hear that rumbling sound? That's rocks being dragged along the bottom—big rocks, Mel. The current is so strong with the melted snow, it'll suck you under and keep you there before you could do anything."

The Cooper's face was worried. Since Jarus was usually eager to swim any time, Mel started to feel uneasy too.

In a little while, the road sloped down, and through the trees, Mel saw the river. It was wider and deeper than the Hallas had been—thirty feet across at least, and wider in some places. Brown water churned and roared and tore at the muddy banks as it thundered on, carrying tree trunks and limbs as if they weighed no more than twigs. White foam flecked its banks.

Mel did not like the looks of it at all.

The trail doubled back several times in a zig-zag pattern down the hill. It crossed the bridge, then wound its way back up the next slope. Mel could see the muddy road etched into the side of the draw, visible between the towering fir trees.

They descended the steep series of switchbacks until they stood before the bridge. It was still in its place, but it sat at an awkward angle, tilting slightly to the right toward the rushing water below. Large boulders had rolled down the opposite hillside, Mel saw, which had twisted the bridge to the side. The wood in the center was partly rotted, and sagged alarmingly close to the churning brown water.

The companions dismounted and paused for a long moment before the bridge. Finally Iriam turned to Jarus. "Well, Jarus, I think you have the most experience with this kind of thing. How would you recommend we cross?"

Jarus stared incredulously at the thundering water, his mouth open. Finally, he answered. "I… all right. We'll have to go single file. Carefully, and slowly. Don't rush across or make any quick movements, just try to ease your weight, one foot to the next." He threw them a quick grin and stepped forward. Mel could tell he was terrified but was trying to appear confident.

The Cooper started out on the crooked bridge, weaving his way around the rotten parts. His light step carried him safely to the other side after a tense minute. He turned to face them on the other bank. "It's safe enough!" he called. "But for goodness' sake, be careful. Especially in that middle section."

Quinn went next. The Elven ranger was the smallest besides Mel and Jarus, and he edged across the bridge slowly, placing his feet in the same places Jarus had. The bridge shuddered and tilted slightly as he reached the middle, and Mel winced. But Quinn soon joined Jarus on the other side.

"It may be better to go two at once," Quinn called across the river. "One of you step forward as the other one is stepping off. That way we can balance the bridge on either end—it will keep it from lurching."

Iriam nodded. "Yes, that will be best. Cross carefully—I shall lead the horses across once the rest of you are over."

Jan and Rygal went next. Once Jan had reached the other side, Mel stepped out, across from Rygal. Quinn was right; the counter balance, with both of them at the ends of the bridge, helped steady the shuddering wood. Mel's mouth was dry, and he focused on taking one careful step at a time. Through the gaps in the wood, he glimpsed the water speeding by underneath.

He had just passed the rotten place in the middle of the bridge when Quinn gave a shout of warning. A split second later, an arrow whizzed by Mel's head, sinking into the wood a few feet past him. Mel looked up sharply, and his stomach lurched as he saw what had caused the alarm. Dwarves, dressed in black leather armor, emerged from the trees on the hill just above them, launching a volley of arrows down at them.

"Get down!" Jan ordered. Rygal sprang the remaining distance to the bank and dropped down behind a tree. An arrow tore through Jan's cloak, and the king quickly ducked behind another tree.

"What are they shooting for?" Mel yelled at no one in particular, frozen in place on the bridge. Iriam and Jan had met with a Dwarve patrol a few days before, and the Dwarves were not involved in the war. Maybe the companions had accidentally trespassed into their lands.

But at the same time the thought crossed Mel's mind, he saw the triangular emblem scrawled on their armor. It was the same symbol that the orcs wore. The Dwarves—this tribe, at least—had joined with the Aces.

"Get across quickly!" Jan called. Red light blazed in his hands. He shot a blast of fire up the hill at the Dwarves. Startled and angry cries came from above, and the archers hesitated a moment.

At the same time, a group of burly orcs burst through the trees on the opposite side of the river. Wielding axes and jagged swords, they attacked Iriam and Aryion. The startled horses whinnied and galloped back into the forest; Aryion started after them, but turned back quickly to join Iriam in combat against the sudden attack. Ice shot from Iriam's palms, and Aryion's sword flashed as they retreated over the bridge carefully. The orcs pressed forward, making the bridge shudder and lurch with their weight.

"Hurry, Mel!" Jarus yelled—his voice was tense with fear.

Mel edged forward, gripping the railing, trying not to think about the thundering river below. An arrow sliced the air past his face, and he fell back a step. His heart was pounding with terror, but he put his head down and ran the rest of the way. Two paces from the bank, his foot sank through the rotten wood, and he toppled forward, clawing frantically at the ferns. Quinn gripped his arm and hauled him forward onto the ground, and they ducked behind a tree.

The Dwarves had stopped shooting now that the companions had hidden behind the trees. Mel could see them advancing down the hill toward the river. The light glinted off their curved swords.

"Form up!" Jan ordered. Drisilas blazed in his hand as the companions prepared for the onslaught.

Mel looked back at the bridge. There were ten orcs, he saw, and they were pursuing quickly. Iriam and Aryion had nearly made it to the opposite bank. At last Iriam shot a blast of ice that knocked the orcs back, and then the two of them ran the rest of the way across.

By this point, the Dwarves had reached the rest of the companions. Mel drew his dagger in a flash and moved to stand by Jarus, their backs to the river. Jan and Quinn stepped forward; Quinn wielded his long-bladed dagger instead of his bow. Between them and Mel, terrifyingly silent, Rygal advanced, slashing his way through the attackers. Dwarve warriors shouted in pain and fury and vengeance as they charged the outnumbered companions.

Mel blocked a Dwarve sword, ducked under the warrior's blow, and fell back as Rygal stabbed the offending warrior through. "Watch behind," Rygal warned shortly. Mel looked over his shoulder. The orcs were hurrying across the bridge. In another moment, they would be trapped.

Then Iriam stepped toward the bridge. "Stay back!" he warned. Deep blue ice flashed from his fingertips as he dropped to his knees and pressed his hands into the ground. Ice spread down the length of the bridge, freezing and expanding the damp wood, warping it even further. The orcs fell, clinging to the frozen wood, as the bridge twisted and buckled like a snake. Then with a deafening crack it split and fell in frozen pieces into the rushing water, taking the screaming orcs downstream.

In the same instant, a Dwarve warrior pushed past Rygal and lunged at Mel. Mel stabbed at him, but the Dwarve seized the front of Mel's jacket and threw him backward. Rygal reached for him, missed—Mel glimpsed the smirk of triumph on the Dwarve's face before the icy brown water closed over his head, and the river dragged him under.

The current gripped Mel instantly, and he was completely in the power of the river. He was swept down, then sharply to the side; his chest slammed into an unseen boulder, and the force of it knocked the remaining air out of his lungs. Water filled his nose, his ears, his eyes—his surroundings were a blur of dark.

Mel surfaced for an instant—out of the corner of his eye, he saw someone plunge into the river after him. "Help," he managed to choke, then slammed into another rock. He clawed at the boulder frantically, but it was slippery with mud and grime, and the current dragged him on.

His back hit a fallen tree scudding downstream, and he clung to it weakly. But exhaustion and the wet bark of the tree made it hard to hold on long. Mel's grip slipped on the wood as he coughed, and he sank underwater again. Then an arm locked around his chest and dragged him to the surface. Gasping for air, coughing up water, Mel fought the restraint blindly for an instant.

"Hold still!" Aryion coughed in his ear. "Try to lay on your back and turn your feet downstream."

Mel did as instructed. Aryion adjusted his grip, holding Mel's arm with one hand. With the other he managed to grab hold of the fallen tree. A rock grazed Mel's back as they drifted closer to the shore.

"Grab that root!" Aryion told him. Mel clawed at the crumbling shoreline until his hand locked on a tree root. Gasping and shivering, he pulled himself on shore and lay on his side, fighting for breath, coughing up water.

Aryion had seized the root too, but was now in danger of being carried downstream with the fallen tree. The rough bark had snagged his cloak, hauling him back by the neck. The ranger clung to the root, trying to undo the clasp with his free hand. But the swirling, twisting current fought against him.

Mel crawled to the river edge and gripped the clasp of Aryion's cloak. His cold fingers unclipped it and sent the cloak downstream with the tree; Aryion fell forward in the shallow water at the bank, gasping for air.

Mel pulled him up, then fell back, worn out. Aryion dragged himself onto the bank and fell flat on his back. They lay there for a moment, both out of breath and coughing up river water.

"Are you… all right?" Aryion asked hoarsely. There was a red line left on his neck from his cloak.

"Yeah," Mel managed to gasp. His body ached from his collision with the rocks, and a red spot of blood showed through the knee of his pants. He lay flat until the dizzying terror faded from his system, and his stomach settled. "Thanks," he added with a cough.

Aryion got to his knees stiffly and pushed his wet hair out of his eyes. Blood ran down his hand from a cut left by the sharp branches. He pressed the wound against his shirt as he surveyed their surroundings. "Well, we're on the south bank," he commented absently. "At least we don't have to cross a second time."

"Good," Mel said heartily. He looked around. The steep hills of the canyon sloped down into a gentler decline, down which the Dûkrane River thundered west. Now that he had his breath back, his thoughts returned to their initial problems. "What about the others?" he asked anxiously. "There were a lot of orcs and Dwarves—do you think they'll will be all right?"

"I think so," Aryion said. "Iriam has already taken care of the orcs, and I doubt the Dwarves will continue the attack for long on their own."

"I thought the Dwarves were allies," Mel said slowly. "Why would they join the Ace-Lord?"

"Probably the same reason the orcs and Jenna did. The Ace-Lord pays well, at least as long as you are useful. Besides that, remember that the alliance between the Dwarves and Liznees is fairly new. Many of the tribes still see Caer Sia as an enemy." Aryion let out a long breath. "Well, either way, the others are hopefully on their way downstream. Let's find the road and wait for them there."

They started up the hill, pushing through the underbrush and branches. Mel's throat felt raw from coughing, and his wet clothes clung to his skin. They had just set foot on the path when Aryion paused. They stood on the crest of the hill, the trees towering up all around them so that it was impossible to see further than a few feet to each side of the road.

"What is it?" Mel asked worriedly. He strained his ears, but he could only hear the thundering of the river. No yelling Dwarves, no clashing weapons.

"Do you smell that?" Aryion asked.

Mel inhaled. A chilly breeze rippled the boughs overhead and ran through his wet hair. It carried a briny scent, salty and with the faint scent of fish. As he smelled it, a gull flew overhead, its eerie cry ringing through the air.

Determined to affirm the sudden hope, they ran down the road, following the gull. The rocky path turned under Mel's feet, but he stumbled on, his eyes on a clear patch through the trees ahead.

Aryion stepped off the road to the left and pushed through the boughs.

They were on a high cliff overlooking a wide bay. Beyond, the sea stretched on for as far as Mel could see. Behind and below them, the Dûkrane River left the forest, tumbling down the rocky cliffs for the remaining few miles before it opened into the sea.

Far out, miles across the water, lay the outline of a long island.

"Kamon," Mel realized, and for the first time in days he felt a stir of hope.

"Kamon," Aryion echoed, relief spreading over his weary face. "Kamon at last."

16

Crossing Wide Waters

The five other companions joined Mel and Aryion shortly after they first glimpsed Kamon in the distance. The Dwarves had been defeated, though not without minor injuries. Rygal had sustained several cuts, but at seeing their destination ahead, he adamantly refused to stop and rest. In fact, any injuries the companions had from the battle were forgotten thanks to relief at seeing Aryion and Mel alive, and from excitement that they were so close to reaching Kamon.

"This path will lead down the cliffs," Iriam told them as they re-grouped. "Step carefully—the rocks are treacherous. Once we leave the forest, we will to go through the town of Barcoast, and purchase passage for the ferry."

"What about the orcs?" Mel asked uneasily. He remembered the group that had been washed down river with the bridge. "If they were immortal, they probably just got carried downstream."

Iriam nodded. "I assume that they will have returned to their commander in defeat. But we can also assume that the Aces now know we mean to travel to Kamon. Thus, we must be cautious. Keep your hoods up as we go through the town, and speak to no one."

"At this point I don't even know who we can trust," Quinn said heavily. "You spoke to the Dwarves just a few days ago, and they seemed neutral. Yet now it seems they've joined with the Aces after all."

"There are many tribes of Dwarves," Jan reminded him. "I hope at least that we still have some allies among their people."

With this in mind, they began the careful walk down the cliffs. The going was slower without the horses, but Mel could tell it might have been harder if they were still riding. The trail circled in a set of switchbacks, going gradually downhill. The loose, slippery rocks made it hard to keep your footing.

After a few hours of going steadily down, passing in and out of the forest periodically, they finally reached the beach. The rumble of the surf and the strong smell of fish hung heavy in the air. The town of Barcoast, Mel saw, was small and scrappy, built on the rocks that overhung the water. The buildings were made of dull red brick, with numerous wood piers sticking out into the bay. Fishing boats and skiffs were moored there.

Mel glanced to his right. To the north, miles and miles across the water, he could just make out where the bay narrowed at the place that the Mata Strait opened out. He pointed at the place. "That's the Strait, right, Jarus?"

Jarus nodded. "Yep. If you sailed that way for a few days you'd reach Mata City." There was longing in his eyes as he spoke of his home. Mel guessed he was thinking of his family.

"Have you ever sailed the whole way down the Strait to the Kamo Sea?" Mel asked him.

The Cooper shook his head regretfully. "No, but I've wanted to do it for years. I've heard it's a fascinating trip from here to Mata City."

A triple-masted ship with white sails waited at the largest pier, prepared to ferry passengers across the water to Kamon. Mel noticed another ship, nearly identical to the first, already sailing towards the island. Business was good in a place like Kamon, with its rich soil and tropical climate. This time of year, Mel guessed that the merchants would be eager to get an early purchase on the island goods.

They walked down the road towards the ferry. Fishermen carrying nets and crab traps pushed past, hardly paying attention to them. People went to Kamon all the time, not just the merchants. It was a fine vacationing spot, especially now with summer just beginning. Aryion offered to purchase ferry tickets.

"Go carefully," Iriam said. "We will wait for you near the pier."

Aryion nodded. "I will. The rest of you, keep your heads down. Try to blend in."

Jan passed Aryion a few coins. "Give a call if there's trouble," he told the ranger. "People tend to be suspicious in towns like these. They might be difficult to barter with."

"I'll come with you," Mel said promptly. He was fascinated by their surroundings. Living in a place like Appledale, trips to the sea were few and far between.

"Let's go then, or the ferry will have gone by the time we are finished discussing it," Aryion said briskly. He turned and walked down the road with Mel trailing. A simple wood shack was set up near the ferry dock. A short, burly fellow sat inside, watching as the two of them drew close. His eyes were widely set, dark and suspicious.

Aryion strode up to him. "Seven tickets for the next ferry to Kamon, please," he said, setting the money Jan had given him on the table in front of the ferry master.

The ferry master eyed him carefully. "Can't say I know your face, ranger," he said. The last word was added with a touch of dislike. Mel looked over uneasily.

Aryion gave a slight shrug. "We just arrived. I'm escorting my nephew home to the island." He jerked his head at Mel.

The ferry master leaned back slowly, glancing between Mel and Aryion. "Humph. Heard that one before," he muttered. He looked at the coins. "Why seven tickets for two people?"

"He plans to come visit this way later," Aryion said without missing a beat.

"Then it'd be four tickets, if yer tellin' the truth. I knew rangers were an odd folk, but I never knew 'em to be bad at the maths." His eyes narrowed. "So, what's your business going that way?"

"I thought standard protocol still applied in these parts," Aryion said levelly. "Take the money, no questions asked."

"Well, these are strange times. You've heard what's happened in

Tinkeeyo, haven't ya? In Caer Sia?" The ferry master's voice sank to a hissing whisper. "We don't trust no one in these parts. Who's to say if you're an enemy of the country? Or a smuggler?"

"I can assure you, I have none of those intentions whatsoever," Aryion said with measured politeness. Mel could tell the ranger was losing his temper. He stepped forward instead.

"Are we going to ride on the boat soon, Uncle?" he asked, trying to sell the story. "I'm excited to see Mom and Dad again."

Aryion caught on and smiled. "Yes, we'll see them in a moment. As soon as I finish doing business with this fine gentleman."

The ferry master hesitated. Jan's prediction earlier had been exactly right. Barcoast had heard every ounce of gossip over the past few weeks, and its people were both suspicious and scared. The ferry master was uneasy to trust these two strangers, no matter what their story was. He folded his arms obstinately. "Can't do it, ranger. Not until I hear the truth of it. Besides, standard protocol doesn't apply here—I asks what I likes."

"Forget protocol, then," Aryion said, exasperated. "You're being paid over three times the amount you would normally for two people. I need seven tickets."

"Not until I hear the facts," the ferry master snapped. "Or see these other people you're getting tickets for. Why don't they show themselves? What've they got to hide—they orcs or Jenna or somethin'?"

"Close enough," said Jan, who had been standing by the side of the ticket shack for the whole encounter. He had expected something of this nature would happen, and gone to listen. Now he stepped forward, and the light reached his face behind his hood.

The ferry master, who had seen quite a lot of strange things in his time, took a moment to register who was standing before him. As he did, his eyes positively bulged, and he staggered against the desk.

"Sire!" he wheezed, not sure whether to bow, salute, or faint. "Beggin' your pardon, sire. No harm meant, no harm, none whatsoever."

"I'm sure," Jan said calmly. "Now, if you will give us our tickets, we will be on our merry way."

The ferry master peered around the side of his shack, as though expecting to see more people hiding there. Seeing none, he looked at Jan wide-eyed. "So you're escorting this lad too?" he asked stupidly, pointing at Mel. "Takin' him to see his family? But I thought the ranger was his uncle."

"Yes, well, I'm the other uncle. Once removed. Something like that." Jan smiled shortly, took the tickets, and swept away as the ferry master tried to make sense of the story.

"I didn't know I had two uncles," Mel couldn't resist commenting as they walked away.

"No, just one. I'm your real uncle," Aryion said. "Jan was adopted."

"Take this and quiet down," Jan said, ignoring the exchange as he handed them their tickets. They reached the other companions, who were waiting by the ferry pier.

"You were right about these being suspicious parts," Aryion said. He turned to Iriam. "It seems the rumors have spread south. The ferry master mentioned Tinkeeyo and Caer Sia."

Iriam's face was grim, but he nodded. "I knew it could not remain secret for long. But perhaps that is for the best. At least now the public are on the alert for anything out of the ordinary."

They waited at a distance while the other passengers milled around by the gate. Finally the sailors lowered the gangplank and ushered them all on board. Mel handed his ticket over, but stopped in his tracks as he saw a poster tacked to one of the lampposts by the pier. The paper was damp and wrinkled from the water, but it bore the drawing of a very familiar face, along with a fine script written in the island language.

Jan saw it too, and nudged Mel forward gently. "We had a few of those made just after we learned he was missing," he said quietly. "I figured most everyone would know his face in the north, but we sent posters to the south just in case."

Mel stared at Dandio's face for a long moment. The picture smiled back at him. Somehow, over the course of the last few days, Mel had forgotten his original motive to come on the quest. "Do you think... do you think he's still alive?" he asked Jan huskily as they stepped on board the ship.

Jan let out a long breath. "I don't know," was all he said.

They went below deck and sat on one of the benches. Several other people had already taken seats, and the room was full of quiet conversation. Mel sat near a small round window. He could see the wide expanse of sparkling ocean, and the distant hump that marked the island.

His thoughts strayed back to Dandio. Knowing the Ace-Lord, there was no telling what would happen to him. If the Aces had captured him at all… he could have simply been killed by outlaws or a wild beast. The thought hurt too much for Mel to accept. That couldn't be, it simply couldn't—and even then, why take the body? No… he was fairly sure there would have been more evidence of a struggle if Dandio had indeed been killed.

Assuming the Aces had taken Dandio, then, there weren't many options. Maybe he had been captured and questioned—maybe the Aces wanted information from him. The thought of Dandio being tortured in some dark fortress was even worse than the idea of him dead. Mel didn't know which he preferred to be true. He hoped, in vain, that perhaps Dandio had returned to Caer Sia while they were out here on the quest. But in that case, he would be captured anyway when the Ace-Lord had taken the city.

He closed his eyes and pressed his head to the glass window, trying to rid his mind of the dark thoughts. The gentle rise and fall of the blue-green water lapped the sides of the ship as they began the voyage. A school of multi-colored fish swam beneath the waves. Gulls and pelicans soared overhead.

Once the ship left the port, Mel and Jarus walked up on deck. The crisp wind dried Mel's damp clothes. It was refreshing after the muggy walk. Jarus scented the breeze, eyes half closed, happily taking in the sounds and scent of the sea again. "Forests and camping are all right in their own way," he commented to Mel with a grin. "But this… this is the way to travel."

"I've never really sailed before," Mel admitted. He had been to the sea, of course, a few times before. But the creaks of the ship, the flutter of the sails, and the slow rise and fall as they rode the waves added to the newness of everything around him.

"Well, you're doing better than most," Jarus informed him. "A lot of people tend to hurl their dinner overboard the minute there's a little ripple, but you haven't done that yet."

"That's probably because I haven't eaten anything since breakfast," Mel said, grinning. "I hope we can get some food at Kamon."

The voyage lasted a little over an hour. Mel stayed up on deck with Jarus, watching the sailors scramble about the ship, and watching as the distant island drew closer.

Finally, he was able to make out details. There were no mountains, only a gentle valley in the middle of four large hills that crested the eastern edge of the island. The white cliffs shielded the rest of Kamon from view. To the north, the hills drooped down to form a sandy beach. Mel could see several flights of stone steps that led up the steep walls.

The dock was built between the white stones and the beach. Two men with curly dark hair and olive skin stood on the dock. Their clothes were lightweight and billowing, and they wore no shoes.

They also wore wreaths of large, colorful flowers around their necks.

"Keelo, friends!" called the first of the men, greeting them in their own tongue. Their eyes were bright and cheery as they helped the sailors bring the ferry alongside the dock.

The companions waited for the other passengers to disembark before following. Mel looked around in awe. The air was considerably warmer than it had been on the Mainland, but not sticky or humid. The sweet scent of flowers and fruit carried on the breeze.

The two islanders bowed in greeting to the companions, and their eyes widened considerably as they recognized Jan.

"Welcome to Kamon, sire," the first speaker said.

"We are honored by your presence on our humble island," added the second.

The trace of a smile touched Jan's face, and he motioned for them to stand. "We are grateful to be here," he said. "But there is little time for warm greetings. I fear there are troubled times in store. If you would show us to your chieftain we would be grateful, for there are matters we must discuss with him."

Both the islanders nodded, concern on their faces as they caught the serious tone in Jan's voice. "Of course, sire," said the second speaker. "Now come." They turned and started up the stairs.

The steps were slick from the waves striking against them, and Mel slipped twice. Once they reached the second set of steps, however, the rock was solid under their feet, and Mel moved with ease.

They were nearly to the top when Mel became aware of a sweet smell. It reminded him of the lilies his mother had planted last spring beside the front porch. They were the first thing Mel smelled every time he left the house. It brought a twinge of homesickness to his stomach. But this smell was far more powerful, and the sweet scent made his mouth water.

Then the steps ended and they took their first paces on Kamon soil.

17

The Isle of Kamon

Mel blinked in the bright sun as they left the stairs behind and reached the top of the cliff. He looked around, his eyes taking in the new sights and colors that made up the island of Kamon.

The terrain was different than Mel had first imagined. Coconuts hung from the boughs of tall palm trees. Pale pink magnolias blossomed further inland. The main part of the forest, Mel noticed, was populated by trees as wide around as houses. Their leaves were wide and flat, their limbs heavy with huge flowers that produced the wonderful smell as they seemed to scrape the sky. Lilies and wildflowers grew amid the shrubbery, flourishing in the fertile ground that made up the heart of the island. The soil was replaced by fine sand on the beach to Mel's right.

As Mel's eyes reached the village, he couldn't help staring. The village of Kamon was, indeed, unlike any other in Orlell. Clusters of huts were built in the tall trees, supported by the thick branches. Woven rope bridges and wooden boardwalks spanned the distance between the huts. Ladders led down to the ground to the winding stone paths that led through the little market.

Visitors and locals alike moved through the streets or walked on the boardwalks above. Colorful booths had been set up near the waterfront. The smell of fruit and smoked fish filled the air as they left the stone steps behind and entered the town.

He realized the two islanders were speaking, and quickly turned his attention back to the group.

"My name is Hasman, and this is my brother Nallis," the first man said. They both bowed again before Hasman continued. "Our chieftain will receive you in the pavilion, if you will follow."

"We thank you," Iriam said, and they walked down the sloping hill and through the shops. Mel studied the market in fascination. The Kamoni villagers returned his glance with a smiles that were friendly but curious. Mel realized how out of place the companions looked here, with their dark, forest colored clothing, most of them streaked in mud and grime from the long journey. It contrasted dramatically with the vivid colors and airy clothing of the islanders.

The pavilion, as Hasman had called it, was actually a large treetop hut, built above the market. The branches of the trees beyond, as big around as Mel was tall, knotted together above the island, so that the entire place seemed sheltered by a canopy of limbs. A spiral staircase wound up the massive trunk. Hasman and Nallis beckoned them forward, and the companions followed them up the winding staircase and into the town of Kamon.

Jarus' eyes were wide. "In Mata City, we have canals instead of roads," he murmured to Mel as they walked up the stairs. "Here, they have trees."

"It's amazing," Mel agreed. There was no other word to describe it.

They entered the pavilion hut. Inside, it looked like a smaller version of the council hall in Flora. There was a round table in the middle of the room. To the right, the wall was made of large, paneled windows that looked out over the market below. The sea, a quarter mile or so from here, sparkled as far as the eye could see. The Mainland was just visible in the distance, yet here, the island seemed isolated, a tropical paradise.

Inside the room were several Kamoni islanders. A tall man looked up as they entered. He wore a thin circuit of beads on his head. Despite the lines of silver in his dark hair, he moved with a youthful energy.

"Welcome, my lords," he said, bowing to both Ĵan and Iriam in turn. "I am Leelo son of Jalen, chieftain of Kamon. For what do we owe the pleasure of your visit?"

"Difficult business, I am afraid, sir," Ĵan said grimly. "But I hope and pray that no harm will come to your people from our visit."

The other islanders exchanged uneasy looks at Ĵan's words. Leelo's face became serious. "We have received some rumors of the happenings in the north," he said. "Could your errand have something to do with the fate of the Forest of Light? Yes," he continued, as the companions reacted in surprise, "even here we have heard of the destruction of the Forest."

Ĵan hesitated and glanced at Iriam, who gave him a quick nod. "Indeed. It is a long tale, but I will tell you." They took seats at the table, and with that, Ĵan told of Dandio's disappearance, of the council in Flora, and the encounter with the Ace and the fall of Caer Sia. He also spoke of the Star-Stone and the Ace-Lord's plans.

Mel had heard the story—in fact, he had lived through most of it. Yet Jan's words of the Aces sent a fresh tremor of fear down his spine. Not fear for himself—strangely enough, he had grown used to feeling afraid for his life now. But looking out at the peaceful market, at the cheerful villagers, and the beauty of Kamon made him worry for what would happen if the Aces came here. Most likely, they were coming anyway—they wanted the Shard, and Mel knew they would do anything to get it.

As though they had guessed his thoughts, Nallis looked at his chieftain uneasily. "We are not warriors, sire," he said regretfully, with a glance at Jan. "What hope should we have if these Aces come here?"

"It is no longer if, but when," Iriam told him gravely. "However, we do not want your people to suffer on our behalf. Thus, it is our request to take the Shard to Caer Sia, and hopefully lead the Aces back north."

Leelo rubbed his chin thoughtfully. "We have guarded the Shard here for generations," he said. "Would not taking it to Caer Sia only aid the Ace-Lord's plans further?"

Iriam nodded. "A valid concern, but you must understand that joining the Shards is our only hope to stop the Aces. How we are exactly to enter Caer Sia, without the Ace-Lord catching us, is still to be determined."

One of the Kamoni advisors spoke quietly to Leelo, who turned to face Iriam again. "How will the Aces take the Shard from here? They cannot touch it—the Star-Stones are deadly to them, as Drisilas was to the Darkness."

"That task, I assume, will be assigned to their servants," Iriam said. "The Aces may not be able to carry the Shard from here themselves, but they are more than capable of sending the Jenna to do it for them."

The word sent a ripple of concerned surprise through the listening Kamoni. "The Jenna have not ventured this far west in centuries," one of the advisors said skeptically. "The march across land would take them months."

Jan spoke, his voice serious. "The Aikala Jenna tribe are skilled sea-raiders, and if they were going to attack, I would expect it to come from the sea. I would not rule them out yet."

Leelo thought for a long moment. "Very well, then. I believe it may be inevitable." He let out a breath. "But what Nallis has said is true. We are not warriors. Our people are harvesters, fishermen, sailors. We can offer you no protection if the Aces come here— much less protect ourselves," he added grimly.

There was a pause. Mel thought of the peaceful little village, helpless and defenseless in the face of a potential attack. Then, suddenly, a thought came to him. "What if we helped you fight them?"

Everyone looked at him, and he faltered. "Help us how?" Hasman asked.

Jan glanced at Mel, looking thoughtful. "That's not a bad idea. We could organize a defensive counter attack. We can help you prepare for battle, if battle comes."

"You will teach us to fight?" Leelo asked.

Aryion looked at Leelo. "Sailors and fishermen tend to be a strong type, sir. Give them weapons to fight with, let us teach them to defend themselves, and we could have a formidable army."

Mel nodded rapidly. He could tell Leelo was interested in the idea—now they just had to convince him. "I bet a battle is the last thing the Aces expect to happen here. They probably think they can just come and take the Shard without anyone putting up a fight. You have the element of surprise on your side, as Dandio would call it."

Leelo spoke with the other islanders for a brief moment. Aryion caught Mel's eye and gave him a quick nod and smile. Mel smiled back, proud to see the ranger's approval.

At last Leelo turned to them again. "This plan is acceptable. Teach us to defend our homes, and we will gladly let you take the Shard back to its twin."

"We thank you," Jan said, inclining his head. "Allow us to speak with your village elders and leaders, and we shall begin planning a counter attack."

"In the meantime," Iriam said, "I would be grateful for the services of your medics. Several of my companions were wounded in a recent encounter with orcs. May we send them to your healers?"

"Of course," Leelo said. "Hasman will show you the way."

They left the pavilion and followed Hasman into the treetop town. Mel focused on keeping his balance as they crossed the many swinging rope bridges between wood boardwalks. Hasman's stride was light and confident, born of years and years of walking these paths.

Hasman gestured ahead. "The inn is unoccupied at present. Please help yourselves to our finest rooms. I will send the medics to tend to your injuries." With that, he jogged away, moving from tree to tree as easily as if he were on land.

The inn, as Hasman indicated it, was different than any inn Mel had ever seen. In reality, it was a cluster of small guest huts, each with two rooms separated by a curtain.

Mel and Jarus walked into one of the huts. Each had a window that looked over the market and the sparkling sea.

Mel dropped his pack on the bed, closed the dividing curtain, and changed out of his clothes, which were filthy and damp from river water. The cut on his knee still ached but no longer hurt, and he noticed a medley of bruises scattered over his body thanks to the rough ride down the rapids.

In a few minutes, a man with a white apron and a satchel entered and introduced himself as the doctor. He bandaged the cut on Mel's knee, then checked Jarus' wounds.

After the medic left, Mel put his shoes on and opened the curtain. He laughed at Jarus, who hadn't moved from the bed. "Wake up, sleepyhead!" he cried. "There's a whole island to explore."

"Well you go explore it, then," Jarus said into the pillow. "When was the last time we slept in beds like these?"

Mel thought a moment. "The council at Flora, I guess."

"But we just slept on the floor then, so it doesn't really count," Jarus said.

Mel thought about it, then realized how long it had been. It had been over a month since a real bed had been available. The idea made him feel very tired, but he shook it off. "Well, I'm going to explore. Tell Iriam if he asks," he added as an afterthought. Then he opened the door and headed outside.

......

The township of Kamon had several similar features to any other city. Mel made his way carefully over the suspended paths, away from the guest huts and toward the main part of the village. He noticed that the houses of the other Kamoni lay on the other side of town—he could see the winding rope bridges through the trees, leading deeper into the forest to different parts of the village.

The main area of town was circular, with the shops making up the edges and a wide wooden path connecting them all together. Mel saw a general store, butcher's, and a bakery, along with many other shops. Vendors had set up small tables outside the shops, selling more merchandise outside. People walked the edge of the circle, going table to table.

Mel followed the crowds, looking around. There were other Mainlanders who had come to the island on summer vacation. Yet here he was on dark and dangerous business. It was a strange thought. He turned his attention back to the scenes around him.

He had a little money in his pocket, and the sweet smells from the bakery drew him inside. He bought a flaky pastry, which tasted delicious and soothed his rumbling stomach.

As he ate, Mel noticed another path, branching away from the township and leading to another circle of huts. He noticed that each of these huts had a staircase leading to the ground, which was unusual. Curious, he walked over to the ring of huts, finishing the last of the pastry.

None of these huts seemed like homes—that much he was quite sure of. They were too small. He had just started to leave when an explosion of hoarse coughing came from within the nearest hut, followed by a weak voice. The words were indistinguishable, but it sounded like someone calling out.

Mel pulled the curtain aside and peeked through the doorway. The curtains were drawn over the windows, so that the interior was quite dark. But he could make out a shape in a bed along the right wall. The shape stirred slightly, then the voice rasped again, "Naomi? Are you here? I need… some water." He broke off in a fit of coughing.

Mel had no idea who Naomi was, but he noticed a pitcher of clean water and a cup on a small table at the foot of the bed. Uncertain but not wanting to leave the stranger unaided, he stepped inside and filled the cup, then gently poured the water into the man's parched mouth. The stranger's breathing became more even, and his eyes closed again as he fell asleep.

This hut, Mel realized finally, was a hospital room. There was another bed a few feet away—he could see another man lying there, asleep. He wondered where the medics were.

At the same time he had this thought, a flare of light came from the side door as the curtain was pulled aside. "Who's there?" a woman demanded sharply. "What are you doing?'

Mel froze, clutching the pitcher. "Oh—I'm sorry—he was thirsty," he stammered quickly. "I didn't know—I was just walking the village."

The young woman's face softened. "Oh. Thank you. You can bring the pitcher here." She disappeared.

Mel followed her outside and down a short path that led to the next hut. This hut was the same size as the other, but better lit, with shelves and tables laden with supplies. Many glass bottles lined the shelves near the window, holding medicine. There were other items too, tools and instruments whose purpose he couldn't understand.

"The others were busy tending your friends, I think," the young woman said, taking the pitcher from his hands. "I had forgotten to check on those two patients. Thank you for giving him water."

Mel nodded quickly, still feeling a little awkward. "I didn't know," he repeated. "I wasn't trying to intrude."

"It is no matter," she replied easily. She was about Mel's height, but seemed around Rygal's age. Her hair was dark and curly, swept back into a messy bun at the base of her neck. She wore a simple linen dress with the sleeves rolled up, and an apron.

"You're… Naomi?" Mel guessed, remembering the name the man in the room had called for.

She nodded. "Yes. And you arrived earlier today, did you not? You met with the chieftain?"

"Yep. I'm Mel." He shook her hand, then nodded in the direction of the first hut he had entered. "Those men—what happened to them?"

"One was hurt in a boating accident a few days ago, and the other is recovering from an infection of the lungs," Naomi told him. "Both are showing quick improvement, and I think they will recover."

"That's good," Mel said, studying the storage room.

"Might I ask a question?" Naomi asked after refilling the pitcher. When Mel nodded, she continued. "I have heard that you and your friends are here for a purpose—you are not simply here to enjoy our scenery." She smiled slightly, then went on. "I was not told much—I have only apprenticed to be a healer for the last five years or so. But everyone has heard the rumors of the happenings on the Mainland, of a dark creature reawakened. If this is true… then why have you come here?"

Mel hesitated, not sure how much he should say. "We're here to… get something. We talked to the chieftain," he said vaguely. "We're here to help your people, and all of Orlell. I don't know what we plan to do. This is only my second quest," he added ruefully.

"Quest?" Naomi repeated, interested. "What do you mean?"

Mel paused, then decided she was trustworthy. Besides, what Iriam had said earlier was right. Better that people knew the truth, so that they could be on the watch for the Aces. If war was coming to Kamon, Naomi would have to know sooner than later. "The Aces have come back," he said slowly. "They took over Caer Sia. They want the Shards, both halves of the Star-Stone."

Naomi's face paled at the mention of the Aces. "Really? But why?" she asked, her voice hushed.

"I'm not sure—I think the Ace-Lord has some sort of plan to use the Shards to channel his powers," Mel said uncertainly.

Naomi straightened a few bottles above the wash basin, clearly not sure how to react. They were interrupted as another woman, bent with age and wrapped in gray linen robes, entered the room. "Madam Tika," Naomi greeted her. "Do you need a fresh vial of ointment for your husband again?"

"Yes, thank you, miss," the other woman said, her voice cracked with age. Her hood hid her frail face from the bright sunlight, and a few strands of silver hair fell in front of her eyes.

Naomi reached for a bottle above the window, while Mel started for the door. The old woman's voice made him turn. "Do you mind helping me back to my home, young man?" she asked.

"Not at all," Mel said quickly. The old woman took the bottle Naomi offered her, then, leaning heavily on Mel's arm, they left the circle of hospital huts.

"Only a few doors yonder," the old woman said softly. "I am pleased to find you here, young one."

Mel looked at her in shock. The woman's voice suddenly rang clear. They stopped in the shadows behind the bakery, and as the woman straightened, the light reached the flashing eyes and proud features of Cahadras.

"Tell Iriam I thought his choice wise," Cahadras said, as Mel bowed hastily. "Dangerous, perhaps, but you are all seven still alive. That is something to be grateful for."

"My lady," Mel stammered, completely thrown. "I didn't know—what are you doing here?"

Cahadras looked at him intensely. "Listen well to my words, New Blood. I was sent here by the High Light. He alone, it seems, still has faith in His creation. Your errand is not in vain. The words of old will reveal all in their proper time. Until that time, stand strong and fear not. Dark events are coming, strange and dangerous, and even I do not see how it will end."

A chill ran down Mel's spine at the implication of the title *New Blood*. "Do you mean the Prophecy?" he asked in a whisper.

"You will see," Cahadras said. "In the meantime, guard the Shard with your life, no matter what comes, and do not speak of what has happened here. I will reveal myself if I am commanded thus."

Mel nodded. He could barely believe what was happening. "Wait… the High Light believes we can win?" he asked incredulously.

The ghost of a smile crossed the Star Queen's face. "He already knows," she replied. "He has already written the history and the outcome of what is to come." She took his hand—Mel felt something small and cold pressed into his palm. Then Cahadras straightened. The crown on her brow flickered, then flashed with golden fire that spread down her frame. Then she vanished—Mel saw a streak of flame that seemed to speed up into the blue sky.

Both awestruck and fearful, he looked down at his hand. A small blue stone sat in his palm, one side round and smooth, and the other jagged, with sharp edges. Cut from its twin long ago.

The Shard.

18

∽ ∽ ∽ ∽ ∽ ∽ ∽ ∽ ∽

Ships from the East

Mel slept restlessly the first night in Kamon. The unexpected appearance of Cahadras, and the sudden burden to carry the Shard, had filled his mind with even more questions. Cahadras had bound him to silence, which was good, because he had no idea how he would explain his possession of the Shard otherwise. The Kamoni chieftain, Leelo, had made a deal with Ĵan to give them the Shard, but only if the companions agreed to help them ready for battle. If Mel suddenly revealed that he had the Shard, the distrust among his companions would return, not to mention what concern the Kamoni islanders would have.

He tried to reassure himself. As it was a command of the High Light, Cahadras had every right to take the Star-Stone and give it to Mel. But Mel wished she had done it a little more publicly. Without proof, it would be his word against everyone else's. Iriam would probably listen and believe Mel's story, but the Neutral had been busy all day yesterday helping Ĵan and Leelo come up with defensive strategies.

If he was grateful for one thing, it was that Cahadras' words had partly answered the question of what his task was in the prophecy.

220

He could assume now that it was his role to reunite the Shards. He had no idea whatsoever how he would do that—the thought of entering Caer Sia, potentially alone, and facing the Ace-Lord terrified him. Here he was, the New Blood, once again realizing how very unqualified he was for any of this.

Mel didn't know what to think. He lay on his back, holding the Shard on his chest, and flitted in and out of sleep for the whole of the night.

Morning dawned bright and sunny. Mel tried to act like nothing had changed, and fought against the urge to constantly feel in his pocket, making sure that the Shard was still there.

The companions met at a breakfast café that morning—minus Rygal. Mel hadn't seen Rygal at all since the meeting with Leelo.

"I think he's in his room," Jarus said slowly when Mel asked.

"Did he ever get his wounds treated?" Mel said with a frown.

"I don't know," Jarus admitted.

Mel took a drink of tea—the Kamoni brewed a sweet, floral beverage from the petals of the massive white flowers on the trees. It tasted delicious, as did the roast ham and fresh fruit on Mel's plate. But his worry for his friend made it hard to enjoy the meal.

"How long will we stay here, Iriam?" Jarus asked.

"A week at least, though if there is an attack, it will be longer," Iriam said. "We cannot leave the island unguarded. Leelo must be persuaded of the safety of his people before he allows us to leave with the Shard."

Mel put a hand on his trouser pocket. The familiar weight of the little stone inside greeted his hand, and he felt a twinge of guilt.

"What about Caer Sia?" Aryion asked. "Even if we had both Shards, what chance do we have of reuniting them there?"

"I am not yet sure," Iriam said, which was the end of the conversation.

Mel left the café and walked along the wood plank roads. There were too many worries brought up afresh this morning. Firstly, his concern for Rygal, and the way grief had completely changed his friend. Secondly, his anxiety of how Iriam—and worse, the Kamoni—would react when Mel revealed that he already had the Shard. And worst of all was the looming threat of the coming conflict: a one-sided fight against the Ace-Lord in which victory seemed absolutely hopeless.

He let out a breath and shook his head. Well, he could deal with the first of those thoughts now. He walked down the paths to the hospitals.

Naomi was inside, as she had been yesterday. "Good morning. Have you eaten?"

Mel nodded. "Yep, I just had breakfast. I have a question. Do you know if the medics… did they help all of my companions yesterday? All seven of us?"

Naomi paused, thinking. "I believe so. If you are unsure, I can ask our lead doctor. Why do you ask?"

Mel explained every one of his concerns for Rygal. Naomi listened without interrupting—she nodded, her brow furrowed intently as he spoke. But her face was sad as Mel finished.

"I can tend to him today," she promised. "But the loss, the hurt, the grief—that is something I cannot help. Only time will do that, time and fellowship."

Mel spent the day with Jarus. They explored most of the market on the ground, and walked through the shade of the forest. He saw Naomi later that evening, and immediately asked about Rygal.

"I've treated the wounds he sustained during the orc fight," was her reply. "And I got him to drink some water. But you must know—he has changed, Mel. No one can suffer so and come out unchanged. In time he will recover, and this rest is doing him good."

And Mel knew this was the best answer he would have for now. He was startled to realize how much he missed Rygal—the bright, cheerful Rygal who used to be. This shadow of his old friend broke his heart.

. . . . . .

The week passed slowly, but not uneventfully. There was always something to do, and Mel's activities varied. He visited with Hasman and Nallis—the two brothers spent most of their time on the cliffs overlooking the sea, keeping lookout and calling out whenever a ship passed by. He walked the dense central forest paths with Aryion and Quinn, learning as much as he could from the two rangers and their skills. He and Jan went spearfishing off the coast with Leelo and several other islanders. He swam with Jarus—the Cooper never grew tired of swimming. The water was cold at first, but in the tropical heat of the day it was always a pleasant relief.

They also worked with the Kamoni to organize a counter attack, in case of battle. The villagers, though uncertain at first, were willing to learn. Thankfully Aryion's earlier observation turned out to be right. While the islanders were a peaceful folk, their bodies were strong and hearty from years of sailing boats and climbing trees.

A troop of archers were trained by Quinn. Another group were trained to act as a shield wall, carrying wide oval-shaped shields. Aryion had the idea to line a group of warriors on the boardwalk nearest to the coast, prepared to hurl projectiles or pour boiling oil upon any attacker unfortunate enough to try to besiege the village from that side. At Quinn's idea, rows of pits were dug within the forest line. Concealed beneath palm branches, the pits would serve as simple but effective traps.

"What we might try," Quinn suggested on the second evening, as they met with Leelo, "is rigging a series of trip wires in the woods. Have them fling darts or stones when sprung. It is how we hunt game in Tinkeeyo."

Hasman and Nallis were greatly interested in this plan, and the following day, Mel saw the two brothers hard at work alongside Quinn, bending saplings and concealing trip wires.

Harpoons and spears, usually used only for fishing, were turned into weapons in the hands of the ready Kamoni. Aryion supervised the training, overseeing a line of warriors as they practiced stabbing and slashing. Mel joined him, both for company and for his own training. The ranger was an impressive swordsman as well as tactician, and he instructed Mel along with the islanders.

The activities helped take Mel's mind off of things, but only a little. Now that his initial shock over the sudden appearance of Cahadras—and the Shard—had passed, he was still confused why Cahadras would choose him to guard the Shard. Surely someone like Iriam or Ĵan would be a better choice. Even if Mel was the supposed New Blood in the Prophecy, as Cahadras evidently believed, that didn't change the fact that he was young and inexperienced.

By the eighth day, he could wait no longer. It was time to talk to Iriam. Mel woke up early and dressed quickly, a nervous twinge in his stomach. The Shard was heavy in his pocket as he walked to the pavilion.

Iriam, Ĵan, and Leelo were already there, bent over a map of the island with mugs of tea. They looked up as Mel entered, a little startled to see him.

"Good morning, Mel," Ĵan said. "Is everything all right?"

Mel forced a smile. "Yes… I just had something to ask. I can wait," he added. He trusted the Kamoni chieftain, but he didn't know how Leelo would react—or if Leelo would believe Mel's story.

"Very well. We are nearly finished." Iriam studied him carefully. Mel half wondered if the Neutral could sense the Shard's presence there. But he said nothing.

Mel sat down on the wood road, his feet dangling over the edge while he waited. The sun was rising to his left, painting the dawn sky with pink and red. Fog hovered over the ocean. The morning was quite chill.

He looked up as someone walked by, and recognized Nallis. The young islander stopped when he saw Mel. "Oh—hello. Forgive me, I did not see you."

"It's fine. Iriam and Jan are talking to Chief Leelo," Mel said, nodding toward the pavilion.

"Ah. Well, I will wait with you." Nallis leaned on the railing, looking at the ocean. His face was worried.

"Is everything all right?" Mel asked.

Nallis let out a breath. "I am sure it is fine. But… it's the ferries. We haven't seen a single ship all morning, which is very strange. At this time of day, the merchants are usually already here to buy and sell. It's nearly sunrise, and the market opens in an hour." He shook his head. "I have never known a merchant to be late to his own sale. Hasman is keeping watch, but we both thought it strange, so I came to report to Leelo."

"Maybe the ferries needed repairs or something," Mel suggested.

Nallis looked doubtful. "If that were so, there are other ships we would have seen. The sea is absolutely silent this morning. There are no fishermen, no merchants."

Mel studied the rolling water and the gradually lifting fog. Nallis was right. On a clear morning like today, the Mainland fishermen should already be at sea. But the ocean was flat and empty like a sheet of parchment—no boats in sight in any direction.

Something about the emptiness chilled him. His mouth was suddenly dry. "We need to tell them," he said, standing and walking back to the pavilion door. At the same second he reached it, he heard the rising lilt of the watchman's horn.

Nallis looked relieved. "They see something—that must be the ferry. Perhaps Barcoast just got a slow start this morning after all."

Mel peered across the water. He could see a shape gradually coming into view. Not just one shape—five, he saw now. Strange ships, not the elegant Coonsian galleons that he had seen before. Their hulls were curved, arching out of the water, their four sails huge and diamond-shaped. The outline of the ships against the horizon looked like exotic, spiked flowers.

"That's not the ferry," he said slowly. He didn't recognize the odd ships.

But Nallis clearly did. His face was white as he flung open the pavilion door, heedless of any protocol that had previously bound him. "Jenna, sir!" he said as Leelo stood in confusion. "Five Jenna ships sighted to the east."

Mel looked at the ships again. They were rapidly getting closer—he could see their flags fluttering from their masts. Three of them were identical, the other two were slightly different. The three flags were striped with yellow, blue, and black, flags unfamiliar to Mel. The other two were yellow and dark blue, and in the center they bore the triangle emblem of the Aces.

His stomach lurched. They had come.

Leelo snapped into action. "Sound the alarm immediately, and rouse the warriors. Prepare the counter attack. Secure the Shard at once." Nallis nodded and sprang away across the boardwalks. Leelo turned to Iriam and Ĵan. "Wake the others. We must fight. We cannot let them get the Shard."

They both nodded and strode toward the circle of huts where the others were staying. Mel ran after them, his hands shaking as he fumbled in his pocket. "Iriam—wait—this is important."

"Come," Iriam said, slowing his stride only slightly so Mel could catch up to him and Ĵan. "Ask your question quickly."

Mel looked at the approaching ships—they were closer now, nearly to the beach. "Something happened the day we got here—I met with someone, and—and—she told me that we had to protect the Shard. And she said I had to guard it with my life."

"She?" Ĵan repeated.

"I have the Shard," Mel blurted, and held it out. "I didn't steal it—I promise—it's a long story, but—"

They both stopped, staring at him and the little stone in absolute bewilderment. Ĵan finally managed to find words. "Mel… we had a deal with the Kamoni. They will not take this news well."

"I didn't steal it, and I don't want it anyway," Mel repeated angrily.

"But you must continue to guard it," Iriam said. His initial surprise had passed, and he was calm again. "If the person who gave it to you is who I think she is, then I cannot intervene. You have been chosen to carry the Shard, in the same way that you are chosen to be the New Blood."

Panic filled Mel's mind for an instant. The Jenna ships had practically reached the beach. They were minutes away from battle, and carrying the Shard felt the same as having a target on his back. The Aces would come for him instantly. "I can't!" he sputtered. "They'll know I have it."

"Perhaps not," Iriam mused, starting forward again.

Jan looked between Iriam and Mel, at a loss. "Iriam, think. He's just a child. If the Aces catch him, they will have caught the Shard as well."

"If the Aces catch him, then we have no hope even with the Shards," Iriam said gravely. "Remember the Prophecy. Remember who Mel is."

"What—" Mel began, desperately needing answers.

"In a moment," Iriam told him, and looked at Jan. "Wake the others. We must hurry if we are to assist the islanders."

Jan nodded, and with a last uncertain look back at Mel, he walked away.

"Please just tell me what I'm supposed to do," Mel said the moment Jan had gone. He looked up at Iriam, feeling very small and very young.

Iriam put a gentle hand on his shoulder. "Cahadras came to you, did she not?" Mel nodded, and Iriam smiled slightly. "Then your orders come from the High Light Himself, or Cahadras would not have given you the Shard. Your actions now will determine much. Keep the Shard safe."

Mel let out a breath. The commotion and shouting below seemed to fade away, and it was only him and Iriam, and the Shard in his hand. "I'm scared," he confessed finally. "I don't want to fail." He looked away to hide the sudden tears that had sprung burning to his eyes.

There it was. The truth behind his hesitation to accept his role as the New Blood, the truth behind his constant stress and anxiety surrounding the Prophecy. He did not know what to do. He was terrified of failure, and he knew the Aces had been using it against him since the moment he had left Appledale.

Iriam's low voice made him look up. "Mel. We trust you. You have so much faith in the actions of others, yet none in yourself. Have courage, and have faith. And know also—there are seven companions for a reason. You are not alone. You will never be alone."

Mel looked up. Jan had returned. Behind him stood Aryion. He saw Rygal, Quinn, and Jarus joining the host of islanders in defense on the beach below. Six friends standing alongside him, prepared to fight and defend and protect. The very thought of their presence was like he had a legion of warriors standing behind him. And he felt braver.

He looked up and met Iriam's eyes. "I'm ready. What's our battle plan?"

19

The Battle on the Beach

Jarus stood beside Quinn, watching with a pounding heart as the rowboats ground against the shore, and the howling host of warriors sprang onto Kamoni soil.

The five ships had slowed several yards off land, and the warriors aboard had poured into the rowboats and rowed the rest of the way to the beach. Two of the strange ships had been full of shouting orcs, brandishing broadswords and maces. Their eyes were pale and blue—enchanted and immortal thanks to the Ace-Lord's spell.

The other three boats were crewed by Jenna. It was the first time Jarus had seen a host of Jenna warriors, yet the sight chilled him to the bone. Their skin was dark brown, their black hair wild and matted like a mane. They appeared somewhat human and somewhat not—their faces were flat, with prominent jaw and cheekbones. Their teeth were black, filed into sharp points, and glinted as they opened their mouths in a shrieking war cry that chilled Jarus to the bone.

"Well, they brought Jenna this time," Quinn muttered.

There was something else, standing and watching from the prow of the lead ship. A tall figure hooded in black, its cloak billowing behind it like smoke, its outline seeming to blur and shift with the scene around it.

"This is bad," Jarus murmured. There were around a hundred Kamoni assembled in defense of the island. The fleet of rowboats that had just arrived carried twice that number, with more enemies waiting on the ships, prepared for a second and third onslaught once the islanders were weakened from the first charge.

The orcs and Jenna sprinted up the beach, heedless of the hail of arrows that were launched from the defenders up hill. Several arrows hit their targets. Jarus noticed that the Jenna seemed wary of the defenders—the orcs simply plowed uphill, ripping arrows out of their wounds and hardly slowing to do it. Then the Jenna followed, attacking in the space between volleys.

Jenna, orcs, and Kamoni clashed on the sand below Jarus and Quinn's vantage point on the edge of the forest. Jarus had seen the orcs fight before. The Jenna were worse. In a howling, slashing frenzy, they attacked like maddened dogs, flinging themselves upon the archers.

"Now!" came Leelo's voice. The Kamoni chieftain stood just behind the small group of archers—the moment the Jenna lunged, the islanders waiting in the trees sent a hail of spears and harpoons at the Jenna's backs. Screeches of pain and rage filled the air. The surviving Kamoni archers drew back, retreating to the safety of the forest.

The orcs surged after them, pursuing the army of islanders. Jarus stepped forward, gripping his knife, slashing and stabbing and fighting to keep his footing while the orcs pressed forward.

"Pull back!" Leelo bellowed from the trees. "Lead them into the forest!"

The Kamoni gave ground, stepping carefully through the underbrush. The orcs plowed on, uninhibited until, suddenly, the ground gave way under their feet as they trod over the carefully concealed pits. The Kamoni warriors had dug these holes days before, filling them with sharp stones and branches, and covering them with palm branches. The orcs plummeted down. Several were impaled and hung there screaming, unable to heal immediately and unable to die at all.

Jarus stepped back to Quinn's side, at the edge of the pits. The scene below turned his stomach, and he quickly looked away. Orc shrieks and howls filled the forest. But the pits only slowed them for a moment. The Jenna came behind, more sure-footed than the orcs, and carefully sidestepped the exposed pits. Now they flung themselves at the islanders, and the fighting continued.

Jarus stabbed the thigh of a stumbling Jenna, and the warrior fell backwards into the nearest pit. Another warrior sprang forward at the same moment, slamming the butt of his spear into Jarus' shoulder. The blow vibrated down Jarus' back, and he staggered, gasping at the pain.

Then Drisilas flashed through the air in front of him, running the Jenna warrior through. Jan pulled the flaming sword free and looked at Jarus. "Are you all right?"

"Where's Mel?" Jarus asked at the same time. "The Aces—they've come for him."

"He's up in the village. I think he went to help evacuate the hospitals," Jan told him.

Jarus felt a surge of relief. At least Mel wasn't alone in the battle somewhere, as he had feared. He moved to Jan's side, his shoulder aching from that last blow. Something was nagging in his mind, but he couldn't place it. A Jenna warrior flung himself at Jan, and Drisilas cut him down, screaming. Jan stepped back, and Jarus finally placed the thought.

"The Jenna… they aren't under the spell," he stammered, baffled.

Jan shook his head—he looked confused too. "I do not know why. Perhaps the Ace-Lord only needed the orcs to be immortal."

That didn't make any sense to Jarus. But there was no time to talk about it now. The surviving Jenna and orcs had regrouped between the beach and the forest. Through the trees, Jarus glimpsed the second group of rowboats—larger than the first—drawing up against the beach. The Ace stood in the prow of the first ship, silent, waiting. Watching as the massive group of warriors advanced up hill.

"High Light help us," Jan murmured. He turned, searching for Leelo in the fray. "Sir, there is no way to effectively defend the beach—it is too wide a space, with no cover. We need to fall back through the woods towards the market. Have your archers assemble on the paths above the market, and we can trap the orcs and Jenna there."

Leelo gripped his spear uneasily. "That is too close to the entrance to the village. I cannot put my people in danger," he said warily.

"The market's cleared out," Quinn said, approaching from behind. "Either way, sir, this part of the island is difficult to defend. There is a chance some of the attackers could get behind and enter the village. It would be better if they were all penned in a central location, where we might be able to surround them."

Leelo finally nodded. "Very well. But I refuse to leave a single wounded warrior behind here."

"We will cover your retreat," Jan said. The fire of his sword reflected in his green eyes.

Quinn accompanied Leelo, who swiftly ordered the retreat back toward the market. Jarus knew that most of the stairways leading up into the trees were in this part of the forest. The last thing they wanted was for the attackers to reach the defenseless villagers sheltered in the pavilion.

He padded behind Jan, watching as the call to retreat reached the fray on the beach. At Leelo's order, the Kamoni retreated back, following their chieftain to safety. The orcs laughed and taunted, clashing their swords against their shields.

"Stay close," Jan warned quietly.

Jarus swallowed. "How are we going to win if we can't kill them?"

Several islanders, refusing to retreat, had moved to stand beside Jan and Jarus. Jan studied the approaching orcs carefully. "We don't necessarily have to kill them to beat them. The pits were effective enough, and there are other traps we have laid."

He quickly relayed this plan to the Kamoni warriors, and they formed into a wide line, standing between the forest behind and the beach in front. The pits lay just in front of them, several still filled with orcs struggling to escape. Jenna bodies lay still and silent inside as well, their blood streaking the sharp stones.

The orcs charged again, trying to force their way through the line of defenders. The Kamoni stood strong, parrying the wild blows. Ĵan stood at the front of the party, Drisilas in one hand and red fire in the other. He sent a crackling blast into the faces of the attacking orcs, and they fell back, howling. Some slipped into the pits, and for an instant the charge hesitated.

"Back!" Ĵan barked hoarsely, and the islanders gave ground again. Jarus followed Hasman, placing his feet where the islanders did, and avoiding the other traps they had devised days before.

More pits claimed the orcs who followed. In other places of the wood, tripped ropes let a hail of poisoned darts fly from hidden places, striking any in their path. Darts whistled over Jarus' head, and he crept as low to the ground as he could. He looked up, and saw another group of islanders assembled on the boardwalks above, raining down anything they could find at the attackers. Buckets full of boiling whale oil were poured upon any orc unlucky enough to walk beneath its flow. Oil and blood slicked the ground.

"Hold!" came Ĵan's order again, and the defenders halted. Jarus moved to Hasman's side, and they watched as the orcs drew close. Ĵan watched, waiting until they were mere paces away. Then he touched the tip of Drisilas to the grease-streaked ground.

With a loud whoosh, the oil ignited. Fire spread through the underbrush, lapped the trunks of the trees, and devoured the orcs who had fallen. The smell of burning wood, then burning flesh, filled the air. Acrid black smoke billowed up, making Jarus' eyes water. He coughed and sprang away, throat burning from the rancid smoke.

Above them, the islanders poured sand down the trunks of the trees that supported the village, protecting the defenders from the flames. The Kamoni and their homes stood behind a wall of fire, while the shrieking orcs on the other side struggled to regroup.

Jarus let out a breath. His stomach heaved at the horror of it all. He tried not to look at the charred bodies on the ground.

"That will hold them for a moment," Jan murmured.

The fire began to die down, and Jarus could see the orcs beyond had formed a line. A tall, scarred orc stood before them, leaning on his massive mace. Unlike the rest of the attackers, his armor was steel, finely polished so that it shone. His black eyes studied the determined islanders for a long moment, then rested on Jan.

"High King," he called out. His voice was low and growling, with a heavy accent. But he spoke the Coonsian tongue fluently. "It seems all I have heard of you is true. You are powerful, clever. But you do not wish for the deaths of your comrades, do you? I think not. In that way, we are much alike."

Jarus looked at Jan. The Liznee king studied the orc carefully. "I have not had the pleasure of meeting you," he called back after a pause.

The orc smiled darkly. "No, indeed. You were not there when we took Caer Sia. Not much of a fight, I am afraid. Still, it was enjoyable putting your unhappy citizens in their place."

Jan straightened. "Have you come to taunt or to parley?"

"Parley, naturally. This is a valiant defense you have organized, but you must know it will fail in the end, and we will kill you all. You will all fall to our swords—and I, Hagshrub, shall lead my warriors into victory."

Hagshrub. The name was familiar to Jarus, though he assumed by now that this was the orc Aryion so hated. Hagshrub smirked as he continued.

"I've come with an offer, sire. Hand over the Shard to me, and I'll call my warriors back. We'll leave the island in peace. Do you value a fragment of stone over the lives of these flowery islanders?"

The Kamoni behind Jan stirred and muttered anxiously. Despite himself, Jarus couldn't help thinking there was some truth in Hagshrub's words. The islanders were outnumbered and outmatched. Perhaps it would be wise to give up the Shard, if only to save Kamon.

Jan seemed to think for a moment, then he shrugged slowly. "For one thing," he said, "I don't have the Shard. For another, I know that the Ace-Lord has bound you and your warriors to his service by your lives, and if you want any chance of escaping that servitude, you will leave Kamon and allow us to reunite the Shards."

Hagshrub's face darkened. "You speak without knowledge. I am bound to nothing but the hope of glory—glory that comes only from the Ace-Lord's reign. And if you will not accept, we will kill you all."

The flames had burned low. Hagshrub shouted an order, and the orcs sprang forward. Jan stepped forward as they moved, red fire crackling in his hands. The blast struck the ground at the closest orcs' feet, sending them staggering backwards. Before they could regain their balance, Jan shot again, and they toppled backwards towards the beach.

The Kamoni surged forward at the same moment. The unexpected charge caused the orcs to fall back even farther. But they recovered quickly, flinging themselves against the wall of wooden shields that the Kamoni held. Swords clashed against sword, against wood, against bone. But the orcs could not break the wall.

More projectiles were flung from above—arrows and spears, and sharp stones. Trapped between the shield wall and the pits, the orcs finally gave ground, pressed back toward the beach.

"Go!" Jan ordered. At his cry, the defenders turned, moving through the trees toward the market and the distant sounds of battle there. The remaining orcs in the forest, many nursing severe burns and stabs, limped back toward the boats. Jarus and Hasman followed Jan, slashing at any orc that hesitated to retreat, forcing them back. Red fire flared in Jan's hand as he sent blast after blast at the ankles of the retreating orcs.

Jarus slashed the leg of a burly orc who had tried to turn back, ducked under a blow from another, and watched as Hasman knocked the offending warrior into one of the pits. "They're giving up," he panted, and hope surged in his chest.

At the instant he said it, Hagshrub sprang from behind a tree and swung his mace into Jan's back.

Jan cried out in pain, reeled forward and fell against a tree. Drisilas slipped from his hands. Hagshrub stepped forward triumphantly, raising his mace again.

But before he could bring the weapon down, Hasman stabbed him in the shoulder with his harpoon. Hagshrub howled in pain and turned furiously on the young Kamoni warrior.

Without thinking, Jarus lunged forward and slashed across the back of Hagshrub's knee. Hagshrub bellowed in pain again and kicked Jarus in the ribs, sending him flying back. Jarus crashed into the scorched underbrush—Hagshrub stepped forward, his wounds closing before Jarus' eyes. Winded, he groped for a weapon, and his paw found a hilt—not his knife hilt, but the hilt of Drisilas, which lay blazing and burning where Jan had dropped it.

Jarus swung the mighty sword up into Hagshrub's face. The orc stopped at the sight of the fire, but it only slowed him down slightly. With a snarl, he swung the mace and knocked Drisilas out of Jarus' paws, then brought his weapon up again.

A blast of red fire hit him squarely between the shoulders before he could bring the mace down. The force of the flame sent him tumbling forward, nearly falling into the pit at the edge of the woods.

Hagshrub gathered his balance and turned, shocked for an instant. Another blast hit him in the chest, and he was flung backwards, rolling down the sandy slope toward the water.

Jan lowered his hand wearily, his fingers still glowing red from the fire.

Jarus leapt to his feet and ran to the Liznee's side. Jan lay chest down at an awkward angle. Spots of blood soaked the side of his shirt, and his breath came in ragged, painful gasps.

"Jan," Jarus murmured, his voice tight with worry.

Hasman knelt by him. "We must move. The orcs will regroup and come this way again."

"I—we can't leave him," Jarus stammered. He put a paw on Jan's shoulder. "Can you move at all? Can you stand?"

Jan gathered his strength and pulled himself to his hands and knees. Yet even that small movement caused him to wince. He fought for breath, then managed to choke, "Can't—walk. Could maybe stand. Don't leave the sword."

"I'll get it," Jarus said. His mouth was dry as he padded over to retrieve Drisilas. The sword left a charred mark on the bloodied ground.

He risked a glance back at the beach. More boats came from the ships. The rest of the Jenna warriors were coming. But his heart nearly stopped as he saw that the Ace led them this time.

Jarus turned back to Jan and Hasman, not knowing what he should do. Jan was badly hurt—he needed medical attention quickly. They needed to go before the Ace got here and killed all three of them.

Then, in an instant, he knew what to do. "Iriam. We need to find Iriam." He looked up at Hasman. "Stay here with him, and try to be quiet. I'll be back as soon as I can."

Hasman nodded and crouched beside Ĵan, gripping his spear. Behind the trees, they were nearly invisible from the beach. But if the Ace led the third charge up through the forest, everything would be over.

He shook the thoughts from his mind and ran through the woods. By the time he reached the market, the sounds of battle had faded slightly. Blood and carnage met his eyes, and bodies of Kamoni warriors and Jenna alike littered the streets. The fighting had paused for the time being—both sides needed to regroup. He noticed a group of orcs and Jenna to the right, near the waterfront. To his left, waiting in the tree line, were the Kamoni warriors.

Jarus' eyes scanned the scene quickly before he spotted Iriam. The Neutral was giving orders to several islanders as Jarus ran over. He noticed the Cooper, and looked relieved. "Ah, there you are, Jarus. I am glad to see you alive."

Jarus shook his head, out of breath. "I'm fine, but Ĵan is hurt. Hasman is guarding him right now, but there's another group of Jenna coming—and an Ace."

There was a groan of despair from the Kamoni at the mention of the Ace. Iriam's face was serious as he turned to Leelo. "This is our final stand. We must face them here. I will deal with the Ace." He turned to Jarus. "Take me there, quickly."

They ran back through the woods. By the time they reached Hasman, Jarus saw that more Jenna had stepped on the beach. The Ace led the group forward, cloak billowing, ice spreading along the sand at its feet.

Jan was barely conscious as Iriam knelt beside him. The Neutral put a hand on his back, carefully assessing his injuries. Then he looked up at Hasman. "I will need your help to get him to his feet. Then you must support him to the medics outside of the market while I confront the Ace."

Hasman nodded. Jan's eyes had flickered at the sound of Iriam's voice, and he managed to raise his head. Iriam spoke, his voice low. "There is a third group of warriors coming. You must try to stand."

Jan nodded and gritted his teeth. Iriam and Hasman both put their shoulders under the king's arms, then raised him up. Jan gave a short cry of pain, then was silent again, his face pale, gripping Hasman's shoulder.

"Go carefully but as quickly as you can," Iriam said. Hasman nodded, and they made their way stiffly through the forest.

Jarus looked back at the beach. The Jenna were not walking through the forest as he had feared—instead they made their way in a purposeful line toward the market square.

"What should we do?" Jarus asked finally, looking up at Iriam.

The Neutral watched the group walk past. "We must join the

others and stand together. Both Mel and the Shard are safe for now, but I doubt the Ace will give up."

Relief filled Jarus at this news, but he also knew Iriam was right. Still, he could not help feeling that they were painfully outmatched.

They returned to the waiting Kamoni. Jarus saw Hasman support Jan inside a small medic tent on the edge of the battlefield. The islanders stood in a group, waiting silently. Leelo stood at their head, and he turned as Iriam and Jarus appeared.

"Jenna warriors, led by an Ace," Iriam told him, confirming the chieftain's guess.

"We cannot hope to defeat this many alone," Leelo said quietly. He looked back at his faithful warriors. The Jenna would outnumber them ten to one.

Aryion had joined them. His sword was streaked with blood. Jarus was about to tell him about their fight with Hagshrub, then decided that now was not the time. Aryion looked over at Leelo's words. "Maybe we don't have to," he said slowly. "The northern towns are no more than a half hour's voyage from here, aren't they?"

A Kamoni general frowned at him. "We will not give up Kamon," he said flatly. "If we will die, we will die on our own land."

"I'm not talking about giving up—I'm talking about getting help. Sail up the Strait," Aryion continued urgently. "Send a cry for aid to every town within an hour's trip—try to get to Yamo if you can. The Hyenin people of the desert are your allies as well as ours."

Hope lit in Leelo's eyes. "That is not a bad plan in the slightest," he mused, and looked at Iriam.

Iriam was nodding. "Yes. Send as many of your sailors as you can spare."

Leelo turned to his waiting warriors and relayed the plan to them. Twenty Kamoni sailors left the main group, moving to the harbor where their ships were safely moored. In a few minutes, Jarus saw the slender vessels slipping out to sea, riding on a southern breeze.

By that time, the third group of warriors, led by the Ace, had arrived.

20

Reparation

"Hand me that bucket, Mel," said Naomi, reaching up from her position on the steps. Mel, who was standing above her on the balcony, leaned over to pass the bucket filled with medical supplies down to her.

His conversation with Iriam this morning had reassured him of one thing. This was not a battle that he would be needed in—not, at least, unless absolutely necessary. The New Blood was too valuable to risk losing, as was the Shard. The little stone thumped against his leg as he moved back and forth, carrying pails of medical supplies out of the hospital supply hut and passing them to Naomi. She passed it to the medic on the steps behind her, and one by one, the pails of precious supplies made its way to the ground.

The doctors had set up a small hospital tent on the back side of the battlefield. But the number of injured were so many that they had quickly exhausted the initial round of supplies. Naomi and two other women had gone back to the supply hut to retrieve more medicine, balms, and bandages.

Mel had gone with them. If he was not going to fight, he was determined to still be of some use. Besides, he would rather be here than watching on the beach. The carnage below sickened him, and it worsened with each minute. Every time he caught a glimpse of the battlefield, he felt a horrible sinking feeling in the pit of his stomach, worried that at any given time he might see Jarus, or Aryion, or Rygal, or any of the others laying still and silent among the fallen.

But he saw no one he recognized among the slain. Not yet. And now, the battle seemed to have quieted down. From his position up on the balcony, he could see the orcs and Jenna standing in the trees beside the waterfront, likely planning their next charge. Closer, nearly invisible in the thick tangle of trees, he caught glimpses of the defenders. Iriam was there, with Leelo. He had seen Aryion and Quinn fighting side by side a moment ago. As for his other companions, he had no idea where they could be.

He picked up another pail and passed it to Naomi, and looked up in time to see Hasman supporting someone through the forest toward the hospital tent. His heart lurched as he recognized Jan. The Liznee king was barely able to keep his footing, stumbling weakly forward.

"Hurry, Mel," Naomi said, and Mel forced his gaze away, turning to get the next pail. Naomi passed it down, then seemed satisfied. "That will be as much as we can get for now. The wounded need these supplies, and quickly."

They walked down the steps, through the short patch of woods, and to what remained of the market. The two armies, Jenna and Kamoni, lined opposite sides of the square, a hundred yards apart.

Now that he was closer, Mel had a better view of the blood-stained sand, of the fallen Jenna bodies, of the many wounded or dying islanders who had been dragged to the shadows of the trees. The hospital tent was at full capacity, and now blankets and mats had been spread out on the forest floor for the wounded. Mel scanned the many injured, but it was impossible to pick out faces from the crowd.

He spotted Jarus among the defenders. The Cooper's tired eyes lit up as he saw Mel. "There you are, Mel. I didn't know where you went. Are you all right?"

"Yes, I'm fine. Are you?"

Jarus nodded in reply. There was blood splattered over his paws, but none of it seemed to be his own.

"Are we all here?" Mel asked him.

Jarus looked around. "I think so. Jan's hurt—I don't know where they've taken him. The medic tent is filled up."

Mel looked at him anxiously. "How did Jan…"

"We ended up running into some orcs," Jarus said wearily. "Hag— one of them hit him in the back with a mace," he finished quickly, glancing back at Aryion.

Mel was less subtle. "Wait—Hagshrub?" he asked, stunned. "He's here?"

Aryion looked over at the name, then at Jarus. Jarus shuffled uncomfortably under his gaze. "I wasn't going to tell you, because— because you're supposed to protect Mel."

The ranger smiled slightly. "Rest assured then, that I won't abandon that duty yet. I already heard that Hagshrub was here, but I have not yet seen him."

Mel felt a flash of gratitude. He knew how much Aryion must want to leave him and pursue his father's killer. But he had stayed here, following orders. Still, he noticed that Aryion gave Iriam a very slight nod—as if verifying that the Neutral was prepared to do anything he could to make sure Aryion had the chance to fight Hagshrub. That, after all, had been their arrangement.

Iriam returned the nod, then turned to face Mel and Jarus. "I am glad to see you here, Mel. How fare the medics?"

"They're busy, but we moved a lot of supplies down," Mel said. "What's our plan here?" He watched as a host of Jenna approached a hundred yards away or so, joining with the first group of orcs that waited in the trees.

"The orcs are still immortal, yet the Jenna can be killed," Iriam said. "Leelo has ordered some of his people to sail north, and try to rally help. Our only task now is to hold off the attackers until help comes."

"And if it doesn't come?" Mel asked slowly. He hated to voice the doubt. But he realized that any help the Kamoni may find would be the town guard of coastal towns. Certainly no warriors capable of beating Jenna, or immortal orcs.

Iriam shook his head. "Then we will trust that as our fate. Until then, we fight."

Mel slipped a hand in his pocket, his fingers closing over the Shard. At the same time he did, he felt a chill run down his spine, felt the unexplainable sensation of unfriendly eyes on him. He looked back at the approaching attackers. Standing in the shadows of the trees was an Ace.

Mel hadn't seen the Ace yet. He must have led the third charge, and remained in the shadows until now. But he was here, and the purple-red eyes were fixed on Mel, less than a hundred yards away.

Hello, New Blood.

Mel closed his eyes, his heart pounding, and fought against the fear as the voice filled his head.

The Ace-Lord does not wish for all these to perish. All he asks for is you—and the Shard. Would that not be a wiser choice? Do you want to see them die? We do not want to kill you—you are invaluable to us. But your friends are less so.

"Iriam," Mel choked, clutching his head. The Neutral turned to him, frowning in confusion for a moment, then he understood what was happening.

You understand our offer, New Blood. My master is generous. Surrender yourself now, and we will leave the island at once. But if you stay to fight, you will watch the deaths of each and every one of your friends here first.

Iriam was speaking, but Mel could hear nothing, only his pounding heart and the echoes of the voice in his mind. His terror overwhelmed him for an instant. His hands clenched into fists at his sides. Something dug into the palm of his right hand—he looked down to see the Shard, glittering and beautiful. The pure blue light inside it caused the voice in his head to falter.

"We are all with you, Mel," came Iriam's voice, low and reassuring.

Mel looked up, meeting the Ace's gaze across the battle field. He spoke softly, knowing that the Ace could hear him none the less. "Tell your master that he won't have me or the Shard today. I will protect it as long as I am able. I promise you that."

The Ace raised his head slightly, displeasure written in his stance. The Jenna began their march forward.

"We need more time," Iriam murmured. He stepped forward, moving through the crowd of islanders until he stood in the open, facing the approaching attackers. The Jenna paused for an instant as Iriam raised his hand. "Halt. I have come to parley."

The Jenna stopped, uncertain. Then someone laughed. A wiry Jenna warrior stepped forward. He wore armor made of leather and steel, and his dark face was scarred from many old battles.

"Parley?" he repeated, the heavy eastern accent making the words nearly indistinguishable. "There is no parley now, Neutral. You should have heeded the offer of my fellow captain Hagshrub if a parley you had wished. Now, you face us. We are the Aikala Jenna. No parley is given nor accepted."

"Nevertheless, I will offer one," Iriam continued calmly. "If you will not listen, perhaps your leader will." He glanced at the Ace.

The Jenna spat angrily. "You will listen to me. I am Irshkhân, leader of the Aikala. I bring the message of the Ace-Lord."

"And what message would that be?" Iriam asked. "To give up and hand over the Shard? You already know our answer to that. Thus, I propose an alternative in place of more senseless fighting." Irshkhân hesitated.

Like a flicker of fog, the Ace moved and appeared before Iriam. His hood had been removed. The face beneath was different than the Ace they had fought before. Half of the face was intact still, with smooth charcoal skin. The other half was withered and skeletal, the eye sunk in the socket, the lip-less mouth tilted up in a smile.

"I'm listening," the Ace said calmly.

The Kamoni had drawn back reflexively from the Ace as he approached. Mel could not help staring. This, he guessed, was the closest resemblance of the ancient strength that had once been the Ace-Lord's. This Ace wore glittering silver armor, with a breastplate emblazoned with the emblem of Kahlifis. The general of the Aces, Mel realized. The Ace-Deputy.

"You know as well as I that the Jenna will think even less of you if you continue sending their warriors to die," Iriam said. "And we have no desire to continue the killing. So let us end this struggle another way. A duel, man to man."

The Ace-Deputy's eyes glittered. "You must know less of the Ace-Lord than I thought. Death means nothing to him. Centuries now he has reveled in death, until he is lord of it."

Chills ran down Mel's spine. Beside him, Aryion gripped his sword, his face drawn and tense.

"However," the Ace-Deputy continued, "I am impatient. So I will accept this offer. What are the terms?"

"Two fighters, one from each side. Each will choose their own men, as is custom," Iriam said.

"I am not fond of mortals' customs as you are, Neutral," the Ace-Deputy informed him coolly. "Let us try a different custom. Let us choose each other's champions." He smiled.

Iriam hesitated for a long moment, then nodded. "Very well. But we must agree, there can be no changing the champions once they accept."

Mel let out a long breath. He was surprised the Ace had accepted. That didn't mean they had won, though. He was nearly certain that the Ace-Deputy had a plan in mind to twist the rules of the duel somehow.

"Allow me to fight, my lord," Irshkhân said eagerly from behind the Ace-Deputy. "Their king is already wounded. I will kill him in an instant." There was an unpleasant gleam in his dark eyes.

"Silence," the Ace-Deputy snapped at him. "Go wait with your warriors. You are not needed here, not yet."

"No choosing among the injured. They will be kept out of further fighting entirely," Iriam said flatly. "On that point I am firm."

The Ace-Deputy paused for a long moment, then he nodded. "Well, then. I shall choose your man first, then you choose one of mine. If that seems reasonable." He smiled mockingly, then looked over Iriam's shoulder to survey the line of warriors. Mel could not help shivering as the eyes swept over them, as if the Ace could see into each of their thoughts.

Then the Ace laughed softly. "How very strange. Your companions are not the pure souls I was led to believe. Who is it among you who bears the Blood Oath? I call him to challenge."

"No," Mel whispered, cold dread seeping through him.

Aryion stepped forward slowly, his eyes on Iriam. The Neutral's face was grim, but he said nothing. The Ace-Deputy's choice was well within the rules of combat. Now it only remained who Iriam would choose as the ranger's opponent.

And Mel knew who it would be. He knew it without a trace of doubt. Aryion had fulfilled his end of the bargain, to protect Mel up till now. Now Iriam must carry through his side of the deal—and that involved making sure that the ranger fulfilled the Blood Oath at any opportunity.

"Your captain Hagshrub it will be, if he is capable," Iriam said quietly.

"No!" Mel yelled this time, staring down the line at Aryion. The ranger's face was impassive, absolutely calm. Not a trace of fear. But he couldn't win. However long the fight lasted, there was no way he would win, not while Hagshrub was immortal under the spell.

And he knew this was exactly what the Ace-Deputy had planned. For the first time, true fear showed on Iriam's face. It was an uneven match, but the Ace-Deputy's choice was well within the rules.

Hagshrub stepped forward, carrying his heavy iron mace. An ugly smile spread over his face as he looked at the ranger. "Well, well. It truly is a small world," he said. "Have you been tracking me all these years? I suppose you had to—you can't give up on a Blood Oath, can you?" A ripple of ugly laughter ran through the orc army. The Ace-Deputy smiled.

Iriam stepped back. He had run out of words. The battle hung on the hope that somehow, the reinforcements would arrive in time to put up a last, futile defense of the Shard.

"Square up, you two," the Ace-Deputy said, almost cheerfully. There was no need—Aryion and Hagshrub already stood facing each other, both holding their weapons. "On my mark… prepare… begin."

The words were spoken in a low voice, but they carried to every listening ear. The second the last syllable died away, Aryion lunged forward, his sword a blur as he landed a series of rapid blows, each plunging between the cracks of Hagshrub's armor. The orc chieftain took a startled step back. A brief cheer rose from the watching Kamoni, but it died just as fast. There was no blood—the injuries simply healed themselves as the immortal orc stepped forward, unconcerned.

Aryion parried the orc's first blow, ducked under another slash, and cut across Hagshrub's face. Hagshrub barely reacted and swung his mace at the ranger's head. Aryion stepped backward, then parried the next blow with a ringing crash.

Mel's heart was in his mouth. The unfairness of the fight infuriated him. Aryion could have won. He should have won already. But the enchantment guaranteed that Hagshrub could—and would—fight for however long was needed. In fact, watching the orc's calm movements, Hagshrub clearly intended to simply wear the ranger to exhaustion, then finish him.

The Ace-Deputy's voice distracted him for a moment. "Captain Irshkhân, return to your task. Be swift."

Irshkhân nodded and barked an order to the Jenna soldiers, who started forward again.

Iriam swung around, disbelief on his face. "This fight is halted for as long as the duel lasts! You cannot go back on your word, Ace."

"The fight is halted?" the Ace-Deputy repeated dryly. "That wasn't part of our deal, was it? No, the agreement was the winner of this duel gets the Shard, and that the wounded will be kept out of the fight. Nothing was said about pausing this battle, or the fate of the survivors."

Iriam's face was livid. Ice sparkled on his fingertips. He started toward the Ace-Deputy, stopped, and instead turned his attention to the Jenna warriors.

The islanders had drawn back with a startled cry as they saw the approaching attackers. Irshkhân led his warriors forward, a wicked smile on his face. Mel shoved the Shard into his pocket and drew his knife. Now was the time. They would have to fight, or all be killed.

"Retreat!" Leelo ordered. "Up into the trees!"

The Kamoni warriors backed away, walking up the spiral staircase that led to the upper village above.

"Remember your people, chieftain," Quinn said uneasily. "We don't want to lead them into the village."

"Hardly anyone remains up there. We can better counter the Jenna from above," Leelo told him briskly. "They can only ascend the steps one at a time."

A flicker of hope lit in Mel's chest. Leelo was right. Now that the wounded had all been moved away, only a few villagers were still in the homes above.

"Barricade the townspeople in the hospital huts," Leelo ordered. "Guard them there. As for the Jenna, let us see how light-footed they are now."

There was a resounding cry of assent from the Kamoni warriors. They sprinted up the steps and sprang along the boardwalks, fleet-footed as deer.

"Let's go, Mel," Jarus said, and the two of them ran up the stairs after the Kamoni defenders.

Leelo was giving orders. His earlier hesitation to fight had vanished with the urgency of the moment. "Archers, go to the pavilion. Open the windows and shoot any Jenna that tries to come up this way. I need thirty men to guard the roads leading to the homes. Another twenty of you, go to the southern cliffs and defend the staircase there. The rest of you, with me."

The Kamoni, used to the brisk orders aboard a ship, split themselves into their respective groups and obeyed swiftly. By the time the first Jenna reached the steps, the defenders were in place.

Mel and Jarus ran after Leelo and the remaining ten islanders in their group. Behind them, the archers in the pavilion launched a volley of arrows upon the Jenna that tried to follow them up the stairs. Most of the arrows met their targets. Jenna warriors screamed in pain and toppled back down the stairs, falling on their companions.

"Where are we going, sir?" Jarus panted to Leelo.

"The Shard must be guarded," Leelo said. "We must reach it before the Jenna do."

"I have the Shard," Mel cried, grabbing his arm. "I have it with me."

Leelo looked at him. Disbelief, then distrust, showed in his eyes. "How did you get it?"

"I—I grabbed it at the start of the battle," Mel stammered quickly. "I saw it a few days ago, and when the fighting started I figured one of us should keep an eye on it. I'm sorry I didn't tell you." This wasn't entirely true, but the truth was too long to explain right now.

Leelo let out a breath. "No—that was a wise decision. In that case, stay close, and guard it with—"

"With my life, yep. I will," Mel finished for him. He was getting a little tired of hearing that.

The archers shot from their position in the pavilion, dispatching many Jenna warriors, but in the gaps of time between volleys, the Jenna surged up the steps and onto the boardwalks. Whooping and howling like wolves, they ran along the bridges, clashing with any Kamoni they met.

"Back to the pavilion," Leelo said to Mel, watching the throng of Jenna as they swarmed through the town. "Stay with the archers until the fight is over."

Mel was about to argue, but decided against it. He ran along the boardwalk leading back toward the beach. To his right, the Jenna clashed with a group of Kamoni led by Leelo. Swords flashed, spears stabbed, and several Jenna toppled off the boardwalk. While the Jenna were surefooted, the momentum of the islanders overcame them and forced them back.

The road Mel was on ran parallel to the one that many Jenna were currently on. Ten paces in front of him, the boardwalk intersected four ways, with the pavilion straight in front of him. But as he ran, he saw a Jenna warrior leave the main body of invaders and jog toward the intersection to cut him off. Mel's heart pounded in fear as he recognized Irshkhân.

The Jenna chieftain's eyes were wild with battle rage. "Going somewhere, New Blood?" he hissed. He smiled, showing his black teeth.

Mel spun back to the intersection and turned onto a boardwalk leading back towards Leelo. Irshkhân sprinted after him, snarling. For an instant, Mel thought about turning and fighting. But he knew he didn't stand a chance against the Jenna chieftain. Irshkhân was older than he was, older and far more experienced in the art of killing. And if Mel was captured, the Shard would be lost too.

Ahead of him, he saw another host of Jenna moving to cut him off. Frantically, he turned onto the next wood path, leading deeper into the village. Irshkhân came after him. His long stride carried him swiftly after Mel. Mel could almost feel his hot breath on the back of his neck, and panic rose inside his chest.

"Help!" he cried, turning onto another path, which led toward the now empty café. "Help! Aryion!" His shrill voice carried over the village. He could not outrun this Jenna. He would be caught, and they would all die. But Aryion was not here to protect him now, as he had been before on the quest. A sound halfway between a sob and a scream rose in Mel's chest, a cry of total desperation. Irshkhân's hand seized the back of his collar just as he entered the café, ripping him backward.

"I'll have the Shard now," the Jenna hissed in his ear. Mel squirmed—there was nothing he could do, no one to come help him.

Then a sword flashed out of nowhere, slashing down the length of Irshkhân's arm and across his shoulder. The Jenna let go of Mel and sprang back, startled—Mel fell sprawling on the floor of the café and looked back.

Cloak billowing, sword glittering, in the same way he had come to save Mel from the serpentine in Appledale months before, Rygal stood in the doorway of the café. His hair was wild, tangled, his face haggard and thin. But there was a fire in his eyes that sent hope surging into Mel's heart.

"You keep away from him," Rygal said hoarsely, glaring at Irshkhân.

The Jenna chieftain seemed stunned by the sudden appearance and attack. But only for a moment—he raised his sword and sprang forward with a growl, clashing with Rygal. They struggled against each other before separating, then they charged each other again. Their swords clashed, the resounding clang of steel on steel filling the little room. Mel struggled to a sitting position, exhausted, watching the fight breathlessly.

Rygal lunged, his sword grazing across Irshkhân's side. The Jenna stumbled back out of the way, cursing the pain, then sprang forward. His blade slashed across Rygal's ribs. Blood streaked Rygal's side, but he barely seemed to notice it, and swung at Irshkhân's head.

The Jenna ducked under the blow, then sprang forward and punched Rygal full in the face. The force of the punch, reinforced by the steel gauntlet that Irshkhân wore across his knuckles, was devastating. Rygal fell back against the wall. This probably saved his life, as his stumbling caused Irshkhân's blade to miss his heart. Irshkhân snarled in frustration, then raised his sword again as Rygal caught his breath.

Mel forced himself to his knees and hurled his knife at the Jenna's back. The little blade slapped uselessly across Irshkhân's shoulder, and he turned sharply, eyes blazing as he came at Mel.

Mel shrank to the floor, helpless and weaponless before the furious chieftain. Irshkhân's boot made contact with his face, knocking him flat on his back. He blacked out for an instant—when his vision focused again, he saw Irshkhân raise his sword. Any orders the Aces had given not to harm the New Blood were gone now—the Jenna's eyes were wild, maddened, as he prepared the final blow.

Then he stumbled forward with a choking hiss. Rygal's sword plunged into his back, impaling him through. The tip of Rygal's sword poked through the Jenna's front—Irshkhân clawed at it, unable to register the fatal wound for a moment. Then Rygal swung him around, flinging him out the door. Irshkhân teetered on the edge of the boardwalk, then toppled backward. Whether he died first of his injuries or from the fall, Mel never knew, nor did he care.

Rygal took a step back, then sank painfully to the floor, breathing hard. His face was bruised and bloodied, and he was bleeding heavily from two separate gashes on his chest. Mel tried to sit up—the world spun, and he fell on his side, blood running from his nose and down his face. "Thank you," he managed to whisper.

Rygal's eyes opened a crack. There was no sign of the old Rygal there, nor was the shadowed shell of the man he had become over the last few weeks either. This was a new man, loyal and brave as ever, broken but healed. "I couldn't save Norrin," he rasped. "But I had to save you." He closed his eyes, then continued. "I'm so sorry. Tell Aryion… I'm sorry."

The distant sounds of battle grew louder. Mel knew they had lost. Even if Aryion had, by some miracle, beaten Hagshrub, the Kamoni could not stand against so many Jenna. Yet he did not feel afraid. Cahadras had been right. The High Light knew how the story would end. And Mel was glad now that He had seen fit to have Mel guard the Shard—for had it not been so, he never would have seen Rygal restored.

His spinning headache from Irshkhân's kick took over his vision, and his eyes began to close. There were voices outside—loud ones, excited ones, triumphant voices. But… not Jenna snarls. He recognized one, quite close, yelling in excitement. Jarus' voice.

"The Coopers! The Coopers have come!"

The cacophony of battle sounds grew louder and louder, until he finally closed his eyes and was left spinning in a silent black oblivion.

21

Aftermath

A ray of light shone through Mel's eyelids, cutting through the darkness and drawing him back to the waking world. The pleasant smell of flowers and tropical fruit reached his nose, making him aware of how hungry he was. He opened his eyes. He was laying on his back in a bed, the soft white blankets pulled up over him. The curtains hanging over the window at the foot of the bed were open a crack, allowing the bright light inside.

He blinked, still groggy, trying to remember where he was.

"Mel? Are you awake?" Jarus' voice came from the left, and Mel looked over quickly. The Cooper was sitting on an empty bed next to Mel's. He looked exhausted, but smiled widely when he saw Mel awake.

"What happened?" Mel mumbled. His voice was thick and muffled through his incredibly swollen nose. He reached inside his trouser pocket, which was—empty. The Shard!

He sat bolt upright, then winced as the movement started the headache over again. "The Shard," he groaned, lying down again as everything came back to him. "The battle—Jarus, I lost the Shard."

"Iriam has it," Jarus reassured him. "Iriam has the Shard. You've been out since yesterday afternoon."

Mel let out a sigh of relief. "Then we won?"

"Yep, we won. Though we wouldn't have, if a fleet of ships hadn't come down the Strait from the Southern towns just in time. And not just them." Jarus added eagerly. "Lord Roan of the Coopers sent a battalion of the best warriors from Mata City, thirteen of our fastest ships, with the newest design." He grinned proudly. "You should have seen it, Mel. Apparently Gareth—he was the man who led the group that went to Elimar, remember? Well, he sent word to Mata City letting them know what we were doing. Lord Roan figured we'd need help, so he sent his ships south. They got here just in time, I can tell you that."

"So—the orcs just left?"

"The Ace-Deputy ordered a retreat. The orcs might be immortal, but once the Coopers got here, there was total panic. So they left."

A memory hit Mel like a thunderbolt. "Aryion—Jarus, what happened to—"

"He's fine," Jarus said reassuringly. "Hagshrub backed out of the duel the minute the Coopers showed up, and tried to run. Aryion started to pursue him, but then let him go so he could help you. He found you and Rygal both injured in the café."

Mel let out a breath of relief. "What about everyone else? Are the other companions all right? What about Jan? Where's Rygal?"

"And I thought Jarus was bad for asking too many questions," came a familiar voice to Mel's right.

Mel turned. Rygal was sitting up slightly in the bed next to Mel's.

He looked pale and tired, his face patterned with dark bruises and cuts, and there were bandages wrapped across his chest and side. But he was smiling. The very sight of him sent a surge of joy through Mel.

"Rygal—you're all right! I wasn't sure—I thought—" he trailed off.

"I'll be fine. A bit sore, though I guess that's to be expected. And I wish I could thank Irshkhân for that punch." Rygal shook his head. The wry humor and crooked smile offered a promising glimmer of the old friend he had known, and Mel felt himself smile too.

"All seven of us are still alive," Jarus continued. "Most of us made it out with only a few cuts and bruises. Quinn got a nasty knock on the head from an orc towards the end of the fight, but he'll be okay." He hesitated for a moment. "Jan took it pretty bad. Broke two ribs, though thankfully there was no injury to his back. But we'll have to stay in Kamon for a few more days until he's well enough to travel again." The Cooper smiled at him. "And as for you two, I think you gave everyone a scare, Mel. But you held onto the Shard, and you made it through."

"Not alone," Mel said, with a thankful grin at Rygal. Then he turned back to Jarus. "What happens now?"

"Nothing for a little while," Jarus said. "Everyone who isn't injured has been helping in the cleanup of the battle. Once that's past, we'll have to figure out our next move." He stood. "I have to get going now. Do you need anything?"

"Well, I'm pretty hungry," Mel said with a rueful smile. "Can you bring me some food? No rush—just when you get the chance," he added.

"All right. Rest up, you two," Jarus said, and left the hospital room, opening the curtains on his way out. The fresh midmorning light made the room feel even more cheery.

"Where were you during the battle?" Mel asked after a moment.

"In every place I shouldn't have been," Rygal said softly. His gaze was distant. "I wanted to find the Ace leading the fight—I wanted to kill him. I was with Leelo's group when they defended the market from the first group of attackers. And… I thought about what was happening, Mel. About what we were fighting for." He looked down at his hands. "I realized I was just fighting for the sake of it. I wasn't thinking about our quest, or saving lives. In that moment, I was no better than the mercenary Jenna."

His simple honesty gratified Mel. "So… then what?" he prompted softly, as Rygal trailed off.

"I went back to the inn. There were townsfolk trapped there by some Jenna, and I helped get them out. When the duel started, I realized that the Ace was trying to capture you—what better way to make sure your guardian couldn't protect you than to involve him in a fight over a Blood Oath? So then I tried to find you. It took me a little while."

"You saved my life," Mel said. "It doesn't matter what you did before." He meant it. Rygal had been lost to them for weeks, following Norrin's death. Now that he was back, Mel could not hold those weeks of sorrow against him.

"Yes, well, there's no excuse for my actions. I am truly sorry." Rygal let out a breath, as though each word was painful. "When I realized… how I was acting… I thought about what Norrin would think, if he knew. I knew it wasn't how he would have wanted me to act."

"I bet he would have been really proud of you, though," Mel told him. Rygal smiled slightly. Tears shone in his eyes.

Naomi came in after a few minutes, bringing lunch for each of them. She checked Mel's swollen nose. "It will mend, but you have suffered a concussion with it. Try to avoid strenuous activity as long as you can," she said, then looked at Rygal. "As for you, you'll have to go easy on yourself for a while, or you will burst the stitches. Go slow and careful."

"I'm not very good at either, but I'll do my best," Rygal said, lying flat on his back.

Naomi shook her head in his direction, but Mel saw her blush.

"I think she likes you," he said to Rygal once Naomi had gone.

Rygal raised his eyebrows. "Don't you start with that. You're as bad as Aryion. You wouldn't know it, but that ranger is the worst matchmaker."

Mel laughed.

They ate lunch, then with permission from Naomi were allowed out of bed. Mel was anxious to check on the other injured companions. Jan was in the room across from Mel and Rygal's, and Aryion was visiting him when they arrived.

The Liznee king was recovering slowly. Breathing was easier for him, but talking was still painful, so he mostly listened.

"How are you feeling?" Mel asked him.

"Better. How is your nose?" Jan asked. His voice was weak, but he looked so glad to see Mel that it made him look stronger.

"It should be fine. They said it wasn't broken," Mel said, and looked up at Aryion. "Do you know where Jarus is?"

"He's down on the beach. A battalion of Cooper soldiers stayed behind after the battle, and they're helping repair some boats," Aryion told him.

"Is he? Maybe I'll go down there to help," Rygal said. "I need something to do. I've laid in bed too long."

"I thought you were supposed to stay in bed," Jan said, shaking his head.

"And I though you weren't supposed to talk, but here we are. Jarus said you're already trying to plan some sort of war council," Rygal said with a wry grin.

"Fair enough," Jan said, and lay back with a smile.

"Did Jarus tell you about the end of the battle, Mel?" Aryion asked.

"Yep," Mel said with a nod. "Sounds like the Coopers came to the rescue. I wish I could have seen it."

"It was magnificent," Jan remarked with a smile.

"There were close to thirty ships," Aryion said. "The Jenna left almost immediately. The orcs stayed a little longer to fight, but they were outnumbered and in the end they fled."

"With the Ace," Ĵan muttered in frustration.

"The Ace-Deputy escaped too? Is that… really bad?" Mel asked uneasily.

Aryion shrugged uncertainly. "Well…not really. Still, the fewer Aces there are left alive, the better. And that Ace commands the army—he will likely cause trouble later."

Ĵan nodded but said nothing more. They spoke less of the battle after that, talking of days gone by and remembering peaceful years before any of them had drawn a sword in battle.

Naomi came in and insisted Ĵan get more rest. Aryion and Mel walked for a moment down the wooden plank roads. It was nearly dusk, and the sky was already starting to turn red in the west.

Aryion paused a moment, staring northeast towards the mainland. "Well, I hear Iriam is already planning our return to Caer Sia. But we'll meet with Leelo first."

"What kind of meeting?" Mel asked, interested.

"I'm not sure," Aryion replied. "Iriam and Ĵan are planning something. We will likely learn more in the next few days, I think."

"Hopefully they have a plan of how we'll get into Caer Sia," Mel murmured.

The ranger nodded. "Yes. And how we will reunite the Shards, without the Ace-Lord catching us."

Mel let out a breath. "I didn't tell you what happened when we first got here—about how I first got the Shard." He quickly explained his encounter with Cahadras. Aryion looked startled to hear it. "I

don't really know what being the New Blood means yet," Mel finished. "But I do know, at least, that I'm supposed to be the one to reunite the Shards." He swallowed hard. The very idea was terrifying.

"You won't have to do it alone," Aryion promised quietly. "Like
Iriam told you before the Kamon battle. We, all of us, are standing
behind you." He gripped Mel's shoulder. "And I'm with you. Hagshrub will wait. This battle, this fight—it is much more important
than fulfilling a Blood Oath."

Mel smiled, heartened by the ranger's words. There was a moment
of silence as they both looked out over the sea, lost in their own
thoughts.

Aryion spoke again, slowly. "Mel… there's something I wanted to
ask you. After the quest, what will you do?"

Mel thought for a moment. "Well, I'll go back home. To Appledale. My twelfth birthday is this fall, you know—so I'll have to pick
a trade school to begin then."

"And… do you know what trade you will choose?" Aryion asked
after a pause.

"Not really," Mel admitted. He gestured at the scene around him.
"This is what I want to do—go on quests like this and protect the
kingdoms of Orlell. But I'm too young to train in the army. And my
parents want me to select a trade—I don't think they'd let 'questing'
count," he added with a grin.

Aryion smiled and looked down. "I just wanted to ask," he said.
"You have the skills, the bravery, and the brains that could make an

impressive warrior, which is a rare combination nowadays. Those traits are essential to ranger training, and—well, unless you want to choose a trade after the quest—that is, I wanted to ask…"

Mel looked up, excited. "Are you asking me if I'd want to train as a ranger?"

"Of course, if you don't want to, it's no matter," Aryion said quickly. "But—I've never had an apprentice, and you could become an incredible ranger with proper training."

Mel felt his face warm with Aryion's praise. Excitement coursed through him at the prospect of such a future. The trade of the rangers offered a life of action, heroism, cunning and planning, and learning the secrets of protecting the kingdom. All the same…he pictured his family, his home in Appledale, his home there. Those old times tugged at his heart. Fear of an unknown future made him hesitate to answer.

Besides, choosing such a trade wouldn't lessen the danger he was in currently. As the New Blood, the Aces would pursue him until they succeeded, or were defeated.

An urge, a call, similar to what he had felt after the battle with the Darkness so many months ago, nudged him toward the life of both adventure and solitude that Aryion offered. But was that what he wanted? More importantly… was that his purpose?

"I'd love to," he said finally. "But I don't know what I'm supposed to do—or what the Prophecy requires of me. So… maybe."

In the end, that was all he could come up with, and he was left lying awake far into the night thinking about it.

The next four days passed slowly. Mel couldn't help much with the construction and rebuilding around the village, so instead he helped Naomi and the other medics at the hospital. Most afternoons were spent cleaning dishes and delivering medicine or food to the many injured. Jarus was busy helping the other islanders most of the time, as was Quinn, so Mel spent his spare time with Aryion or Rygal. The three of them met on the evening of the fourth day in the hospital room Mel and Rygal shared.

"All the same, it was the Ace-Deputy," Rygal growled as Mel entered the room. "Imagine if we'd managed to capture him."

"Well, we'll probably get a chance to fight him again in Caer Sia," Aryion reminded him. "There are still ten Aces, not counting the Ace-Lord."

"Are you still frustrated about that?" Mel asked Rygal, grinning.

Rygal shook his head. "There's nothing we can do about it now, I know. Still, we might have got information out of him. Maybe about Dandio."

"D'you suppose the Aces are holding Dandio in Sia?" Mel asked.

"Yes, that would be likely, if…" Rygal cut himself off abruptly, and there was a moment of silence. Rygal hadn't finished, but Mel knew what he was going to say: If Dandio was still alive.

The long silence was broken as Aryion, thankfully, changed the subject. "Well… I have some interesting information for you both. I talked with Jan and Iriam last night, and got a better idea of what our plan is. Apparently there was a goblin—one of the servants to that Jenna chieftain Irshkhân—who was captured in the battle."

Rygal frowned slightly. "There's little reason for captives," he said, "and there's no reason at all for the Ace-Lord to ransom a minor servant."

"We don't want this captive for ransom," Aryion said. "This goblin surrendered to the Kamoni voluntarily. Later, they got more word out of him. Turns out, this goblin servant was there during the attack on Caer Sia—a first-hand witness to the battle. Ĵan was quite interested when he heard about it, and we are to hear the goblin's report tomorrow during the meeting."

Rygal raised his eyebrows, impressed. Mel didn't understand. "Why would that matter?" he asked. "I mean…the attack already happened, so why would a report of it be so important?"

"Because there's a lot about the attack we don't know," Rygal replied. "How the Aces got in, how bad the damage was, and—most importantly—what happened to the survivors. If we can get the answers to those questions, then we can start planning out the best way to enter the city to reunite the Shards."

Mel had a hard time falling asleep that night. The beginnings of an idea had begun to grow in his mind. He figured he should come up with some sort of plan, being both the New Blood and the one who would have to reunite the Shards. He didn't want any more people to die defending him. It was time for him to face his own fate—no matter what it would be.

The council took place the following morning, just after break-fast. They met in the pavilion, which was miraculously unharmed, thanks to the archers that had sheltered in it. One of the windows had been broken, but it let in a refreshing breath of sea air. Chairs had been set up around the round table.

Jan was seated and was talking to Leelo, who sat to his left. To Mel's relief the High King looked much recovered. The medic's treatments and Jan's own physical strength had saved his life, although there was still a secure bandage around his ribs. Iriam was on Jan's right. The rest of the companions entered and took their seats around the table. On Leelo's side of the table was Hasman and another islander, who had assumed command of the counter attack during the battle and was now the unofficial battle master.

Mel sat down on the far right side of the table, and Jarus sat down next to him. The Cooper looked excited. As Mel heard Jan and Iriam discussing battle strategies, and Quinn and Aryion talking about weapons, he had the strange sensation that he belonged here, alongside his comrades. These men—all of them were seasoned warriors, veterans to the cause. Now Mel had joined their ranks. Strangely enough, he had never felt more at home.

Iriam spoke to the ten people assembled. "Whatever news the captive brings, we must remain collected. Threats and intimidation will likely have an adverse effect—besides, we are hardly any more frightening than his previous master."

"You're too modest, Iriam," Jan said with a half-smile. "But this is true. This goblin might be the only hope we have to answer our questions."

Leelo turned to Hasman. "Bring in the prisoner," he said. Hasman nodded and moved to the door.

Mel glanced at the others. They all had the same expression—concerned, serious, yet cautiously hopeful. He straightened, tense with anticipation. They were about to interrogate a soldier who had witnessed firsthand the attack on the capital. It was worth hoping that he might also have news about the survivors. Most importantly, the goblin's news might just hold the key of how to join the Shards, and save Caer Sia.

22

The Fate of Caer Sia

Hasman reappeared in a few minutes, followed by two islander soldiers who led a small, pale creature in chains into the pavilion.

Mel had never seen this particular breed of goblin before. It wasn't muscular like the orcs, nor thin and wiry like some of the goblins he'd seen in Hagshrub's group. This goblin was short and thin, only around four feet tall, with tan-gray skin and a pale yellow mess of paltry hair. His ears drooped slightly at the ends, and looked somewhat like a pig's. He was clad in a stained, tattered tunic and a belt that was much too big for him. His eyes were round and watery and bulged slightly, giving him the appearance of a shrunken, scrawny, two-legged frog.

For a moment he stood there, gawking at the companions, then let out an unhappy whimper.

Iriam studied him for a moment, then spoke briskly. "Speak, and leave off with that whimpering. What is your name and rank in the Ace-army?"

The goblin gulped. His voice was stuffy and whining. "I am called Orig, sir, just poor old Orig. And I doesn't have a rank. Just clean stuff for Master, see?" He sniffed loudly.

"Tell us about your master, then," Ĵan said.

The goblin bobbed his head in his direction. He seemed unable to maintain eye contact for longer than a few seconds. "Captain Irshkhân, Master Irshkhân of the Aikala Jenna. Been his slave for ten years, I has."

"Well, you are his slave no longer," Ĵan informed him. "Your master was killed in the battle. You were not by his side when he fought, however."

"No, sir, not me, sir," Orig said. He did not show much remorse at the news of Irshkhân's death. Mel didn't blame him. The idea of serving the maddened Jenna chieftain for ten years made him almost feel sorry for the goblin captive.

"You allowed yourself to be captured," Ĵan said slowly, trying to ease more information out of the goblin. "Why?"

Orig blinked, thought for a moment, and shuffled his feet uneasily, making the chains clink.

"We are not going to hurt you," Iriam said. "If you answer our questions, you will be free to return to your homeland. But," he added, as Orig's face broke into a hopeful grin, "we will not tolerate lies. Any information you have in regards to the battle in Caer Sia is vital to us."

The name of the capital made Orig visibly wince. "Sia, Sia," he muttered unhappily. "There isn't much of it now, you know. Awful, really awful, but we did gets some good wine there." He brightened. "Good wine. The Jenna drank most of it."

"Well, we're past the worst of the news, I suppose," Ĵan said dryly. "But tell us. How did the attack happen?"

Orig paused, thinking how best to begin, then spoke. "It was cold an' gray when we got close to Sia. I didn't hear much about the plan itself. My orders were to stay with the Jenna during the battle. I didn't have no option here, y'see, sirs," he added hastily. "I didn't want to fight. When the news was out that we'd be attacking, every-body else got real excited about it—especially the orcs." He frowned. "But then, the orcs don't really have a say what they do. They aren't like the Jenna."

"They are enchanted, you mean? With the immortality spell?" Ĵan asked.

Orig nodded. "Enchanted, yeah, that's what. But I'd call it cursed." He wrinkled his nose. "Master Irshkhân didn't want nothing to do with it. None of the Jenna wanted it."

"Why not?" Aryion asked slowly.

"Well, they're not just immortal, you know," Orig said. "The spell—curse—it changes 'em. They know everything about fight-ing, every way to kill. Kinda enhances their overall performance in battle." He looked uncertain. "But they don't have a single memory of their past. They don't even remember who a person was in their lives, not even family."

"But… that spell is not on all of the orcs," Aryion said. He looked confused.

Mel looked at him, not understanding the ranger's logic. "How do you know?"

"Hagshrub knew me," Aryion said. "When we fought—he knew who I was. He was immortal, yes, but he still had his memory."

At Hagshrub's name, Orig nodded quickly. "I heard Captain Hagshrub didn't get his mind wiped—he just got half of the curse, I guess. Maybe the Aces needed his mind clear so he could get the Shard. Or somethin' like that." He frowned, looking uneasy. "I'm not sure why."

Leelo rubbed his chin thoughtfully. "I wonder if the Ace-Lord would let the leaders of the army—the captains—keep their memories, if only to keep their minds clear. The other servants are blood-thirsty, but not especially cunning—you saw how easily they fell victim to our traps on the beach."

Mel wasn't sure that was right either. The companions had already noticed that the other orc captains were enchanted, as shown in the previous battles. For Hagshrub to receive only the enhancements of the spell was unusual.

"We will have to see," Ĵan said, and looked at Orig again. "This enchantment is not on any of the Jenna, then?"

Orig nodded quickly. "Yeah, there was no spell binding the Jenna. Master Irshkhân wanted it so. The spell can only happen if you're willing, and Master didn't want nothing holding his people. He just wanted the payment they'd get after the battle. The Ace-Lord didn't like that, but he agreed." He shivered at the name, and Iriam turned to him sharply.

"You have seen the Ace-Lord? What is he like?"

"Oh, he's dreadful," whimpered Orig. "All tall and black. But…
he can make himself look like whatever he pleases. Usually though,
he's tall and black, and wears a crown. And he looks like something
dead. Ghostly, that's what." He shivered again.

Orig's description had not been all too helpful, since he had basically described an average Ace, but Jan didn't push it. "Forgive our
interruptions. Please continue."

The goblin nodded obediently and picked up the story. "Well,
there'd been a plan made up by another man—though he wasn't
under the spell. The Ace-Lord needed him to think clear, so he
devised the strategy. Hagshrub liked it, but Irshkhân thought it was
too careful. He wanted to charge headlong into the city, thinking
everyone would just run."

"You know that the opposite would happen," said Jan in a dangerous voice. Orig nodded his head rapidly.

"I knows this. Irshkhân eventually was convinced of it too, so we
stuck with the plan. We headed to the city. As I said before, it was
cold and gray. And when we got there, there was this big event happening." He glanced at Jan. "You knows of this holiday event, sire?"

Jan frowned as well and shook his head slightly. "No, we have
none at that time of year. Describe it."

"There was a coffin," Orig said. "Covered in flowers. But no body.
And no grave. The people were crying though, and they was saying… they was saying things like, 'High Light watch you, Dandio,'
and 'What on Orlell will we do without you?'"

The name hit Mel in the stomach, but he didn't know what event Orig could possibly be describing. But Ĵan had flinched—his face, previously calm, was blank with shock. It was so rare to see any fear on Ĵan's face at all that a sinking sensation of dread ran through Mel. He could not speak, too afraid to voice his questions, too afraid to know the answer.

"What…what was happening, Ĵan?" Jarus asked tentatively.

Ĵan took a deep breath. "It was a traditional service called a *tumral*," he said. "When a warrior goes missing in action, his second-best sword is placed in a coffin, which is then covered in flowers. After some brief words, the coffin is burned." His eyes were distant as he spoke the next words. "That service was for Dandio."

It took Mel a moment to realize what this implied. All this time, they had assumed Dandio had been captured by the Aces. But now the reality that he could have been killed on his journey home was out in the open, and it seemed terribly likely. Dandio could be dead. The stubborn hope in Mel's heart faltered.

Aryion turned to Ĵan. "Do you believe Dandio is dead, then?" he asked quietly.

Ĵan spoke stiffly, as though every word was torn from him. "We… have little hope of believing he is alive. He could have been killed by the Aces months ago, or by something else." Then he straightened abruptly, and the familiar light of determination was back in his eyes. "On the other hand, we have no evidence proving that he is dead, and I know for a fact it takes a lot to kill Dandio. I shall not stop hoping unless I see his body with my own eyes."

There was hope in his words, and Mel was able to relax. But only a little.

Orig hesitated a moment before continuing. "Hagshrub ordered the charge, and everyone started moving at once. I just followed master Irshkhân, because I didn't know what else to do. But he was running faster than me, and I fell behind. By the time we were out of the trees, the people had seen us. A lot of them had weapons, and soldiers came from the castle. They started to fight, or protect the women and children. The orcs went first, and the Jenna followed, since they weren't about to get themselves killed for no reason. Then I saw a woman turn to fight them—a Liznee, tall and dark-haired."

"That would be Dandio's wife Ajaha," Jan said, and his voice was tight with anticipation as he waited to hear of her fate.

"Yes, well, she didn't run. She tried to fight. She blasted two orcs with that red lightning stuff you Liznees shoot, and tried using a dagger. But Hagshrub got behind her and grabbed her arms, then chained her up. The other orcs were jeering her, but they wouldn't get too close. Hagshrub took her away. That was when another girl, this one a lot younger, went after them. She had a sword—the same sword that had been in the coffin. She looked a lot like the woman though."

"And that would be Dandio's daughter Asescia," Jan said, sounding even more worried.

"And she started fighting, too," Orig said in awe. The idea of anyone opposing Hagshrub was extraordinary to him. "She didn't shoot any lightning, but she did use that sword, and cut a big gash on Hagshrub's side. The other orcs went after her, and she fought them, but once she realized they couldn't die, she started retreating. The other woman yelled at her to run, so she did, still carrying the sword."

"So she escaped?" Jan asked.

"I'spose so," Orig said. "She ran towards the east guard tower. But…that got torn down, sirs," he said hesitantly. "The towers around the courtyard were torn down. Ten Aces were there, not counting the Ace-Lord, and they blasted the walls down. But they left the castle standing, and I saw the Ace-Lord come up the steps into the courtyard. That was where the orcs brought the survivors."

"And Ajaha?" Iriam asked.

"She was taken to the courtyard, with the other prisoners," Orig said. "I lost sight of her for a while—the walls came down and there was so much dust and smoke."

Mel felt a shiver of dread run down his spine. So Ajaha could be dead as well. Dandio, Ajaha, and Asescia. All royalty, all missing in action. Jan's face was white. He seemed to have lost the strength to ask any more questions—the agony of not knowing was written in his expression.

"I was in the courtyard for a while after that," Orig continued. "Keepin' an eye on things—with the Jenna. They stole most everything of value from the prisoners. The Ace-Lord went into the castle. His deputy stayed in the courtyard, and then I saw the Liznee woman again— whatever you said her name was."

"Ajaha," Jan said tensely.

Orig nodded. "Hm, right. Her. Forgot her name. Anyway, the Ace-Deputy walked up to her and started askin' her questions. He wanted to know about a Shard, and a scroll."

"A scroll?" Mel echoed, though he could already guess what the Aces were seeking. The second copy of the Prophecy—likely, the only surviving copy.

The goblin nodded impatiently, looking annoyed at the interruptions. "Yeah, and I was confused too. 'We're here to get the Shard, not a scroll,' I thinks to myself. But turns out, the Ace-Lord wanted both all along. I'm not sure why he didn't tell everyone else, though. The part about the scroll was kept a secret."

"What about Ajaha?" Jan demanded.

"Well, the Ace-Deputy walks up to her—she was kneeling down, chained up. And he says *'What is your name, woman?'* So, she tells him. And then he says, *'You wear the garb of a courier. Thus, you are learned in the matters of history, are you not?'* And the Liznee woman sort of nods. She just looked angry. But the Ace-Deputy kept asking her questions. *'What do you know of the Prophecy of Three?'* he asks. *'Where are the scrolls of prophecy kept in the palace?'* But she didn't tell him anything. Then he… he grabbed her and pulled her up, dragged her inside the castle. I don't know what happened to her."

The sinking feeling returned to Mel's chest, but he knew it was nothing compared to the fear Jan had to be feeling at this moment.

There was a long pause before Iriam spoke. "What have they done with the prisoners?"

"They kept 'em below, in the dark," Orig said with a shiver. "At least, everyone in the castle is kept down there. Nobles and soldiers and such. But they can't fit all the civilians in there, so the Ace-Lord lets them stay in their homes—as long as they stay there."

"Could any of them have escaped the city?" Iriam asked.

"Doubt it. There's a patrol of orcs that guard all the main roads," Orig told him. "They're under orders to kill anyone that tries to leave the city. At night, the Jenna are allowed to… to enforce curfew, as Master Irshkhân called it. They kill anyone they catch out on the streets after dark. And they plunder anything that isn't already broken."

Mel let out a deep breath. The infiltration into Caer Sia was beginning to sound more and more impossible. The city was under constant watch—orcs by day, Jenna by night, and likely the Ace-Lord keeping an eye on every minute in between. "Do you know anything about the Shard, Orig?" he asked.

The goblin looked at him, slightly surprised. "The Shard? Not particularly. The Ace-Lord got it sometime during the battle—or rather, he had someone get it for him. The Aces can't touch the Shards, you know."

Mel nodded. "Yep, we know. But where do they keep it? Is it in the castle?"

"Dunno," Orig said with a shrug. "I think the Ace-Lord stays with it all the time. Probably been keepin' it in the same place as the scrolls they found."

"The scrolls?" Mel said, sitting up straight as he caught the plural. "What scrolls? Where did they get them? What's the Ace-Lord doing with it?"

Orig flinched back under the onslaught of questions. Jan and Iriam had also reacted at the news. Iriam leaned over the table. "Orig, this is of the utmost importance. If you have any news about the scrolls or the Shard, you must tell us."

Orig fidgeted with the hem of his filthy tunic. "The… the Ace-Lord keeps both of 'em somewhere in the castle. I don't know where. No one was allowed. No one is allowed to wait on the Ace-Lord anyway—only the Ace-Deputy. But I know one of the other Aces put the other scroll in there too."

"Two scrolls?" Jan said, incredulous.

Mel's mind was racing. This could only mean one thing—both copies of the Prophecy of Three were now in Caer Sia. But why? Why hadn't the Ace-Lord just destroyed it, as they had first thought? If the Prophecy held the hope of the mortals… then why let it exist at all?

Then the answer came to him. Cahadras' words from the council in Flora echoed in his mind: *"Deception is the Aces' strongest trait."*

"They're not going to destroy the Prophecy," he said out loud, and the others looked at him. "They're going to twist it. The Ace-Lord knows he can't counter the words of the High Light—so he's going to spread his version of the Prophecy instead, one where it looks like he wins."

The Ace-Lord could not destroy or combat the hope of the Prophecy. He was smart enough to see it as a threat. So instead, he would taint it. Poison it. Replace its truths with his lies and offer it as proof of his victory—and under such words, the world would fall.

But the realization, though dark, planted an idea that began to take root in Mel's mind.

"What is the state of Caer Sia now, Orig?" Iriam asked.

"Well, the Ace-Lord keeps to himself in the castle, like I said," Orig replied. "The other Aces keep inside during the day. They don't like the sunlight, but they'll go out at night. The Ace-Deputy brings the words of the Ace-Lord to the townsfolk every few days, and he always offers the chance to join the Ace-army."

"As if they would," Quinn said doubtfully, but Orig shrugged.

"A lot of them have, actually. Under the enchantment, they can forget about everything. They can walk the streets freely, feel the wind on their faces. They have freedom."

"Freedom through bondage," Jan mused. He shook his head. "The choice would have to be made eventually. If they believe that the Ace-Lord is the right side to join with, nothing can change their minds. I do know that we will accept them back, if they manage to escape that bondage."

Iriam looked at Orig and nodded slightly. "Thank you for your report. You are free, but know that should you return to the Aces, you will be considered an enemy. Go east, back to the desert lands, and stay clear of Coonsia."

Orig nodded rapidly, looking very grateful.

The Kamoni guards led the goblin out of the room again. Silence fell for a few moments.

"What will we do, Iriam?" Quinn asked finally. "I fear that any attempt to go north would only succeed in giving the Ace-Lord the second Shard."

Iriam nodded slowly. "We will have to enter secretly. But even if we avoid the patrols, I doubt we could avoid being seen by the Ace-Lord. He will be watching for us."

"No," Mel said softly. "He'll be watching for me. He knows I'll come with the Shard." He let out a deep breath, trying to put his thoughts into words. "If the Ace-Lord knows the Prophecy, he's going to do everything he can to make sure I fit myself into his interpretation of it. It's exactly what he's done up till now—making us seem to do the right thing, even though we're just following his plan. Like what Cahadras said at the council."

"What can we do against that, then, except avoid his plan?" Jarus said.

"No, that's what he expects," Mel said. "I won't. I'll do what he wants. He knows the New Blood is meant to join the Shards—he wants the Shards joined, not to save Caer Sia, but to channel the Dark Realm. The Aces can't join the Shards on their own. They need someone—a mortal." He swallowed. The words felt strange, but the confidence with which he spoke them filled him with determination. "They need the New Blood."

He saw the uneasiness on the faces of his companions—worry for him. Iriam's face was thoughtful. "The Blue Stone was given to the Cantrians," he mused. "It is fitting. The Aces need a Cantrian to rejoin the Shards, and thus become the Twelfth Ace."

Mel inhaled, calming his racing mind, and spoke calmly. "I need to join the Shards. Let me keep the Ace-Lord occupied, and you can use that time to get the prisoners free and deal with the Jenna. There are enough people in Caer Sia to fight—they just need the chance."

"Mel, think. You cannot stand alone against the Ace-Lord," Jan said uncertainly.

"I'm the New Blood," Mel told him firmly. "Isn't that what I'm supposed to do?" He looked at the other companions. "I think if all six of you try to come with me, the Aces will kill us all. But if I go… alone… I might be able to buy enough time for you to save the townsfolk… and maybe figure out how to defeat the Ace-Lord."

There was a long silence. Iriam spoke finally. "For this purpose you were chosen, but not by any of us, I think," he said grimly. "No, from what I have heard of your actions during the quest to return Drisilas, and from what I have seen of you thus far on this venture… it is fitting that it should be your task. The High Light has chosen you, Mel Smallbutton, to guard the Shard. Will you see this task through?"

Mel met his eyes. He felt nervous, uncertain, yet resolved. The High Light had chosen him. The High Light alone knew the end to his story… but the thought did not make him feel afraid. However it all ended, as long as he fulfilled his mission, as long as the Shards were joined and the people of Coonsia safe from the Aces… it didn't matter what happened to him.

That, he understood, was the heart of a hero.

"Yes," he answered. His voice was steady.

A slight smile of approval crossed the Neutral's face, and he nodded. "Very well. Then we must tarry here no longer. The time has come to return north."

PART 3

Caer Sía

23

The Task of the New Blood

Evening in Caer Sia…

Voices drifted into the half-conscious mind of the scribe master. Irritating voices. They had woken him from a dream, a pleasant dream in which he seemed to float in the darkness, while a face with violet eyes had spoken softly, gently, asking strange questions.

Questions he barely knew the answers to, but the face never seemed to grow angry.

Now he was no longer floating. Cold rock dug into his back, and cold iron gripped his wrists, sending brief flares of pain as he moved slightly.

The scribe master blinked, but the darkness behind his eyes was no different than the one in the waking world. He had no idea where he was. This was clearly not the library of Caer Sia, which was the only place he could remember at the moment. He had gone there to study, to tidy up, to sort and shift through the piles and piles of records that were held within the castle's library. And then… and then…

Nothing.

"Hello?" he called out. His voice was oddly hoarse, and it echoed through the darkness of the stone room. The echoes made him once again aware of the sounds that had drawn him back to reality. Someone was speaking a little ways away from him.

"I grow tired of asking this." That voice was familiar. The scribe master knew that this voice belonged to the face in his dreams. Yet the tone was no longer gentle—the words were harsh and lowered. "Isilas will not protect him from us, you know this. His sword has no strength against our master. We wish for all three Stones. Surely you know it would be better to hand it over."

A vague shuffling noise, then a choked cry—

"I cannot determine if you are too stubborn or too stupid to answer us. What can you possibly gain from remaining silent?"

A second voice, so weak it was hard to hear the words, croaked in reply. "Loyalty."

"A shame," said the first voice. There was a dull thump followed by another weak cry, this one in pain. "We will get the truth either way, Liznee," the first speaker said softly.

A faint white light flared somewhere in the strange stone passage. The scribe master squinted. The light showed a barred door, one of many in a dripping, dark maze of stone that made up the bowels of Caer Sia. The light cast a shadow on the wall of his cell—a hooded figure stooping toward someone on the ground.

The scream split the silence, and in the same instant the scribe master remembered. He remembered the cries in the streets, the toppling of the towers, the thousands of warriors that poured into the valley of the city where they killed everyone they could catch. He remembered turning away from the bookshelf, moving to the window to watch the invaders charge through the courtyard. Then he had turned away, rushing for the door of the library –

But a hooded stranger had stood there already, tall and shrouded, wearing the shadows of the room like a cloak and sending them billowing at his feet like smoke. He had said nothing—only taken the scribe master's arm and smiled so that the light glinted on a silver crown and the infinite darkness of the face beyond.

The scribe master sprang upright as the scream cut off. A shadow darker than those in the room ghosted its way through the door of his cell and swept toward him. The violet eyes flashed crimson.

His scream joined the echoes of the first.

. . . . . .

The room was empty again, aside from the bed and the colorful curtains. It had been prepared for the next guest who would come to the island, most likely on summer holiday or for a pleasant visit with family.

A week had passed since the battle, and while the logistics of war remained a tangled riddle, Kamon itself hardly showed signs of the struggle. The Coopers who had come after the battle had worked alongside the islanders for days, until the white sands and flowery coastline returned to its immaculate state.

Mel's satchel leaned against the door as he studied the room. Now that war had come and gone, and the attackers driven back to the north, the sensation of peace and serenity had returned to Kamon. He was sorry to leave it, with its beaches and sun and wide open sky.

Jarus was standing by the window, looking out across the island. A warm breeze blew in, ruffling his fur. "I'll miss this place," he remarked.

"Yes," Mel echoed. There was a pause. "I'd sure want to come back here," he added.

Jarus smiled. "Well, it's just south of Mata City. Perhaps we can plan a vacation here after this is all over. You'll travel to Mata City to meet my family, and then we'll all go south and stay at Kamon."

"Yes," Mel said eagerly. "And then we could travel over land awhile back to Appledale."

"Stop at Caer Sia along the way," Jarus put in.

"And maybe Elimar." Mel laughed. "Yeah, maybe that would work out."

"I'll check my schedule," Jarus said with a grin, but his face fell as they left the room. Talking about the future was a heavy subject. There was no telling what would happen in the next few days. The journey north was a treacherous one under normal circumstances. Even if they reached Caer Sia safely, the battle would have only just begun. The confrontation of Ace-Lord and the New Blood.

Mel let out a breath, trying to shake the dark thoughts from his mind.

The other companions were waiting on the beach, along with a small, two-mast boat docked for them. "Not the ferry?" Mel asked in surprise.

Rygal shook his head. "Not this time. We're getting out at the northern most point of the bay, miles from Barcoast. The fewer people that see us leave, the better."

Mel remembered the ferry master and the questioning glances of the other passengers on board the ferry. Rygal was right. If the Aces believed the companions were still on Kamon, they might not expect them to come so quickly.

It was a futile expectation, since Mel guessed that the Ace-Lord was not easily surprised. But it was better than arriving on the coat-tails of rumors.

A small crew of Kamoni sailors guided the slender ship out into the open sea and north, toward the wide mouth of the Strait. The day was warm but clouded. Jan was still recovering, and remained below decks, planning the rescue of Caer Sia's civilians with Iriam and Aryion. Jarus and Rygal were speaking in lowered tones by the starboard rail.

Mel leaned against the opposite rail, watching the waves roll by. He had too much on his mind to want to talk to anyone. By this point, his parents would have received his last letter—he had sent them a note right after the battle on Kamon. He had left out most of the details, only stating that there had been a change of plan which had delayed their journey to Caer Sia. This was partly true. The details of the battle itself could wait for another time. As for his role in the Prophecy... well, that was something he couldn't explain with paper and pen.

He looked up as Quinn walked over. The Elven ranger smiled at him and looked out over the water. "We are planning to fortify the city when we arrive," he said. "Jan hopes that the cannons on Sia's walls are still intact—if they are, we can turn them against the orcs."

"They might still be there," Mel said, remembering the line of cannons on the bulwarks of the castle. "If they weren't destroyed, the orcs won't know how to shoot them."

"True. I hope this is so," Quinn said. There was a few minutes pause, then Quinn spoke slowly. "I heard that Aryion offered to train you."

Mel looked up. "Oh—yes, he did. I just—I'm not sure what I want to do yet," he stammered. He hoped he hadn't offended either ranger.

But Quinn only nodded quickly. "That seems a wise choice. After all, none of us know what lies ahead."

Mel nodded, wishing he could explain his inner conflict. His hesitations about his future were only part of the problem. Choosing to be trained would likely include Aryion—and many other rangers—in the Aces' strategy to capture the New Blood. It could put more people in danger. But then, returning home to his family would do that too. In that case, his priority had to be defeating the Aces, and then he could finally feel safe. Rid himself of his pursuers once and for all. That made facing the Ace-Lord even more urgent than before. But even if he survived such an encounter, what after?

"I don't know what to do," he admitted finally, voice soft.

Quinn hesitated. "Mel…I know that it is still a long way off before we reach Caer Sia, but if I might offer you some advice…" he paused awkwardly, then continued. "Take Aryion up on his offer. He's never trained anyone, but I can say he's one of the best. Trained by him, you could become that skilled. And—well, you know Aryion. But his obsession over killing Hagshrub seems to have faded a little. He even talks about renouncing the Blood Oath."

"What?" Mel asked, stunned. "You can renounce a Blood Oath? How?"

"Most people don't," Quinn said slowly. "Under certain circumstances, a warrior can choose to renounce his Oath. In doing so, he gives up his sword as well, and essentially gives up on battle all together."

"Aryion wouldn't be a ranger, then," Mel said uncertainly. "Rangers can't just retire from fighting."

"True, but he seems to think it worth it. He could teach you what he knows and no longer have the Blood Oath dictating his life. It is a surprising choice, but he's been thinking about it." Quinn glanced down at him. "He's changed a lot since he met you, Mel."

"He has?" Mel asked in surprise. He hadn't realized the effect he'd had on the ranger. But now as he thought about it, he realized Quinn was right. When Mel had first met Aryion, the ranger had been grim and quiet, solemn and vengeful. But over the past weeks, he had become much more pleasant to be around. He smiled more often, talked less of killing. And now he thought it was worth giving up everything he loved about being a ranger if only to regain control of his own life.

Quinn was nodding. "Yes," he said quietly. "Go see your family, of course, after this is all over. But then it might benefit you to seriously consider Aryion's offer."

The thought lingered with Mel until the boat glided up against a small dock an hour or so later. There was no town here, just a few shacks and an old weathered dock. The companions disembarked, thanking the Kamoni islanders again for their help and hospitality. Then they turned and began the trek north.

After the weeks spent in the Kamon sun, Mel was chilled to the bone as they started walking. It grew cooler and cooler as they got farther from the tropical bay, and the sky clouded over. Eventually, Mel's body adjusted to the change in temperature, and as they walked, he warmed up. There were several mainland features that he loved just as much as Kamon, he realized—the smell of the wet leaves, the sun peeking through the dark clouds, the towering trees.

They stopped an hour or so before nightfall in a grove of dense hemlocks. Mel was so tired, mentally and physically, that he didn't eat any supper and was asleep seconds after lying down. The few dreams he had were scattered and incoherent, and he remembered nothing except feeling confused and frightened.

When he woke, his blanket was dusted in dew. Quinn had built a small fire, and Iriam was looking through the maps with Jan. The companions ate a quick breakfast, then started out again.

The day passed slowly. The road led steadily higher in elevation, away from the low-lying shores of the bay. Scrawny trees clung to the rocky ground, warped and twisted by the winds that tore through the gorge toward the sea. The companions toiled on, over each ridge, while the wind and sun beat down. By the time they stopped and took shelter in a small grove of trees for midday meal, Mel was out of breath, and his legs ached. He could tell the others felt the same.

But time was of the essence. The companions had thrown the Aces off their trail—for now—but stopping for too long could be dangerous. Remembering this gave Mel more energy, and he stood and resumed their brisk pace.

He passed the time talking with Jarus. The Cooper seemed just as eager as Mel was to forget about the upcoming struggle, so Mel listened to Jarus ramble on about Mata City.

After another hour or so, the forest opened out into a vast expanse of emptiness. The ground rolled over a gentle series of hills, a wide brown-gray sea with a fringe of green to the right. Low shrubbery and sage covered the ground, and wild daisies swayed in the light breeze. Mel tripped over a stump—the number of logs and stumps scattered over the ground suggested the existence of a forest here, once. Before the trees had been cut down and turned into homes for the southern settlements.

"Is that the Magno Forest?" he asked out loud, pointing toward the dark line of trees miles to the east.

Rygal nodded. "Part of it—the Old Wood, as they call it down here. And it used to be where the Darkness lived."

Mel looked up at him uneasily. "It was?"

Quinn answered from behind. "Few of us saw it there, but these roads were dangerous to travel at night. This used to be the fastest road from Kamon to Tinkeeyo, my hometown. It was too dangerous to travel in the days of the Darkness." He smiled at Mel. "It is only in the last few months that the road has become safe again. We have you to thank for that."

Mel grinned, a little embarrassed. "Well, at least we don't have to worry about the Darkness any more. But what if the Aces are there instead?" He didn't know much about the mind of the Darkness—if it had had one—and he knew even less about the plans of the Ace-Lord. But it made sense to him that if the Darkness had had a lair, the Aces might find shelter there to gather their forces.

"It is unlikely," Iriam said from ahead, "but it is a valid concern. That is why we intend to bear north, following this road, and then cut east once we are past the Darkness' old haunts."

They continued walking. Mel glanced at Jarus—the Cooper looked like he was thinking hard, but did not voice his ideas.

"What is it, Jarus?" Rygal asked presently.

Jarus looked up, frowning. "I didn't say anything."

"No, but you've been muttering to yourself for the last few minutes or so."

Jarus looked at Mel again. "It's just… I've been thinking, Mel."

"Write this down, Rygal. Jarus has been thinking," Mel teased with a grin.

The Cooper shook his head, ignoring the jibe. "I don't know if it works like this, but I wondered if you could tell us how you beat the Darkness. You and Jan," he added, raising his voice to carry to the Liznee king, who was walking in the back of the party.

"What do you mean?" Mel asked.

Jarus shrugged slightly. "The Darkness was a Netrocrian too, right? I mean—it's not exactly the same as the Aces, but we've already seen they have similar strengths—maybe they have similar weaknesses."

"I've been wondering that for a while too," Quinn said, looking at Mel and Rygal.

"I only watched from a distance," Rygal said, shaking his head, "and I could barely explain what happened even then."

They all looked at Mel. Mel shook his head slowly. "But we didn't beat the Darkness. You know that. The Ace-Lord ordered it to surrender."

"True," Jarus said. "But either way, it's dead now. And you held your own in that fight, obviously. Otherwise, why else would the Ace-Lord have ordered it to surrender?"

Mel hadn't thought of this. He couldn't claim defeating the Darkness as his own victory—no, the Ace-Lord had clearly made the wraith give up. But that had only been after Mel himself had entered the fight, after the Darkness had seized him and pulled him inside itself…

He shuddered as unwanted memories flooded his mind.

"Both the Blue Stone and the stone of Drisilas are deadly to the Aces," Ĵan said. "The only Star-Stone safe to them was the Jewel, since that stone was given to the Netrocrians."

Aryion, who was walking behind Mel, turned to face Ĵan. "We know that the Netrocrians cannot touch the Stones, at least not while the Stones are in their natural state. The Ace-Lord must have some plan to turn the Shards to his will, if he cannot touch them."

"I believe he does," Iriam said quietly from ahead. He said nothing more, but met Mel's eyes down the road. Mel's heart pounded as he understood. It seemed every day now he learned something more terrifying about what the Ace-Lord planned for him. There was another reason the Aces wanted him. Not just to be the New Blood that joined their forces—he would be the pawn used by the Ace-Lord to join the Shards, the mortal Cantrian required by the Prophecy. Then he would transform into an Ace when the Dark Realm's powers flowed through the Stones. The Twelfth Ace.

He could not find words to voice the truth now. "If… if the Ace-Lord wants the three Star-Stones, that means he wants Drisilas, too, right?" he stammered instead.

"Most likely," Ĵan said. One hand rested on the hilt of his sword.

"What about the Jewel?" Jarus asked. "We destroyed it."

"Not that it would matter to the Ace-Lord," Rygal said grimly. "He's the Lord of the Dead. The Jewel's power had to go somewhere when we broke it—it didn't just disappear."

There was a long silence. The road crested another ridge, and began a descent of switchbacks down the stone slope. Mel's boots skidded in the gravel, and he focused on the path. It was a difficult task thanks to the thoughts filling his mind.

"I agree with Jarus," he said. "The Aces will probably have some of the same weaknesses that the Darkness did. They can't touch the Stones, and they're vulnerable to fire." He glanced at the others. "Any other things we can think of?"

There was a pause. "Hope," Quinn said slowly, sounding a little puzzled. "After all, their greatest strength is the fear of mortals. They can't defeat hope."

"If only hope fit in a scabbard," Aryion said wryly.

"No," Rygal said, "but it fits in a scroll."

Mel looked at him, impressed. "What do you know about the Prophecy, Rygal?"

"Not much." Rygal let out a breath. "Norrin... Norrin talked about prophecies, sometimes. The messages of the High Light. He studied them, each and every one of them. I wish I'd paid better attention. But I do remember what he would say regarding them—that words are powerful, and words from the Land Immortal are even more so." He threw a crooked grin at Mel. "If you're one of those words, Mel, you'd do well to stop underestimating yourself."

These truths hit Mel in the chest, one after the other. He was startled to feel hope surging through his veins, warm and comforting, challenging the doubt in his mind. "Add hope to our list then," he said softly. "The Aces are weakened by fire, by the Stones, and by hope."

"And the New Blood," Aryion added with a half-smile. The other companions nodded and echoed their agreement. Mel blushed, but he was touched to see the faith they all had in him. He still felt daunted by the task ahead—rightly so, but it was easier knowing he had them all at his back.

• • • • • •

They set up camp in a small grove of trees as night fell. The sloping hills were left behind, and now all that remained was the flat, bare expanse of wilderness before they would enter the Magno Forest.

Mel and Aryion took first watch. Darkness fell quickly under the clouded sky. There were no stars, and the rising moon was visible only through a wreath of clouds. The two of them sat, backs to the fire, watching the shadows play across the open land.

"How far are we from Caer Sia?" Mel asked finally.

"I am not sure," Aryion answered. "Two days, maybe. We will enter the Magno Forest tomorrow, and those roads are better made, so our going may be faster."

"Good," Mel said softly, without much conviction. The faith of his companions was comforting, yes, but it didn't ease the worry he felt about facing the Ace-Lord. Iriam had carried the Shard since the Kamon battle. Mel was grateful to him. It was easier to keep his mind off such matters without a constant reminder in his pocket.

"Do you have a plan?" Aryion asked at length.

Mel let out a slow breath. "Oh, I'll figure something out."

Strangely, while he had given ideas for the companions to enter Caer Sia, he hadn't thought about his own strategy too much. Get in, join the Shards, get out without being killed. That summarized it. Much easier said than done.

"You know they will expect you," Aryion said.

"Probably. But I don't think they'll expect me to come by myself," Mel replied. He paused. "And I don't think they'll expect me to fight them. Every time I've seen the Aces, I haven't fought back. I just… run away."

"You are not planning to run, then?" Aryion asked.

"No," Mel said, putting as much fire as he could manage into that word. "I'm done running. Besides—if I want any sort of life after this quest is over, I'll have to face my job as the New Blood eventually."

Aryion nodded thoughtfully but said nothing more. They sat in silence for the remainder of their watch, listening to the distant moan of the wind as it whistled over the empty land. By the time Quinn and Jan relieved them of watch, a few stars had begun to shine through the clouds.

Despite the long walk, it took Mel awhile to fall asleep. He lay on his back, thinking about the Shards, and Caer Sia, and the Ace-Lord, for several hours. Finally, as the waxing moon broke through the clouds, he slipped into sleep.

24

An Ally of the North

"We may want to cut east now," Jan said.

The sun had just begun to rise, bathing the grove of trees in pale light. A breeze rippled over the wasteland, sending the gray clouds scudding north across the sky. Mel swallowed his last bite of biscuit and looked up at the Liznee king. Jan folded up the map he had been studying and looked at Iriam.

The Neutral frowned slightly. "If we cut east too quickly, we might miss the road north to Caer Sia. That will lead to days of wandering the Magno Forest."

Jan had said nothing about their current route last night—in fact, everything seemed well. They were making good progress to Caer Sia, and here on the flatlands, it was easy to see the roads that crisscrossed the land like the stitching of a huge quilt. Mel was confused. "Why do we need to go east now?"

Quinn sat down by the ashes of the fire across from Mel. He had finished his breakfast already, and had quickly packed up the gear. "That is the debate of the morning," he said, shaking his head.

"I'd think you would agree with me, at least, Iriam," Jan said. He sounded irritated.

Mel glanced a question at Rygal. "What did I miss in the two minutes it took me to put away my bedroll?"

Rygal stood and stretched. "Remember when we crossed Deadman's Flats, and we had to choose between speed and safety? That's pretty much the discussion today. Iriam thinks this route is better, since we avoid the southern half of the Magno Forest and enter Caer Sia from the west. But now Jan says it could be safer to go east, through the forest, and enter the city from the south."

Mel blinked, trying to make the directions all make sense in his mind. "So… is this route dangerous?"

"Not yet," Quinn said. "Except…" He trailed off and arched an eyebrow at Jan.

"I am not trying to complicate the plan," Jan said. He let out a breath, looking absolutely exhausted. His face was drawn and tired, and the dark circles under his eyes seemed more pronounced this morning. "Entering Caer Sia from the west would mean we have to go through the main part of the city—the most populated. From Orig's report, I'd guess those roads would also be patrolled heavily by the orcs."

"The orcs will be watching for us either way," Iriam told him. "If we no longer have the element of surprise, we can keep the element of speed on our side. This is the fastest road to Caer Sia."

Mel looked between Jan and Iriam. It was the first time their leaders had disagreed during the entire journey. He doubted the discussion would escalate to an argument, but it did put the rest of the companions in an awkward place.

Jarus finished packing the cooking supplies. The camp had been gathered, now the only question was where they would go.

"We do not have to decide yet," Iriam said, clearly trying to calm Jan. "The crossroads is several miles from here."

"At which point we *will* have to decide. I do not like putting things off," Jan said shortly. He sat down stiffly, one hand on his side.

Iriam turned to the other companions. "Well, if we will decide now, let us have it over with. Here is our choice. This road we are currently on leads north, then heads east to Caer Sia. However, Jan is right. There is a likelihood that the west side of the city will be guarded the heaviest."

He nodded toward the distant tree line. "Our other option is to take the next road east, through the Magno Forest. It is a longer road, but we might arrive at a less guarded part of Caer Sia—and closer to the castle."

"But it could add another day's worth of travel," Jan said, rubbing his brow.

"Indeed. And were it the choice of safety alone, I would agree with you. But I feel speed may be more important at the moment." Iriam turned to the companions again. "Still, you five have as much of a right to decide as we do. What are your thoughts?"

"Well… we don't know if there are orcs in that part of the city, more than anywhere else," Quinn ventured after a pause.

"Right," Jarus said. "I don't know. I feel at this point, the Aces are already expecting us eventually. They won't think we'll just give up."

"I don't like shortcuts," Aryion said. "The Magno Forest road may be longer, but we will also have better cover."

Iriam nodded thoughtfully. "Rygal?"

Rygal shook his head briskly. "No more shortcuts. I'm with Jan and Aryion."

Aryion's eyebrows shot up. "Who are you, and what did you do to Rygal?"

"Mel?" Iriam asked.

Mel stared at the embers of the fire, drawing out the silence. "The east road," he said finally. "I trust Jan about Caer Sia."

Iriam nodded shortly. He did not seem disappointed—though it was hard to read the Neutral's face normally anyway. "Very well. Then we must be off. That road is a longer distance, but let us see how much time we can take off the journey."

They headed out at a brisk pace, passing out from under the grove of shabby trees and moving out on the flatland again. Jan walked in the back of the party, a hand on Drisilas' hilt, lines of worry etched in his face. Mel slowed his pace. "Is everything all right?" he asked awkwardly.

Jan let out a breath. "Yes. I am sorry for worrying you. It's just... this place." He gestured vaguely at the area around them. "We are only a little east of the Salem Flats... that is where the Liznees fought the Aces last time, you know. Led by my father the king. And that way," he nodded right, back toward the Old Wood, "we fought the Darkness there. We thought we beat it then, you know. The Red Dawn, myself, and... Dandio."

The name dropped into the silence. Jan said nothing more. Mel had never seen him so broken down. The king had lost his city, his people, and possibly his brother to the Aces.

"He might have made it," Mel ventured slowly, trying to be encouraging. "Like you said in Kamon… it takes a lot to kill Dandio." He forced a smile.

Jan nodded shortly and cleared his throat, as if dismissing the topic. "Well. Yesterday we spoke of the weaknesses of the Aces. What of their powers? Some of us have seen them already. What should we be wary of?"

"Their ice," Jarus said, waving a paw vaguely in the air. "And the one we fought before—it could make sounds. Voices."

Mel shivered as he remembered that. "Yeah—and I bet they'll try to use that one when we get to Sia. If it works, we could all end up separated."

"What kind of voices?" Quinn asked.

"Voices of people you love," Jarus said quietly. "Voices of them calling for help. Sounds of them in pain." He fell silent.

Mel quickly moved past the memory. "The Aces can take your Essence, too, right? We… saw that before." He swallowed. "Iriam, you and Jan can block that. What about the rest of us?" He waved his hands in front of him. "We can't shoot the Essence out of our hands to block." He was starting to feel helpless again. The Ace-Lord could snuff out his life in an instant.

"You will have the Shards, Mel," Iriam said. "They will offer you some protection from the Ace-Lord's powers. But you will have to learn to master their strength."

Mel didn't understand what this meant. Aryion looked at Iriam. "And the rest of us? We cannot counter this power of theirs."

"No, but this power has a cost on the Aces, too," Iriam said. "It draws a great amount of strength from them. I believe they will use it sparingly, but nonetheless, we must watch each other's backs. And beware of the white ice. That is the only warning you will have that they are going to use this power."

Another pause. A cloud had covered the sun. The heaviness of the conversation seemed to have settled on Mel's mind, too.

They reached the crossroads, and turned east, moving toward the Magno Forest. The land drooped down into a flat valley, leaving the rolling hills behind. The bright patches of wildflowers and fresh green growths contrasted with the dull colors of before. It was quite pretty. But Mel did not like it. They were exposed here, with no cover, not even the shabby trees to offer hiding. He imagined Aces emerging from the shadows near the forest edge, and shuddered.

It was a little past midday when they unexpectedly reached another crossroads. The road no longer led east—instead, it split two ways, one leading north, one leading south. They halted, while Iriam and Jan reviewed the maps. But much like Rygal's shortcut weeks earlier, the crossroads was unmarked on the maps. There was no way to know which way to go.

"How old are those maps, anyway?" Jarus asked, frustrated. "This must be the third time this has happened."

"Roads change," Aryion said wearily.

"This is no good," Jan said, irritated. "We must have gone too far north and not far enough east. I don't know how we missed the right path, but either way I fear we are in the middle of nowhere now."

"There was no other path indicated on the maps, nor any that we passed," Iriam said, shaking his head. "But you are right. At this rate, we shall end up in Badwater and have to walk east along the coast to enter Caer Sia."

"At which point, we'll be back to entering the west side of the city," Aryion said. He looked at Rygal. "Know any shortcuts in this area?"

Rygal shook his head, arms crossed over his chest. "No one's come this way in years, like Quinn said yesterday. We have the Darkness to thank for that. In fact, the correct road might have been destroyed years ago."

"Well, we know we don't want to go back south," Mel said slowly. "Shouldn't we just go north and… hope for the best?"

"We could leave the road entirely," Rygal suggested. "The land's flat enough that we can see where we're going. Why not go east until we reach the Forest, then find the road again once we're across this valley?"

"Try walking the Magno Forest without a road, and let me know how that goes for you," Quinn said dryly.

"I think we have something else to worry about," Aryion said suddenly, his voice low.

Everyone looked at him. Mel's hand flew to the hilt of his knife, his heart pounding. Aryion nodded to the ridge behind them. As Mel followed his gaze, he caught his breath.

Crouching on the ridge, watching the seven companions in the valley below, was a massive winged creature. The white light glinted off its silver scales, the frill of green feathers, the bat-like wings that reached before it, claws gripping the rocks.

"Kragon," Mel whispered. He had seen such a beast once before—and he never wished to see one again. Tentative allies with the Liznees, they were massive, power-hungry beasts, twice as intelligent and twice as dangerous as a dragon.

Quinn reached for an arrow, but he moved uncertainly. The kragon spread its wings and glided down the ridge toward them. It came slowly, low to the ground.

"Get down!" Aryion warned.

The companions dropped to their knees in the shrubs. Quinn raised his bow as the kragon landed twenty paces away. The dull light glinted on the broadhead.

"Wait!" Jan ordered. He stood slowly. Drisilas blazed in his hand, but he did not attack, only moved to stand before the great beast as it drew close.

The kragon was even bigger up close. A thin band of gold was set on its head, over the frill of feathers. There was something vaguely familiar about this kragon that Mel couldn't place. But Iriam had straightened too.

The kragon's golden eyes flicked over Ĵan and Iriam briefly. There was neither hostility nor friendliness in the look.

"Lord Fireclaw," Ĵan said finally, inclining his head slightly. His tone indicated that Fireclaw was neither friend nor enemy.

The kragon lowered his head in a polite bow. "Ĵan Ki," he growled. The voice was heavily accented, almost incomprehensible due to the gravelly snarl. It sounded halfway between the shrill cry of an eagle and the purr of a massive cat.

Now Mel remembered the battle with the Darkness and Drona, when Lord Fireclaw had led his loyal kragons in battle against the renegade Adderstrike. Mel had only caught glimpses of the aerial struggle, but he recognized the kragon lord. The only question that remained was who the kragons had sided with in this conflict.

"You were not in Caer Sia, ven came the Dark Ones, I see," Fireclaw observed.

"No. Now, we must know. Are you friend or enemy in this war?" Ĵan asked. Red fire glowed in his hand, and ice sparkled on Iriam's fingertips as they awaited the answer.

Fireclaw let out a short bark of growling laughter—a bizarre sound. "Think you that ve joined vith the Dark Ones? They who are enemies of old?"

"I am glad to hear it," Iriam said, looking satisfied.

Mel felt a quick flash of relief. So the kragons were still on their side, even if the Black Dwarves were not.

Ĵan turned to the other companions, who had stood and approached cautiously. "Don't worry. This is Fireclaw, Lord of the Kragons." The others bowed.

"How fare your people, my lord?" Iriam asked.

Fireclaw inclined his head respectfully to the Neutral. "Driven south ve have been, to Tinkeeyo. Spoken vith the Dark Lord have I, two times now."

"You have spoken with the Ace-Lord?" Ĵan said, stunned.

"Vished he an alliance vith us. Vished that kragons fight along-side Aces." Fireclaw shook his head, snarling. "Forgotten he has the deaths in battles of old. Ve do not forget."

"How has he taken that news?" Iriam asked.

Fireclaw gave another growling laugh. "As he should. Know vell the Prophecies, do my warriors. Vary of us the Ace-Lord vill be."

While Mel doubted the last sentence, it was heartening to know that they had the kragons on their side. Clearly, the Aces were not eager to pick a fight with them, either, since they knew the truth of the Prophecy. That was a good thing to know too.

Fireclaw stretched his back like a massive cat. "I searched for you in Sia, Ĵan, but you vere not dere, so I looked around de area. Now I find you. But I sense you vounded." His ears flicked back as he eyed the Liznee.

"Slightly," said Ĵan, who was used to the kragon's way of speech. "But there is something I need to know. You said you flew over Sia. What is it like there?"

Fireclaw's ears flicked back again, this time in anger. "Ah, is very bad dere. Many Dark Ones, and dere be that nasssty Ace-Lord." At which point he launched into a string of snarling, hissing curses that Mel was rather glad he couldn't understand. The kragons had long ago battled the Aces, and their hatred for the Ace-Lord burned hot and red.

Jan waited patiently. "Then the Aces are still in Sia? All eleven?" he asked when Fireclaw had finished.

"Yesss," the kragon hissed. "All them. The prisoners are kept in de castle."

"Where?" Iriam asked immediately.

"I am not sure," Fireclaw replied. "Dere be the dungeon, but that is below the ground and I could not see. But they are alive. I heard this from the orcs who guard the keep." He paused warily. "You vill return then? Despite the Aces?"

"We must," Iriam said. "Aces or no, the Shards must be reunited."

Fireclaw lashed his tail worriedly on the ground, but in the end, he seemed to agree that this needed to be done.

"I have a favor to ask of you, my lord," Jan said slowly. "I would be in your debt."

Fireclaw looked at him intently. "Threaten all of Orlell, the Ace-Lord does. I am at your service. Vhat ask you?"

"We're rather off track," Jan said. "It will take another day's travel before we reach Caer Sia, if we go through the Magno Forest."

"By then it be too late," Fireclaw growled, shaking his head.

"Yes..." Jan agreed. An idea had come into Mel's mind almost the same moment he had learned that Fireclaw was on their side. He guessed it was the same plan Ĵan had, but clearly, the king was trying to think of the most diplomatic way to voice the question.

Fireclaw, however, was to the point. So was Iriam; the Neutral glanced sidelong at Ĵan, a wry smile playing over his face, then looked back at the kragon.

"My dear friend Fireclaw," he said smoothly. "How would you mind… escorting us the rest of the way to Sia?"

. . . . . .

Requesting a ride on the back of the Kragon Lord, Mel understood, was not a small favor. He half worried that Fireclaw would react angrily, once Iriam explained the idea. But Fireclaw had only nodded his huge head slightly.

"This arrival be dangerous," was his only objection. "Sssee us coming, the Aces vill."

Iriam, of course, had already thought of a solution. They soon decided that Fireclaw would carry them within half a mile of the city, and the companions would enter from the south. With the Aces watching the west, there was a chance the companions would be able to enter unnoticed.

"It's all a gamble, of course," Ĵan said.

"So was the whole quest," Aryion pointed out. With the travel course decided, they headed over to the waiting kragon.

Mel had ridden on the gryphon, Nella, when Rygal had rescued him and Misty in Appledale. Riding on a kragon was a different matter entirely. Fireclaw had a frill of green feathers that ran down his back to his tail, and upon first glance, Mel decided that he could hold onto that. But the wispy feathers were hard to hold onto—about as easy as clutching a handful of hair. Not only that, the tough, glossy-gray scales that covered Fireclaw's body were uncomfortably slick, and Mel could feel himself sliding at every slight movement. He gritted his teeth and held onto Aryion's shoulder with one hand and the kragon's spines with the other.

Fireclaw straightened and gripped the bags of supplies in his massive talons. He turned his head and eyed the companions with slight amusement. "No fear!" he croaked. "If you fall, I vill catch you, yessss?"

This was not particularly comforting, Mel thought, studying the huge claws.

Fireclaw spread his wings and launched forward. His huge, ash-gray wings pounded the air, and they gained altitude so quickly that, for an instant, Mel's ears popped and he couldn't hear a thing.

Then Fireclaw leveled out and soared northeast. Mel was so focused on moving his jaw around to try and clear his ears that he didn't realize exactly how high they were. Then his ears cleared—what a relief—and he looked down to see an ocean of rippling green evergreens spreading out for miles upon miles. The world spun slightly, and Mel's stomach flipped. He tightened his grip and swallowed hard.

Aryion squirmed slightly. "Mel—loosen your grip a little. You're positively clawing my shoulder."

"S-s-sorry," Mel said through chattering teeth. He let his grip on Aryion's shoulder slip—slightly—and looked down again. His terror passed. Despite the buffeting gales of wind, he felt more balanced on Fireclaw's back. The Diamond Cap mountains rose before them, their heads tearing through the clouds, speckled with leftover snow. Distantly, Mel could see the slight droop in the land, where the mountains bowed before the valley of Sia.

"Look at that," he whispered in awe.

"No thank you," Jarus mumbled from behind him. Mel turned to look at him. The Cooper's eyes were squeezed shut, and his fur was blown and plastered against his body.

"Hold on," Mel said encouragingly. "At least we don't have to walk anymore."

Jarus peeked down at the view, then promptly shut his eyes again. "Light above," he choked, frantically shaking his head. "The sky is no place for a Cooper. Give me a rushing river—a frozen lake—I'd take a blasted hurricane over this. Confound that missed path! C-c-confound this wind!"

"This isn't so bad," Rygal said mildly. He was seated directly behind Iriam, sheltered from the wind by the Neutral's tall frame. "It's not every day one gets a view like this."

"C-confound the view," Jarus said, teeth chattering.

Despite the chill, Mel had to laugh.

25

The Approaching Storm

On they flew, soaring northeast, while the Magno Forest stretched on like a great carpet below them. Lord Fireclaw showed no sign of weariness, his powerful wings carrying them on.

The flight lasted a few hours, Mel guessed, though his cold and stiff muscles made it seem longer. He'd wanted to wrap up in his cloak, which was flapping uselessly behind him, but that would mean letting go of his hold, and that was unthinkable. But when Caer Sia came into view, Mel forgot entirely about the cold, about his aching back and streaming nose.

A huge black thundercloud crouched over the city, overshadowing the nearby mountains. The occasional crackle of lightning came from within, followed by a roll of thunder that echoed over the forest. Fireclaw dipped low to avoid it. The sun had begun its downward descent in the west, yet as they swept under the shadow of the cloud, the sun disappeared entirely and they were enveloped in a cold gray light. Mel shivered. This was a different cold, a different chill that spoke of hidden deeds and an evil too dark to even be spoken of.

And so they entered the conquest of the Ace-Lord.

Fireclaw descended gradually, then tucked in his wings and dropped down into the trees. Mel caught a glimpse of the spires of the castle ahead, before his vision was obscured by branches. Fireclaw landed lightly on the ground, and the companions slid stiffly off his back. Mel fell to his knees, his legs and feet numb after the long flight. The ground crunched slightly as he did; he saw the grass was crusted in ice. He rose to his feet stiffly.

Fireclaw shook himself, stretching his wings. Ĵan and Iriam both bowed slightly to him. "We thank you, my friend," Ĵan said. "Know that you are always welcome in Sia's halls."

The kragon nodded his acknowledgment. "May prayers carry your quest," he rumbled. His gaze traveled to the companions. "Be vary once vithin. No creature you have faced yet, the Ace-Lord is like. Clever he is, cunning as a volf. Be vary."

"We will," Iriam said. He studied the kragon lord, thinking. "My lord, I also ask that you send your warriors here as soon as possible. The civilians must be protected, and there will be many Jenna to face."

Fireclaw smiled, his long teeth glittering. "As you asssk," he hissed, then lifted into the air and sped south. A breath of wind rippled the trees as he vanished into the dark clouds.

The companions stood in a small circle, looking down the road. No one spoke. There were no words to say, nothing to ease the tension. Here they were. The doorstep of Caer Sia. Mere miles away from the Ace-Lord himself.

There was a heavy silence. Iriam spoke finally. "You came on this quest not looking for glory, not looking for fame, but because of the call. We have little idea of what we are about to face today. But know that the High Light has brought us thus far, and I trust that He will guide us now. Can you trust Him?"

Another pause, this one solemn and thoughtful. No one spoke, yet Mel sensed the firm resolve and persistent determination. He felt it himself, and nodded slightly.

A faint smile crossed the Neutral's face. "Good," he said, then turned to Mel. "Take the Shard. You know what you must do. We will do everything we can to help you on your way."

Mel slipped the Stone into his pocket. It hung there like a weight. He fought down the fear and uncertainty that rose in his chest.

Ĵan looked at the others. "Our plan is risky, I admit. But it is our best chance," he said. "We will walk to the southeast guard tower. There will likely be rubble scattered across the roads there, so watch your step and keep quiet. After that we will enter the city itself, slowly and quietly."

"What about the Shards?" Mel asked. He remembered, from what Orig had said, that the Shard was kept somewhere inside the castle. Guarded by the Ace-Lord himself, in fact.

"The southeastern steps will likely be your best choice," Ĵan told him. "They lead up the hillside to the courtyard."

"But where…" Mel started, then stopped. There was no way they could know where exactly in the castle the Shard would be kept. But he also realized that he wouldn't have to find it. The Aces would lead him to the second Shard. The Ace-Lord would need both the New Blood and the Shards together.

They set off up the road, through the forest. The walk itself, though not as long as others on this journey, had to be the most stressful. The going felt painfully slow, and while the forest path offered shelter from any watching eyes, the frozen leaves and twigs scattered across the road seemed to cry aloud their presence with each rustle. Mel moved as slowly and carefully as he could, nerves as taut as a bowstring, ears straining for any sound of the enemy.

They left the forest behind as the city came into view. The outlying houses that they passed were silent, the windows dark. These were the peasants who kept farms on the edge of the city proper. When Mel had traveled this way before, the farms had been alive with activity. Now everything was ominously silent. He wondered what had happened to the simple folk that had lived here. The Aces could not imprison everyone inside Caer Sia's dungeons.

Had the orcs and Jenna killed them all? He hoped not.

The afternoon sun vanished as they went on. Fog hung heavy over Caer Sia. In the gray light, Mel could only see a few hundred yards ahead at a time. The companions moved quickly and quietly, creeping from house to house, remaining on the edges of the road. The silence became still more ominous as they entered the outskirts of the once-great capital. Buildings had been torn down, houses burned, windows smashed. Mel could not help staring at what remained. The wreckage was surreal to him, as though the city had been made of sand and been washed out with the receding tide.

Glass crunched under his feet, and he quickly turned his focus back to the present.

Ahead, Iriam raised a hand and motioned for them to stop. The seven companions moved behind a crumbled brick wall that had once been part of a house. Mel peeked over the bricks as a patrol of Jenna marched down the road across the block. They seemed focused on their task—which was good. But Mel could tell from their straight-set postures and swift, searching glances that they would be eager to kill anyone they found out-of-doors.

What had Orig called it? "Enforcing curfew?" It was barely past midday. Why hadn't they seen any civilians yet?

Fear dried his mouth, and he swallowed hard. "Where is everyone?" he whispered to Rygal.

Rygal's face was grim; he shook his head slowly, as confused and worried as Mel was.

"This way," Jan said, leading them down a cross street and away from the sounds of the Jenna patrol. On they went, weaving past the wreckage. Twice more they passed patrols, one of Jenna and one of humans. Mel studied the faces of the human soldiers as they passed near the companions. Their eyes were pale blue, hollow and vacant as their minds. They stared straight ahead, their faces blank.

They reached the city square, and Iriam called a halt. A community park and garden grew here, surprisingly untouched by the wreckage. The roads ran parallel on opposite sides of the park, which sloped down in a gentle valley. A creek trickled weakly through the draw. Roses and brambles had overgrown the garden and taken hold of the trees, forming a tangled thicket.

The thicket offered decent shelter from any watching eyes, and the companions stopped just off the road.

"Where are the civilians?" Jarus asked softly. "Orig said they were allowed to wander during the day, as long as they stayed in the city."

"He must have been mistaken, or else we would have seen someone else by now," Aryion murmured. "Not only that, what are the Jenna doing out? Orig said the Jenna only patrolled at night, but we've seen two groups of them already."

"I doubt he was lying. More likely, the Ace-Lord has changed things since Orig was last here," Jan said. His brow was furrowed in concern.

Rygal looked at Iriam, worried. "If our information is outdated, there's no telling what we're getting into. How much of our plan was based on Orig's report?"

"Not all of it, I can assure you," Iriam said, as calmly as ever. "I do not know what they could have done with the civilians. Nor can I guess why the patrols have changed. If our information is incorrect, this means we must be all the more cautious."

Mel took a drink of water to calm his racing thoughts. If Orig's report was outdated… did that mean the Ace-Lord had moved the Shard, too? What if the civilians had been killed? The total silence seemed to roar in his ears, adding to his growing anxiety.

He let out a breath and looked around. The park was not large—maybe two acres or so. The spires of the castle, around a mile away, were just visible through the trees to his right. More cross streets and buildings made up the space between them and the palace. Some buildings still stood, others had been destroyed entirely. Large heaps of rubble skirted the roads.

He turned away. The guard tower, he noticed, stood on the edge of the park directly across from where he sat. At least it had. Now it had been toppled, lying propped at an angle by the roof of a building.

"We should keep moving," Ĵan said. "Whether or not the civilians are here, the Shards must be joined."

Mel glanced toward the castle again. Soon, they would leave the houses and buildings behind, crossing the open road to get to the castle courtyard. Cover would be severely limited there, he thought, remembering the battle with Drona and the Darkness. Perhaps he could distract any watching Aces, and allow his companions to enter another way.

They had just stood and prepared to start moving when Quinn motioned them all to stop. "Get back—keep still!" he hissed.

Mel shrank back under the tree boughs, drawing his knife in a flash. Quinn pointed slowly at the ruined guard tower. Mel strained his eyes, but he couldn't see anything. The overall gray of the wreckage and the fading light made it hard to see anything.

"What is it?" Iriam asked in a low voice.

"He's gone back behind the rocks again, he'll come back into view in a moment…" Quinn muttered, then nodded forward.

Mel's eyes were drawn to the movement more than anything else. The figure blended perfectly in with the ruin. Moving slowly, he climbed up the ruined pillar.

"It's too small to be an orc," murmured Jarus. He looked up at Quinn. "It could be a Jenna…but it would be a small Jenna."

"Too small," Quinn agreed.

"And the Jenna have no reason to sneak around like he's doing," Rygal pointed out with a frown. "They've conquered the city with the Ace-Lord. Probably a beggar, or a thief come to plunder the ruins."

"I doubt a common beggar could climb like that," Aryion told him. "Might be a thief, I suppose. Either way, I think we can assume he's been here before. Look how easily he's climbing."

There was a long silence as the companions watched. The climber reached the top of the wrecked pillar and paused there, looking to the east. He wore ill-fitting gray clothes that draped awkwardly on his slight frame.

"Shall I shoot?" Quinn asked uncertainly, reaching for an arrow.

"Don't shoot him," Rygal said. "He might have information about the castle and the Aces."

"Rygal is right," Iriam said quietly. "Nor should we kill a person whose motives we have yet to learn." He thought for a moment. "We will cross to the other hill, and after that see if we cannot gain some information from him. But be cautious. We cannot let him sound the alarm."

They moved in single file down the hill toward the tiny creek. As they reached the basin of the park, Mel glanced up, trying to see. The fallen guard tower was still visible, but he couldn't see anyone there anymore. "Where'd he go?" he asked as quietly as he could.

"I think he went down the other side," Quinn whispered back. "Keep an eye out." He had set an arrow to the string. Capturing the stranger was ideal, Mel knew, but they might not have the opportunity. Nor could they afford to compromise their position.

They reached the top of the other hill, next to the ruined tower. Beyond, the city stretched on in a grid of side streets and battered shops. To Mel's right, he could see the wide field next to the castle, where they had battled the Darkness before. The thunder of the sea was closer now, making it harder to hear.

"There's another patrol coming," Aryion cautioned, and the companions ducked down behind a heap of rocks. Mel kept his head down, facing the building that the tower had fallen on. An upper story window had been knocked out—Jenna, probably, plundering whatever the building had held before.

"Those are orcs," Jarus muttered, as the patrol passed. Mel glanced over to watch the soldiers fade into the fog. He hadn't seen their eyes, but he could assume they were enchanted. This could be a problem.

"Where's our mystery thief?" Jan asked, as the companions formed a small circle.

Quinn fingered the fletching of his arrow, looking agitated. "I don't know. I saw him climb to the other side of the guard tower, but I didn't see him climb down again."

"Maybe he crossed the street before the patrol walked by," Mel suggested.

"Or," Aryion said in a low voice, "maybe he's watching us from the upper window right now."

He said it so calmly it took Mel an instant to register the words. When he did, his heart skipped a beat, and it took all his will power to not turn and look. Doing so would likely frighten the stranger away before they had the chance to question him.

"Can you see him?" asked Jan, who had his back to the building.

Aryion, facing him, nodded slightly. "He is wearing a cloak and hood, like we are, so I cannot see his face. He's rather small. We would probably be able to capture him, but I think he'll slip away before we can catch him."

"He has left the window now," Iriam said, just as Aryion finished.

Mel could not help himself—he looked back. The broken window was empty now. From inside the building came the faint sound of movement. Jarus' ears perked up.

Then he saw someone slip through the sagging door frame and stand in the shadow of the guard tower, hunched slightly in the small space, watching them silently. But Mel guessed, from his tense stance, that he planned to flee.

"If he gets to the road, he could alert the patrol," Quinn said, his voice still low but rising in urgency. He gripped his bow.

Jan turned, faced the stranger in the shadows, and spoke softly. "We are not here to hurt you. Come out quickly, before the patrol catches us."

His low voice was gentle but commanding. Halfway through his words, Mel saw the figure start, then move forward. The stranger crept out from under the guard tower, cautiously, a hand reaching back for the sword he wore slung across his back.

Then instead, the hand pushed back the hood, and the weak light reached the face beneath.

The face was filthy, patch worked with bruises and grime. But the bright eyes and frightened expression beneath were familiar at once, and Mel realized they had mistook something about the stranger. It was a girl.

And not just any girl. The ragged figure before them was Asescia Ki, heiress of Caer Sia.

26

They That Remained

For a second no one spoke. Mel stared at the Liznee girl in shock before he realized who he was seeing. Her dark hair hung matted and gray with dust, her clothes were in ribbons, but she was here.

"Are you real?" she asked, barely above a whisper. Her green eyes were riveted on Jan.

For answer, Jan stepped forward and gathered her into his arms, holding her tightly. Allie's arms hung at her sides for a moment before she returned the hug. Her frame trembled with both fear and relief.

"Are you all right?" Jan asked after a moment. He pulled away and looked her up and down. "We heard about the attack—we feared you were dead."

Allie nodded, swallowing hard. Tears made bright paths down her dirty face. "They came—Aces, and so many others. That was weeks ago. It's been… horrible." She pressed her hands into her eyes and took a shaking breath. "We see things—the Aces try to—the Jenna will—"

"It's over," Jan told her gently. "We're here. I'm back."

"Where's my father?" Allie asked. "Do you know…"

Ĵan shook his head. "Not yet. The Aces may have taken him, but we don't know. We must stop them before we can save him." He took a breath and turned to the others.

The other companions had watched in silence. The relief and joy of finding the young Liznee alive temporarily overshadowed all else.

Iriam drew them back to reality. "That patrol is coming back. We must hide."

"In here," Allie said, leading them through the broken door frame and inside the building. Rubble scattered the floor. Mel side-stepped it carefully.

"Asescia, what do you know of the other survivors?" Iriam asked. "Where are they keeping the hostages?"

"I'm not sure," Allie said. She let out a breath. "In the attack, I—I couldn't see much. It all happened so fast. Mum told me to run." She stopped, tears shining in her eyes.

"Where did they take her?" Ĵan asked.

"I don't know," Allie said unhappily. "I ran to the east tower, to try and find help. The orcs had already killed everyone here. Then they tore down the tower. They were sure everyone here was dead, so I hid here during the battle." She clenched her fists. "I couldn't do anything—I couldn't help them—"

"If you had, you would have been killed, or captured," Iriam said. His words were blunt, but his tone gentle. "We have good reason to believe your mother still lives. We have heard that the Aces are holding most of the courtiers in the dungeons."

A little light came back to the Liznee girl's eyes. She turned, seeming to register that the other companions were all here too. "Where did you all go? After the council at Flora?"

"We went to get the other Shard," Mel said, keeping his voice low.

Allie's eyes widened. "That's what the Aces are here for? But why?"

"The Ace-Lord wants the Star-Stones," Rygal said wearily. "He lost the Jewel, so now he's going after the Shards. And it sounds like he already has one of them."

"Have you… have you seen the Ace-Lord, Allie?" Mel asked hesitantly.

The girl shook her head. "No, not yet. The Aces only walk the streets at night. So I've been here, with the others."

"The others?" Jan repeated.

Allie led them down a flight of stairs, into darkness. "Anyone we could find. Glentree did his best." She turned up the wick of an oil lamp on the table.

As Mel's eyes adjusted, he stared in awe. The room was filled with people—men, women, and children. Most of the men wore the armor of the Red Dawn. They stared in stunned silence at the companions.

"Look what the cat dragged in," came a familiar voice, and a hulking man limped forward. One arm was in a sling, and a bandage was wrapped around his head. But his wide, crooked grin and twinkling eyes were the same as ever.

"Glentree," Jan said, smiling as he clasped the huge man's hand. "I should have expected you'd pull through."

"Not as well as I'd 'oped," Glentree said, shaking his head. "This is the best form of counter attack I've managed to get together, and it hasn't gone too well the last few days. Got caught by a Jenna patrol out after dark two nights ago." He grinned fiercely. "They'll remember it—I bashed their 'eads in, and we managed to steal some weapons. But they took a toll." He nodded at his injured arm.

"You've done everything you could, old friend," Jan said.

"What should we do, sire?" a soldier behind Glentree asked doubtfully. "The Jenna guard the streets, and the Aces seem to be plotting a new scheme. Only this morning they rounded up the rest of the townsfolk and took them away."

"Took them where?" Iriam asked.

"We don't know," Glentree said. "But they aren't to be killed. Just kept locked up someplace."

"I think they might have taken them to the city square," Allie said slowly. "That way, they can watch everyone in one group."

"But why?" Glentree mused.

"Because they know we're coming," Mel guessed slowly. He had been mulling over this question for a while now. "The Ace-Lord is waiting for me. He's waiting for me to bring him the Shard—and he doesn't want any of the townsfolk in the way."

"Or he wants to make you choose between saving the civilians and joining the Shards," Rygal murmured.

"Probably both," Mel agreed. He didn't know his role in the Prophecy yet, so the Ace-Lord would do everything he could to add to that confusion. Of course, Mel had his companions to help the civilians. His task now lay with the Shards alone.

He looked at Iriam and saw the Neutral nod slightly, almost as though he had guessed Mel's thoughts.

Jan turned to Glentree again. "How many here are fit to fight?"

"I'd guess fifty or so, maybe more," Glentree replied, scratching the stubble on his chin as he thought. "The patrols haven't found our spot here yet. But they'll be on us the minute we march for the castle. The Aces get braver and stronger at night, and it's almost dusk."

"If we wait until morning, it might be too late," Iriam said grimly. "We do not know what the Ace-Lord plans for the civilians. Know also, that we have something among us that the Aces cannot overcome." There was a ripple of questioning murmurs before he finished. "The New Blood has come with the second Shard."

Only a few of them understood the implication of the New Blood, but everyone knew about the Shard. The crowd stared with wide and hopeful eyes.

"Here is our plan," Iriam said. "We will go past the square and approach the castle from the south, keeping under cover as far as we can. Once in place, we will attempt to free the civilians, while Mel enters the castle to reunite the Shards." He nodded at Mel, who nodded back—he felt very small in the Neutral's shadow.

"That's a problem, Iriam," Glentree said. "The south side is pretty sparse for cover. The west would be better—but you'd have to go through the courtyard, right past the Aces."

"Not if you're on the west side of the castle," Allie said unexpectedly. She looked at Mel. "There's a way in on the south—a small door that will let you enter through the servants' quarters. Then you can get into the upper levels and find the Shard."

"Which side door?" Jan asked, surprised.

"You know," Allie said with a small shrug. "If you go down that little flight of stairs from the dungeons and down the hallway…"

"Oh, *that* side door," Jan said with a note of distaste in his voice. "The one with squeaky hinges that lets in drafts all winter long and never shuts all the way." The corner of his mouth twitched. "Well, perhaps it will finally serve some purpose. That will work well if Mel can get in that way."

"I'm guessing the side door isn't a likable object?" Mel asked with a grin.

She shook her head wearily. "Oh, no. My dad complains the most about it, but whenever the carpenters offer to fix it, he tells them not to worry." Her smile faded at the mention of Dandio.

"There's still the issue of avoiding the guards," the first soldier pointed out, glancing at Iriam. "If we are seen, the Aces will tighten their guard of the civilians. It'll be even harder to rescue them then."

"True," Iriam murmured, looking thoughtful.

Aryion looked up. "What if instead of surrounding the square, we join the group of civilians there? We can pass the plan around the prisoners. At Iriam's signal, we can charge the guards, and Mel can sneak to the castle."

"That sounds risky. I like it," Glentree boomed, a familiar light coming back into his eyes.

Iriam hesitated, but finally agreed. "Very well. But do not give yourselves away until the very last moment. We must all be in place, and ready to attack." He looked at Mel. "Wait to start your approach until after the fighting begins. In that way, you can slip away unnoticed."

"Hopefully," Mel said, forcing a smile. It helped ease the tension, but only a little. This plan would likely work well to free the civilians, but it involved putting themselves into the hands of the Aces, at least for a few minutes. He wondered if the Ace-Lord would be there, and shuddered. They might be able to sneak past the other Aces, but he doubted they would fool the Ace-Lord.

"Let's get going, then," Rygal said.

"Anyone who is fit to fight, step forward," Jan said. Glentree's guess turned out to be close. There were fifty-two men and women who were ready for battle. Glentree stepped forward too, ignoring his injured arm as he hefted his battle axe with his free hand.

"Onward, then," Iriam said with a slight smile, and led the way back up the stairs.

. . . . . .

Iriam instructed they split into smaller groups as they approached the city square. Even from this distance, Mel could hear the low, uneasy murmurs of the massive crowd that was gathered there. If all of them arrived at once, the Aces would notice. Better to arrive in small groups of fives or tens, so that it was less noticeable.

"The lead Ace tends to give orders," Allie whispered to him as they walked. "The one with half a face—he seems to be in charge. I think he's the Ace-Lord's commander."

"Must be the Ace-Deputy," Mel said. "He led the attack on Kamon."

Allie raised her eyebrows. "But you beat him then?"

"Sort of. He retreated," Mel said. "I didn't see it. I was busy trying to not be killed by a Jenna chieftain."

"Well, fair enough," Allie murmured. Her face was pale and drawn with fear. Mel could not imagine the horrors she must have been through in the weeks since the attack. It was a miracle she and the other warriors were alive at all.

"We're going to beat them," he said, trying to raise her spirits. "Most likely, you'll never see the Ace-Lord. I'm going to face him myself."

"That's either very brave or very stupid," Allie said with a tentative smile.

"I think we're a healthy mix of both," Rygal said from behind them.

"Just as long as we get these Aces out of Caer Sia, and rescue everyone else, I don't care what happens," Allie said vehemently.

Mel nodded in agreement. Everything had led up to this—every life that had been lost, every battle that had been won. He would see the fight through to the end—join the Shards, or die trying. He smiled to himself. Keep that thinking up, and you'll basically have a Blood Oath, he thought. He turned, trying to find Aryion. The ranger had joined Iriam and Glentree's group of ten, traveling down a side street to reach the city square a little after Mel's group did.

He studied the faces around him. Five of them in his party—Jan, Allie, Rygal, himself, and a Red Dawn captain whose name he didn't know. Across from them, traveling another street, occasionally visible through gaps in the broken buildings, was the group of ten, which included Jarus and Quinn. He felt strange, having his companions separated. With the exception of the Kamon battle, he'd had them all with him this entire journey, and felt exposed and unprotected without them.

A sudden trumpet blast made him jump. Nerves jangling, he shrank into the shadows of a building next to Allie and Rygal. The trumpet sounded three more times before the screeching echoes fell away in the silence.

"Did they see us?" Mel whispered in the sudden silence.

Allie listened, then shook her head slowly. Understanding had dawned in her eyes. "No… no, I don't think so. I've heard that before—it makes sense why they wanted everyone in the square now."

"Why?" Jan asked.

"It's an execution," Allie said. "The Aces have them every few days, killing prisoners who don't behave or… or powerful people they know to be against them. They've killed five of Father's generals already." Her voice trembled.

Mel felt sick. It was exactly something the Ace-Lord would enjoy.

A public execution of Caer Sia's heroes, killing them one by one, only further displayed his power and ultimate control of the city. More importantly, it would continue to crush the hopes of the people.

"Come on," Jan said, and they moved forward again. The street led between the ruin of two buildings, which framed the square in a V-shape as Mel peered through the fog.

The living civilians of Caer Sia filled the square, standing uneasily. They were a ragged group, nearly three hundred strong. Once-fine clothes had been torn to shreds in the aftermath of the attack. Barefooted children huddled near their parents. A baby cried somewhere in the crowd, quickly shushed by its mother as a Jenna guard glared at them.

"Keep your heads down," Jan cautioned. Mel slowed his pace and shuffled forward, trying to look as though he belonged here, as though he was just another piece in the horror that had become these people's lives. This had become reality for everyone here. Not for much longer, though, he promised himself, and felt a spark of hope again.

They joined the crowd on the edge of the square. A flat-roofed building stood directly in front of them. On top of it, robes billowing like smoke, stood the Ace-Deputy. Mel's stomach twisted, and he quickly adverted his glance. What if the Aces could sense him here? Could they sense the Shard?

They could sense fear, at least, but in the huge crowd, fear was abundant, and Mel doubted the Ace-Deputy could sense his in particular. The Ace-Deputy seemed focused on the task at hand.

Next to the Ace-Deputy was a burly, glassy-eyed orc, leaning on a massive axe. Three Jenna guards stood around the prisoner. A sack had been pulled down over the prisoner's head—likely to add to his fear, so that he did not know when the axe would strike. His wrists and ankles were chained, but there was something in his stance that made Mel doubt he'd resist. This poor soul had been so long in the captivity of the Aces that by now, any hope had been drained out of him.

The sight wrenched his heart. "Could… do you think we could save him?" he asked softly, though he already knew the answer. They had to wait for Iriam's signal, which would be at a point where the guards were relaxed. That point, Mel guessed, would be right after the axe swung. Then, with the execution finished and the guards distracted, their attack would come out of nowhere, and catch the Jenna by surprise.

Jan let out a breath. His face showed the conflict within him. It was a terrible decision to make, but it had to be done. "You know I would say yes. But it is too risky. We cannot reach the rooftop without the Ace-Deputy seeing us, and then they would know what is happening. At that point, the Aces would be alerted, and the Shard would be lost."

As horrible as it was, Mel knew Jan was right. The nasty business of war called for sacrifice, for the greater good. Saving this man would only bring about more death. This was how it had to be.

The Ace-Deputy surveyed the crowd, a sickly sweet smile on his hideous face. "People of Caer Sia," he called, his voice carrying over the square. "You are summoned here today to witness justice. A fine, pleasant thing it is, to exact justice in the name of security. Let this man's life be a testimony to such security, and to the truth that the only future you have is in your king and master, the Ace-Lord."

The orcs and Jenna clashed their weapons and bowed at the name. Mel was startled to see a few civilians do the same. He couldn't imagine believing the Ace-Deputy's words. But weeks of hearing and seeing the things these people had probably made it easier. Their spirits had been broken down, their hearts and minds turned to the only thing that offered some security—and that was in their captors' strength. Freedom through bondage, as Jan had said in Kamon.

"Mortal people of Sia," the Ace-Deputy called out again. "Witness this noble sacrifice so that security can prevail."

He nodded to the executioner. The burly orc pushed the prisoner forward. The man's legs gave out and he collapsed weakly to the rooftop.

Mel wanted to look away. But he forced himself to watch. The Ace-Deputy was right—it was a sacrifice. But it was a sacrifice that would end in good. Mel promised himself that.

A Jenna guard hauled the man to his knees roughly, and pulled off the sack. At the same time, the clouds shifted slightly, and a pale ray of sunset reached the prisoner's face.

The world skewed sideways.

Mel could not breathe, could not speak, could only stare in horror until he was sure what he was seeing was real. It was no illusion. He faced the dreadful truth. The prisoner kneeling before the executioner's axe was their lost hero. *Dandio Ki.*

27

The Storm Breaks

Dandio looked horrible. His face was thin and pale, patterned with bruises. His left eye was so swollen he could hardly open it, and blood trickled from a fresh cut on his lip. He was battered and weak from weeks of darkness and little food and who knew what other horrible tortures.

But he was alive.

Alive.

And now he knelt, ready to die before the city that had mourned him mere weeks ago.

Allie gasped when she saw her father and stepped forward. Rygal stopped her, but Mel could tell he was ready to follow her lead. Now the entire company was at a loss. This was not a turn of events any-one had foreseen. It was either allow Dandio to die, or risk the fate of the world for his rescue.

The call was not his to make, but that did not help him feel any better. His heart raced as he stared at Dandio, moments away from death.

"Jan, what's the plan?" Rygal asked, keeping his voice measured and calm.

"The… plan…" Jan muttered vaguely. Mel looked at him. The king's eyes were blank with shock as he stared at his brother twenty yards away.

"You know this man, good mortal people of Sia," the Ace-Deputy drawled. "Observe, then, his death, and know that he will be greeted well in the realm of our master."

Mel could only stare. To him, the horror came not from Dandio's weakened state, but from the look in his eyes. That passionate spark of green had been extinguished, and now they were dull and lifeless, like pieces of charcoal. They were the eyes of a man who had completely given up all hope.

"One life. One blood for the survival of the few. One soul for the Realm Beyond," the Ace-Deputy intoned. It was clearly a practiced ritual. The orc with the axe stepped forward and pulled down the collar of Dandio's jerkin, exposing his neck. Dandio barely reacted.

"Father…" Allie choked, trembling with rage and fear. Rygal restrained her—his face was white.

The orc stepped back and raised the axe.

"Jan, what's the plan?" Rygal demanded, louder this time.

"HANG THE PLAN!" Jan shouted—he leapt forward, red fire crackling in his left hand as he drew Drisilas in a flaming arc. The people sprang out of the way with cries of alarm and surprise. The Jenna on the rooftop echoed their surprise. Jan ran, faster than Mel would have believed; leaping upon the heaps of rubble, he sprang onto the roof before the executioner.

Rygal and Allie charged after him. Mel stood at a loss for an instant, then, realizing that the plan had been abandoned entirely, chased after them.

The executioner stepped back, startled, then raised the axe with a bellow. Jan didn't even flinch; he swung Drisilas sideways. Momentum and furious strength fed the blow. The flaming sword passed cleanly through the executioner's body. The orc stood upright for a moment, unable to register what had happened to him, then fell in two halves down to the crowd below.

The Jenna howled and flung themselves at Jan. Jan swept a ray of red flames at them, knocking one of them off the rooftop and leaving the other two screeching and clutching their burns.

Dandio's head snapped up at the familiar voice, and Mel saw hope kindle anew in his green eyes as he saw Jan. The fifty-two civilian warriors leapt from their places in the crowd, some of them attacking the guards, others rushing to join Jan on the roof.

A roar of hope and excitement rose from the crowd. Mel saw that several of the watching captive civilians had turned on the shocked guards, stripping them of their weapons before they could do anything.

The Ace-Deputy was so startled by the sudden fire that at first, he barely moved. Then he lunged at Jan. Ice sparkled in his hands— white ice, glittering and hungry and eager for Essence.

"Watch out!" Mel screamed, knowing there was no way to counter that blast. It would strip Jan's life right out of him like a cider press, as it had Norrin's.

But a ray of deep blue ice hit the Ace-Deputy in the arm before he could let the fatal shot fly. The Ace-Deputy staggered to the side, hissing, and looked around in shock. Seeming to materialize from the shadows themselves, Iriam moved to Jan's side. His hood was drawn over his face, his black robes billowed, and ice leapt from his fingertips in a swirling, dancing storm of glittering blue. Mel felt a thrill of fear and excitement as he beheld the Neutral, for the first time, in true power.

The Ace-Deputy straightened, recovering quickly. "You should not have come, Iriam," he hissed. Ice crawled from his fingers, running up and down his arms, weaving in and out of his armor like snakes.

Iriam brought both his arms down in a sweeping motion. Ice leapt from the beams at the Ace-Deputy's feet and slammed into him like a wave. The force sent the Ace-Deputy toppling from the roof in a cloud of fog and ash.

A ragged cheer rose from the watchers. "Form up quick!" came Glentree's bellow. "They'll be back soon, I'll warrant." His soldiers raced through the crowd, helping move the vulnerable and passing weapons to whoever was prepared to fight.

Mel stood below the building, one hand gripping his knife and the other clasped protectively over the pocket that contained the Shard. A trumpet blast jarred his attention to the left. The Jenna that had blown the signal earlier now stood on a rooftop, raising the alarm. Quinn's arrow sank into his neck a moment too late.

"Well, everyone's heard that," Rygal panted. He stood on a pile of rubble above Mel, sword in hand, eyes scanning the square. "I bet the Aces mobilize fast, too."

On the roof above him, Drisilas sheered through Dandio's bonds as if they were made of butter. Dandio got to his feet weakly, his hollow eyes scanning his brother's face. "Is this real?" he asked finally, his voice so hoarse it was barely recognizable.

"I was about to ask you that," Jan told him with a wry smile. "You're the ghost, after all." He clasped his brother's hand tightly.

Dandio let out a shaking breath. "They'll come soon. The Aces—there's ten of them in the castle. They'll come heed the call."

"Indeed they will," Iriam said. Dandio jumped slightly at his voice—he hadn't noticed the Neutral. Mel could tell he was still processing everything that was happening. Iriam studied him carefully. "If you are not well enough to fight, you should lead the others to safety."

"How do you feel?" Jan asked.

Dandio stooped and lifted the executioner's axe, hefting it experimentally. "I'd feel better taking out some Jenna, if it's all the same to you," he said absently. He noticed Rygal and Mel. "Light above, how many of you are here? What have I missed?"

"Nothing major," Jan said. "Now let's go. I hear them coming."

Mel heard them too, but not in the same way that he felt them. The sun sank below the western horizon, and the shadows deepened. A chill unlike any he had ever experienced flowed through him. The clatter of many feet came down the road, and in another instant a host of orcs and Jenna appeared.

"Form up!" Iriam ordered. He leapt from the rooftop to stand before the army of civilians. "Beware the Aces' white ice. The orcs cannot be killed. We must try to trap them, or push them back into the river."

He had just finished speaking when a dark shadow crept over the square, plunging them into gray darkness. A chill ran down the back of Mel's neck. He knew what was coming.

Through the swirling fog came the Ten. Ice coated the ground at their passing. Their armor glittered silver in the last light of day. Some stood solid and strong, like the Ace-Deputy. Others were more decayed, wraiths hung together by sinew and tattered cloth. Ten sets of purple-red eyes stared at the defenders in critical amusement.

How they loved such resistance. Hope was not always bad for their victims. A little of it at a time, like salt, to heighten the sweet taste of fear in their mouths when that hope was crushed. And crush it they would. But first, a feast of fear, made all the better by the mortal's stubborn resistance to feel it.

Mel watched the Aces approach through the fog. It was a chilling sight, but it made him realize something else. "He's all alone," he thought. The Ace-Lord, waiting alone in the castle. Waiting patiently for Mel to come to him.

There was no time to see anyone else, no time to say good bye.

He'd had his companions at his back this entire quest, but now he must stand alone. The New Blood against the Lord of Death.

He met Rygal's eyes, and saw the young warrior nod slightly. No words were said. They both understood the solemnity of what was happening.

Mel took a breath and walked away, towards the line of Aces. None of the Aces moved to stop him. They shifted out of his way without so much as giving him a glance, and drew together again once he had passed, continuing their advance toward the weary defenders. They would not harm their master's prize.

Mel walked across the lowered drawbridge and entered the castle.

. . . . . .

It was very dark inside. The only light came from the fading gray outside. The lamps were not lit in the hallways. Of course, Mel thought. The Aces hated fire, after all. And the dark did not hinder them. They welcomed it, commanded it like a tamed wolf.

The only sounds came from his feet on the tiled floors. Orig's report, he saw, was correct here. The castle was barely touched by the destruction that had plagued the city. It made sense to him. The Ace-Lord used it as his personal dwelling place, and a safe fortress to keep the Shard and the Prophecies.

Mel's heart was racing, and he took a deep breath to steady himself. No fear. He would not give the Ace-Lord that satisfaction. He would join the Shards, and die calmly.

Yes, he would die. He didn't doubt that. The Ace-Lord needed him to join the Shards and become the Twelfth. Mel would only fulfill one half of that plan, and that was joining the Shards. After that, he would have to deny the Ace-Lord's offer to become the Twelfth, and he doubted the Ace-Lord would let him walk away after that.

Maybe the Shards would form some sort of shield. He hoped so. Either way, his companions outside were counting on the fact that the Shards would drive away the Aces, ending the battle and the occupation of Caer Sia. Thinking about that made him move a little faster.

"All right," he said out loud. His low voice echoed in the empty halls. "If I were a long-dead maniac, where would I hide the Shard?"

That didn't help much. He racked his brain, not sure where to go. The castle was huge—four stories tall, with numerous rooms. The Ace-Lord could be anywhere. He likely loved this palace. From Cahadras' story, the Ace-Lord had always wanted to rule—he had always wanted a…

"A throne," Mel said aloud, and the answer hit him. He hadn't gone to the throne room during his brief stay here before. But he remembered vaguely that it was on this level, near the heart of the castle.

So on he walked, until he reached two copper doors, beautifully engraved. Ice shimmered on the handle.

Mel stopped. Calmed his racing heart. And remembered with each breath that this was what he was meant to do. Here he was. Thus far he had come. He did not feel afraid. He held the little blue stone against his beating heart, letting its strength feed his will to continue.

Mel opened the door and let out a breath.

There, in the center of the room, on a small silver table, sat the second Shard.

It was practically identical to its other half, glittering blue and pure light. Its glow filled the room. Below it, resting on the floor, were two scrolls.

Holding the Shard from Kamon, Mel stepped forward. As he did, a thought barged into his mind that this was far too easy, that he should have looked around the room before moving, that he should have noticed the way the silver table seemed to shift and move as though he was viewing it through a film of water.

But he did not register any of these thoughts. Not until he stepped fully into the room. In another instant, the color washed out of the scene before him and he hung suspended in a swirling black void.

28

The Twelfth Ace

Mel clutched the Shard to his chest, fighting back his gasp of panic. All was black and gray, and all was silent. Just as it had been inside the Darkness. This was bad, very bad.

"Let me out!" he yelled. His voice echoed in the void.

Suddenly he found he was no longer suspended. His feet rested on the cold tile of the throne room. He could see the table and the second Shard and the scrolls, through a wall of swirling gray and white fog. The room around him was the same—but the color had been muted, so that everything was black and white. Through the windows, the scene beyond was a black oblivion, with a few white stars winking tiny pinpricks of light.

"Good evening."

Mel spun around. A tall figure stood before the table, his black robes fluttering and joining with the shadows that skirted his feet.

"I have been waiting for you, New Blood." The voice was deep, much clearer than the echoes that had haunted Mel's dreams since the confrontation inside the Darkness. He stood frozen in place, staring at the figure before him.

The fog between them shifted, and through the monotonous gray scale came the glimmer of purple-red eyes. They were set in a chiseled face with skin the color of charcoal. White hair fell in a straight shining wave past the shoulders, over the silver armor. A triangle-shaped emblem was emblazoned on the breastplate, and the polished chain mail clinked slightly as the figure folded his hands and faced him.

"What is this?" Mel demanded, shivering at the cold.

The Lord before him smiled. "This is my glory. Sheer power and strength, a power that filled the foundations of the world long before your ancestors were birthed. And so it shall be again, in my kingdom. This mortal world shall be rid of fear and sickness and all that torments your meager lives at present."

"You're the one that brought it into the world," Mel flung at him. He stared at the shining figure in front of him, startled by the noble strength and majesty in his bearing.

"I?" the Lord asked, arching an eyebrow. "Indeed not. Do you not see, child? I mean to liberate the world. As I liberated my servants. Eternal life, with no more fear. They need not fear death, for even in death, I will be their Master."

Mel edged a little closer to the table. It was glimmering and shifting through the gray fog. That… that wasn't the illusion, he realized. The Aces could not touch the Shards—they must not be able to replicate them in an illusion, either. "I think you and I have different definitions of life," he said slowly.

The Lord laughed softly. "Ah, a diplomatic answer. Enlighten me, then, mortal child. How is your simple existence better than what I offer?" He spread his arms. The fog rippled through his silver hair, sending his robes billowing, and a faint light glittered off the crown on his brow.

Mel looked at the table again. It stood there, on the edge of the illusion. His best way out. He looked back at the glittering Lord. "I don't know much," he said slowly, drawing out time. "But I've seen what you can do—and none of it is good. Not even this illusion you've drawn up for me."

He raised the Kamon Shard and lunged for the table. There was a blinding blue flash, a snarling hiss, and the illusion dissolved around him. Mel crashed into the silver table, sending the other Shard spinning across the tile floor. The dazzling return of color and light dazed him for an instant, and he got to his feet shakily.

"Illusion?" the cloaked figure murmured, his voice cold. "I thought you might prefer the illusion."

Mel turned toward the voice. The weak light reached the speaker as he stepped from the shadows. The robes were ragged, torn and tattered from the wear of a thousand years. The armor was tarnished. But the face—the form—

His face was shrunken, black as midnight, the cheeks hollow and rotted around the bone. Red eyes flashed from sunken sockets. The mouth was much too wide, the teeth broken and decayed like fangs. Flesh and sinew stretched thin over the neck, exposing the white bone in places. He raised a hand, allowing ice to glimmer from the claw-like fingers.

Kahlifis, the Ace-Lord, the Master of Death in his true form.

Mel's stomach heaved from the horror of it. He clutched the table for support.

The Ace-Lord stepped forward, tilting his head to the side slightly as he walked. "At last," he said. His voice was hoarse and echoing. He smiled, and the flesh of his face pulled back to expose every jagged tooth in his black mouth. "At last comes the mortal I have waited so long to see. You truly are extraordinary, child." His eyes flicked to the Shard in Mel's hand. "And you have brought the second Shard. Yes, very extraordinary. I am quite proud of you."

"Stay back," Mel gasped, lowering the Shard at him.

The Ace-Lord studied him. "Still just as determined, I see. But there is a fine line between bravery and foolishness, child." He waved a hand. "Put the Shard down, and let us speak. I have a proposal for you."

Mel's hands shook as he clutched the Kamon Shard. His head was throbbing, his heart racing. He glanced behind—the other Shard had slid a few feet away, lying glittering on the floor.

"I'm not going to do it, Ace-Lord," he stated, flinging the words at the wraith. "I'm the New Blood. I'm not the Twelfth Ace, and I'll die before I join you."

"Indeed you will," the Ace-Lord said calmly. "That was always the plan. My plans never go awry. How else do you suppose it has come to this moment? Foolish child. Do you believe I would hang my conquest on the whims of a mere mortal boy?"

Mel sprang away, reaching for the second Shard. Before he could reach it, someone snatched it up. A sword clipped his back as he stumbled forward. With a cry of surprise, Mel turned.

The figure before him, holding the Sia Shard, was—Hagshrub.

"You!" Mel said, totally confused. "What are you doing here?"

"Awaiting my reward, of course," the orc chuckled. "Once I kill you." He raised his curved sword, stepping forward.

Mel stepped back. Something had gone wrong. He had missed something, something vitally important. "I—you can't," he stammered. "I'm the one they're hunting. You can't kill me." He looked at the Ace-Lord.

The Ace-Lord smiled, making his red eyes glitter. "An arrogant thought, and far too assuming. You deceive no one. You say you do not want to be the Twelfth Ace, and the spell will only work if you are willing. Why should I force you if I have another willing servant, prepared to take your place?"

Hagshrub grinned.

Mel's mind spun. "But... I'm... I'm the one," he repeated. "All this time—you wanted me to be the Twelfth Ace..."

"You would have been ideal, of course," the Ace-Lord said, almost casually. "But luck favors the adaptable, as I have learned. Captain Hagshrub will do quite well. All that remains is to lift the enchantment of immortality on him, so that the role of the Twelfth is fulfilled." He nodded at the scrolls.

Mel stepped back. "I thought I was in the Prophecy," he insisted, desperate to find some hole in the Ace-Lord's plan. "I'm the one—I'm the New Blood."

"You might have been," the Ace-Lord replied. "But Hagshrub will be the Twelfth. Then, he will kill the New Blood, and thus end the Prophecy's inspiring but misinformed words."

"That Prophecy of yours only calls for a mortal Cantrian to join the Shards," Hagshrub said, his wicked grin widening. "I fit that criteria, same as you, boy. Better, because I'm ready to join his forces. Immortal and deathless forever—an Ace, more powerful even than the Stars."

Mel clutched the Shard tighter. True fear rushed through his veins as he realized the truth. He had not been brought here for some epic showdown. He had been lured here, like a sheep to the slaughter. Brought here to deliver the Shard before being killed. Because in the end, he was still just an eleven-year-old, inexperienced, fear-filled boy. Hagshrub had been chosen for the Twelfth, his mind as clear as ever so that he could embrace the evil choice.

"Stand, Captain Hagshrub," the Ace-Lord commanded. Hagshrub turned to him, closing his eyes and holding out his hands. The Ace-Lord struck him with a blast of violet light that dissolved the second it hit him. Hagshrub reeled backward, gasping. Lines appeared instantly on his face, and he moved much slower, an old and weary mortal again.

"Your immortality has been surrendered," the Ace-Lord said. "Now, take what is meant to be yours."

Hagshrub turned and moved toward Mel. He gripped the Sia Shard in one hand, and with the other lowered his curved sword at Mel.

Somewhere below them came a distant creak, then a thud of a closing door. Mel barely registered the sounds as he set his stance before the orc, heart racing. He would not give up. He must get the Shards together and join them before Hagshrub did so.

He lunged in with his knife. Hagshrub deflected the blow and struck—Mel blocked it, but the force of the strike jarred all the way up his arm. He staggered back, nearly dropping his blade.

"Still resisting," the Ace-Lord observed in an amused tone. "Still trying to fight."

Mel straightened, gasping for breath. He could not beat Hagshrub. That much he realized. The orc was bigger, stronger, and had killed his whole life long.

"Give it up, boy," Hagshrub snarled. "Give me the Shard and I'll make your death quick and painless."

Mel gritted his teeth and lunged again, slicing a gash across Hagshrub's forearm. Hagshrub hissed, startled by the pain, and struck Mel across the face with his other hand. Mel's head snapped against his shoulder, sending his ear ringing. He crashed to the floor, his vision blurring and spinning.

Hagshrub's blade rested on Mel's chest. "Little fool," the orc growled, smiling like a wolf. He lowered the blade. The cold steel bit into Mel's skin, and he closed his eyes, ready for the killing blow.

Then the copper doors slammed closed, followed by the sound of boots on the tiled floor. Mel opened his eyes in time to see a sword plunge into Hagshrub's shoulder. The orc screamed, dropping the Shard, stumbling back.

Standing strong, eyes blazing, was Aryion. Mel hadn't seen him coming, couldn't guess how he had known that Hagshrub was here, or how he had found them. Yet he was here. Guarding his charge and staring his father's killer down.

The ranger wrenched his sword free. "Get up, Mel," he ordered, his eyes never leaving Hagshrub's face.

Hagshrub stared at him in shock for an instant. But he recovered quickly, and the fight, so long in the coming, finally began in a blur of steel.

The Shards—

Mel tore his eyes away from the sword fight and scooped both Shards up. They glowed blue and warm in his hands. He rushed to the little silver table, slipping on the ice-coated tile.

The Ace-Lord flung a ray of ice that hit him in the stomach, sending him sprawling. Gasping for air, he stood and pressed the Shards together. They blazed, white hot in his hands. He cried out and dropped them, looking in shock at his blistered fingers. Then he grabbed them again, placed them on the silver table, and pressed both halves together.

Nothing happened.

Mel stared at the two Shards, not sure what he had expected. A wall of protective fire, maybe, or some sort of shield—something to shoot and hit and destroy the Aces. Instead, a small ray of blue light glowed in the core of the joined Shards, filling the crack between them so that they appeared as one.

Hagshrub, seeing it, snarled and sprang for the table. Aryion leapt between him and Mel, deflecting the orc's blow. Hagshrub kicked the table and the Shards were bumped apart. Mel pressed them back together, wincing at his burned fingers, and watched in fascination as the light began to glow again.

"Foolish choice, New Blood."

Mel turned, saw the Ace-Lord raise both hands and lower them at him—it was too late for him to run, too late to duck out of the way.

He flinched back, waiting for the end, for the ice to run him through or to strip the Essence from his body.

What actually happened was far worse.

A wall of darkness hit him, and he stumbled back. He blinked— the darkness stayed. The world twisted, and he stumbled, fell, and floated. The void had embraced him again—but it was no longer silent. Deep in the black oblivion, he heard voices.

"Mel! Help me!" Misty's high-pitched scream from his left; he pressed through the shadows, swimming through the darkness—

I gave you a warning, child, the voice thundered through the shadows.

Mel was flung upward by an unseen draft. The world twisted again, and he was falling, falling through the inky blackness. He clawed at the air, terrified by the sickening sensation of toppling, but there was nothing to clutch. Misty's distant screams died as he fell into—water. Or something that felt like it.

Your bravery is strong. Your fear is stronger.

Mel fought to the surface of the invisible pool. This wasn't real. It was another illusion. It had to be, because somewhere in the blackness, he could still see the blue of the Shards—

Their power is useless against me.

He heard the Ace-Lord's echoing laugh, and saw the glittering form of Kahlifis suspended in the air before him, silver hair floating ghost-like around his face. Misty's shrieks echoed through the air again. It was so real—they couldn't have caught her, but—

"Misty!" Mel cried out. The screams vanished, and instead of liquid all was air as he toppled again, clawing for an invisible handhold. Suddenly the darkness was gone, and a blinding light struck his eyes. He saw a flash of reality before the Ace-Lord wrenched him forward, the claw-like hand gripping Mel's forehead.

Look at what you are, boy, the voice boomed in his mind. *Look at the pain you have caused.*

Pale ice rushed through Mel's mind, hauling memories to the surface. His helplessness as he watched Llyrion die. Dandio, lying covered in blood beside the serpentine's body. The charred skulls of Terrax's warriors grinning, left in ruins at the wake of the Darkness.

Then, recent memories of every horrible thing he wished to forget. The lies he had told his family. The betrayal and anger he had felt at Aryion's revelation. Norrin crumpling to the ground, Rygal's tormented scream, Irshkhân's maddened eyes as he seized Mel's jerkin—and this time, no one ran to his rescue. The Jenna's face contorted until it was no longer Irshkhân's, but the Ace-Lord's, smiling a hideous smile in his face.

The ice turned white hot in Mel's mind, searing and burning. He screamed and fell, clutching his head. The Ace-Lord loomed over him. His words cut through the ringing pain in Mel's ears.

"Now you see, child?" he asked, his voice low. "You are nothing. Everything you have done, you have done because I willed it. You will die, another pawn in my glorious game. Another mortal, forgotten after a few hundred years."

Mel lay on his chest, gasping. The Shards glittered blue a few feet away. The Shards. Once their powers were joined, he could use them against the Ace-Lord… but how long…

"You're wrong about the mortals," he choked. "You'll die… we'll beat you, with the Shards."

"I?" the Ace-Lord echoed, dragging him forward so that their faces were inches apart. His decayed face contorted in another evil smile. "You forget, boy. I cannot die."

The world evaporated again, and Mel was flung backward. This time, it was no longer dark. Colors and patterns swam in a feverish dream about him, a cacophony of chaos. It was like those recurring dreams just before falling asleep, where the proportions of everything around him were ballooned out of shape and reality was nothing more than a construct. Fire and ice clashed around him, shattering into fragments of a dazzling rainbow with razor edges. A song played somewhere far off in the distance, a song he did not recognize.

Then the colors were washed out again. The ice in his mind painted a picture of blues and blacks, a living scene centuries old that swam into focus. Kahlifis stood over a wide field, where a thousand corpses rotted.

This is my legacy, boomed the voice in his mind. *And I have made it my glory.*

"Let me out!" Mel screamed, squeezing his eyes shut against the horror of the images. The world went black again, and the sounds reappeared—an explosion of pain and panic all echoing at once, resounding in his mind, the voices of everyone he had ever loved rising in a roar that thundered in his brain. His sanity writhed in a cage of ice. He clapped his hands over his ears and screamed until the spinning stopped abruptly and he was flung on his back on the floor.

"Get up, New Blood," the Ace-Lord commanded above him. "Get up and face me like a man."

Mel could not stop the sob that tore from his throat. His hands shook. He gripped his knife and stood, meeting the Ace-Lord's horrible face. Tears of pain blurred his vision, but he lowered his knife and planted his feet.

The Ace-Lord reached for him. Mel slashed at his hands and

dodged, rolling to his knees next to the table. The Shards were glowing now, pulsating blue and radiating power and heat. He reached for them, and his hands came away further blistered.

"You cannot touch them," the Ace-Lord hissed. "I know your thoughts. You are unworthy. You have no true strength. In the end… you are only yourself."

The words cut to Mel's core. They called out and named every one of his fears and failures. The stubborn spark of hope in his chest flickered weakly.

The clatter of steel falling to stone drew his attention—Aryion had disarmed Hagshrub, and lowered his blade at the orc. Hagshrub flinched back, his eyes wide with fear.

At the same time, the Ace-Lord seized Mel again. The searing pain tore through Mel's head, as though his skull would split in two. He screamed, writhing in the Ace-Lord's grasp.

Then through a blur of pain he saw Aryion turn away, leaving Hagshrub cowering by the wall. The ranger's sword flashed as he sprang forward, Mel's name on his lips as he attacked. His voice was lost in Mel's ringing ears.

The Ace-Lord dropped Mel and sprang away from the sword, more startled than threatened by the sudden attack. Aryion lowered his blade, moving between Mel and the Ace-Lord. The Ace-Lord laughed softly. "How touching, Oath-bearer. Do you believe you can redeem yourself now, after all that has transpired?"

Mel propped himself weakly on his elbows. "No… no…" he

gasped, motioning desperately for Aryion to run. He struggled to stand—the world heaved under his feet, and he fell again.

The Ace-Lord shoved Aryion back with a flash of pale blue ice, then seized Mel again. Mel saw the ranger regain his balance and gather himself to charge again. The room began to swim into blackness behind Mel's eyes; in another moment, he would be lost to the void.

But before it went to darkness he saw Hagshrub stand. Saw him spring forward. Saw him bury his dagger to the hilt between Aryion's ribs.

Mel's vision went out as the shadows lifted him, preparing to spin him into the void again. His aching mind registered what he had just seen, watched Hagshrub's sudden attack happen over and over, and realized… realized it was real.

The voice, mocking and amused, echoed in his mind. *He will die because of you, child.*

"No!" Mel yelled. A shock of anguished fury rushed through his system. His mind rejected the illusion. It was not real. He grounded his mind on the distant blue of the Shards and dragged himself back into reality, through the fog that filled his brain, until he crashed onto the tile again.

The strain of it took his breath away. His vision focused to see Aryion stumble sideways, a hand pressed to the cruel gash in his side. Hagshrub laughed. It was the last expression on his face. Aryion lunged with his last strength, so fast his sword was a blur as he hewed Hagshrub's neck. The orc's head sailed back several feet and hit the floor. The body remained upright briefly, then crumpled slowly to the ground.

Aryion fell on his back against the steps, his sword sliding from his grasp.

Face me, New Blood.

Mel didn't care about the voice. He ran to the ranger, his heart racing in a sudden rush of fear. "Aryion—Aryion, hold on—"

Face me!

Icy ropes gripped Mel's arms before he reached Aryion, spinning him around, dragging him back to the Ace-Lord. Mel squirmed until his hand was free; he slashed at the wraith's face with his knife. The Ace-Lord caught his blade midair with one hand. He held it for an instant, then ice spread down the length of the blade and shattered it.

"You foolish, interfering mortal," the Ace-Lord hissed. "Before, I had told Hagshrub to make your death swift and painless. Now, your soul will suffer in my realm forever."

He pressed a hand against Mel's chest. White ice glistened on his fingers. Mel felt a mighty tug deep inside his chest, as though his heart was being wrenched from his body. He screamed at the pain. Stars swam in his vision. He thrashed in the Ace-Lord's grasp, but there was no end to it, nothing he could do –

Until his frantically reaching hand rested on something hot.

A flash of blue light shot out of Mel's chest, into the Ace-Lord's hand. The Ace-Lord reeled backwards, hissing, staring in shock at his seared fingers.

Mel fell back, and his fingers closed over the joined Shards—the Blue Stone made whole again. He drew in a ragged breath, realizing that he was still alive. The Stone was warm in his grasp. He put a shaking hand to his chest, unable to explain what had just happened.

The blue light, the power, it had come from him, channeled through his Essence, almost as if… as if…

His mind struggled to put his thoughts in order. *Guard them with your life,* came Iriam's voice from another time. Guard the Shards… guard his life… his heart and the Shards… the Ace-Lord wanted his heart and mind, not just because of the Prophecy but because—because—

"What have you done?" the Ace-Lord whispered, his hoarse voice filled with venom.

Mel looked at the Stone in his blistered hand as he finally understood. The Prophecy needed a Cantrian—a mortal, whose Essence did not rely on the elements, but relied purely on the magic of the Land Immortal. The Stone required a conduit to channel their strength. Someone to harness their strength while relying on none of their own. Someone to rely on faith and trust in the Words of old. Someone impressionable, while still staying loyal and strong for what they knew to be true.

The Stone required the New Blood.

This was his task. To channel that power and hope, so that the strength of the Blue Stone flowed through him.

"Listen to me, mortal," the Ace-Lord said, stepping forward. His voice was low and urgent, smooth and tempting. "It is not too late. You know you cannot expect to win this struggle against my forces. I offer you this chance once more only. You have joined the Shards. You may yet become the Twelfth. Surrender yourself and allow me to fill you with my power."

He reached out. Cold filled the room, sending chills down Mel's back. For an instant, the gray light faltered, and he saw Kahlifis, in his glory, offering Mel the choice. Offering him power beyond his wildest dreams.

Then the Stone flashed radiant blue light, and Mel saw the truth. A withered, rotted being older than the world. Powerful, yet weak. Immortal, yet dead. Filled with strength, but a shell of a being without a soul or a heart.

"No," he said.

The word dropped into the silence.

"I'm not going to become an Ace," Mel said. "What you said before was true. I'm not strong, I'm not worthy, I don't have any sort of power. But I have do have the hope of the Words of old."

The Ace-Lord recoiled, his face a mask of shock and hate.

"I know the Prophecy," Mel pressed on. "I know enough of it to know my choice—and that choice was never you. I am the New Blood. I wield the Blue Stone, and its power flows through my life."

The Ace-Lord laughed softly. "You know not what you throw away."

"Yes, I do," Mel shot back, limping forward. New strength flowed through him despite his wounds. "I throw away the darkness that obsessed you, the ice that engulfed you, and the servitude that binds your servants. That's worth it. It's worth it if there's still freedom to fight for."

The Ace-Lord snarled and brought his hands to his sides in a sweeping motion. Ice sprang up the walls of the throne room, shattering the glass windows, and filled the room in gray light. Fog leapt up between Mel and the Ace-Lord, who no longer appeared as a wraith, but as the silver-clad warrior who stood prepared to fight.

Ice shot from the Ace-Lord's palms. Mel raised the Shards at the same time. The icy blast slammed into the Shards. Blue fire sprang from the core of the Stones, meeting the ice with a deafening crackle. Mel stood, quailing only at the blinding light, shielding his eyes with his other hand.

Then the Ace-Lord's ice shattered under the Stone's power. Razor-sharp darts of ice sailed through the air, raining down on Mel, and he staggered at a flare of pain that shot up his leg. But he stood strong. Blue fire licked across the tile, melting the illusion of glory cast by the Ace-Lord. The silver form of Kahlifis screamed in fury as his appearance returned to the long-dead spectre he had become.

"This is not over, New Blood," he snarled, as the illusion faded for the last time. "We will return. The Stones will be mine, and the Prophecy cannot save you forever."

He sprang back and sent a wave of ice that knocked Mel backwards into the wall. Dazed, Mel looked up in time to see the Ace-Lord raise his face to the high ceiling. The crown on his brow spread liquid darkness down his frame, engulfing him and spiriting him away.

Thunder shook the castle. Through the broken window, Mel saw a dark streak travel across the sky, joined by ten others. The Aces had left Caer Sia. Driven away by the combined power of the Shards.

All was still and silent but for the falling rain.

29

∽ ∽ ∽ ∽ ∽ ∽ ∽ ∽ ∽

The Power of the Stone

The cold stone floor bit into Mel's back as he lay flat, gathering his breath, while the last strands of the illusion faded away. Finally, his vision steadied, the world ceased heaving, and reality again seemed certain. The burns on his hands, and the Blue Stone, glowing and pulsating light in his grasp, reassured him that it had all happened.

The Ace-Lord was gone. Through the open window, Mel saw rain falling in a cleansing shower over the broken city. The sounds of battle, which had come distantly to his ears earlier, were silent now. What had happened? How had it ended?

The Aces had left, but he doubted the Jenna and orcs had gone. His heart skipped a beat. Were any of his friends still alive?

That question he needed answered now.

He sat up stiffly, then cried out as white-hot pain shot through his body from his thigh. That last blast from the Ace-Lord had done damage. A blade of ice was embedded in the front of his leg. Blood already soaked his pant leg, streaked across the tile, joining with Hagshrub's and—

He struggled to his feet, took a few steps and fell, and crawled the rest of the way to Aryion's side.

376

The ranger lay on his back, dragging gasps of air. He coughed, and blood ran from the corner of his mouth.

"Aryion… hold on…" Mel wheezed. His hands shook as he fought to staunch the rapid flow of blood.

Aryion's eyes flickered open weakly, and focused on Mel's face. He tried to speak, but the action set him coughing again. Blood wet his collar.

"Hold on," Mel repeated. He shifted his weight, and the piece of ice sank deeper into his leg. The pain dizzied him for an instant, threatening to plunge him into unconsciousness. For a moment, darkness tugged at the edges of his vision, only this time, the oblivion was comforting, peaceful and calm. It beckoned to him, so that he forgot about the throbbing pain in his leg and his head. It would be so easy to lie down and give up.

"No!" he yelled, shaking his head to clear it. "We're gonna make it… we're going to get out of here and… get to Iriam… he can help…"

He moved behind Aryion, locking his arms under the ranger's and dragging him across the tile. Aryion did not cry out or cough again. He was still now, his dark eyes half closed.

"Hold on," Mel murmured again. There was no strength behind the word, no real power. Just the stubborn mantra of someone unable to accept the inevitable truth.

His knees gave out and he fell, lying flat on his back beside Aryion. Too much blood. He knew it already. Knew it meant the end for both of them, here, alone in the throne room.

"We're going to make it," Mel whispered, and forced himself to his knees again. His words came in short gasps as he struggled toward the door. "I swear—on my life—we're going to get out of here—and make it—and—and—"

His words faltered. He could not find Aryion's pulse. The lump, which had begun to rise in his throat, stifled his voice for an instant. He choked out a hoarse sob. "And—and—you're going to train me—I'm going to be a ranger, but only—only if you train me—please—please—"

The world blurred, and Mel fell again. Tears ran down his weary face. He gripped the ranger's wrist, felt the weak flutter of his heart beat as both their lives drained away.

Then with his other hand, he clutched the Blue Stone. Closed his eyes. And summoned any strength he had left to command their power. Calling on their pure magic and healing forces. That was what they'd been made for, wasn't it? They had been given to the Cantrians, their power gifted to the ancients.

"Please," Mel whispered, even as his own vision faded. "Please." This time it was a prayer, a plea to the Writer of the Prophecy, the very Author of hope itself, spoken with the last amount of strength he possessed.

He did not know how to use the Stone's power. But he finally understood. This was why the Stones had been made. Not to be used as weapons, as Kahlifis had twisted the Jewel. But to protect, to comfort, to heal. To bring hope to the mortal world.

Perhaps that tied into his role as the New Blood, too. In him there lived a power stronger than his own, stronger than the darkness around him. With that power, he chose, with every breath, to breathe hope or fear into the world. With the power, he chose to break down, or to heal.

His task. His name. His fate.

It aligned with the little he knew of the Prophecy, a promise older and more powerful than death itself.

The Stone blossomed a blue beam of light as he held it, pure light that cut through the darkness in the room. A light that seemed to sink into his skin, rushing through his body, as though carried by the blood in his veins. It embraced his faltering strength. It sang with the Essence of his heart. It disintegrated the blade of ice in his leg and stitched the flesh back together.

And it made Aryion's returning heartbeat the last thing Mel was aware of.

30

ॐ ॐ ॐ ॐ ॐ ॐ ॐ ॐ ॐ

The Blue Stone

Mel opened his eyes. Sunlight blinded him for a moment. I'm back on Kamon, he thought vaguely. Except the distant roar of the sea was different somehow, as was the soft bed that he lay in.

"I'm starting to think you have a knack for fighting wraiths," came a familiar voice.

Mel sat bolt upright.

Dandio sat on the foot of his bed. He was thinner, his voice not as strong as it used to be. But the smile was the same.

"You," Mel panted, his brain struggling to make sense of what he was seeing. "I thought—you were—what—"

"How do you feel?" came Jan's voice. The king entered through the door to Mel's right. There was a bandage wrapped around his side, but he seemed all right aside from that.

"I'm…" Mel turned to look at Dandio again. The long suspense and unknowing, the rumors and worries, everything faded away by the simple truth. The relief and joy overwhelmed him for a moment, and tears ran down his face. "I'm fine. We won. You're back," he stammered.

"Is he awake?" came Jarus' anxious voice from the doorway. The

380

Cooper limped inside. His rear paw was bandaged, but he paid it little attention. "Mel! I've been waiting to hear all about it. We didn't see much, y'know—the Aces sort of ghosted away right before it started raining, so we knew that you must have used the Shards. But then it took a little while before the Jenna and orcs gave up and retreated too, so…"

"What happened?" Mel demanded. "Is everyone okay? Who's hurt? Where were *you*?" he added to Dandio, then rounded on Ĵan. "What about the Shards? Where are they?"

"I think he set a record with that one, Dandio," came Rygal's voice. The young warrior leaned against the door frame. "Most Questions Asked in Ten Seconds. Write that down."

"You," Dandio said to Rygal, very slowly and patiently, "are a difficult man."

"Him and Jarus are competing for that award, I think," said Quinn, appearing beyond Rygal's shoulder.

"Which award?" Jarus asked. "The questions, or the difficult-ness?"

"Difficult-*y*, Jarus," Ĵan corrected wearily.

Mel felt like he was going to explode. "Is no one going to tell me what in the world happened?"

"Part of it, maybe."

Mel whipped around at the familiar voice.

Aryion stood in the doorway. He was dressed in clean clothes, his cloak swept back so that he seemed less withdrawn in the shadows. But that wasn't the main difference Mel had noticed. Aryion was smiling. A real smile, not the half-smirk, but a true joy that lit his dark eyes as he looked at Mel.

"Is he awake?" came Allie's voice through the doorway. The princess appeared, a little breathless. "Mel, I want to hear the whole thing," she began at once. "How did you do it? What happened?"

"First," Jan said with a smile, as Mel had drawn breath for yet another string of questions, "I will tell you our side of the battle."

Mel sat up. The wound in his leg had vanished, and aside from a slight headache, he felt better than he had in weeks. The others made themselves comfortable sitting next to him on the bed, or in the few chairs in the room, or on the floor.

Mel listened, enraptured, as Jan spoke of the battle. Once the ten Aces had arrived, the fighting became even more intense. The civilians scattered in an effort to avoid the deadly white ice. The Aces had still taken a toll, as Jan recounted, with a grave face, those who had been lost. A small group had gathered in the courtyard of the castle, not sure what to do, until Rygal reminded them of the cannons on the walls. Then they had fought up the bulwarks and rained fire upon the orcs and Jenna in the streets. After this, the Aces vanished. The orcs retreated soon after; immortal or no, they had no desire to continue the fighting if they were not being paid. The Jenna were slower to leave; either foolish enough to challenge the warriors of Sia alone, or hopeful of looting and raiding the castle. Jan suspected both.

"They gave up when the kragons arrived," Jan finished. "Lord

Fireclaw led his forces here just after the Aces left, and the Jenna fled. They went east, hopefully back to Sikhazi."

"Then the Ace-Lord's lost a large portion of his army," Allie said, sounding satisfied.

"Where's Iriam?" Mel asked, realizing he hadn't seen him.

"Covering for Jan at the moment," Dandio said, smiling in his brother's direction. "Actually, he and Glentree are discussing a defensive strategy—a way to protect Caer Sia from the Aces in the future, so that they can't transport themselves inside the city again. Iriam thinks there may be an old spell in the archives that he can perform, something given to us by the Stars in the old days."

"That's good," Mel said, hoping he was right. "What about the Aces? Do we know where they've gone?"

"Our sources say to the southwest," Jan said. "They seem to have disappeared somewhere near the Salem Flats—ironically, not far from where they first appeared."

"That's something the Ace-Lord would do," Dandio said. "Probably thinks it an amusing coincidence."

"But… do you think they will come back?" Mel asked worriedly.

"Eventually, yes. But I doubt they will attack again soon," Jan said. "The first stage in this war is complete, and now both sides will have to recuperate before another action is taken."

War. Mel felt tired just thinking about it.

"Tell us about the fight with the Ace-Lord, Mel," Jarus asked hopefully. "What happened? How did you do it?"

Mel explained a little of the battle, summarizing most of it. The horrific visions in and out of the void, and the Ace-Lord in his true form, were both terrifying to recount. "I didn't really do much," he admitted as he finished. "It was all the Shards—the Blue Stone. I just had to be the person holding it—and their power channeled through me."

"You did very well," Aryion told him.

Mel had several questions for the ranger. He had only seen glimpses of the duel with Hagshrub.

From Aryion's perspective, he had been considering the possibility that Hagshrub was in fact the Twelfth Ace for a while. "I'd been wondering about it since Kamon," he explained. "Why not clear Hagshrub's mind, and have another mindless soldier in his army? I also knew that the Ace-Lord was no fool. He wouldn't risk his entire strategy of turning you into the New Blood unless he was sure that was your choice."

"And it never was," Mel said.

"No," Aryion said. "Then the fight started, and Hagshrub was nowhere in sight. I went through the side door Asescia mentioned to get to the throne room."

"Well, I'm glad you did," Mel breathed, remembering Hagshrub's last moments with a shudder. He shook his head. "I'm not sure I'm up for talking about it all yet, though."

"Indeed," Jan said, standing. "Rest will do you good." He ushered the others out of the room, leaving only Dandio and Aryion.

Mel looked at the Liznee warrior, still in awe to see him. "Dandio… where were you?"

Dandio let out a breath. "Well, your guesses were not all off. I was captured in the Forest of Light, on my way back to Sia. The Aces kept me imprisoned… later, they took me to Caer Sia."

"What happened then?" Mel asked, intrigued.

Dandio smiled faintly. "I'm not sure I'm up for talking about it all yet," he replied, echoing Mel's words.

And Mel knew better than to press him.

Dandio asked a few more questions, mostly about the Shards. Mel answered everything he could, though he couldn't really explain what had happened.

"I think… in the end… I realized I was trying too hard to do it on my own," he said, wrapping up his story. "To stop the Ace-Lord, to heal Aryion—I was thinking too much, when I needed to just let go and let the Stone's power do it all for me." He shrugged, a little surprised by his own words.

Aryion looked thoughtful. "I suppose that makes sense. Like Cahadras said at the council—the Stone had that power since the dawn of time, power from the Land Immortal. The type of power that the Ace-Lord couldn't overcome."

He smiled, then left the room with Dandio.

· · · · · ·

It was no easy task to rebuild a shattered city. There were homes to rebuild, people to help, lives to piece back together. Jan oversaw most of this himself, along with Dandio. The return of the long-lost hero further inspired the people of Caer Sia, so that the work continued to be done and the city began to thrive again.

Darker matters needed to be dealt with, too. With the Ace-Lord's return now publicly known, messages were sent to the allies of Coonsia telling of the reunion of the Shards and the recovery of Caer Sia. It was a rallying call to every kingdom, summoning the allies of the Liznees to stand together against the coming darkness.

On the third day since the battle, Ĵan called a meeting. The companions gathered with Dandio and the other war leaders of Caer Sia, as well as Dandio's wife Ajaha, who led Caer Sia's couriers. With the city reclaimed and the Shards joined, the meeting would address the question hovering in Mel's mind—what would come next.

"Allies will come," Glentree stated fiercely. "This war won't be won without 'em."

"Many have already answered the call," Ajaha said. She sat beside her husband, their fingers intertwined. "After seeing the outcomes of this battle, they will know our only course is joining together in resistance."

"Does that mean war is returning already?" Jarus asked, a little uneasily.

"Not yet," Ĵan said. "We have entered a pausing point of the war, where both sides will work to mobilize. We receive word from our sources every day about the progress of the Ace-Lord."

"Progress?" Mel repeated. He didn't like the sound of that. "Are they coming to attack us?"

Iriam smiled reassuringly. "The Ace-Lord has suffered a grave defeat. He must have the Star-Stones, and I do not doubt he is already plotting his next move. But until then, we will stand ready for him."

"That we will," Glentree said with a fierce grin. "And next time, it won't be Caer Sia all on her own."

"Indeed not," Quinn agreed. "I ride to Tinkeeyo tomorrow morning, to inform the city leaders of what has happened here. I am also instructed to return this." He raised a scroll.

Mel's heart skipped a beat. It had been three days added to the weeks on the quest, thinking and wondering about the Prophecy. Yet now, for the first time, he felt a strange hesitation to ask anything about it at all.

"Lord Roan will have to hear of this, too," Jarus said. "I'm to sail for Mata City after Quinn leaves."

"And I bring word back to King Casper of the Direns in Gayrile," Rygal said. "The Guardians will come, I can promise you that."

After the meeting, Jan asked both Mel and Aryion to stay behind. "I hear you plan to train as a ranger, Mel," the king said, looking impressed.

Mel nodded with a smile. "Yep. I'm not really sure what that means, though," he added uncertainly.

"It will be significantly harder than facing the Lord of Death," Aryion said, straight faced. But the light in his eyes betrayed a smile.

Jan smiled at them both. "Well, I have a particular assignment for you, to look into after you return from Appledale. It's not a pleasant task, but it must be done."

Mel looked up with a surge of unease. "Is it the Aces? Are we going to attack them?"

"No, not yet. I will give you both particulars later. But Mel at least has some history with this person I need you to find. Though not the Ace-Lord, he is still a threat."

Something about the way he said that reminded Mel of another conversation, one he'd had with Dandio after he'd first left Appledale. His heart sank. "Terrax?"

"I'm afraid so," Jan said. "Lammar—he is an informant for the Guardians of Gayrile—picked up news on his whereabouts. How Lammar got the news, your guess is as good as mine, but regardless, Terrax is said to be in the south, near the Crime Rings of Esile City."

Terrax of Elvengate. The name brought both fear and hate to Mel's mind. He wasn't too surprised—it made sense that the Elven outlaw would turn up again. "Will we go after him? How far is it to Esile City?"

"Not yet," Jan said. "I only wanted to make you both aware, so you can prepare. But first, Mel, go home to your family, begin your training, be ready."

"And I will speak with my contacts in Elimar," Aryion said. "Some of Terrax's comrades were imprisoned there—they may have more news about him."

"Good. Dandio will have more information for you after you return," Jan said.

The looming emotions of both excitement and fear hovered over Mel the rest of the day as he thought about the coming mission. His first task as a ranger. He wanted to leave that moment, but Jan and Aryion were right. The task could wait for now. There were other things at hand.

The following morning, Mel said farewell to Jarus, Quinn, and Rygal. The three of them would travel in different directions back to their homes. In the span of the quest, he had grown to trust and admire each of them. Despite the horrors they had faced, despite the darkness they had fought, they had endured through the struggle. No matter what was to come, Mel knew, somehow, that they would continue to endure. As it was written in the Prophecy of Three.

The Prophecy. There lay the source of his remaining questions.

"What will happen now, Iriam?" he asked, as he and the Neutral met in the library. 'What about the Prophecy—and the New Blood?"

Iriam allowed the scroll he had been reading to close and looked up with a slight smile. "The first stage of the Prophecy has been set, and the events foretold have been fulfilled, through your actions."

"They have?" That surprised him. "But—I didn't do anything. I didn't even know what that Prophecy asked of me."

"And so you fulfilled your place," Iriam said. He paused. "The Prophecy tells of a moment where a New Blood brave stands alone. You faced the Ace-Lord alone, just as you are, with the powers of the Stone flowing through you. It also explains that before the

Ace-Lord's downfall, a Nameless New Blood will know their call. You passed the Ace-Lord's tests without even the Prophecy itself to influence you. You know your call now—to guard the Stone."

"I'm supposed to guard the Stone?" Mel repeated, startled.

"Indeed. The Prophecy is most insistent." Iriam fingered the worn edge of the scroll thoughtfully. "You are the mortal Cantrian, without title or rank to your name. This gives you another trait, often overlooked in today's age," Iriam said. "Humility. You come unassuming, open and willing to the Stone's power. Thus, you will be the one who carries the Stone from now until the Aces are defeated."

Mel shook his head slowly. "Do I… do I get to read the Prophecy now, then?" he asked. It was odd, how now that the moment had come, he was hesitant to read the Prophecy. Before now, his choices, good or bad, had been his own. It felt strange to read a Prophecy where the rest of the events of the war were dictated.

"I will leave that choice to you," Iriam said, taking a step back from the table. "The New Blood's role has been fulfilled. If you wish to read the Prophecy of Three in full now, I permit you. However, I do offer this as warning," he added, after a pause. "The Prophecy's words are dark ones, speaking of many strange events that even I cannot unravel at this point in time. Not only that, certain things must yet happen before the second stage can be in place."

Mel frowned, his hands hovering over the scroll. "When will the second stage happen?"

"It may happen tomorrow. It may happen in years. I cannot be sure. I think we can assume it will be within the next year. I doubt the Ace-Lord will wait long." Iriam folded his hands on the table.

"How will we know when the next stage is going to happen, then?" Mel asked after a moment.

"There are certain events that will precede it, certain people entering the war from both sides," Iriam told him. "The first stage is complete—the New Blood stood strong through the Ace-Lord's tests. And the Blue Stone has a guardian again."

"Then who's the next person in the Prophecy?"

"I cannot say yet. We could speculate, but without context, I cannot say what effect the Prophecy's words would have upon you. The future carries a certain weightiness, more so when one begins living only for a time yet to come. Instead, I believe it is wisest to live each moment as it comes, living each day with expectation and not letting the future consume you."

Mel hesitated, touching the worn parchment. He longed to know its words, longed to know what it said of himself and others. And yet… was that his place? How long had he obsessed over his role as the New Blood, afraid of failing, afraid of what was coming? Any actions he could control within the Prophecy were past now. What was to come would involve different events, different people.

He didn't feel afraid of the Prophecy anymore. He only felt very tired. And the option to wait gave him relief.

Despite his own curiosity, he moved away. "I don't think I should read this now. Not at least until the second stage is about to begin."

Iriam nodded slowly, and Mel thought he saw approval flicker briefly over the Neutral's face. "A wise decision. You still have much to learn," he added with a wink. He replaced the scroll on one of the shelves and selected a different one.

Mel looked up at him, thinking. "After the last quest, I wanted Rygal to send me news of everything happening here. Could you… maybe… could you tell me when you think the second stage is set, so I have time to read the Prophecy before?"

A slight smile crossed Iriam's face, and he nodded. "Indeed. I shall send for you the moment you are needed. In the meantime," he paused thoughtfully, "do not let the Prophecy worry you. Allow yourself to rest. Of the Three, only one has come into the picture now, and he has fulfilled his role quite well."

Mel felt himself smile.

Three, his mind echoed as he turned away. It was a recurring number.

Three stages, or things to happen.

Three people to fulfill those events.

Three Star-Stones, given to the rulers of the ancient world, now reappearing in his lifetime. Intertwining with his life in some strange destiny written before the world was formed.

How strange it all was. How truly, deeply magic.

The New Blood slipped into the hall, no longer afraid of what was to come.

Epilogue

"I thought I might find you here," came Dandio's voice.

Mel turned. The tall Liznee entered the throne room soundlessly to stand beside Mel. Before them, the Stone glittered and shone in its place on the small silver table. The evening sun blended with the pure blue light in its core, shining a thousand sparkling facets around the room.

"You spoke with Iriam, I hope," Dandio said after a pause.

Mel nodded and took a deep breath. It was strange. His questions about himself had been answered. His questions about the Prophecy could wait for now. In all reality, he figured he should feel relieved and joyous.

And yet something still nagged in his mind. An urge to do something.

"I don't know what to do, Dandio," Mel said finally.

Dandio studied him. "In what way?" he asked gently.

His low, caring tone helped calm Mel's turmoil of thoughts. Still, Mel hesitated before speaking.

"I'm not sure," he said at last. "We beat the Aces, at least for now. The Shards are joined, Caer Sia is safe, and you're back. But… there's something else. I feel like I need to do more. I can't leave—this," he said, gesturing vaguely.

He meant the world of questing, of adventure and loss and sacrifice. He couldn't leave that behind. He had tried to do that after the quest for Drisilas, and this is where it brought him. No, he knew he was meant to see this struggle—the entire war—through to the end. Until the Ace-Lord was ultimately defeated.

The realization tore at his heart as he pictured what he had given up. His family, his simple life—gone now. He wasn't the little boy who dreamed of quests anymore. He was one of seven companions. The New Blood. The Keeper of the Stone. Nothing would ever be the same again.

"I don't know what to do," he said after a pause. "After tomorrow… I don't know what my future holds."

"The future is a big word," Dandio said thoughtfully. He paused. "You can spend a lot of time mulling over your thoughts for tomorrow, for the next day, for the day after that. So much time that you lose sight of what is before you for today. With each day, with every breath you receive, you also receive a choice of what you are going to do with it."

Mel nodded slowly, processing this truth. It was similar to what Iriam had said earlier. That helped ease a little of his worries. One day at a time was easier to comprehend than planning out how to conquer the future. He felt a little braver. "Iriam gave me the chance to read the Prophecy," he said slowly.

"And what did you make of it?" Dandio asked.

"I didn't read it—not yet," Mel said. "I know that sounds strange. But I know I've fulfilled my role in it. I think… when the time comes, I'm ready to face whatever the Prophecy has."

"I think that's a wise choice," Dandio said, studying Mel's thoughtful expression. He's growing up, the Liznee thought. And yet he is still every bit as determined to be the person he is called to be. Dandio was proud of him. "What will you do in the meantime?" he asked in the silence that followed.

What would he do? Mel knew this answer, and smiled. "I'm going with Aryion. He's offered to train me as a ranger—the closest thing to being a warrior while still being in a trade school. Jan mentioned something about a mission for us, too, but he said not to worry about it yet."

"Well, that's certainly a good start," Dandio said.

Mel nodded, gratified to see the Liznee's approval. "After that—after that, I'm not sure. I do know where I'm called," he said, nodding toward the Blue Stone. "We don't know when the second part of the Prophecy will happen, but we do know the hope that there will be an end to the war. I think… I think if we focus on that… focus on the hope, and not the darkness that comes… I think that's how we'll win." He trailed off, a little surprised by his own speech, the simple act of stating it reaffirming his own conviction.

"I think so, too," Dandio agreed softly.

Silence fell in the room. They stared into the swirling depths of the Blue Stone, lost in their own thoughts.

In the west, the sun sank beneath the horizon, bathing the world in one last ray of light.

In a hidden place in the wastelands, the Lord of the Dead waited, plotting his next move in this deadly game he now played with the stubborn mortals of Orlell.

In Mata City, Jarus entered the court of Lord Roan, eager to bring both the good news and the bad.

In Appledale, Mr. Joseph Smallbutton sat down with his wife to read the letter from their son.

In the halls of Caer Sia, Iriam spoke the Words of an ancient time, a prayer that rose to the Land Immortal.

And so it was, at that moment, in that simple point of time in the wide world, as evening fell.

The New Blood will return...

Glossary/Pronunciation Guide

Aces...................... a race of Netrocrians who grow stronger through fear

Ajaha Ki (ah-ZHA-ha KEE)......................Dandio's wife and a skilled courtier and politician

Appledale ....small town in Daffodalion

Aryion Paya (ARE-ree-on PY-ah)................... ranger. Also known as the Hummingbird

Asescia Ki (ah-SESS-see-ah KEE) ....the daughter of Dandio and Ajaha, hieress to the crown of Caer Sia. Also known as Allie.

Caer Sia (care SEE-uh)..................the capital of Coonsia, home of the Liznee people

Cahadras (cah-HAD-drass) .... queen of the Stars

Cantrians (CAN-tree-ins)......................the most common type of Essense-filled being; includes humans and elves

Coonsia (COON-see-uh) ....country on the Mainland of Orlell

Cooper......a race of four-legged creatures that dwell by the northern coast of Coonsia

Daffodalion (DAFF-oh-DAHL-lee-in) ....Coonsia's neighbor, the largest country on the Mainland

Dandio Ki (dan-DYE-oh KEE) .... skilled Liznee warrior, and the commander of Caer Sia's army. Brother of the king.

Flora.. large city in Daffodalion

Fyrocrians (FY-roh-CREE-ins)..... a type of Essence-filled individual whose power manifests as fire and light

Hagshrub (HAG-shrub) ....orc chieftain

Iriam (EER-ree-ahm)...................... *Neutral, leader of the company*

Jan Ki (ZHAN KEE)................................. *High King of the Liznees*

Jarus Puddlepaw (JARE-us Puddlepaw)... *Cooper of Mata City*

Jenna... *a wild race of tribal warriors from Sikhazi*

Kamon (kah-MONE)...............................*tropical Coonsian island city*

Leelo (LEE-loh)...*cheiftain of Kamon*

Liznee (LIZ-nees) .... *a race of silver-skinned Fyrocrians native to Coonsia*

Mel Smallbutton... *young boy from Appledale*

Netrocrians (net-tro-CREE-ins)............. *a type of Essence-filled individual whose power manifests as ice and darkness*

Neutral...*a race of Netrocrians who remained loyal in the Dividing War. Thought all but extinct now*

Norrin(NOR-in).........................*leader of the Guardians of Gayrile*

Quinn Fireleaf...*Elven ranger*

Rygal of Gayrile (RYE-gull) ....*young warrior and member of the Guardians of Gayrile*

Sikhazi (si-KAHZ-zee)... *eastern country, home of the Jenna*

Acknowledgments

I would like to thank a few key people that saw this book into completion.

Mom, your early edits were spot-on as always. Thanks for your criticism, your notes, and your smiley faces scribbled next to paragraphs you enjoyed.

To the entire Orlell Launch Team, you guys are the best. You are the driving force behind this book, and I have you to thank for helping it reach a wider audience.

Thank you to everyone at IngramSpark, for making the publication process a bit less tedious.

To my writing students of 2023, you bring so much energy and excitement. Thanks for your enthusiasm and encouragement (and for catching a few spelling errors of mine).

To the family and friends who support me in each step of my writing journey, thank you a thousand times. I value you each as Star-Stones.

And, of course, to my husband Levi, who listened to each draft of this book and offered your ideas and feedback. Thanks for every late-night plot brainstorm, every long-drive book ramble, and for all the care and thought you put into these stories and characters.

2 Timothy 1:7